MW01174819

THRILLING WONDER STORIES™

SUMMER 2007

Winston Engle, editor

THRILLING WONDER LLC

————

LOS ANGELES, CA

also from Thrilling Wonder LLC

THRILLING WONDER VINTAGE SERIES

Space Salvage, Inc. by Cleve Cartmill (August 2007)

THRILLING WONDER CLASSICS SERIES

The Legion of Space by Jack Williamson (September 2007)

Editor's Dedication:
To my mother,
to Marshall,
and to Marc and Elaine,
who all believed in my Thrilling Wonder Story.

Cover painting by Iain McCaig.
Inspired by a 1952 cover for *Planet Stories* by Allen Anderson.
Copyright © 2007 Iain McCaig.

www.thrillingwonderstories.com

ISBN-13: 978-0-9796718-0-7

VOL. XLVI, No. 1   A THRILLING PUBLICATION   Summer 2007

THRILLING WONDER STORIES

STRANGER THAN TRUTH

EDITOR/PUBLISHER – WINSTON ENGLE
CONSULTING EDITOR – MARC SCOTT ZICREE
EDITORIAL ASSISTANT – PAMELA DAVIS

The Wonders of Wonder

by Winston Engle

The Golden Age of Science Fiction began one summer day in 1981.

Well, it did for me, and as this is my magazine, you'll just have to humor me.

It began when I read *The Voyage of the Space Beagle,* by A.E. van Vogt, as I sat on a chaise longue in the backyard. I spent hours out there every day that summer in an effort to finally get a suntan. That part didn't go so well; rather than tanning, my skin peeled off in long, rubbery strips. But I did, at least, come away with a new appreciation for science fiction.

I'd experienced science fiction before, of course. I'd seen *Star Wars* as many times as my parents would take me to the theater, and *The Empire Strikes Back.* I'd watched *Battlestar Galactica* and *Buck Rogers* on TV, and even though I was only eight when the former premiered, I quickly decided that, special effects aside, they were... well, not what you'd call exactly *good.* (Not that this kept me from watching them. I even suffered through all

two hours of the legendarily hideous *Star Wars Holiday Special,* for pity's sake.) I'd even read two-thirds of C.S. Lewis' *Space Trilogy* (in a cluelessly self-administered, Blockbuster Video-like case of "If you liked *The Chronicles of Narnia...*"), but found the third the very exemplar of *heavy going.*

But it was *The Voyage of the Space Beagle,* at age eleven, that introduced me to the power of written SF to impart that transcendent giddiness of exciting new universes I'd never imagined opening up, that they call "the sense of wonder." And for me, the Golden Age of Science Fiction began. (Appropriately enough, some historians of SF mark the beginning of the actual Golden Age with the issue of *Astounding* in which "Black Destroyer"— the original version of the first quarter of *Space Beagle*—appeared.)

Peter Graham famously said that the Golden Age of Science Fiction is twelve. But as a child, I tended to precociousness (as long as the subject didn't involve social skills or physical acumen). In fact, to be wholly accurate, my first mind-opening experience with science fiction came the year before, when I was flipping through channels during an ad break in the national news (I told you I was precocious), and discovered *Doctor Who.*

But whereas *Doctor Who* was pretty much *sui generis, Space Beagle* led into a whole galaxy of inspiring written SF. I read *I, Robot* and *The Martian Chronicles* (although, taste lagging behind intellect, I was disappointed by its differences from the TV miniseries) and *The Shrinking Man,* and scads more. I started watching *Star Trek* after seeing *Wrath of Khan* as many times as my parents would etc. (I'd never watched the show much. It was on early Sunday morning, for a start, and whenever I did tune in, they always, but always seemed to be either sneaking around a 1960s airbase, or facing down a multi-colored cube.)

What I read was primarily Golden Age stuff because I drew from my father's library, and these were the selfsame books he'd read in his own teens and pre-teens. I did read other SF—I devoured the *Dune* (then) trilogy; I happened on *The Hitchhiker's Guide to the Galaxy,* and my humor was never the same—but what I loved in SF was what I found in Asimov, and van Vogt, and Heinlein.

And that was what I kept reading—that, and latter-day products of the Golden Age authors. Eventually, science fiction fell away from its predominant share of my reading, but it was always there.

Fast-forward to 1999. I'm living in Los Angeles. I'm getting mighty fed up with pitching allllmost, but never quite, successfully to *Deep Space Nine* and *Voyager.* I'm part of a roundtable of people on various rungs of various entertainment-industry ladders. And they say to

me, in essence, why don't you make your own damn movie? And I think about this short story I'd read in 1990 that I always thought would make a great short film.

That story was "A Can of Paint," written in 1945 by, as it happens, A.E. van Vogt. And, despite various twists and turns, and wanting approximately every couple of weeks to chuck it all and wallow in my own despair, and several bouts of, at least in effect, actually chucking it all and etc., I wrote a script, interested a producer and director, got money together, and spearheaded the final push to get that puppy to the finish line to premiere at the San Diego Comic-Con one summer day in 2004.

It ultimately played 25 film festivals, won numerous awards for special effects, music, and Best Science Fiction Short, and, from friends and relatives, elicited hearty cries of, "So, what next?"

What next, indeed? I worked on some original screenplay ideas, and also returned to heavy reading of SF, this time in a (deliberate) hunt for material. I read further works of my old favorite authors, started in on others I'd never gotten to, and started reading the SF magazines, both contemporary and from the '50s. And I quickly realized something. Although the contents weren't all classics by any means, I found I preferred any whole issue of, say, *Galaxy* to one of any current magazine.

This time, I didn't need the roundtable to tell me, why don't I make my own damn magazine?

But what to call it? I considered a brand-new title, but then thought a title from Back in the Day would not only clearly establish my intentions, it would get attention in itself. I considered acquiring the recently-defunct-again *Amazing Stories.* Then a friend of a friend reminded me that there are bunches of long-dead magazines without baggage of subsequent decades of history—like *Famous Fantastic Mysteries,* or *Future Science Fiction,* or, say, *Thrilling Wonder Stories.*

I paid little attention to this at first. I'd read issues of *Thrilling Wonder,* and enjoyed them, but... a magazine, in the twenty-aughts, called *Thrilling Wonder Stories?* Get real.

But slowly, the name started to grow on me. There was a certain kind of science fiction I was looking for, a certain point of view I wanted my magazine to put across, and I came to realize that what it was, was thrilling wonder stories. For me, it became not just a title, but a descriptor.

Thrilling. There was a time it went without saying that the primary virtue of a science fiction magazine, or pretty much any fiction, was to entertain, for the reader to set it down at the end and say, "Well, I enjoyed that!"

Mike Ashley, in his second volume on the history of SF magazines, *Transformations,* quoted Michael Moorcock, in an editorial for *New Worlds,* as saying that his writers "are trying to cope with the job of analysing and interpreting various aspects of human existence, and they hope that in the process they succeed in entertaining you."

To me, these are reversed priorities. I'd much rather read something merely entertaining than something that succeeds in being Frightfully Fraught with Meaning at the price of being, to use a Hitchhiker's phrase, nourishing but nasty. Besides, I frequently find entertainment that sneaks up on meaning to be more convincing than fiction where the meaning comes first, and the story is built around it. Perhaps it's because meaning often sneaks up to us in life. Or perhaps I'm outing myself as a philistine. It doesn't matter that much to me. All I know is, *The Hitchhiker's*

Guide to the Galaxy, or a good Robert Sheckley story, like "The Monsters," has plenty to say about various aspects of human existence, and that's while trying first and foremost to be funny.

More people than I want to remember have argued with me, starting with the basic and unshakable belief that the one and only virtue is realism. Which seems like an odd, quixotic thing to argue about *science fiction,* but there you go. Usually "realism" equates in these arguments with "being brutal and nasty." Because That's Just How Life Is, they say. Besides that this strikes me as an emotionally impoverished point of view, I have enough despair already, thanks all the same.

In this magazine, and guaranteed not to cause despair, is "Three's a Crowd..." the first of a series of rip-roaring space adventures from Eric Brown. R. Neube, in "Love Seat," brings us an amusing look at the future of celebrity, and a unique spin on better living through technology. And non-humans face mystery, murder, and secrets as they search for their origins in Constance Cooper's "Tomb of the Tyrant Emperor." They're trying to entertain you, and they hope that in the process they succeed in analyzing and interpreting various aspects of human existence.

Wonder. It's not that I want *Thrilling Wonder Stories* to be all happy fluffy bunnies in space (although, now that I write it, the idea of a *few* happy fluffy bunnies in space kind of amuses me). It's more a matter of point of view. Wonder, I think, is the ability to look at something, and feel joy and excitement... whether in place of, or in addition to, dread and anxiety. Project that from the now into the future, and it becomes closely aligned to hope. And if you have it, you can find wonder even in the end of the world.

One of my favorite short stories (one I

discovered in reading those back issues of *Galaxy,* by the way) is "A Pail of Air," by Fritz Leiber. That story begins after the end. Earth has been sent hurtling into interstellar space. The atmosphere has frozen out. Billions have died horribly. A family of four, living in a tiny room behind an improvised airlock, are, as far as they know, the last living humans. But the heart of the story is examining why, in the bleakest, most challenging circumstance, life is not only worth living, but perpetuating (the children were born into this new world). The ending (which I won't give away) is actually kind of superfluous next to the question of how they maintain hope.

I also enjoy *A Canticle for Leibowitz,* by Walter M. Miller, Jr. It's dark, but it demonstrates some hope for human progress—in a ten steps forward, nine steps back kind of way. Humanity may crawl its way back from nuclear destruction over 1,500 years only to do it all again, but at least Modernity Mark 2 lasts long enough to put colonies into space, so that the next collapse isn't total.

In this issue's "Farthest Horizons," Geoffrey Landis takes speculation about an interesting question in quantum physics, and though the consequences are problematic, he makes us feel good and excited about it. The hero of Ben Bova's "Jovian Dreams" changes his life in a pretty thorough sort of way to personally experience the wonders of Jupiter. And in "Dark Side," new SF writer Kevin King imagines an unknown bit of spaceflight history his hero faces with curiosity, courage and, yes, hope.

Stories. I mean "stories" as opposed to vignettes, or character studies, or meditations on an idea. Things with, as your English teacher told you, a beginning, a middle, and an end. I've read pieces with fascinating ideas about future developments, which the author illustrates a little by showing us an event, a scene. But I feel that if you want to go deeper into how a world works, and how it affects the lives and basic assumptions of the people in it, and the choices they have to make, you just have to put something at stake, have the hero make some kind of decision. In short, tell a story.

To use, for once, a current example that's not in this magazine, Eric Brown's Kethani cycle is all about this kind of storytelling. People have to face new possibilities and choices in the wake of an alien contact that completely changes their ideas about life and death.

Or, to go back to the '50s again, Wyman Guin's "Beyond Bedlam." He could have settled for a travelogue of his future where schizophrenia is universal and mandatory. But by giving the protagonist something to figure out, he takes us through its hows, whys, and wherefores in a way he couldn't have otherwise.

A concept is sort of a promise, and a real story is that much better thing—a promise fulfilled.

I'd just like to emphasize before I go, I wouldn't presume to say that what I've described is "real" science fiction, in contradistinction to other types I would deny a place in the canon. To paraphrase Walt Whitman (and Harlan Ellison, whose frequent use of the original made me aware of it), science fiction is large; it contains multitudes. This is not a manifesto, so much as a definition of terms, so I can say this simple thing:

I enjoy thrilling wonder stories—and *Thrilling Wonder Stories*—and I hope you do, too. Go to the back yard, get in your chaise longue, and have a Golden Age.

And for pity's sake, put on some sunscreen. • • •

Tomb of the Tyrant Emperor

by Constance Cooper

Illustrated by Kevin Farrell

It was the final day of our trek, according to Lastwell, our guide, and on the horizon we could already see the dark hump of the Dead Mound lying like exhausted prey at the end of a chase. The sky was raw blue, scraped clear of clouds by the jawbone of the World's End Range to the north. A chill, dry wind ruffled our fur.

It was so cold up on the Plateau that we had to wear protective covers on our hands and feet. Those members of the expedition who were too vain to do without facial braids had to wrap their muzzles as well, where the chill struck at the partings in their fur. Whenever one of the sumpter beasts let loose a shower of dung, the pellets froze mid-air and rattled off the path like beads.

I had ample opportunity to study this last phenomenon, walking as I was at the rear of the line with Kettle the drover. We had hired her shortly after leaving the central provinces, and over the course of our travels I had found her far better company, in many ways, than the more educated Free in our party. Although I'd put in time at the Academy myself, years of working with miners had given me a taste for plain speaking which was not shared by my other travel companions.

Kettle also seemed to possess a more inquiring mind than even the historians among us. Upon first meeting me and hearing my qualifications, she didn't subject me to yet another lecture on how important it was that the contents of the Dead Mound not be damaged. Instead she was full of lively questions about how I would place my powder and calculate the charges, and how the extreme temperatures would affect my work. Later we conversed about everything from music in the capital to the habits of prey in our home ranges.

Of course, it could have been nothing more than kindness. Even with her silvered fur unbraided and frizzing comically out from her jowls, Kettle was obviously a Caretaker; it took only a few moments of conversation to discern her pack role. In her middle years, with her pack's offspring safely grown, she'd hired on with us to care for the sumpter beasts and meat animals, but she couldn't help looking after every person in the expedition as well. She even worried about Solfatara, the abrasive young religious zealot the Conclave had foisted on us for political reasons.

"I've never met a Singularist before," Kettle told me as we padded along. "He must feel lonely, being the only one in the group—maybe that's why he's so sarcastic all the time. I'm sure I could make him feel better, if he would just talk to me."

"You should be glad he doesn't. You must be the only one of us he hasn't tried to convert." I wondered if Kettle knew that Solfatara referred to her and Lastwell as "bumpkins" and worse when they were out of earshot.

"Well, you can't blame him for trying, can you?"

"Of course I can. I'm a Cataclysmist myself, so I'm in the minority most places I go, but you don't hear me arguing with everyone all the time."

Kettle suddenly darted ahead and returned an errant beast to the herd with a practiced grip at the base of its jaw.

"Yes, but you don't have so much to argue about," she said breathlessly. "I mean, I was raised Insurrectionist—very strict, heart and liver to the Rebel Leaders every tenth kill—but I can keep an open mind. I can try to see your point of view and imagine that maybe the Tyrants were wiped out by some natural event. But to be like Solfatara, to say that they never even existed—I just can't do that."

Religious argument was a regular pastime among the others, but it was the first time I'd heard Kettle come close to it. Could she finally be feeling it, too—the tension of being so near our goal, close to revelations that could confirm or shatter her own beliefs?

I sidestepped as a flurry of dung pebbles skittered down the slope in our direction. Our way was steeper now, and over the shaggy backs of the animals I could see the other five Free of our party strung out along the flank of the hill. As usual they were walking in twos for ease of conversation, with one odd man out—currently the young Butcher, Brickburrow, separated from his mentor Steampool while the senior historian conferred with our guide.

"I agree, Solfatara's position is absurd," I told Kettle. "Who knows? Soon we may be able to prove him wrong."

"But that's just what worries me! Poor Solfatara—how's he going to feel if we actually find any Tyrant remains?"

I snorted. "If that happens, we'll be too busy to worry about Solfatara."

We reached the Dead Mound later that day. It was an immense lava tunnel, the farthest-reaching finger of a nameless, worn-out volcano. But there was none of the homelike feeling one usually associates with thermal areas. There was not a single hot spring or green leaf to be seen—only scanty pockets of snow, and here and there a spatter of lichen.

We picked our way over steepening ridges. Finally Kettle sent me up to the head of the line with a message for Steampool. "Tell him we're camping here, unless he wants frozen meat for his supper. That's what he'll get if one of the beasts breaks a leg, because I won't let an animal suffer till evening just to keep his food warm.

"Oh, but don't say it like that! Be polite!" she called after me as I hurried ahead.

We reached the stubby western end of the mound not long after. Steampool and Brickburrow broke into a lope to arrive there first. When the rest of us caught up, Steampool had already removed his hand covers and was running his strong fingers over the stone.

He was a striking figure against the dark wall. His fur had yellowed, away from the chemical cleansers available in the sophisticated baths of the capital. But even without his snowy coat, he looked every bit as imposing as when he paced the walkways of the Academy.

"Masonry," he rumbled.

It was true. The end of the mound was a wall of massive fitted blocks, so eroded that it resembled raw stone.

"So worn, it is!" commented Gull Gliding, the foreign scholar. Her voice was as cool as ever, but her exotic gray eyes shone. "Especially for this area of little water. It is of great antiquity, surely, a discovery of much importance."

Solfatara pulled down his face cover. "Ha! Can you really call this a *discovery,* when we had a guide to lead us right up to it? Or maybe you've already forgotten Defender Lastwell's contribution?"

Lastwell stiffened. "The scholar meant no offense."

Steampool's resonant voice cut in. "Solfatara is correct," he said. "This is not a discovery."

All eyes went back to him; even Brickburrow, who had been engrossed in examining the wall, turned to listen.

"It seemed like one, back at the Academy." Steampool shrugged ruefully. "When I translated the manuscript describing this place, it was like nothing I'd ever heard of before. And when Brickburrow helped me piece together more references, and even rough out a map—well, those of you from the capital probably remember the uproar."

I hadn't read Steampool's academic paper, but the speculations had soon made it into the popular press. The prospect of a tomb was novel enough; the very idea of the wasted meat and uncracked bones, hidden away in stone with no way to return their richness to the land, had produced shocked hisses in every braiding-parlor of the city. Surely not even an emperor would be so perverse?

But what really set the capital bubbling was the hint that the buried monarch might be an actual member of the Tyrant species. What would it be like to gaze on the massive leg-bones, the monstrous, heavy-jawed skull of one of our ancient oppressors? What would it mean to bring the Tyrants, those shadowy archetypes from the dawn of history, into the clear scientific light of the present day?

And the politics! How would Tyrant remains affect the current Conclave, which had been so conscientious about representing every religious group, even the oddball Singularists?

"When we started planning this trip, it felt like we'd be walking off the edge of the world," Steampool continued. "But we were ready to leave the comforts of pack and range, to travel into strange lands, to endure rough trails and unfamiliar meat. For as we Free begin this new era of inquiry and innovation, we must know the truth about our past."

As Steampool raised his stately head and turned his deep-set eyes on us, it was easy to see how he had persuaded the Conclave to finance the expedition. Even Solfatara's ears were tilted forward in agreement.

"You all saw how things changed, the farther we went from the cities and centers of progress. As we traveled we sought out folklore that echoed our research—and we began to find it. Children's scare-stories of Tyrant ghosts underground; whispers of monsters in Plateau caves. We started getting silences and turned backs in the villages. There were folk who darted their eyes toward the east at the mention of a Tyrant tomb.

"But there were other Free who helped us—folk who had traveled beyond their birth range, or had managed to get books from the central provinces. They told us their local legends, and helped us find our way. And finally, at the edge of the Plateau, we found Defender Lastwell, who alone in his village was willing to go against centuries of fear and superstition to show us what his people call the Dead Mound."

Lastwell scuffed his feet against the ground. He was a smallish, wiry male

with the curly coat one sometimes sees in remote, inbred communities. He had been understandably shy ever since joining our group, but his story had gradually come out: how in his youth he had left his tiny, nine-pack range and traveled far away to Silver Springs, a larger settlement which he referred to as "the city." He had eventually returned home, joined a pack, and now served as schoolteacher to his community.

"No reason this place should be forbidden," Lastwell mumbled. "Nothing but superstition." Defiantly, he edged up to the wall and placed both hands against the stone.

Steampool's eyes shone. "There we see it," he said quietly. "What was it that really led us here? Not just our own scholarship or persistence. It was the new openness and learning that have spread outward from the capital in our generation." He brushed the ancient wall with one big hand. "I say it again: this is not a discovery.

"It is a victory."

While the others examined the stonework, Steampool took me aside. "Tracker, how long will you need to get this wall down?"

Two Free with pickaxes probably could have chipped out a doorway within a day, but I didn't need to tell Steampool that. I had realized when he invited me on this trip that sundering the wall with explosives was very important to him. For political or poetical reasons, he wanted it to be the most modern technology that brought down the barrier between us and the past.

"A few hours," I told him. "But I'd recommend waiting a day before we go in. The air could be foul, and there might be delayed rockfalls."

"Hmm." Steampool surveyed the rest

of the team: Brickburrow, with his lanky arms swinging as if he'd like to tear into the wall with his bare claws; Gull Gliding, writing furiously in her spiky Coastal script; Solfatara, pacing intently; and Lastwell, sitting motionless and staring at the wall. "I doubt I could enforce a whole day's wait. What if you blew the wall this evening? Would it be safe to go in by morning tomorrow?"

"I'd think so."

Solfatara was incredulous. "I thought the Tracker was supposed to be a demolitions expert. Boom!" he shouted, making Lastwell jump. "How long could it take?"

"It's crucial that we all be rested and alert when history is made," Steampool said sternly. "As soon as we bring up Tracker Sweetwater's equipment, we'll be heading back to camp for meat and sleep. Everything will be easier tomorrow in the daylight."

Lastwell dipped his head in agreement. "Sensible, I say. Better not to enter in the dark."

Although his words were nearly the same as Steampool's, something in his intonation made me realize that we were standing at the closed mouth of a tomb— a cold and ancient hollow that might well contain the long bones and outsized jaws of a Tyrant. By now, a ridge of stone had laid a black shadow across the lower half of the wall, and the ruddy sunset light above showed the end of the Dead Mound as a red-gummed muzzle, baring a grin of interlocked black teeth.

The others seemed to share my feelings. Even Solfatara was uncharacteristically efficient as he packed up his notes.

It was a simple job, one any of my students could have managed. Steampool had invited along a senior engineer in much the same spirit as he had planned to use explosives instead of hand tools to open the tomb. Those who want the tech-

nical details of my work that night can refer to the paper I later published in *Excavator & Miner's*. Suffice it to say that I did the most professional job I could in that desolate place, with no one to hold the lantern or even keep me company as the sun sank into a bloody stain on the horizon.

After the roar of the detonation, the dust spread in a great pale cloud like an animal's hot breath, lit red by the last sunset glow. My Tracker stubbornness drove me back toward the mound only far enough to see that my efforts had indeed opened that stony maw.

The familiar layout of our camp and the circle of Free around our lantern seemed as welcoming that night as coming home to my own pack. Meat-sharing was over, but Brickburrow had set aside a portion of the supper beast for me, including a large share of the liver. Everyone had heard the powder go off, and they were elated to hear that I had been successful, but soon enough they resumed their favorite arguments.

"—nothing but a powerful archetype, a reflection of the age-old desire of the youngster to break free of its birth-pack," Solfatara was saying. "The symbolism is *obvious*. The supposed Tyrants, larger and stronger, holding sway over us until we finally mature and assert our independence—"

"Not all believe so in the Uprising," Gull Gliding corrected him haughtily. She was the other Cataclysmist of our group, a Diluvian, like most folk from the Shore. A scholar of great repute in her home country, she had made it clear that this discovery was too important to be left to inland barbarians. This far into the trip, still no one had dared to inform her that her foreign braid pattern was similar to that used by inland children.

"Ah yes, the Cataclysmic view," Solfatara exclaimed. "But still the symbolism holds true. The young ones who are separated too soon from their parental group by circumstances beyond their control—forced to take on adult responsibilities before they feel ready—"

Gull Gliding's ruff rose. "You try to say, Cataclysmists are immature? You were raised Insurrectionist, I will guess. Perhaps you still feel so, beneath."

"I do still think there may have been an Uprising," Solfatara admitted, studying the silver claw-guards that he affected.

"An Uprising, but no Tyrants?" I asked him.

"That's right. No separate species, no race of monsters. If we did have oppressors—they were us."

"Free could never be that vicious," Brickburrow protested. "We don't eat each other, for one thing; it's unnatural."

Lastwell raised his head. "Tyrants existed, and they were crueler than we can imagine. My people remember." Locks of his loose cheek fur, still showing traces of his Defender's braids, coiled around his thin face. "Mind you, I'm not superstitious. I don't believe they had any supernatural powers. If there's a Tyrant buried in that cave up there, unsealing it won't make any difference to him. He's not hungry, he's long dead—he can't come marching out tonight looking for prey."

No one spoke for a moment as we all listened to the wind hooting across the tumbled stone of the escarpment, the sighs and snufflings of the herdbeasts and the creaking of the ropes that held them on their tether line.

"Eh, Lastwell, we'll all sleep sound after that," Brickburrow said, showing his crooked front teeth.

"Now, now." Steampool's voice was reassuring and full of humor. "If any of us are restless tonight, it'll be from excitement. We all know old bones can't hurt us."

Later, as I nestled down among the warm, curled bodies of my fellows in the sleeping tent, I wondered if Steampool really believed that. What we discovered in that mound might well challenge the dearest beliefs of thousands of Free. The time-worn, almost comfortable arguments would be revived with a new fervor, and who knew what tumult might erupt? The folktales we had struggled against to get here spoke of a terrible evil that would emerge if the tomb was unsealed. Perhaps, as Solfatara might say, those legends had a symbolic truth.

And I was the one who had opened it.

In the morning I woke to raised voices. "He tells us to wait, and then he sneaks on ahead! Just what I'd expect from that posturer." Solfatara pushed his way into the sleeping tent with an angry gesture.

"It is arrogant," Gull Gliding agreed coldly as she entered behind him. She was fiercely rebraiding her cheek fur, slim fingers pulling the hair mercilessly tight.

"He thinks he is the one who knows best, always. I have his learning and more, but he does not listen to my advice. The site must be explored slowly with many observers! I have told him this often." This last was unnecessary; we had all witnessed their clashes.

Brickburrow, just awakened, raised his head. "What's going on?"

"Sounds like Steampool's missing," said Lastwell. "Must've already gone up to the tomb, that's all. Probably wanted to be the first inside. No other explanation," he added, ears flicking.

"Oh, surely not," Kettle protested, uncurling from her spot beside me. "It's not like him, to try to grab the glory that way."

Brickburrow looked down quickly, but not before I saw a bitter expression twist his face. Then he took a deep breath, stretching his long arms. "Well, arguing won't find him any quicker, eh?" He looked around, meeting eyes, making sure everyone remembered that he was the secondary leader of the expedition. "But it does seem like the mound is the first place to look.

I had imagined that when we first entered the Dead Mound, it would be a weighty occasion. I had pictured us wearing resolute expressions, groomed as meticulously as our circumstances allowed, equipment in impeccable order, conscious of the eyes of future generations upon us.

Instead we rushed up to the site in a ragged line, fur tangled and braids unraveled, foot covers sloppily tied and eyes sandy with sleep. Our stomachs were rumbling, empty of even a morning cup of broth, and we had to pause along the way for those who had forgotten to use the latrine before we left. As we reached the gap torn in the wall, poor Lastwell destroyed our last vestige of dignity by spewing up his supper on the threshold.

Brickburrow tried to save the moment with a few well-chosen words. "Taboos instilled in childhood are not easily overcome," he managed. "As we step over this vomitus, let us consider it the rejected aliment of superstition and irrational fear that we are leaving behind. Eh?"

I couldn't help thinking that Steampool would have done better.

We stooped and squeezed through the rough doorway with the minimum of decorum, entering an antechamber floored with fitted blocks and roofed in raw stone. What we saw there, in that startling stillness as we left the wind outside, made us forget all about our search for Steampool.

Our yellow lantern light, and the diffuse daylight spreading from the entrance hole,

fell upon a gaunt but towering form posed beside a tall doorway. Draped in the hide of some unknown, stripe-coated animal, it appeared to be a clay statue—or no, it was an immense scare-doll, of leather dried over a framework of wire—or no— I was not the only one to cry out as I finally made sense of what I saw. What I had thought a leather mask was a long-dead face, fur shaved short, flesh and skin shrunken to the bone like a piece of freeze-dried meat.

Which, of course, was exactly what it was.

None of us had expected that the arid, frigid climate of the Plateau could preserve a corpse with such horrific faithfulness while ages passed outside. But looking at the ancient figure, none of us doubted that we had indeed uncovered a relic of the remote, near-mythical past.

For as we continued to stare, more details emerged: the massive, heavy-jawed skull beneath the bristly fur; the muzzle, so blunt it seemed deformed; the striped fur that was not a covering after all, but the guard's own pelt; and most of all, the huge, hulking size of it even in its shrunken state, the sunken eye-pits that peered darkly out at a level far above any of our heads.

The only sound was a dry retching from Lastwell as we gazed at the figure that was so appallingly like a Free, and yet grotesquely unlike.

Solfatara was the first to speak. "Well," he said in a brittle, cheerful voice, "I guess I was wrong."

That single Tyrant corpse was probably enough to found a new school of study at the Academy. But none of us would have joined this expedition without a strong streak of curiosity, and it wasn't long before the second doorway beckoned us.

Our lantern light was unsteady on the dark walls as we filed through the fitted arch, well within the reach of those long, dessicated arms.

We emerged into a hall forested with Tyrants.

An aisle stretched ahead into darkness. Lined on either side, tens of dozens of mummified bodies stood, their withered hands clutched together in gestures of obeisance, long bony fingers sewn together by time as tightly as soaked rawhide wrapping a knife hilt.

"No braids," Brickburrow murmured. "But look at those wristlets and throat-guards, the intricacy of the knotwork. Perhaps that was how they indicated pack-role."

"You inlanders with your pack-roles," Gull Gliding snorted. "Why do you assume they had such? Your prejudices make you blind, I think."

"Of course you're right, scholar," Brickburrow conceded. "Their family structure may be completely alien. Though I'm sure we can deduce something from the presence here of their young."

I had not noticed until then that the Tyrants' shriveled remains were of varying sizes. Their visages were uniformly wrinkled, their eyes like sun-dried berries in leather pouches, giving an impression of great age; but among the groves of giant forms were some of our own height or less, with the outsize hands and feet of childhood.

"Was it a plague?" Kettle asked softly. "What could have carried off so many families at once?"

Brickburrow shifted uncomfortably. "You're forgetting, Kettle, we have reason to believe this is the tomb of a Tyrant emperor. It could easily have demanded that its favorite servants, um, accompany it into death."

"Possible, also, that a demand was not needed," Gull Gliding put in. "They believed, perhaps, that it was an honor to be so chosen."

I had thought the gullied faces ranked around us horrific enough, but I shivered to picture living Tyrants sidling through the hall on their thick-boned legs, swinging their huge-jawed heads from side to side, propping and bracing the dried bodies of the slain servants to form this tableau.

Our cluster of lantern light crawled down the dark walkway like the glow at the tip of a burning fuse. The Tyrant bodies, dry lips pulled slightly back from brown slabs of teeth, seemed to sneer silently down at us.

At the end of the hall a throne of stone blocks loomed up like a mountain above a plain. Upon the summit, its stick-arms extended indolently along the armrests, presided the sere form of what had to be the Tyrant emperor.

Its face, with ancient flesh furrowed over the broad, blunt muzzle, surveyed its domain with an inscrutable gaze. At the ends of the armrests its palms were turned toward us, long fingers spread sideways as if accepting adulation. Knobbled toes twisted upwards from feet that seemed disproportionately large for its frame.

"Righteous Pestilence," I swore softly as we approached, our heads tilted upward in fascination. "Is it—a child?"

"So it seems," said Brickburrow. "Yes, compare the size."

"Intriguing! An indication, surely, that the position of Emperor was one of inheritance." Gull Gliding moved closer, eyes gleaming with scholarly delight—and then recoiled, lantern swinging wildly, with a strangled cry higher in pitch than I had ever heard her utter.

Lying in the darkness at the foot of the Tyrant's throne was the bulky, motionless body of a Free, luxuriant fur braided in the rippled pattern of a Stalker, mighty chest unstirred by even a hint of breath.

We had found Steampool.

"**E**veryone out!" Lastwell howled. "Before the curse strikes us too!" His panic was contagious, and we hastily withdrew, tripping on our foot covers and stepping on each other's toes. Outside the tomb, we milled around, stunned, while Lastwell crouched trembling nearby.

"Fools!" Gull Gliding panted. "To so believe in curses!"

"I notice you moved as fast as anyone," said Solfatara, wrinkling his nose as he scraped crumbs of frozen vomit off his foot covers.

"Poor, poor Steampool," Kettle mourned. "At least it was quick—it looked like it was, anyway—"

Brickburrow raised his arms. "Please. We've had a terrible shock, but there's no need to talk of curses. It's obvious what happened. Stalker Steampool was so eager to explore the tomb, he not only didn't wait for the rest of us—he also ignored the Tracker's warning about bad air. I just thank the Rebels that the fumes had already cleared by the time we all went in." Brickburrow turned to me. "Isn't that right?"

"It's possible," I said slowly. "But there's only one way to find out."

"Don't go back in there," Lastwell pleaded.

"Oh, we can't just leave his body inside, can we? I couldn't bear to think of him trapped in there, with all those hungry-looking Tyrants staring down at him..." Kettle's voice trailed off.

"We won't leave him." Brickburrow beckoned to me and Solfatara. "Tracker. Killer. Will you accompany me?"

We set down the six lanterns we had brought in a semicircle around Steampool's body, making it look obscenely like the prey of honor set out for a Firsthunt celebration.

"It could be bad air," I said slowly. "The way his hands are near his throat. But see how his head is lying—"

Solfatara squinted down at the corpse. "His throat braids are all messed up. He'd never have left camp looking like that. Not even in the middle of the night. I'd say he was strangled. Or maybe his neck was broken."

Despite ourselves, we looked up at the Tyrant emperor seated calmly above, underlit face tilted slightly toward the dark ceiling, bony fingers spread wide.

Brickburrow gave a humorless laugh. "I'd almost like to believe that thing did it," he said. "But I don't think it has the muscle tone, eh?"

"But we do," I completed his thought. "Any of us."

There was little more to be told from Steampool's body, even after we moved it outside. It was almost completely frozen, but that would not have taken long.

Brickburrow took me aside. "If this was murder, we need to know who did it," he said. "You're our Tracker. You find out."

"What? But there's no dust in the tomb," I stalled.

"Don't be so literal. You're the best one for the job, and you know it. Please, Sweetwater. We can't have this pack falling apart now. We've got important work to do."

My neck fur rose. His mentor had just been murdered, and he had "important" work to do?

"I'll Track," I said gruffly.

At Brickburrow's direction, I headed back toward camp with Lastwell and Kettle. The wind was restless, shifting and picking at our fur from different directions, and the low morning sun flashed in and out of view as we passed between humps of stone. I felt hollow and strange as I tried to organize my thoughts.

Who besides Steampool had left the sleeping tent last night? I had no idea. I had slept unusually well myself, knowing my main task was done.

"Kettle," I began, raising my voice over the whisper of the wind. "Do you remember who left the sleeping tent last night?"

She shrugged unhappily. "Not really. I went out a couple of times to check on the animals, so I could easily have missed someone going in or out."

"I didn't sleep." Lastwell's voice was shrill. "Didn't sleep that whole night long, thinking what might come out of that mound. Just about everyone went out, one time or another. But not me. Didn't dare."

Lastwell's memory proved unreliable on how long each Free had been out of the tent, but he did think that Gull Gliding and Steampool had left together.

"Shouldn't be wasting your time on these questions, though," Lastwell told me. "Obvious who killed the Stalker: that Solfatara fellow! Only one who's got the temper for it."

"Oh? How do you think it happened?"

"Simple. Steampool goes out to sneak a look at the tomb, and Solfatara follows him in, worried he's going to fake up some Tyrant bones or something. Gets the shock of his life, being Singular or whatever it is he calls himself. All Steampool would have to do is tease him about it, the way he always does—always did. All it would take. Solfatara's a Killer, after all. It would come easy to him. Must've happened like that. The Tyrants are nothing but long bones and leather, no way they could—"

His voice had become uneven again, and under Kettle's accusing glance, I fell silent for the rest of the walk back.

Later, after we had eaten and Lastwell had retired shakily to the sleeping tent, I sought out Kettle again. She had taken the herd to forage in the long trench between two reaching arms of rock. The heavy-lidded food animals were pulling at the lichens that splotched the stone like ill-kept fur. Most of the sumpters were clustered near Kettle, who was brushing down her favorite one with short, fierce strokes.

I elbowed and pushed my way between the shaggy backs and rumps. My best relationships with beasts, I'm afraid, have always come when they are lying before me in pieces on a platter.

"Kettle—you heard what Lastwell said. Do you think Solfatara could have killed Steampool? Could the shock of seeing the Tyrants have unbalanced him that much?"

Kettle ran the brush slowly over the smooth pads of the animal's cheeks. "I can't believe anyone in our expedition could kill a Free—unless they were defending their pack, of course," she added hastily. "Tracker, are you sure it wasn't fumes?"

I didn't answer.

Two of the meat animals chose that moment to compress me between their hot sides, and Kettle had to rescue me with a deft hand at the nerve points on their necks. Watching her skill, I couldn't help thinking that despite her modest size, Kettle would have been just as capable of bringing down Steampool as any of the rest of us. Maybe more so.

Back at the camp, I learned from Lastwell that the other three had arrived, gathered food and equipment, and swept off back to the tomb site, talking excitedly of what they'd found. I noticed, as I trudged up to the mound for the second time that day, that we had already worn a track into the thin soil.

I found Solfatara resting outside the entrance, close enough to the wall to shelter from the wind, gnawing on a stick of jerky.

"I should probably be in there, observing," he told me. "But I can only spend so long with those dried-up corpses." He grinned whitely. "On the other hand, the *Tyrant* remains don't bother me at all."

I didn't laugh. "No one would blame you if you were uncomfortable around the Tyrants—"

"Oh, I'm embarrassed as *anything*. And of course they aren't the prettiest things to look at. Those long legs with the flesh all shriveled to nothing..." He took an unenthusiastic bite from the jerky, looked at it, then laid it down on the ground.

"But I was raised without any of that spittle about lingering Tyrant spirits. Now that I know the Tyrants were real—well, I still can't see them as pure evil, the way most Free do. They were just intelligent animals, even if they did treat us like livestock."

"You certainly seem to be in better shape than Lastwell," I observed.

"Lastwell. Now, there's a sad cub." Solfatara pulled off one of his claw-caps and examined the perfect, snow-white tine beneath. "Although—doesn't he seem a little too *convenient,* sometimes? There we were, in that little bloodspot of a trading outpost, and suddenly the ideal guide pops up and offers to take us right to the tomb. And this is a village that has a morbid fear of Tyrant curses—a village that probably is the *reason* no other explorers ever got this far."

"You make it sound like we were lucky they didn't murder us all in our sleep."

"They couldn't have done *that.* We're too high-profile, sent by the Conclave and all. But imagine how they must have felt, thinking we were going to doom them all by disturbing the emperor's grave. I still remember their eyes."

Indeed, that last stay had been very unpleasant, except for the luck of meeting Lastwell.

Solfatara squinted up at the sun. "They'd talked to us. They knew we wouldn't be satisfied until we'd looked inside their Dead Mound. But maybe we could be frightened so badly that we'd seal it up again and go running back to the cities, with a story that would keep everyone away for another generation. Maybe, oh, something about the Tyrant emperor strangling our leader with its own dead hands."

"You're saying that Lastwell could have lured Steampool into the tomb, killed him, and set things up to look like the emperor did it?"

I was hoping that when I said it, the theory would sound more far-fetched, but my mind was sickly totting up the many times Lastwell had set everyone on edge by referring to Tyrant curses, usually right before bedtime. His nausea upon facing the tomb this morning—only superstitious fear, or perhaps fear mixed with guilt? And the way he had induced a panic when Steampool's body was found... his dismay at seeing that we weren't paralyzed with fear, that we planned to go back in....

"It's something to think about, isn't it?" said Solfatara. "These country mouse-eaters aren't really *rational,* like us—you never know what their delusions can make them do. You might want to be more careful around Kettle, too—she's not from the cities either, you know."

I made myself nod to Solfatara before turning and plunging through the broken space in the wall, into dimness which seemed almost welcoming. Surely Solfatara was only being spiteful, in his own imaginative way. I berated myself for even considering his ideas, even as I revolved them in my mind like a Butcher studying a diseased organ.

At least I had found out one thing, I thought as I entered the throne room. Solfatara was not in shock.

A lantern was set midway down the aisle, and another rested near the base of the throne where Steampool's body had lain. Their flames were almost motionless within their isinglass shields. The smooth light fell on the sticklike limbs of the Tyrant multitude as if they were no more than a thicket of dead wood. The air smelled of burning tallow and nothing else.

I picked up the first lantern, and it swung in my hand. In an instant, the dreamlike mood was gone. The moving light glanced off the edges of great-toothed jaws, the sides of legs covered in ropes of gristle, so that they seemed to crawl with stealthy movement like maggots in meat. As I hurried toward the throne, foot covers shushing far too loudly against the floor, I imagined that I could almost hear a sibilant whispering, growing ever louder, in some unknown tongue.

Then I realized that it was not my imagination. The hissing came from a faintly glowing doorway in the wall to the left of the throne. It was Gull Gliding, of course, talking to herself in the barbaric dialect of the Shore.

Embarrassed, I turned toward the other doorway, also dimly illuminated, that lay on the opposite side of the throne.

As I stepped through the arch, my light fell on a snarling face, inches from my own, its fangs bared. I choked back a cry, and heard Brickburrow's dry laugh.

"Gave you a start, eh, Tracker?"

The grimacing face belonged to a mid-sized predator similar to the tuft-eared deercatcher of my native range. Its eyes were wrinkled black slits.

The chamber was lined with shelves of such trophies—some complete bodies, some mere heads, beaks, or severed paws. As I looked further, I saw works of art: platters made from etched shoulder blades, strings of threaded vertebrae and carved bone beads, draped pelts which, even in this light, retained tatters of beauty. There were eggshells of freakish size, painted in intricate geometric patterns. There was a pair of drinking horns etched with birds, and—

"Merciful Plague!"

Brickburrow sighed happily. "Isn't it amazing? A perfect illustration of how they must have regarded us. Not even servants—just cattle, or even furniture." Before him—and obviously the subject of the current sketch in his notebook—was the corpse of a Free on hands and knees, looking for all the world like a small table—and indeed, a length of beaded leather lay draped over its back.

The body seemed pathetically small, compared to the dead Tyrants. Its face gazed impassively at the floor, and its hands were knuckled into impotent half-fists. I could hardly bear to look at it. "Should we bury it, do you think?"

Brickburrow looked aghast. "No, no, it's far too valuable for that. This could be one of the most important specimens in the whole site! It has to be treated with respect. Many papers will be written, I can promise you that. But first things first, eh? Inventory, inventory...."

Brickburrow closed his notebook. "I'm sorry, Tracker, I tend to get carried away. What have you found out so far?"

I had intended to question Brickburrow as I had the others, but I found myself recounting my previous conversations.

"Hmm. I don't put much stock in any of those theories." Brickburrow lowered his voice, and glanced toward the door. "But I do find it interesting that Gull Gliding and Steampool were seen leaving the tent together."

"Kettle tells me that wasn't unusual for them—pest knows why."

"Oh, come on, Tracker, are you really that naïve? A sexual liaison, of course."

"What? But it's not the season," I said automatically, and then felt foolish. "Wait—you don't mean—I've heard of such things, but—"

Brickburrow stroked his narrow muzzle in a worldly-wise gesture he had probably copied from Steampool. "I assure you, in certain circles in the capital, those kinds of drugs are easily available. And Gull Gliding's from the Shore, after all. Who knows what she might consider normal?"

"But they weren't even fond of each other," I protested, remembering their fiery shouting matches. Their passionate arguments, their glee whenever they thought they'd won a point....

"I suppose it's possible," I conceded. "But do you think Gull Gliding killed him, then?"

Brickburrow's ears flattened. "Rebels know, I wouldn't choose a tomb as a place for a rendezvous, but if they fancied forbidden thrills—well, you can't get much more forbidden, eh? Then maybe they argued over how to preserve the site. She has strong opinions on that," he added darkly.

As I approached the other lighted doorway, I tried to throw off Brickburrow's distasteful suggestions, but the images clung like cobwebs on the whiskers.

This chamber was empty except for the straining form of Gull Gliding holding her lantern as high as she could reach, her arm trembling from fatigue.

"Ahh, Sweetwater, you are coming at the best time! Might you hold this, please?" Her face, its absurd child's braids dangling like icicles, was more animated than I had ever seen it. As I held our lights where she indicated, I saw why: the stone blocks that formed the wall were grooved and crazed with an unintelligible pattern that had to be some sort of script.

"Extraordinary!" I marveled.

"Yes, this we had not expected, never. None of our legends even hint that the Tyrants were literate. So much knowledge, lost in the time of the flooding! And more destroyed after, when we Free wanted only to forget our captivity. As a Free, I have sympathy; but as a scholar, I regret."

"I don't suppose you can actually read it?"

"No, of course I cannot. Frustrating!" She scanned the wall with narrowed eyes. "And yet, there are familiarities. I will like to compare this with the chirography of the Far Western mountain Free..."

I cleared my throat. "Scholar, I'm sorry to interrupt your work, but I've got a few questions."

"Ah, yes, this burden the so-wise Brickburrow has chosen to lay on you. Proceed."

Gull Gliding did not precisely recall who had left the sleeping tent the previous night, but her recollections were in line with the others.

"Did you see Steampool go out, scholar?"

"Yes, he went in and out several times. I noticed because I was sleeping next to him. He was—most warm." Her eyes stayed on the wall markings. "Once I even followed him outside, to ask if he was well. But he did not wish my company, he made it clear. He was looking far away, even as he ordered me back into the tent."

"And did you go back in?"

"Yes. I always went back in." She traced the line of a swirling letter, conscientiously not touching the stone.

"Do you have any ideas about who might have killed him, scholar?"

She turned her eyes back to me, and for a moment they looked as ancient as the arcane symbols graven on the wall. "Who else but the one who has hated for years? The one who did the messy, bloody work, only to have Steampool take the glory? Yes, one may even say, the Butcher's work. You see how I have learned about your inlander packs."

I recalled again that Gull Gliding came from the decadent Shore, a land of fish-eaters who lacked the very concept of the hunt. Their language, she had told us, did not even contain different pronouns for the six pack roles. She laughed at how the Conclave had taken such pains to fill out a proper work-pack for our expedition, and claimed not to understand why Steampool selected our supper beast each day, Solfatara killed it, and Brickburrow carved it up.

Could she truly not understand that for a Butcher, it was natural to spend time on details, to do the painstaking, careful work, while a Stalker oversaw the larger sweep of analysis?

How horrible if she was right, though— if Brickburrow was so unhappy with his own nature that he would kill his closest colleague!

There are Free, of course, who fit more than one pack role. There's a good bit of Killer in most Stalkers, and I know I've some Butcher in me. But a Butcher can never be a Stalker; they're just too different. Brickburrow could never hope to have Steampool's charisma, or his incisive insight.

Had that been reason enough to kill him?

Brickburrow made us leave the tomb site before full dark, so we wouldn't waste candles lighting our way back. Clearly he

also felt that we should be conserving our strength; upon returning to camp he ordered all work to cease and supper preparations to begin immediately.

"You'll act as Stalker, naturally, won't you, Sweetwater?" he asked me.

I had expected this, but didn't relish the idea of pushing in among the meat beasts for the second time today. Luckily I was spared that annoyance. "Kettle's taken the herd out to graze again," Lastwell told me. "Probably ran out of things to do here, after she swept the campsite."

"She what?"

"Took a broom to the bare rock, after she finished cleaning out the tent. This was after she reorganized all our supplies, rendered down the fat from last night's carcass, and dug us a new latrine. Couldn't seem to stop." Lastwell shook his head. "Slept all day, myself. Anyhow, at least she left a supper beast back for us."

It was one of the most docile meat animals, fortunately, and I silently thanked Kettle as I tugged the creature across to where Brickburrow had set up the Butcher's bar.

It was a simple travel set, with wide tripod feet for the two support poles, since here they could not be staked into snow or earth. The crossbar was wood as well, with the plainest of bosses on the ends, and the hoists were not chain but rope, stained and weathered from our journey. As I helped Solfatara fasten the noose around the forelegs of the sleepily blinking animal, I couldn't help thinking of the city compound of my home pack, where the Butcher's bar was the lowest branch of a living tree. And our range outside the capital, teeming with prey, soft with lush grasses under the moist snow—how different from this bleak wasteland!

"I choose this for us," I said brusquely, the Stalker's line feeling lumpy on my tongue.

Solfatara distracted the beast with soft words, and broke its spine with one decisive twist of his arms. "I make it ours," he said.

Brickburrow and Solfatara took up the hoist rope, and the pulley creaked as they drew the animal's forelegs upward. There is a certain stage in this process, when the beast seems almost to be standing upright like a Free, that always makes me shudder, and I felt glad when the beast was finally dangling in the air like proper food.

Brickburrow picked up his skinning knife from the cloth where he had painstakingly laid it out next to his whetstone and saw. "I divide it among us," he intoned, and raised his hand.

It was at that moment that the frayed rope gave way.

Solfatara shouted in dismay, and leaped backward barely in time to avoid being pinned under the plunging weight of the dead beast. Brickburrow dodged as well, luckily not slashing anyone with the knife in his wildly waving hand. The animal collapsed onto its hindquarters with a soft thud, and for a surreal moment imitated a seated Free as it had earlier imitated a standing one. Then it toppled onto its side, coming to rest in a position hideously similar to that in which we had found Steampool that morning.

"Deluge," Gull Gliding swore softly.

"Never seen such a bad omen!" Lastwell's voice was hoarse with horror. "Ought to pack up and leave this place. Tonight!"

I gazed down at the heavy head of the supper beast, with its tongue protruding slightly over its blocklike teeth, and suddenly my thoughts gave a quiet click, like the tiny sound the beast's spine had made when Solfatara twisted its neck.

I stood stricken for a moment, then whirled around. "We need to get up to the tomb site! Right now!"

"What's wrong?" Brickburrow asked, easily catching up to me on his gangly legs.

I didn't have breath to explain. "It's Kettle," I panted. "She may be in terrible danger."

We were almost all the way to the mound when we found the dead sumpter. It sprawled in the trail, one hoof still wedged in the crevice that had snapped its leg. Kettle had mercifully broken its neck. I was impressed that she had managed to get the animal even this far over the treacherously piled rock.

I crouched down and examined the scuffed trail. "She kept going on foot, and she was carrying something heavy." I touched the blurs left by sacks. "Here's where she unloaded it from the sumpter."

"But what was it?"

"I'm very afraid it might be bags of blasting powder."

We were almost too late.

Kettle was crouched at the base of the emperor's throne. The tomb was lit only by a single lantern at her feet, and we could clearly see the crawling orange worms at the end of each fuse, squirming away across the floor.

"Defenders! Hold her!" Brickburrow rapped out. Lastwell and Gull Gliding seized Kettle's arms. Brickburrow raced to each fuse and amputated the glowing end, using the skinning knife he seemed startled to discover still in his hand.

"You were going to blow up the tomb, with yourself *inside?*" Solfatara asked Kettle incredulously.

Kettle's eyes darted around the dark hall, as if she hoped one of the silent Tyrants would answer the question. "Yes!" she blurted. "I don't deserve to live, after what I did to Steampool!"

There was a sudden babble of voices,

bouncing off the cave walls and the heads of the Tyrant mummies.

Brickburrow waved his arms. "Everyone! Quiet down. Kettle, tell us what happened, eh?"

Kettle drew in a breath. "He—he must've followed me from the camp," she said in a low voice. "I didn't mean to kill him! But the tomb was already scary enough, and then he came up behind me...."

"But what were you doing in here, anyway?" said Brickburrow.

"I was curious, that's all. Everyone else had already been up to the mound, while I was stuck setting up camp. If I'd known what would happen—" Kettle slumped in the Defenders' grasp.

"Should've just told us!" Lastwell scowled. "We know you, Kettle. Must've been an accident. Would've been a pretty short term of reparation."

"But that wouldn't be right!" Kettle burst out. "I'm a Caretaker, and I killed someone I was taking care of. No punishment is enough! I ought to die. I don't even deserve to have my body taken back to my home range. I figured I should bury it here, with the Tyrants. They're the only other creatures as wicked as me."

We all had pity in our faces as we looked down at Kettle's hunched, shaking body. But I do believe no one had more sympathy than me as I laid a hand on her shoulder.

"Poor Kettle," I said softly. "It's not going to work, I'm afraid. I know why you really wanted to blow up the tomb.

"And I know why you killed Steampool."

Although everyone must have been staring at me by that time, the only eyes I noticed were Kettle's, stark with despair.

"I didn't figure it out until tonight," I told her. "We had a bit of trouble with our supper beast—the rope on the Butcher's

bar gave way, and the animal fell to the ground. For a moment before it tipped to the side, it looked almost as if it were sitting like a Free. I thought about how odd it was to see a beast sitting, that usually goes on all fours. And that made me realize that a Free on hands and knees has essentially the same posture as a Free sitting with arms outstretched.

"Except for a few details...."

While the others were still frozen with confusion, I strode to the chamber of trophies. The mummified Free was as light in my hands as a dried-leather basket. I carried it back, shuddering at the feel of its papery skin and sticklike bones, and set it down carefully on the cold floor. Then I lifted the dead child off the throne.

The ancient Free fit as if the throne had been designed for it—as indeed it must have been. The hands curled negligently over the ends of the armrests, and the face which had seemed to look blankly at the floor now regarded the hall full of dead servitors with a dispassionate gaze.

As a final touch, I took the dry body of the child and set it, on its hands and knees, as a footrest beneath the heels of the Free. It was exactly the right height.

I turned and looked into the appalled faces of my companions.

"This," I told them, "is what Kettle and Steampool saw, when they entered the tomb last night."

"But—that makes no sense! How could the emperor be one of us—" Solfatara fell silent.

"Unless we were the ruling species," said Brickburrow thickly. "And the others were our slaves. You were right after all, Solfatara. The Tyrants were us."

From Solfatara there came a stream of low cursing; from Lastwell, whimpers of disbelief; from Gull Gliding, a hiss of indrawn breath, and from the rest, only stunned silence.

"You see?" Kettle cried out in anguish. "I couldn't let Steampool tell what he saw! I just couldn't!"

"So you killed him," I said quietly. "And then you switched the corpses around—that must have been a grim job. All to protect us from the truth."

"To protect *everyone,*" Kettle said.

There was silence while we all stared up at the throne.

"The hands do make more sense that way," Brickburrow said as if to himself.

"I suppose we can't call them *Tyrants* anymore, can we?" said Solfatara. "We'll have to think up some new name."

"That's the least of our problems," I put in. "What's going to happen when it comes out that every religion on the continent is wrong? That our whole culture is based on a lie? That our brave ancestors were slaveholders?"

"It's worse than that." In the lantern light Kettle's eyes were dark hollows, like the sockets of the Tyrant dead. "You still haven't figured it all out, have you? Yes, we were the ruling species. Yes, we kept the others as slaves. Probably we ate them too. But that's not all.

"We were the ones who wiped them out.

"Maybe they tried to revolt. Or maybe, over the generations, we bred their stock for intelligence—to be better servants— and suddenly we got scared that we'd succeeded too well. For whatever reason, once the killing started, it spread until we'd slaughtered them all.

"Why else would we have tried so hard to forget? Why else would we have destroyed every record of them, down to their bones? The guilt was too much to bear.

"We must've tried so hard to justify the massacre—to ourselves, to our children— that eventually we came to believe that the victims had deserved to die, that they had been the oppressors. Killer Solfatara, you with your psychological theories, what do you think of that?"

Solfatara shifted his weight. "It sounds pretty valid, actually," he mumbled.

"So the tomb did have a curse, after all," said Lastwell. "Can't even imagine what'll happen when the truth gets out."

"But it doesn't have to!" Kettle pleaded. "We can blow up the whole mound, and say we never found it. If we don't, just imagine what it'll do to everyone, across the whole continent, to find out that we Free are capable of such— such atrocity." She closed her eyes in pain. "I know what it's done to me."

"You're right to be afraid," I said slowly. "It's going to be more terrible than we can imagine. But I'm remembering what Steampool said. In this new age of technology, we must face our past."

Gull Gliding signed agreement. "The Tracker is correct. In this modern time, with the explosive powder, the steam-driven engines, the new drugs... More than ever we need to be aware of what we are capable."

"No more curses," Lastwell said roughly. "No more monsters and ghosts. Been enough of that."

"Ha! Why are we even *discussing* this? It's not as if any of us could ever *keep* this kind of secret." Solfatara picked at a tangle in his fur.

"Then we're decided." Brickburrow pulled his lanky frame erect, and his voice had a gravity I had not heard him manage before. "We'll get the Conclave to send guards for the site. We should publish as soon as we can, and widely. And if you're agreed, scholars—we should give Steampool full credit for the discovery."

"And the victory," I said. • • •

JACK WILLIAMSON
1908-2006

Introduction: If You Don't Know Jack

by Winston Engle

Jack Williamson's career spans virtually the whole existence of science fiction as a genre. During nine decades, he has managed to stay not just active and relevant, but essential.

That's the opening of the blurb I wrote in my head for the story I hoped Jack Williamson would write for the first new *Thrilling Wonder Stories.* Even aside from his standing as one of the living legends of SF, the idea of opening this enterprise with a new story from a man who wrote for the premiere issue of this magazine's progenitor, *Science Wonder Stories,* in June 1929, gave me goosebumps.

But time and fate can be cruel sons-of-bitches, and I reached his niece, Betty, three days after he had died. Me being me, my first reaction was deep embarrassment at what felt, somehow, like a gross social faux pas. Once I was off the phone, then I had the crushing disappointment and, again me being me, general feelings of futility. And I had to work through that before I could see the obvious.

Let's review why I'd wanted the story. First, he was a great writer. Although never a household name like Isaac Asimov or Ray Bradbury, Williamson had an enormous influence on generations of writers... such as Asimov and Bradbury. He wrote the archetypal space opera, *The Legion of Space.* But as the style and preoccupations of science fiction changed over the decades, Williamson made the effort to change along with them while

maintaining his own essential voice. He won a Hugo and a Nebula for his novella, "The Ultimate Earth," at age 93.

Second, he wrote for *Science Wonder Stories, Air Wonder Stories, Wonder Stories, Wonder Stories Quarterly,* and *Thrilling Wonder Stories,* only missing out *Science Wonder Quarterly.*

So why not celebrate Jack Williamson with a cross-section of his work in the various iterations of this magazine? We begin, appropriately, with his first appearance, winning "First Honorable Mention" in Hugo Gernsback's essay contest on "What Science Fiction Means to Me" with "Tremendous Contribution to Civilization." Then we present "The Moon Era," a lovely and lyrical novella from the February 1932 issue of *Wonder Stories.* It managed to grip me when I first read it, when I was proofreading the input from the Optical Character Recognition program, when I was laying out the pages, and *then* when I was proofreading them. (By that point, I ordinarily can't see anything about a story anymore besides whether the words are spelled correctly, and whether QuarkXPress managed to turn all the straight quotation marks into the right types of curly ones.) Along the way, we have a bit of autobiography, and story excerpts showing his familiarity scientific ideas few other writers would catch onto until much latter.

So when we're done, it's my hope that, if you don't now, you will have begun to know Jack, and be happy you do. • • •

What Science Fiction Means to Me: Tremendous Contribution to Civilization

by Jack Williamson

S cience fiction is a wonderful new art. It displays new vistas, new ideals, new worlds. It lifts us above the dull, painful routine of the work-a-day world into the glorious realm of deathless romance. It carries us to the land of our dreams and lo! they are dreams no longer, but splendid, fascinating realities. Dreams moulded into concrete life! Dreams solidified into definite realities by the scientific touch woven into the delightful pattern of the dramatic plot, colored with the magic of literary style, enhanced with vivid illustration—until we forget they are dreams!

There lies the appeal of the science fiction book. The cover's promise of weird and thrilling adventure! Lifelike illustrations. Stirring associations recalled by the word! Throbbing memories of a thousand worlds of romance! Living hope, vibrant expectation, of visits to spheres unique and new! Certainty of meeting the real living forms of a million ideas whose vague shadows have flitted, dim and indefinite, through our fancies since youth!

In an illimitable universe, through time, there is a mathematical certainty that every possible combination of circumstances will be actual fact. Then every science fiction story, with a faultless basis of fact, has been or will be true. To be sure, we do not often meet the story that is perfect in proven fact—if ft were, it would not be science fiction. But all science fiction, in a larger sense, is true.

It is the space flier that bears us most often to the world of golden adventure. It is as real an achievement as the locomotive or the airplane. Science discloses a wide universe. When man has found means to explore it, he has conquered his environment. The space flier is a great creation, even if one is never built. The release of the mind from the earth to which it has been eternally chained has a real spiritual, inspirational value. That is the great gift of science fiction.

And the realization of the space ship is a definite possibility. If the progress of the last century is multiplied through ten thousand years, the result is beyond our comprehension. Fifty years ago gunpowder was the best force Verne could find for the propulsion of a rocket to the moon. Already such possibilities as radium and the disrupted atom have been added. Slowly we come to understand space and gravitation. To understand completely is to master. Science fiction has met and solved every problem connected with building a machine to guard man against the cold and the emptiness of space. The proposition is ready for the inventor. In the space ship, science fiction has made a tremendous contribution to civilization. And it is but an outstanding one of a thousand creations, many of which are already realized.

Daily, science fiction gains popularity. That is because it explores the new frontiers. Man has conquered the sea and the air. The last blank spaces vanish from the map. In the march of conquest, we turn to

Originally appeared in Science Wonder Stories, *June 1929.*
Copyright © 1929 Stellar Publishing Corp.
Used by permission of the Estate of Jack Williamson.

other worlds. Human interest has suddenly expanded beyond the globe. For all the ages man has gazed in wonder at the riddle of the moon, and felt the mystery of the stars in measureless space. Now he thinks of conquest.

A new era dawns. Dreams of men reach out to other worlds of space and time. The new unknown of science is calling. The ships of man will follow his dreams as the caravan followed the dreams of Columbus. Science will answer the call, with a thousand new inventions—inspired by science fiction. • • •

Williamson on Black Holes

(Here, in 1939, Williamson almost coins the term "black hole" 28 years early. —Ed.)

My voice was ragged with outraged protest:

"Not deliberately—into the Hole? That's suicide."

The Hole was what we called it, in the argot of the spaceways. For it was crudely pictured as a hole in space. A deadly phenomenon. Essentially a closed field of special space-time curvature, as the astrophysicists described it, a blind whirl-pool in the ether, its resistless vortices could trap anything from a photon to a planetoid. • • •

As Williamson Sees Himself

Born 1908, at a mining camp in Arizona Territory. Carried mule-back, aged-six weeks, to Rancho La Loba, deep in Sonora's Sierra Madre. A wheelless land, of scorpions, mountain lions, and renegade Apaches—but it took revolution to send my parents back to the States.

Arrived in New Mexico by covered wagon. When drouth of '18 struck the Llano Estacado, drove chuck wagon for father's trail herd. Now I write in a shackon the ranch, still find relaxation in the saddle.

Science fiction is the answer to why I don't write westerns. For nothing else has quite equalled the thrill of Merritt's *Moon Pool.* Ambition to write dates from age five, when informed that Mark Twain got a dollar a word—even, astonishingly, for easy words like *if* and *is.* (Family's skepticism not yet wholly overcome.)

Like travel; have knocked about a bit, mostly with Edmond Hamilton. But chief interest remains science fiction. Now working on second million words—and hope to make them better than the first.

For I believe that science fiction will come to fill a very important niche in a scientific age, that the possibilities in depicting the dramatic impacts of science and human beings have hardly been explored. • • •

left: illustration for "Passage to Saturn," quoted left.

right: as Thrilling Wonder *readers saw Williamson— photo accompanying the above piece in the June 1939 issue.*

Williamson on Wormholes

top: Jack Williamson gets the cover for "Through the Purple Cloud," quoted right.

bottom: illustration for "Through the Purple Cloud." Both by Frank R. Paul.

"Williamson on Black Holes" from "Passage to Saturn," Thrilling Wonder Stories, June 1939. Copyright © 1939 Standard Magazines, Inc., renewed 1966 Jack Williamson.

(Unfortunately, "pinhole" isn't as evocative as "wormhole," or he could have coined a name for them 26 years early. —Ed.)

"The plane, you know, flew into a circle of purple light that appeared suddenly ahead of us. It may have been a sort of a gate to this otherworld, through the fourth dimension. This planet may be so far distant in space from our own world that it is in another universe, yet touching it in the fourth dimension."

"How could that be?" Juanita asked in a puzzled tone.

"I don't know whether I can explain it very clearly. But a favorite method in such discussions is to form an analogy in dimensions of a lower order. Suppose we were two-dimensional beings, with length and width, but no thickness. Suppose our world were on the surface of a sheet of paper. And suppose this planet were on the other side of the sheet, just opposite.

"Being two-dimensional beings, we could not conceive of the third dimension, which is the thickness of the paper. We could not know of the other world so near, nor could we reach it except by going around the edge of the sheet.

"But suppose somebody stuck a pin hole in the paper, through the two worlds on opposite sides. Then we might blunder through, into a new world outside of our knowledge, just as the plane flew through the purple cloud into this strange place. So we must have fallen through a hole in the fourth dimension!" • • •

The Moon Era

by JACK WILLIAMSON

Illustrated by Frank R. Paul

We were seated at dinner in the long dining room of my uncle's Long Island mansion. There was glistening silver plate, and the meal had been served with a formality to which I was unaccustomed. I was ill at ease, though my uncle and I sat alone at the table. The business of eating without committing an egregious blunder before the several servants took all my attention.

Originally appeared in Wonder Stories, *February 1932*
Story copyright © 1931 Gernsback Publications, Inc. Copyright renewed 1958 by Jack Williamson

It was the first time I had ever seen my uncle, Enfield Conway. A tall man, stiffly erect, dressed severely in black. His face, though lean, was not emaciated as is usual at his age of seventy years. His hair, though almost perfectly white, was abundant, parted on the side. His eyes were blue, and strong; he wore no glasses.

A uniformed chauffeur had met me at the station, in the afternoon. The butler had sent an entirely unnecessary valet to my luxurious room. I had not met my uncle until he came down to the dining room.

JACK WILLIAMSON

Jack Williamson has properly been called a first-rate writer of colorful tales. His "Alien Intelligence," published in the early days of SCI-ENCE WONDER STORIES, placed him, in the estimation of our readers, in the class of A. Merrit and other masters. The present story carries on Mr. Williamson's gripping portrayal of the possibilities of science on other worlds.

It is quite within reason that our moon, now dead and barren, was once the scene of flourishing life. Although no water now exists there, nor air shields from the moon the intense solar rays, in another age the moon may have been bountifully endowed by nature. If that is true, then the picture of the Eternal Ones drawn by our author is certainly a colorful portrayal of what the lunar civilization may have been like. And the picture of the Mother, and her exciting and bizarre adventures with our hero, are, in our opinion, among some of the best drawn by any author of science fiction.

—from WONDER STORIES, February 1932

"I suppose, Stephen, you are wondering why I sent for you," he said in his precise manner, when the servants had carried away the last course, leaving cigars, and a bottle of mineral water for him.

I nodded. I had been instructor of history in a small high school in Texas, where his telegram had reached me. There had been no explanation; merely a summons to Long Island.

"You are aware that some of my patents have been quite profitable."

Again I nodded. "The evidence surrounds me."

"Stephen, my fortune amounts to upwards of three and a half million. How should you like to be my heir?"

"Why, sir—I should not refuse. I'd like very much to be."

"You can, if you wish, earn that fortune. And fifty thousand a year while I live."

I pushed back the chair and rose to my feet in excitement. Such riches were beyond my dreams! I felt myself trembling.

"Anything—" I stammered. "I'll do anything you say, to earn that! It means—"

"Wait," he said, looking at me calmly. "You don't know yet what I require. Don't commit yourself too soon."

"What is it?" I asked, in a quivering voice.

"Stephen, I have been working in my private laboratory here for eleven years. I have been building a machine. The best of my brains have gone into that machine. Hundreds of thousands of dollars. The efforts of able engineers and skilled mechanics.

"Now the machine is finished. It is to be tested. The engineers who worked with me refused to try the machine. They insist that it is very dangerous.

"And I am too old to make the trial. It will take a young man, with strength, endurance, and courage.

"You are young, Stephen. You look vigorous enough. I suppose your health is good? A sound heart? That's the main thing."

"I think so," I told him. "I've been coaching the Midland football team. And it isn't many years since I was playing college football, myself."

"And you have no dependents?"

"None—but what is this machine?"

"I will show you. Come."

He rose, agilely enough for one of his seventy years, and led the way from the long room. Through several magnificent rooms of the big house. Out into the wide, landscaped grounds, beautiful and still in the moonlight.

I followed silently. My brain was confusion. A whirl of mad thought. All this wealth whose evidence surrounded me might be my own! I cared nothing for luxury, for money itself. But the fortune would mean freedom from the thankless toil of pedagogy. Books. Travel. Why, I could see with my own eyes the scenes of history's dramatic moments! Finance research expeditions of my own! Delve with my own hands for the secrets of Egypt's sands, uncover the age-old enigmas of ruined mounds that once were proud cities of the East!

We approached a rough building—resembling an airplane hangar—of galvanized iron, which glistened like silver in the rays of the full moon.

Without speaking, Uncle Enfield produced a key from his pocket, unlocked the heavy padlock on the door. He entered the building, switching on electric lights inside it.

"Come in," he said. "Here it is. I'll explain it as well as I can."

I walked through the narrow doorway and uttered an involuntary exclamation of surprise at sight of the huge machine that rested upon the clean concrete floor.

Two huge disks of copper, with a cylinder of bright, chromium-plated metal between them. Its shape vaguely suggested that of an ordinary spool of adhesive plaster, from which a little has been used—the polished cylinder, which was of smaller diameter than the disks, took the place of the roll of plaster.

The lower of the massive disks rested on the concrete floor. Its diameter was about twenty feet. The cylinder above it was about sixteen feet in diameter, and eight feet high. The copper disk above was the same size as the lower one.

Small round windows stared from the riveted metal plates forming the cylinder. The whole was like a building, it burst on me. A circular room with bright metal walls. Copper floor and copper roof projecting beyond those walls.

My uncle walked to the other side of this astounding mechanism. He turned a projecting knob. An oval door, four feet high, swung inward in the curving wall. Four inches thick. Of plated steel. Fitting very tightly against cushions of rubber.

My uncle climbed through the door, into the dark interior. I followed with a growing sense of wonder and excitement. I groped toward him through the darkness. Then I heard the click of a switch, and lights flashed on within the round chamber.

I gazed about me in astonishment.

Walls, floor, and ceiling were covered with soft, white fiber. The little room was crowded with apparatus. Clamped against one white wall was a row of the tall steel flasks in which commercial oxygen is compressed. Across the room was a bank of storage batteries. The walls were hung with numerous instruments, all clamped neatly in place. Sextants. Compasses. Pressure gauges. Numerous dials whose functions were not apparent. Cooking utensils. An automatic pistol. Cameras. Telescopes. Binoculars.

In the center of the room stood a table or cabinet, with switches, dials, and levers upon its top. A heavy cable, apparently of aluminum, ran from it to the ceiling.

I was gazing about in bewilderment. "I don't understand all this—" I began.

"Naturally," said my uncle. "It is quite a novel invention. Even the engineers who built it did not understand it. I confess that the theory of it is yet beyond me. But what happens is quite simple.

"Eleven years ago, Stephen, I discovered a new phenomenon. I had happened to charge two parallel copper plates, whose distances apart had a certain very definite relation to their combined masses, with a high tension current at a certain frequency.

"The plates, Stephen, were in some way—how, I do not pretend to understand—cut out of the earth's gravitational field. Insulated from gravity. The effect extended to any object placed between them. By a slight variation of the current's strength, I was able to increase the repulsion, until the plates pulled upward with a force approximately equal to their own weight.

"My efforts to discover the reason for this phenomenon—it is referred to in my notes as the Conway Effect—have not been successful. But I have built this machine to make a practical application of it. Now that it is finished, the four engineers who helped design it have deserted. They refused to assist with any trials."

"Why?" I asked.

"Muller, who had the construction in charge, somehow came to the conclusion that the suspension or reversal of gravity was due to motion in a fourth dimension. He claimed that he had experimental proof of his theory, by building models of the device, setting the dials, and causing them to vanish. I would have none of it. But the other men seemed to accept his ideas. At any rate, they refused with him to have any part in the tests. They thought they would vanish, like Muller says his models did, and not come back."

"The thing is supposed to rise above the ground?" I asked.

"Quite so." My uncle smiled. "When the force of gravitation is merely suspended, it should fly off the earth at a tangent, due to the diurnal rotation. This initial velocity, which in these latitudes, amounts to considerably less than one thousand miles per hour, can be built up at will, by reversing gravitation, and falling away from the earth."

"Falling away from the earth!" I was staggered. "And where is one to fall?"

"This machine was designed for a trip to the moon. At the beginning of the voyage, gravitation will be merely cut out, allowing the machine to fly off on a tangent, toward the point of intersection with the moon's orbit. Safely beyond the atmosphere, repulsion can be used to build up the acceleration. Within the gravitational sphere of the moon, positive gravitation can be utilized further to increase the speed. And reversed gravitation to retard the velocity, to make possible a safe landing. The return will be made in the same manner."

I was staring at him blankly. A trip to the moon seemed insane, beyond reason. Especially for a professor of history, with only a modicum of scientific knowledge. And it must be dangerous, if those engineers— But three million—what dangers would I not face for such a fortune?

"Everything has been done," he went on, "to insure the comfort and safety of the passenger. The walls are insulated with a fiber composition especially worked out to afford protection from the cold of space, and from the unshielded radiation of the sun. The steel armor is strong enough not only to hold the necessary air pressure, but to stop any ordinary meteoric particles.

"You notice the oxygen cylinders, for maintaining that essential element in the air. There is automatic apparatus for purifying it. It is pumped through caustic soda to absorb the carbon dioxide, and through refrigerator tubes to condense the excess moisture.

"The batteries, besides energizing the plates, are amply powerful to supply lights and heat for cooking.

"That, I believe, fairly outlines the machine and the projected voyage. Now it is up to you. Take time to consider it fully. Ask me any questions you wish."

He sat down deliberately in the large, cushioned chair, beside the central table, which was evidently intended for the operator. He stared at me alertly, with calm blue eyes.

I was extremely agitated. My knees had a weak feeling, so that I desired to sit down also, though I was so nervous that I kept striding back and forth across the resilient white fiber of the floor.

Three millions! It would mean so much! Books, magazines, maps—I should have to economize no longer. Years—all my life, if I wished—abroad. The tombs of Egypt. The sand-covered cities of the Gobi. My theory that mankind originated in South Africa. All those puzzles that I had longed to be able to study. Stonehenge! Angkor! Easter Island!

But the adventure seemed madness. A voyage to the moon! In a craft condemned by the very engineers that had built it. To be hurled away from the earth at speeds no man had attained before. To face unknown perils of space. Dangers beyond guessing. Hurtling meteors. The all-penetrating cosmic ray. The burning heat of the sun. The absolute zero. What, beyond speculation and theory, did men know of space? I was no astronomer; how was I to cope with the emergencies that might rise?

"How long will it take?" I demanded suddenly.

My uncle smiled a little. "Glad you are taking it seriously," he said. "The duration of the voyage depends on the speed you make, of course. A week each way is a conservative estimate. And perhaps two or three days on the moon. To take notes. Photograph it. Move around a little, if possible; land in several different places. There is oxygen and concentrated food to last six months. But a fortnight should see you nearly back. I'll go over the charts and calculations with you."

"Can I leave the machine on the moon?"

"No. No atmosphere. And it would be too hot in the day, too cold at night. Of course an insulated suit and oxygen mask might be devised. Something like diving armor. But I haven't worked at that. You will be expected just to take a few pictures, be prepared to describe what you have seen."

I continued to pace the floor, pausing sometimes to examine some piece of apparatus. How would it feel, I wondered, to be shut up in here? Drifting in space. Far from the world of my birth. Alone. In silence. Entombed. Would it not drive me mad?

My uncle rose suddenly from the chair.

"Sleep on it, Stephen," he advised. "See how you feel in the morning. Or take longer if you wish."

He switched off the light in the machine. Led the way out into the shed. And from it into the brilliant moonlight that flooded the wide, magnificent grounds about the great house that would be one of the prizes of this mad adventure.

As he was locking the shed, I gazed up at the moon. Broad, bright disk. Silvery, mottled. Extinguishing the stars with argent splendor. And all at once it came over me—the desire to penetrate the enigmatic mystery of this companion world, that men have watched since the race began.

What an adventure! To be the first human to tread this silver planet. To be the first to solve its age-old riddles. Why think of Angkor, or Stonehenge, of Luxor and Karnak, when I might win the secrets of the moon?

Even if death came, what did it matter against the call of this adventure? Many men would trade their lives eagerly for such a chance.

Suddenly I was strong. All weakness had left me. All fear and doubt. A few moments before I had been tired, wishing to sit down. Now vast energy filled me. I was conscious of an extraordinary elation. Swiftly I turned to my uncle.

"Let's go back," I said. "Show me as much about it as you can tonight. I am going."

He gripped my hand tightly, without a word, before he turned back to the lock.

CHAPTER II
Toward the Moon

It was in the second week, after that sudden decision came to me, that I started. At the end my uncle became a little alarmed, and tried to persuade me to stay longer, to make more elaborate preparations. I believe that he was secretly becoming fond of me, despite his brisk precise manner. I think he took the opinion of his engineers seriously enough to consider my return very uncertain.

But I could see no reason for longer delay. The operation of the machine was simple; he had explained it quite fully.

There was a switch to close, to send current from the batteries through the coils that raised it to the potential necessary to energize the copper disks. And a large rheostat that controlled the force, from a slight decrease in gravity, to a complete reversal.

The auxiliary apparatus, for control of temperature and atmosphere, was largely automatic. And not beyond my limited mechanical comprehension. I was certain that I should be able to make any necessary repairs or adjustments.

Now I was filled with the greatest haste to undertake the adventure. No doubt or hesitation had troubled me since the moment of the decision. I felt only a longing to be sweeping away from the earth. To view scenes that the ages had kept hidden from human eyes, to tread the world that has always been the symbol of the unattainable.

My uncle recalled one of the engineers, a sallow young fellow named Gorton. On the second morning, to supplement my uncle's instruction he went over the machine again, showing me the function of every part. Before he left, he warned me.

"If you are idiot enough to get in that darned contraption, and turn on the power," he told me, "you'll never come back. Muller said so. And he proved it. So long as the batteries and coil are outside the field of force between the plates, the plates act according to schedule, and rise up in the air.

"But Muller made self-contained models. With the battery and all inside. And they didn't rise up. They went out! Vanished. Just like that!" He snapped his fingers.

"Muller said the things moved along another dimension, right out of our world. And he ought to know. String of degrees a mile long. Into another dimension. No telling what sort of hell you'll blunder into."

I thanked the man. But his warnings only increased my eagerness. I was about to tear aside the veil of the unknown. What if I did blunder into new worlds? Might they not yield rewards of knowledge richer than those of the barren moon? I might be a new Columbus, a greater Balboa.

I slept a few hours in the afternoon, after Gorton had gone. I felt no conscious need of slumber, but my uncle insisted upon it. And to my surprise, I fell soundly asleep, almost as soon as I lay down.

At sunset, we went down again to the shed in which the machine was housed. My uncle started a motor, which opened the roof like a pair of enormous doors, by means of pulleys and cables. The red light of the evening sky streamed down upon the machine.

We made a final inspection of all the apparatus. My uncle explained again the charts and instruments that I was to use in navigating space. Finally he questioned me for an hour, making me explain the various parts of the machine, correcting any error.

I was not to start until nearly midnight. We returned to the house, where an elaborate dinner was waiting. I ate almost absently, hardly noticing the servants of whom I had been so conscious upon my arrival. My uncle was full of conversation. Talking of his own life, and asking me many questions about my own, and about my father, whom he had seen last

when they were boys. My mind was upon the adventure before me; I could answer him only disjointedly. But I was aware that he had taken a real liking for me; I was not surprised at his request that I postpone the departure.

At last we went back down to the machine. The white moon was high; its soft radiance bathed the gleaming machine, through the opened roof. I stared up at its bright disk. Was it possible that in a short week I should be there, looking back upon the earth? It seemed madness! But the madness of glorious adventure!

Without hesitation, I clambered through the oval door. A last time my uncle wrung my hand. He had tears in his eyes. And his voice was a little husky.

"I want you to come back, Stephen."

I swung the door into its cushioned seat, upon massive hinges, tightened the screws that were to hold it. A final glance about the white-walled interior of the machine. All was in order. The chronometer by the wall, ticking steadily, told me that the moment had come.

My uncle's anxious face was pressed against one of the ports. I smiled at him. Waved. His hand moved across the port. He left the shed.

I dropped into the big chair beside the table, reached for the switch. With my fingers upon the button, I hesitated the merest second. Was there anything else? Anything neglected? Anything I had yet to do on earth? Was I ready to die, if so I must?

The deep, vibrant hum of the coils, beneath the table, answered the pressure of my finger. I took the handle of the rheostat, swung it to the zero mark, where gravitation was to be cut off completely.

My sensation was exactly as if the chair, the floor, had fallen from under me. The same sensation that one feels when an elevator drops very abruptly. Almost I floated out of the chair. I had to grasp at the arm of it to stay within it.

For a few moments I experienced nauseating vertigo. The white crowded room seemed to spin about me. To drop away endlessly beneath me. Sick, helpless, miserable, I clung weakly to the great chair. Falling... falling... falling. Would I never strike bottom?

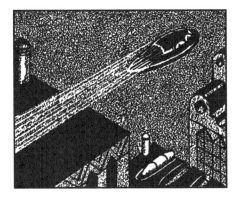

Then I realized, with relief, that the sensation was due merely to the absence of gravity's familiar pull. The machine had worked! My last, lingering doubt was killed. Strange elation filled me.

I was flying away from the earth. Flying.

The thought seemed to work a miracle of change in my feelings. The dreadful, dizzy nausea gave way to a feeling of exhiliration. Of lightness. I was filled with a sense of power and well-being, such as I had never before experienced.

I left the great chair, floated rather than walked to one of the windows.

Already I was high in the air. So high that the moonlit earth was a dim and misty plain before me. I could see many lights; the westward sky was aglow, above New York. But already I was unable to pick out the lights at my uncle's mansion.

The machine had risen through the opened roof of the shed. It was driving out into space, as it had been planned to do! The adventure was succeeding.

As I watched, the earth sank visibly. Became a great concave bowl of misty silver. Expanded slowly, as the minutes went by. And became suddenly convex. A huge dark sphere, washed with pale gray light.

Presently, after an hour, when the dials showed that I was beyond the faintest trace of atmosphere, I returned to the table and increased the power, moving the rheostat to the last contact. I looked at charts and chronometer. According to my uncle's calculations, four hours at this acceleration were required, before the controls were set again.

I returned to the window and stared in amazement at the earth, that I had left vast and silver gray and motionless.

It was spinning madly, backward!

The continents seemed to race beneath me—I was now high enough to see a vast section of the globe. Asia. North America. Europe. Asia again. In seconds.

It was madness! The earth spinning in a few moments, instead of the usual twenty-four hours. And turning backward! But I could not doubt my eyes. Even as I watched, the planet seemed to spin faster. Ever faster! The continental outlines merged into dim indistinctness.

I looked away from the mad earth, in bewilderment. The firmament was very black. And the very stars were creeping about it, with visible motions!

Then the sun came into view, plunging across the sky like a flaming comet. It swung supernally across my field of vision, vanished. Appeared again. And again. Its motion became ever swifter.

What was the meaning of such an apparent revolution of the sun about the sky? It meant, I knew, that earth and moon had swung about the star. That a year had passed! But were years going by as fast as my chronometer ticked off the seconds?

Another strange thing. I could recognize the constellations of the Zodiac, through which the sun was plunging. And it was going backward! As the earth was spinning backward!

I moved to another window, searched for the moon, my goal. It hung still among spinning stars. But in its light there was a flicker, far more rapid than the flashing of the sun across the wild heavens. I wondered, then knew that I saw the waxing and waning of the moon. Months, passing so swiftly that soon the flicker became a gray blur.

The flashing past of the sun became more frequent. Until it was a strange belt of flame about the strange heavens, in which the stars crept and moved like living things.

A universe gone mad! Suns and planets spinning helpless in the might of a cosmic storm! The machine from which I watched the only sane thing in a runaway cosmos!

Then reason came to my rescue.

Earth, moon, sun, and stars could not all be mad. The trouble was with *myself!* My perceptions had changed. The machine—

Slowly it came to me, until I knew I had grasped the truth.

Time, true time, is measured by the movements of the heavenly bodies. Our day is the time of earth's rotation on its axis. Our year the period of its revolution about the sun.

Those intervals had become crowded so thick in my perception that they were indistinguishable. Then countless years were spinning past, while I hung still in space!

Incredible! But the conclusion was inevitable. And the apparent motion of earth and sun had been backward.

That meant—and the thought was staggering—that the ages were reeling backward. That I was plunging at an incalculable rate into the past.

Vaguely I recalled magazine articles that I had read, upon the nature of space and time. A lecture. The subject had facinated me, though I had only a layman's knowledge of it.

The lecturer had defined our universe in terms of space-time. A four-dimensional "continuum." Time was a fourth dimension, he had said. An extension as real as the three of what we call space, and not completely distinguishable from them. A direction in which motion would carry one into the past, or into the future.

All memory, he had said, is a groping back along this dimension, at right angles to each of the three of space. Dreams, vivid memories, he insisted, carry one's consciousness in reality back along this dimension, until the body, swept relentlessly along the stream of time, drags it forward again.

Then I recalled what my uncle had told me of the refusal of his engineers to try the machine. Recalled Gorton's warning. Muller, they both had told me, had declared that the machine would move along a fourth dimension, out of our world. He had made models of the machine, and they had vanished when the power was turned on.

Now I knew that Muller was right. His models had vanished because they had been carried into the past. Had not continued to exist in the present time.

And now I was moving along that fourth dimension. The dimension of time. And very swiftly, for the years went past too fast for counting.

The reversal of gravitation, it came to me, must be some effect of this change of direction in time. But I am not a scientist, I can explain the "Conway Effect" no better than my uncle, for all the wonders that it has brought into my life.

At first it was horribly strange and terrifying.

After I had thought out my explanation of the mad antics of the earth and sun and moon, and of the hurrying stars, I was, however, no longer frightened. I gazed out through my small round ports at the melting firmament with some degree of equanimity.

I continued to watch the charts my uncle had prepared, and to make adjustments of the rheostat when they were indicated by the chronometer.

And presently, feeling hungry, I toasted biscuits on the electric stove, cut off a generous slice of a cheese that I found in the supplies, opened a vacuum bottle of steaming chocolate, and made a hearty and very satisfactory meal.

When I had finished, the aspect of the space about me was unchanged. Crawling stars, already forming themselves into constellations the most of which were unfamiliar. The sun a broad belt of burning gold, counting off the years too swiftly for the eye to follow. A living flame that girdled the firmament. The earth was a huge gray sphere, spinning so swiftly behind me that no detail was visible.

And even the moon, hanging in space ahead, was turning slowly. No longer was the same familiar face toward me, and toward the earth. Already I had reached a point in past time at which the moon was turning on its axis more rapidly than it revolved about the earth. The tidal drag had not yet completely stopped the moon's apparent rotation.

And if already the moon was turning, what would it be when I reached it? Hurtling into the past as I was, would I see oceans cover its dry sea-floors? Would I see an atmosphere soften the harsh outlines of its rugged mountains? Would I see life, vegetation, spread over its plains? Was I to witness the rejuvenation of an aged world?

It seemed fantastic. But it was taking place. The speed of rotation slowly increased as I watched.

The hours slipped past.

I became heavy with sleep. The two days before the departure had not been easy. I had worked day and night to familiarize myself with the machine's operation. The nervous strain had been exhausting. The amazing incidents of the voyage had kept me tense, sapped my strength.

The chart told me that no change was to be made in the controls for many hours. I inspected the gauges which showed the condition of the atmosphere in the chamber. Oxygen content, humidity, temperature, were correct. The air smelled sweet and clean. I completed the rounds, found everything in order.

I adjusted the big chair to a reclining position, and threw myself upon it. For hours I slept, waking at intervals to make a tour of inspection.

Sometimes, in the following days, I wondered if I should be able to go back. Muller's models had carried no operator, of course, to start them on the flight back through time to the starting point. Would I be able to reverse the time-flight? If I followed the directions on the operating chart, on the flight back, would I be flung forward through the ages, back to my own era?

I wondered. But the speculation brought forth no conclusion. A strange, unique experience was mine. Glorious adventure. Death was not too high a price to pay.

It did not even occur to me to attempt to turn back earthward, when I found that I was slipping through time. And I did not have sufficient control of the machine to have done so, had I wished. Dependent upon the chart for navigating instructions,

I could not have plotted a return path from the midway point. And I knew no way to stop my flight, except by using the repulsion of the moon's reversed gravitation.

My flight lasted six days, by the chronometer.

Long before the end, the moon was spinning very swiftly. And the edges of its outline had become hazy, so that I knew it had an atmosphere.

I followed the charted directions, until I was in the upper layers of that atmosphere. The moon's surface was sliding very rapidly beneath me, and the atmosphere with it, due to the swift rotation of the satellite. Consequently, fierce winds screamed about the machine.

I hung in the atmosphere, merely using enough power to balance the moon's comparatively feeble gravitational pull, until the pressure of that rushing wind swept me with it. The mistily indistinct surface slowed, became motionless beneath me.

With power decreased still further, I settled slowly, watching alertly through the ports.

A towering, crimson mountain loomed above the mists below. I dropped toward it, increasing the power a little. At last I hovered motionless above a narrow, irregular plateau, near the peak, that seemed covered with soft scarlet moss.

Slowly I cut down the power. With hardly a shock, the machine settled in the moss.

I was on the moon! The first of my race to set foot upon an alien planet! What adventures might await me?

CHAPTER III
When the Moon Was Young

With the power cut off entirely, I ran to the ports. There had been no time to scan my surroundings during the uncertainties of the landing. Now I peered out eagerly.

The moonscape was as strange a sight as man had ever seen.

The machine had come down in thick green moss that looked soft as a Persian rug. A foot deep it was. Dark green fibers closely intertwined. In an unbroken carpet it covered the sloping plateau upon which I had landed, and extended almost to the top of the rugged peak to northward.

To the south and west lay a great valley, almost level, miles across. Beyond it rose a dim range of green hills, rugged summits bare and black. A broad river, glinting white in the distance, flowed down the valley, from northwest, into the south. Then there must be an ocean in that direction.

Strange jungle covered that valley, below the green moss of the mountains. Masses of green. Walls of yellow lining the wide smooth river. Dense forests of gigantic plants, weirdly and grotesquely strange. They grew more luxuriant, taller, than similar plants could upon the earth, because a much feebler gravitation opposed their growth.

Equally strange was the sky.

Darker than on earth, perhaps because the atmosphere was thinner. A deep, pure, living blue. A blue that was almost violet. No cloud marred its liquid azure splendor.

The sun hung in the glorious eastward sky. Larger than I had known it. Whiter. A supernal sphere of pure white flame.

Low in the west was an amazing disk. A huge ball of white, a globe of milky light. Many times the diameter of the sun. I wondered at it. And realized that it was— the earth! The earth young as Venus had been in my time. And like Venus, shrouded in white clouds never broken. Were the rocks still glowing beneath those clouds, I wondered? Or had the life begun—the life of my farthest progenitors?

Would I ever see my native land again, upon that resplendent, cloud-hidden planet? Would the machine carry me back into the future, when I attempted return? Or would it hurl me farther into the past, to plunge flaming into the new-born and incandescent world?

That question I put resolutely from my mind. A new world was before me. A globe strange and unexplored. Why worry about return to the old?

My eyes went back to the broad valley below me, along the banks of the broad river, beneath the majestic range of green mountains. Clumps of gold, resembling distant groves of yellow trees. Patches of green that looked like meadows of grass. Queer, puzzling uprights of black.

I saw things moving. Little bright objects, that rose and fell slightly as they flew. Birds? Gigantic insects? Or creatures stranger than either?

Then I saw the balloons. Captive balloons, floating above the jungles of the valley. At first I saw only two, hanging side by side, swaying a little. Then three more, beyond. Then I distinguished dozens, scores of them, scattered all over the valley.

I strained my eyes at them. Were there intelligent beings here, who had invented the balloons? But what would be the object of hanging them about above the jungles, by the hundred?

I remembered the powerful prism binoculars hanging on the wall beside me. I seized them, focused them hurriedly. The weird jungle leaped toward me in the lenses.

The things were doubtless balloons. Huge spheres of purple, very bright in the sunlight. Anchored with long red cables. Some of them, I estimated, were thirty feet in diameter. Some, much smaller. I could make out no baskets. But there seemed to be small dark masses upon their lower sides, to which the red ropes were attached.

I left them and surveyed the jungle again.

A mass of the yellow vegetation filled the lenses. A dense tangle of slender yellow stems, armed with terrible rows of long, bayonet-like thorns. A thick tangle of sharp yellow thorns, it seemed, with no more stalk than was necessary to support them against the moon's feeble pull. A wall of cruel spikes, impenetrable.

I found a patch of green. A mass of soft, feathery foliage. A sort of creeper, it seemed, covering rocks, and other vegetation—though it did not mingle with the yellow scrub. Enormous, brilliantly white, bell-shaped blooms were open upon it here and there.

A flying thing darted across my vision. It looked like a gigantic moth, frail wings dusted with silver.

Then I made out a little cluster of curious plants. Black, smooth, upright stalks, devoid of leaf or branch. The tallest looked a foot in diameter, a score in height. It was crowned with a gorgeous red bloom. I noticed that no other vegetation grew near any of them. About each was a little cleared circle. Had they been cultivated?

Hours went by as I stared out through the ports, at this fascinating and bewildering moonscape.

Finally I recalled the pictures that my uncle had requested me to make. For two or three hours I was busy with the cameras. I made exposures in all directions, with ordinary and telescopic lenses. I photographed the scene with color filters. And finally I made motion pictures, swinging the camera to take a panoramic view.

It was almost sunset when I had done. It

seemed strange that the day was passing so swiftly, until I looked at the chronometer, found that it was not keeping pace with the sun, and decided that the period of rotation must be rather less than twenty-four hours. I later found it to be about eighteen hours, divided into days and nights of very nearly equal length.

Darkness came very swiftly after sunset, due to the comparatively small size and quick rotation of the moon. The stars burst out splendidly through the clear air, burning in constellations utterly strange.

A heavy dew was soon obscuring the ports. As I later discovered, clouds almost never formed in this light atmosphere. Nearly the entire precipitation was in the form of dew, which, however, was amazingly abundant. The tiny droplets on the glass were soon running in streams.

After a few hours, a huge and glorious snow-white sphere rose in the east. The earth. Wondrous in size and brilliance. The weird jungle was visible in its silvery radiance almost as in daylight.

Suddenly I realized that I was tired, and very sleepy. The anxiety and prolonged nervous strain of the landing had been exhausting. I threw myself down upon the reclining chair, and fell into immediate oblivion.

The white sun was high when I woke. I found myself refreshed. Keenly hungry. And conscious of a great need for physical exercise. Accustomed to an active life, I had been shut up in that little round room for seven days. I felt that I must move, breathe fresh air.

Could I leave the machine?

My uncle had told me that it would be impossible, because of lack of atmosphere. But there was plainly air about me, on this young moon. Would it be breathable?

I pondered the question. The moon, I knew, was formed of materials thrown off the cooling earth. Then should its atmosphere not contain the same elements as that of earth?

I decided to try it. Open the door slightly, and sniff experimentally. Close it immediately if there seemed anything wrong.

I loosened the screws that held the heavy door, tried to pull it open. It seemed fastened immovably. In vain I tugged at it, looked to see if I had left a screw, or if something was amiss with the hinges. It refused to budge.

For minutes I was baffled. The explanation came to me suddenly. The pressure of the atmosphere outside was much less than that within the machine. Since the door opened inward, it was the unbalanced pressure upon it that held it.

I found the valve which was to be opened to free the chamber of any dangerous excess of oxygen that might escape, and spun it open. The air hissed out noisily.

I sat down in the chair to wait. At first I felt no symptoms of the lessening pressure. Then I was conscious of a sensation of lightness, of exhilaration. I noticed that I was breathing faster. My temples throbbed. For a few minutes I felt a dull ache in my lungs.

But the sensations did not become unduly alarming, and I left the valve open. The hissing sound gradually decreased, and finally died away completely.

I rose and went to the door, feeling a painful shortness of the breath as I moved. The heavy door came open quite easily now. I sniffed the air outside. It bore a strange, heavy, unfamiliar fragrance which must have been carried from the jungle in the valley. And I found it oddly stimulating—it must have been richer in oxygen than the air in the machine.

With the door flung wide, I breathed deeply of it. At first I had thought merely of strolling up and down for a while in the moss outside the machine. But now I decided, quite suddenly, to hike to the lower edge of the green-carpeted plateau, perhaps a mile away, and look at the edge of the jungle.

I looked about for equipment that I should take, got together a few items. A light camera, in case I should see something worth taking. The binoculars. A vacuum bottle full of water, and a little food, so that I should not have to hasten back to eat.

And finally I took down the automatic pistol on the wall, a .45 Colt. It must have been included with the machine's equipment merely as a way of merciful escape, in case some failure made life in the little round compartment unendurable. There was only one box of ammunition. Fifty cartridges. I loaded the weapon, and slipped the remainder into my pocket.

Gathering up the other articles, I scrambled through the oval door, and stood upon the rim of the lower copper disk, drawing the door to behind me, and fastening it.

And stepped off, upon the moon.

The thick, fibrous moss yielded under my foot, surprisingly. I stumbled, fell into its soft green pile. And in scrambling to my feet, I forgot the lesser gravity of the moon, threw myself into the air, tumbling once more into the yielding moss.

In a few minutes I had mastered the art of walking under the new conditions, so that I could stride along with some confidence, going clear of the ground at every step, as if I had worn seven league boots. Once I essayed a leap. It carried me twenty feet into the air, and twice as far forward. It seemed that I hung in the air an unconscionable time, and floated down very slowly. But I was helpless, aloft, sprawling about, unable to get my feet beneath me. I came down on my shoulder, and must have been painfully bruised had it not been for the thick moss.

I realized that my strength upon the moon was quite out of proportion to my weight. I had muscles developed to handle a mass of 180 pounds. Here my weight was only 30 pounds. It would be some time, I supposed, before I could learn the exact force required to produce the result desired. Actually, I found myself adapted to these new conditions in a surprisingly short space of time.

For a time I was conscious of shortness of the breath, especially after violent exertion. But soon I was accustomed to the lighter air as well as the lesser gravitation.

In half an hour I had arrived at the edge of the red plateau. A steep slope fell before me to the edge of the jungle, perhaps two-thirds of a mile farther below. A slope carpeted with the thick fiber of the green moss.

A weird scene. Clear cerulean sky, darkly, richly blue. Huge white globe of the hot earth setting beyond the farther range of green mountains. The wide valley, with the broad silvery stream, winding among golden forests, and patches of green. The purple balloons floating here and yon, huge spheres swaying on the red cables that anchored them above the jungle.

I seated myself on the moss, where I could overlook that valley of eldritch wonder. I remained there for some time, staring out across it, while I ate most of the food that I had brought, and half-emptied the bottle of water.

Then I decided to descend to the edge of the jungle.

The sun was just at the meridian—the whole of the short afternoon, four hours and a half, was yet before me. I had ample time, I thought, to go down the slope to the edge of the jungle and return before the sudden nightfall.

I had no fear of getting lost. The glittering armor of the machine was visible over the whole plateau. And the jagged, triple peak to the northward of it was a landmark which should be visible over the whole region. There should be no difficulty about return.

Nor, while I realized that the jungle might hide hostile life, did I fear attack. I intended to be cautious, and not to penetrate beyond the edge of the jungle. I had the automatic, which, I was sure, gave me greater power of destruction than any other animal on the planet. Finally in case of difficulty, I could rely upon the superior strength of my muscles, which must be far stronger, in proportion to my weight, than those of native creatures.

I found progress easy on the long, mossy incline. My skill at traveling under lunar conditions of gravity was increasing with practice; I found a way of moving by deliberate, measured leaps, each carrying me twenty feet or more.

In a few minutes I found myself approaching the edge of the jungle. But that was not so sharp a line as it had appeared from above. The first vegetation other than the moss was scattered clumps of a plant resembling the cactus of my native Southwest.

Thick, fleshy disks growing one upon another, edge to edge. They were not green, however, but of a curious pink, flesh-like color. They bore no thorns, but were studded with little black protuberances or knobs of doubtful function. The plants I first approached were small and appeared stunted. The lower clumps seemed larger, and more thickly spaced.

I paused to examine one. Walked around it curiously. Photographed it from several angles. Then I ventured to touch it with my foot. Several of the little black knobs broke—they proved to be thin-walled vesicles, containing a black liquid. An overpowering and extremely unpleasant odor assailed me, and I retreated hastily.

A hundred yards farther on, I came upon the green creepers. Thick stems coiled like endless serpents over the ground, with innumerable fronds rising from them, terminating in feathery sprays of green. Here and there were huge white blooms, nearly six feet across, resembling great bells of burnished silver. From them, evidently, came the heavy perfume that I had noticed upon opening the door of the machine.

The creepers formed an unbroken mass of green, several feet deep. It would have been impossible to penetrate it without crushing the delicate foliage. I decided to go no farther in that direction. The creeper might have such means of protection as the malodorous sacs of the fleshy plants above. Or dangerous creatures, counterparts of terrene snakes, might lie concealed beneath the dense foliage.

For some distance I followed along the edge of the mass of creepers, pausing at intervals to make photographs. I was approaching a thicket or forest of the yellow scrub. A wall of inch-thick stems, each armed at intervals of a few inches with dagger-like thorns, all interwoven. A hundred feet high, I estimated. Interlaced so closely that a rat would have had difficulty in moving through it without impaling himself upon a needle-sharp spike.

Then I paused to watch one of the purple balloons, which seemed swaying toward me, increasing the length of the red anchor-cable which held it to the jungle behind. A strange thing, that huge purple sphere, tugging at the thin scarlet cable that held it. Tugging almost like a thing alive, I thought.

Several times I photographed it, but its distance was so great that I feared none of the images would be satisfactory. It seemed to be moving toward me, perhaps carried by some breeze that did not reach the ground. Perhaps, I thought, it would soon be near enough for a good picture.

CHAPTER IV
The Balloon Menace

I studied it closely, trying to see if it had an intelligent pilot or occupant. But I was unable to settle the point. There was certainly no basket. But black arms or levers seemed to project in a cluster from its lowest part, to manipulate the cables.

Nearly an hour, I waited, watching it. It moved much closer during that time, until, in fact, it was almost directly overhead, and only a few hundred feet high. The red cable slanted from it back into the jungle. It seemed to be loose, dragging.

At last I got a picture that satisfied me. I decided to go on and examine the tangle of yellow thorn-brush or scrub at closer range.

I had taken my eyes from the purple balloon, and turned to walk away, when it struck.

A red rope whipped about me.

The first I knew, it was already about my shoulders. Its end seemed to be weighted, for it whirled about my body several times, wrapping me in sticky coils.

The cable was about half an inch in diameter and made of many smaller crimson strands, fastened together with the adhesive stuff that covered it. I recall its appearance very vividly, even the odd, pungent, disagreeable odor of it.

Half a dozen coils of the red cable had whipped about me before I realized that anything was amiss. Then it tightened suddenly, dragging me across the red moss upon which I had been standing. Toward the edge of the jungle.

Looking up in horror, I saw that the rope had been thrown from the purple balloon I had been watching. Now the black arms that I had seen were working swiftly, coiling it up again—with me caught neatly on the end.

The great sphere was drawn down a little as my weight came upon it. It seemed to swell. Then, having been dragged along until I was directly beneath it, I was lifted clear of the ground.

I was filled with unutterable terror. I was panting, my heart was beating swiftly. And I felt endowed with terrific strength. Furiously I writhed in my gluey bonds, struggled with the strength of desperation to break the red strands.

But the web had been spun to hold just such frightened, struggling animals as myself. It did not break.

Back and forth I swung over the jungle, like a pendulum. With a constantly quickening arc! For the cable was being drawn up. Once more I looked upward, and saw a sight to freeze me in dreadful stupefaction of horror.

The whole balloon was a living thing!

I saw its two black and terrible eyes, aflame with hot evil, staring at me from many bright facets. The black limbs I had seen were its legs, growing in a cluster at the bottom of its body—now furiously busy coiling up the cable that it had spun, spider-like, to catch me. I saw long jaws waiting, black and hideously fanged, drooling foul saliva. And a rapier-thin pointed snout that must be meant for piercing, sucking body juices.

The huge purple sphere was a thin-walled, muscular sac, which must have been filled with some light gas, probably hydrogen, generated in the body of the creature. The amazing being floated above the jungle, out of harm's way, riding free on the wind, or anchored with its red web, lassoing its prey and hauling it up to feast hideously in the air.

For a moment I was petrified, dazed and helpless with the new horror of that thin snout, with black-fanged jaws behind it.

Then fear bred superhuman strength in me. I got my arms free, dragging them from beneath the sticky coils. I reached above my head, seized the red cable in both hands, tried to break it between them.

It refused to part, despite my fiercest efforts.

Only then did I recall the pistol in my pocket. If I could reach it in time, I might be able to kill the monster. And the gas should escape through the riddled sac, letting me back to the surface. I was already so high that the fall would have been dangerous, had I succeeded in my desperate effort to break the web.

The viscid stuff on the cable clung to my hands. It took all my strength to tear them loose. But at last they were free, and I fumbled desperately for the gun. A red strand was across the pocket in which I had the weapon. I tore at it. It required every ounce of my strength to slip it upward. And it adhered to my fingers again. I wrenched them loose, snatched out the automatic. It touched the gluey rope, stuck fast. I dragged it free, moved the safety catch with sticky fingers, raised it above my head.

Though it had been seconds only since I was snatched up, already I had been lifted midway to the dreadful living balloon. I glanced downward. The distance was appalling. I noticed that the balloon was still drifting, so that I hung over a thicket of the yellow scrub.

Then I began shooting at the monster.

It was difficult to aim because of the regular jerks as the ugly black limbs hauled on the cable. I held the gun with both hands and fired deliberately, very carefully.

The first shot seemed to have no effect.

At the second, I heard a shrill, deafening scream. And I saw that one of the black limbs was hanging limp.

I shot at the black, many-faceted eyes. Though I had no knowledge of the creature's anatomy, I supposed that its highest nervous centers should be near them.

The third shot hit one of them. A great blob of transparent jelly burst through the faceted surface, hung pendulous. The thing screamed horribly again. The black arms worked furiously, hauling me up.

I felt a violent upward jerk, stronger than the regular pulls that had been raising me. In a moment I saw the reason. The creature had released the long anchor cable, which had held it to the jungle. We were plunging upward. The moon was spinning away below.

The next shot seemed to take no effect. But at the fifth, the black limbs twitched convulsively. I am sure that the creature died almost at once. The limbs ceased to haul upon the cable, hung still. But I fired the two cartridges remaining in the gun.

That was the beginning of a mad aerial voyage.

The balloon shot upward when the anchor cable was dropped. And after it was dead, the muscular sac seemed to relax, expand, so that it rose still faster.

Within a few minutes I must have been two miles above the surface. A vast area was visible beneath me: the convexity of the moon's surface, which, of course, is much greater than that of the earth's, was quite apparent.

The great valley lay below, between the

green mountain ranges. Splotched with blue and yellow. The white river twisting along it, wide and silvery. I could see into other misty valleys beyond the green ranges, and on the curving horizon were more hills, dim and black in the distance.

The plateau upon which I had landed was like a green-covered table, many thousands of feet below. I could distinguish upon it a tiny bright disk, which I knew was the machine that I had left so unwisely.

Though there had been little wind at the surface, it seemed that I rose into a stratum of air which was moving quite rapidly into the northwest. I was carried swiftly along; the floor of the great valley glided back beneath me. In a few minutes the machine was lost to view.

I was, of course, rendered desperate at being swept away from the machine. I kept myself oriented, and tried to watch the landmarks that passed beneath me. It was fortunate, I thought, that the wind was driving me up the valley, instead of across the red ranges. I might be able to return to the machine by following down the great river, until the triple peak, near which I had left the machine, came into view. Despair came over me, however, at the realization that I was not likely to be able to traverse so vast a stretch of the unknown jungles of this world, without my ignorance of its perils leading me into some fatal blunder.

I thought of climbing the web to that monstrous body, and trying to make a great rent in the purple sac, so that I should fall more swiftly. But I could only have succeeded in entangling myself more thoroughly in the adhesive coils. And I dismissed the scheme when I realized that if I fell too rapidly, I might be killed upon striking the surface.

After the first few minutes of the flight, I could see that the balloon was sinking slowly, as the gas escaped through the bullet-holes in the muscular sac. I could only wait, and fix in my mind the route that I must follow back to the machine.

The wind bore me so swiftly along that within an hour the triple peak that I watched had dropped below the curved horizon. But still I was above the great valley, so that I should be able to find my way back by following the river. I wondered if I could build a raft, and float down it with the current.

The balloon was carried along less rapidly as it approached the surface. But, as I neared the jungle, it was evident that it still drifted at considerable speed.

Hanging helpless in the end of the red web, I anxiously scanned the jungle into which I was descending. Like that which I had first seen, it was of dense tangles of the thorny yellow scrub, broken with areas covered largely with the luxuriant green creeper.

Never would I be able to extricate myself alive, I knew, if I had the misfortune to fall in the thorn-brush. And another danger occurred to me. Even if I first touched ground in an open space, the balloon, if the wind continued to blow, would drag me into the spiky scrub before I could tear myself free of the web.

Could I cut myself free within a safe distance of the ground, and let the balloon go on without me? It seemed that only thus could I escape being dragged to death. I knew that I could survive a fall from a considerable height, since the moon's acceleration of gravity is only about two feet per second—if only I could land on open ground.

But how could I cut the web? I was without a knife. I thought madly of attempting to bite it in two, realized that that would be as hopeless as attempting to bite through a manila rope.

But I still had the pistol. If I should

place the muzzle against the cable and fire, the bullet should cut it.

I reached into my pocket again, past the adhesive coil, and found two cartridges. Though they clung to my sticky fingers, I got them at last into the magazine, and worked the action to throw one into the chamber.

By the time I had finished loading, I was low over an apparently endless jungle of the yellow thorns. Swaying on the end of the web, I was swept along over the spiky scrub, dropping swiftly. At last I could see the edge, and a green patch of the great creepers. For a time I hoped that I would be carried clear of the thorns.

Then they seemed suddenly to leap at me. I threw up my arms to shelter my face, still clinging fiercely to the pistol.

In an instant, I was being dragged through the cruel yellow spikes. There was a sharp, dry, crackling sound as they broke beneath my weight. A thousand sharp, poisoned bayonets scratched at me, stabbed, cut.

Intolerable agony racked me. I screamed. The razor-sharp spikes were tipped with poison, so that the slightest scratch burned like liquid flame. And many of the stabbing points went deep.

It seems that I struck near the edge of the thicket. For a moment I hung there in the thorns. Then, as a harder puff of wind struck it, the balloon leaped into the air, dragging me free. I swung up like a pendulum. And down again, beyond the thorny scrub—over a strip of bare sand beside the thicket.

Bleeding rapidly from my cuts, and suffering unendurable pain from the poison in my wounds, I realized that I could not long remain conscious.

Moving in a haze of agony, I seized the red cable with one hand, put the muzzle of the automatic against it, pulled the trigger. The report was crashing, stunning. My right hand, holding the gun, was flung back by the recoil—I should have lost the weapon had it not been glued to my fingers. The cable was jerked with terrific force, almost breaking my left hand, with which I held it.

And it parted! I plunged downward, sprawled on the sand.

For a few minutes I remained conscious as I lay there on the hard, cold sand—the first soil, I recall thinking vaguely in my agony, that I had seen not covered with vegetation.

The clothing had been half stripped from my tortured body by the thorns. I was bleeding freely from several deeper cuts—I remember how dark the blood was, sinking into the white sand.

All my body throbbed with insufferable pain from the poison in my wounds. As if I had been plunged into a sea of flame. Only my face had been spared.

Weakly, dizzy with pain, I tried to stagger to my feet. But a coil of the red web still clung about my legs. It tripped me, and I fell forward again, upon the white sand.

Fell into bitter despair. Into blind, hopeless rage at my inane lack of caution in leaving the machine. At my foolhardiness in venturing into the edge of the jungle. Fell into gentle oblivion....

A curious sound drew me back into wakefulness. A thin, high-pitched piping, pleasantly melodious. The musical notes beat insistently upon my brain, evidently originating quite near me.

On first awakening, I was aware of no bodily sensation. My mind was peculiarly dull and slow. I was unable to recall where I was. My first impression was that I was lying in bed in my old rooming place at Midland and that my alarm clock was ringing. But soon I realized that the liquid piping notes that had disturbed me came from no alarm.

I forced open heavy eyes. What startling nightmare was this? A tangle of green creepers, incredibly profuse. A wall of yellow thorns. A scarlet mountain beyond. And purple balloons floating in a rich blue sky.

I tried to sit up. My body burst into screaming agony when I moved. And I sank back. My skin was stiff with dry blood. The deeper wounds were aching. And the poison from the thorns seemed to have stiffened my muscles, so that the slightest motion brought exquisite pain.

The melodious pipings had been abruptly silenced at my movement. But now they rose again. Behind me. I tried to turn my head.

Recollection was returning swiftly. My uncle's telegram. The flight through space and time. My expedition to the jungle's edge, and its horrible sequel. I still lay where I had fallen, on the bare sand below the spiky scrub.

I groaned despite myself, with the pain of my stiff body. The thin musical notes stopped again. And the thing that had voiced them glided around before me, so that I could see it.

A strange and wonderful being.

Its body was slender, flexible as an eel. Perhaps five feet long, it was little thicker than my upper arm. Soft, short golden down or fur covered it. Part of it was coiled on the sand; its head was lifted two or three feet.

A small head, not much larger than my fist. A tiny mouth, with curved lips full and red as a woman's. And large eyes, dark and intelligent. They were deeply violet, almost luminous. Somehow they looked human, perhaps only because they mirrored the human qualities of curiosity and pity.

Aside from red mouth and dark eyes, the head had no human features. Golden down covered it. On the crown was a plume or crest of brilliant blue. But strange as it was, it possessed a certain beauty. A beauty of exquisite proportion, of smooth curves.

Curious wing-like appendages or mantles grew from the sides of the sleek, golden body, just below the head. Now they were stiffened, extended as if for flight. They were very white, of thin soft membrane. Their snowy surfaces were finely veined with scarlet.

Other than these white, membranous mantles, the creature had no limbs. Slim, long, pliant body, covered with golden fur. Small, delicate head, with red mouth and warm dark eyes, crested with blue. And delicate wings thrust out from its sides.

I stared at it.

Even at first sight, I did not fear it, though I was helpless. It seemed to have a magnetic power that filled me with quiet confidence, assured me that it meant only good.

The lips pursed themselves. And the thin, musical piping sound came from them again. Was the thing speaking to me? I uttered the first phrases that entered my mind, "Hello. Who are we, anyhow?"

CHAPTER V
The Mother

The thing glided toward me swiftly, its smooth round golden body leaving a little twisting track in the white sand. It lowered its head a little. And it laid one of the white mantles across my forehead.

The strange red-veined membrane was soft, yet there was an odd firmness in its pressure against my skin. A vital warmth seemed to come from it—it was vibrant with energy, with life.

The pipings came again. And they seemed to stir vague response in my mind, to call dim thoughts into being. As the same sounds were repeated again and again, definite questions formed in my mind.

"What are you? How did you come here?"

Through some strange telepathy induced by the pressure of the mantle upon my head, I was grasping the thought in the piping words.

It was a little time before I was sufficiently recovered from my astonishment to speak. Then I replied slowly, phrasing my expressions carefully, and uttering them as distinctly as I could.

"I am a native of Earth. Of the great white globe you can see in the sky. I came here on a machine which moves through space and time. I left it, and was caught and jerked up into the air by one of those purple, floating things. I broke the web, and fell here. My body was so torn by the thorns that I cannot move."

The thing piped again. A single quavering note. It was repeated until its meaning formed in my mind.

"I understand."

"Who are you?" I ventured.

I got the meaning of the reply, as it was being piped for the third time. "I am the Mother. The Eternal Ones, who destroyed my people, pursue me. To escape them, I am going to the sea."

And the thin, musical tones came again. This time I understood them more easily.

"Your body seems slow to heal its hurts. Your mental force is feeble. May I aid you?"

"Of course," I said. "Anything you can do—"

"Lie still. Trust me. Do not resist. You must sleep." When the meaning of the notes came to me, I relaxed upon the sand, closed my eyes.

I could feel the warm, vibrant pressure of the mantle on my forehead. Vital,

throbbing force seemed pulsing into me through it. I felt no fear, despite the strangeness of my situation. A living wave of confidence came over me. Serene trust in the power of this being. I felt a command to sleep. I did not resist it; a strong tide of vital energy swept me into oblivion.

It seemed but an instant later, though it must have been many hours, when an insistent voice called me back from sleep.

Vitality filled me. Even before I opened my eyes, I was conscious of a new and abounding physical vigor, of perfect health; I was bubbling with energy and high spirits. And I knew, by the complete absence of bodily pain, that my wounds were completely healed.

I opened my lids, saw the amazing creature that had called itself the Mother. Its smooth golden body coiled beside me on the sand. Its large, clear eyes watching me intently, with kind sympathy.

Abruptly I sat up. My limbs were stiff no longer. My body was still caked with dried blood, clothed in my tattered garments; the sticky scarlet coils of the web were still around me. But my ragged wounds were closed. Only white scars showed where they had been.

"Why, I'm well!" I told the Mother, thankfully. "How'd you do it?"

The strange being piped melodiously, and I grasped the meaning almost at once. "My vital force is stronger than your own. I merely lent you energy."

I began tearing at the coils of the crimson web about me. Their viscid covering seemed to have dried a little; otherwise I might never have got them off. After a moment the Mother glided forward and helped.

It used the white, membranous appendages like hands. Though they appeared quite frail, they seemed able to grasp the red cable powerfully when they were folded about it.

In a few minutes I was on my feet.

Again the Mother piped at me. I failed to understand, though vague images were summoned to my mind. I knelt down again on the sand, and the being glided toward me, pressed the white, red-veined mantle once more against my forehead. An amazing organ, that mantle, so delicately beautiful. So strong of grasp when used as a hand. And useful, as I was to learn, as an organ of some strange sense.

The meaning of the pipings came to me clearly now, with the warm, vibrant mantle touching my head.

"Adventurer, tell me more of your world, and how you came here. My people are old, and I have vital powers beyond your own. But we have never been able to go beyond the atmosphere of our planet. Even the Eternal Ones, with all their machines, have never been able to bridge the gulf of space. And it has been thought that the primary planet from which you say you came is yet too hot for the development of life."

For many hours we talked, I in my natural voice, the Mother in those weirdly melodious pipings. At first the transference of thought by the telepathy which the wonderful mantle made possible was slow and awkward. I, especially, had trouble in receiving, and had many times to ask the Mother to repeat a complex thought. But facility increased with practice, and I at last was able to understand, quite readily, even when the white membrane did not touch me.

The sun had been low when I woke. It set, and the dew fell upon us. We talked on in the darkness. And the earth rose, illuminating the jungle with argent glory. Still we talked, until it was day again. For a time the air was quite cold. Wet with the abundant dew, I felt chilled, and shivered.

But the Mother touched me again with the white membrane. Quick, throbbing warmth seemed to flow from it into my body, and I felt cold no longer.

I told much of the world that I had left, and of my own insignificant life upon it. Told of the machine. Of the voyage across space, and back through eons of time, to this young moon.

And the Mother told me of her life, and of her lost people.

She had been the leader of a community of beings that had lived on the highlands, near the source of the great river that I had seen. A community in some respects resembling those of ants or bees upon the earth. It had contained thousands of neuter beings, imperfectly developed females, workers. And herself, the only member capable of reproduction. She was now the sole survivor of that community.

It seemed that her race was very old, and had developed a high civilization. The Mother admitted that her people had had no machines or buildings of any kind. She declared that such things were marks of barbarism, and that her own culture was superior to mine.

"Once we had machines," she told me. "My ancient mothers lived in shells of metal and wood, such as you describe. And constructed machines to aid and protect their weak and inefficient bodies.

"But the machines tended to weaken their poor bodies still further. Their limbs atrophied, perished from lack of use. Even their brains were injured, for they lived an easy life, depending upon machines for existence, facing no new problems.

"Some of my people awoke to the danger. They left the cities, and returned to the forest and the sea, to live sternly, to depend upon their own minds and their own bodies, to remain living things, and not grow into cold machines.

"The mothers divided. And my people

were those that returned to the forest."

"And what," I asked, "of those that remained in the city, that kept the machines?"

"They became the Eternal Ones—my enemies.

"Generation upon generation their bodies wasted away. Until they were no longer natural animals. They became mere brains, with eyes and feeble tentacles. In place of bodies, they use machines. Living brains, with bodies of metal.

"Too weak, they became, to reproduce their kind. So they sought immortality, with their mechanical science. And still some of them live on, in their ugly city of metal—though for ages no young have been born among them. The Eternal Ones.

"But at last they die, because that is the way of life. Even with all their knowledge they cannot live forever. One by one, they fall. Their strange machines are still, with rotting brains in their cases.

"And the few thousands that live attacked my people. They planned to take the Mothers. To change their offspring with their hideous arts, and make of them new brains for the machines.

"The Mothers were many, when the war began. And my people a thousand times more. Now only I remain. But it was no easy victory for the Eternal Ones. My people fought bravely. Many an ancient brain they killed. But the Eternal Ones had great engines of war that we could not escape, nor destroy with our vital energy.

"All the Mothers save myself were taken. And all destroyed themselves, rather than have their children made into living machines.

"I alone escaped. Because my people sacrificed their lives for me. In my body are the seed of a new race. I seek a home for my children. I have left our old land

on the shores of the lake, and I am going down to the sea. There we shall be far from the Eternal Land. And perhaps our enemies will never find us.

"But the Eternal Ones know I have escaped. They are hunting me. Hunting me with their strange machines."

When day came, I felt very hungry. What was I to do for food in this weird jungle? Even if I could find fruits or nuts, how could I tell whether they were poisonous? I mentioned my hunger.

"Come," the Mother piped.

She glided away across the white sand, with easy, sinuous grace. Very beautiful, she was. Slim body, smooth, rounded. Compactly trim. The golden down was bright in the sunlight; sapphire rays played over the blue plume upon her head. The wondrous, red-veined mantles at her sides shone brilliantly.

Regarding her strange beauty, I stood still for a moment, and then moved after her slowly, absently.

She turned back suddenly, with something like humor flashing in her great dark violet eyes.

"Is your great body so slow you cannot keep up with me?" she piped, almost derisively. "Shall I carry you?" Her eyes were mocking.

For answer I crouched, leaped into the air. My wild spring carried me a score of feet above her, and beyond. I had the misfortune to come down head first upon the sand, though I received no injury.

I saw laughter in her eyes, as she glided swiftly to me, and grasped my arm with one of the white mantles to assist me to my feet.

"You could travel splendidly if there were two of you, one to help the other out of the thorns," she said quaintly.

A little embarrassed by her mockery, I

followed meekly.

We reached a mass of the green creeper. Without hesitation, she pushed on through the feathery foliage. I broke through behind her. She led the way to one of the huge white flowers, bent it toward her, and crept into it like a golden bee.

In a moment she emerged with mantles cupped up to hold a good quantity of white, crystalline powder which she had scraped from the inside of the huge calyx.

She made me hold my hands, and dropped part of the powder into them. She lifted what she had left upon the other mantle, and began delicately licking at it with her lips.

I tasted it. It was sweet, with a peculiar, though not at all unpleasant, acid flavor. It formed a sort of gum as it was wetted in my mouth, and this softened and dissolved as I continued to chew. I took a larger bite, and soon finished all the Mother had given me. We visited another bloom. This time I reached in, and scraped out the powder with my own hand. (The crystals must have been formed for the same purpose as the nectar in terrene flowers—to attract raiders, which carry the pollen.)

I divided my booty with the Mother. She accepted but little, and I found enough of the sweetish powder in the calyx to satisfy my own hunger.

"Now I must go on down to the sea," she piped. "Too long already have I delayed with you. For I carry the seed of my race; I must not neglect the great work that has fallen upon me.

"But I was glad to know of your strange planet. And it is good to be with an intelligent being again, when I had been so long alone. I wish I could stay longer with you. But my wishes are not my master."

Thoughts of parting from her were oddly disturbing. My feeling for her was partly gratitude for saving my life and partly something else. A sense of comradeship. We were companion adventurers in this weird and lonely jungle. Solitude and my human desire for society of any sort drew me toward her.

Then came an idea. She was going down the valley to the sea. And my way led in the same direction, until I could see the triple peak that marked the location of the machine.

"May I travel with you," I asked her, "until we reach the mountain where I left the machine in which I came to your world?"

The Mother looked at me with fine dark eyes. And glided suddenly nearer. A white membranous mantle folded about my hand, with warm pressure.

"I am glad you wish to go with me," she piped. "But you must think of the danger. Remember that I am hunted by the Eternal Ones. They will doubtless destroy you if they find us together."

"I have a weapon," I said. "I'll put up a scrap for you, if we get in a tight place. And besides, I'd very likely be killed, in one way or another, if I tried to travel alone."

"Let us go, Adventurer."

Thus it was decided.

I had dropped the camera, the binoculars, and the vacuum bottle when the balloon-creature jerked me into the air. They were lost in the jungle. But I still had the automatic. It had remained in my hand—stuck to it, in fact—when I fell upon the sand. I carried it with me.

The Mother objected to the weapon. Because it was a machine, and machines weakened all that used them. But I insisted that we should have to fight machines, if the Eternal Ones caught us, and that fire could be best fought with fire. She yielded gracefully.

"But my vital force will prove stronger than your rude slaying machine, Adventurer," she maintained.

We set out almost immediately. She glided off along the strip of bare sand beside the wall of thorny yellow scrub. And began my instruction in the ways of life upon the moon, by informing me that there was always such a clear zone about a thicket of the thorn-brush, because its roots generated a poison in the soil which prevented the growth of other vegetation near them.

When we had traveled two or three miles, we came to a crystal pool, where the abundant dew had collected at the bottom of a bare, rocky slope. We drank there. Then the Mother plunged into it joyously. With white mantles folded tight against her sides, she flashed through the water like a golden eel. I was glad to remove my own garments, and wash the grime and dried blood from my body.

I was donning my tattered clothing again, and the Mother was lying beside me, at the edge of the pool, with eyes closed, drying her golden fur in the sunshine, when I saw the ghostly bars.

Seven thin upright pillars of light, ringed about us. Straight bars of pale white radiance. They stood like phantom columns about us, enclosing a space ten yards across. They were not above two inches in diameter. And they were quite transparent, so I could see the green jungle and the yellow wall of thorn-brush quite plainly through them.

I was not particularly alarmed. In fact, I thought the ghostly pillars only some trick of my vision. I rubbed my eyes, and said rather carelessly to the Mother:

"Are the spirits building a fence around us? Or is it just my eyes?"

She lifted her golden, blue-crested head quickly. Her violet eyes went wide. I saw alarm in them. Terror. And she moved with astonishing speed. Drew her slender length into a coil. Leaped. And seized my shoulder as she leaped, with one of her mantles.

She jerked me between two of those strange columns of motionless light, out of the area they enclosed.

I fell on the sand, got quickly to my feet.

"What—" I began.

"The Eternal Ones," her sweet, whistling tones came swiftly. "They have found me. Even here, they reach me with their evil power. We must go on, quickly."

She glided swiftly away. Still buttoning my clothing, I followed, keeping pace with her easily, with my regular leaps of half a dozen yards. Followed, wondering vainly what danger there might have been in the pillars of ghostly light.

CHAPTER VI
Pursuit!

We skirted a continuous wall of the spiky yellow scrub.

The strip of clear ground we followed was usually fifty to one hundred yards wide. The mass of yellow thorn-brush, the poison from whose roots had killed the vegetation here, rose dense and impenetrable to our right. To the left of our open way limitless stretches covered with the green creeper. Undulating seas of feathery emerald foliage. Scattered with huge white blooms. Broken, here and there, with strange plants of various kinds. Beyond were other clumps of the yellow scrub. A red mountain wall rose in the distance. Huge purple balloons swayed here and there upon this weird, sunlit moonscape, anchored with their red cables.

I suppose we followed that open strip for ten miles. I was beginning to breathe heavily, as violent exercise always made me do in the moon's light atmosphere. The Mother showed no fatigue.

Abruptly she paused ahead of me, and glided into a sort of tunnel through the forest of thorns. A passage five feet wide and six feet high, with the yellow spokes arching over it. The floor was worn smooth, hard-packed as if by constant use. It seemed almost perfectly straight, for I could see down it for a considerable distance. Twilight filled it, filtering down through the unbroken mass of cruel bayonets above.

"I am not eager to use this path," the Mother told me. "For they who made it are hostile things. And though not very intelligent, they are able to resist my vital force, so that I cannot control them. We shall be helpless if they discover us.

"But there is no other way. We must cross this forest of thorns. And I am glad to be out of sight in this tunnel. Perhaps the Eternal Ones will lose us again. We must hasten, and hope that we encounter no rightful user of the path. If one appears, we must hide."

I was placed immediately at a disadvantage upon entering the tunnel, for I could no longer take the long leaps by which I had been traveling. My pace became a sort of trot. I had to hold my head down, to save it from the poisoned thorns above.

The Mother glided easily before me, to my relief not in such haste as before. Slender and strong and trimly beautiful—for all her strangeness. I was glad she had let me come with her. Even if peril threatened.

I found breath for speech.

"Those ghostly bars," I panted. "What were they?"

"The Eternal Ones possess strange powers of science," came the thin, whistling notes of her reply. "Something like the television you told me of. But more highly developed. They were able to see us, back by the pool.

"And the shining bars were projected through space by their rays of force. They meant some harm to us. Just what, I do not know. It is apparently a new weapon, which they did not use in the war."

We must have gone many miles through the tunnel. It had been almost perfectly straight. There had been no branches or cross-passages. We had come through no open space. Roof and walls of yellow thorns had been unbroken. I was wondering what sort of creature it might be, that had made a path through the thorns so long and straight.

The Mother stopped suddenly, turned back to face me.

"One of the makers of the trail is approaching," she piped. "I feel it coming. Wait for me a bit."

She sank in golden coils upon the trail. Her head was raised a little. The mantles were extended stiffly. Always before they had been white, except for their fine veining of red. But now soft, rosy colors flushed them. Her full red lips were parted a little, and her eyes had become strange, wide, staring. They seemed to look past me, to gaze upon scenes far-off, invisible to ordinary sight.

For long seconds she remained motionless, violet eyes distant, staring.

Then she stirred abruptly. Rose upon tawny, golden coils. Alarm was in her great eyes, in her thin, melodious tones.

"The creature comes behind us. Upon this trail. We have scant time to reach the open. We must go swiftly."

She waited for me to begin my stumbling run, glided easily beside me. I moved awkwardly. With only the moon's slight gravitational pull to hold me to the trail, I was in constant danger from the thorns.

For tortured hours, it seemed to me, we raced down the straight passage, through the unbroken forest of yellow thorns. My heart was laboring painfully; my breath came in short gasps of agony. My body was not equipped for such prolonged exertions in the light air.

The Mother, just ahead of me, glided along with effortless ease. I knew that she could easily have left me, had she wished.

At last I stumbled, fell headlong, and did not have energy to get at once to my feet. My lungs burned, my heart was a great ache. Sweat was pouring from me, my temples throbbed, and a red mist obscured my sight.

"Go—on," I gasped, between panting breaths. "I'll try—to stop—it."

I fumbled weakly for my gun.

The Mother stopped, came back to me. Her piping notes were quick, insistent. "Come. We are near the open now. And the thing is close. You must come!"

With a soft, flexible mantle she seized my arm. It seemed to me that a wave of new strength and energy came into me from it. At any rate, I staggered to my feet, lurched forward again. As I rose, I cast a glance backward.

A dark, indistinguishable shape was in view. So large that it filled almost the whole width of the tunnel. A dim circle of the pale light of the thorn forest showed around it.

I ran on... on... on.

My legs rose and fell, rose and fell, like the insensate levers of an automaton. I felt no sensation from them. Even my lungs had ceased to burn, since the Mother touched me. And my heart ached no longer. It seemed that I floated beside my body, and watched it run, run, run with the monotonously repeated movements of a machine.

My eyes were upon the Mother before me.

Gliding so swiftly through the twilight of the tunnel. Trim, round golden body.

White mantles extended stiffly, wing-like, as if to help carry her. Delicate head raised, the blue plume upon it flashing.

I watched that blue plume as I ran. It danced mockingly before me, always retreating. Always just beyond my grasp. I followed it through the blinding mists of fatigue, when all the rest of the world melted into a gray blue, streaked with bloody crimson.

I was astonished when we came out into the sunlight. A strip of sand below the yellow wall of thorns. Cool green foliage beyond, a sea of green. Sinister purple balloons above it, straining on crimson cables. Far off, a scarlet line of mountains, steep and rugged.

The Mother turned to the left.

I followed, automatically, mechanically. I was beyond feeling. I could see the bright moonscape, but it was strange no longer. Even the threat of the purple balloons was remote, without consequence.

I do not know how far we ran, beside the forest of thorns, before the Mother turned again and led the way into a mass of creepers.

"Lie still," she piped. "The creature may not find us."

Gratefully, I flung myself down in the delicate fronds. I lay flat, with my eyes closed, my breath coming in great, painful, sobbing gasps. The Mother folded my hand in her soft mantle again, and immediately, it seemed, I felt relief, though I still breathed heavily.

"Your reserve of vital energy is very low," she commented.

I took the automatic from my pocket, examined it to see that it was ready for action. I had cleaned and loaded it before we started. I saw the Mother raising her blue-crested head cautiously. I got to my knees, peered back along the bare strip of sand, down which we had come.

I saw the thing advancing swiftly along

the sand.

A sphere of bright crimson. Nearly five feet in diameter. It rolled along, following the way we had come.

"It has found us!" the Mother piped, very softly. "And my vital power cannot reach through its armor. It will suck the fluids from our bodies."

I looked down at her. She had drawn her slender body into a golden coil. Her head rose in the center, and the mantles were outspread, pure white, veined with fine lines of scarlet, and frail as the petals of a lily. Her great dark eyes were grave and calm; there was no trace of panic in them.

I raised the automatic, determined to show no more fear than she, and to give my best to save her.

Now the scarlet globe was no more than fifty yards away. I could distinguish the individual scales of its armor, looking like plates of horn covered with ruby lacquer. No limbs or external appendages were visible then. But I saw dark ovals upon the shell, appearing at the top and seeming to drop down as the thing rolled.

I began shooting.

At such a distance there was no possibility of missing. I knelt in the leaves of the green creeper, and emptied the magazine into the globe.

It continued to roll on toward us, without change of speed. But a deep, angry drumming sound came from within it. A reverberating roar of astonishing volume. After a few moments, I heard it repeated from several points about us. Low and distant rumblings, almost like thunder.

In desperate haste, I was filling the clip with fresh cartridges. Before I could snap it back into the gun, the creature was upon us.

Until it stopped, it had presented a sphere of unbroken surface. But suddenly six long, glistening black tentacles reached out of it, one from each of the black ovals I had seen evenly spaced about the red shell. They were a dozen feet long, slender, covered with thin black skin corrugated with innumerable wrinkles, and glistening with tiny drops of moisture. At the base of each was a single, staring, black-lidded eye.

One of those black tentacles was thrust toward me. It reeked with an overpowering, fetid odor. At its extremity was a sharp, hooked claw, beside a black opening. I think the creature sucked its food through those hideous, retractable tentacles.

I got the loaded clip into the gun, hastily snapped a cartridge into the chamber. Shrinking back from the writhing tentacular arm, I fired seven shots, as rapidly as I could press the trigger, into the black-lidded eye.

The deep drumming notes came from within the red shell again. The black tentacles writhed, thrashed about, and became suddenly stiff and rigid. The sound of it died to a curious rattle, and then ceased.

"You have killed it," the Mother whistled musically. "You use your machine well, and it is more powerful than I thought. Perhaps, after all, we may yet live."

As if in ominous answer, a reverberating roll of distant drumming came from the tangle of yellow thorns. She listened, and the white mantles were stiffened in her alarm.

"But it has called to its kind. Soon many will be here. We must hasten away."

Though I was still so tired that movement was torture, I rose and followed the Mother, as she glided on along the sand.

Only a moment did I pause to examine the very interesting creature I had killed.

It seemed unique, both in shape and in means of locomotion. It must have developed the spherical shell of red armor through ages of life in the spiky scrub. By drawing its limbs inside, it was able to crash through the thorns without suffering any hurt. I supposed it contrived to roll along by some rhythmic muscular contraction, inside the shell—such movement being much easier on the moon than it would be on earth, because of the lesser gravity. Where it could not roll, it dragged or lifted itself with the long, muscular appendages that I have called tentacles.

Since we were in the open air again, I was able to resume my progression by deliberate, measured leaps, which carried me forward as fast as the Mother could move, and with much less effort than I had spent in running. I had a few moments of rest as I glided through the air between leaps, which compensated for the fiercer effort of each spring.

From time to time I looked back, nervously. At first I could see only the scarlet shell of the dead creature, there by the green vines where we had killed it. Always smaller, until it was hardly visible.

Then I saw other spheres. Emerging from the tangle of yellow thorn-brush. Rolling along the strip of bare soil, to congregate about the dead being. Finally I saw that they had started in our direction, rolling along rather faster than we could move.

"They are coming," I told the Mother. "And more of them than I can kill."

"They are implacable," came her piping reply. "When one of them sets out upon the trail of some luckless creature, it never stops until it has sucked the body fluids from it—or until it is dead."

"Anything we can do?" I questioned.

"There is a rock ahead of us, beyond that thicket. A small hill, whose sides are so steep they will not be able to climb it.

If we can reach it in time, we may be able to scramble to the top.

"It will be only temporary escape, since the creatures will never leave so long as we are alive upon it. But we shall delay our fate, at least—if we can reach it in time."

Again I looked back. Our pursuers were rolling along like a group of red marbles, at the edge of the yellow forest. Gaining upon us—swiftly.

The Mother glided along more rapidly. The white mantles were stiffly extended from her golden sides, and aglow with rosy colors. The muscles beneath her furry skin rippled evenly, gracefully.

I increased the force of my own leaps.

We rounded an arm of the tangle of scrub, came in sight of the rock. A jutting mass of black granite. Its sides leaped up steep and bare from a mass of green creepers. Green moss crowned it. Thirty feet high it was. Perhaps a hundred in length.

Our pursuers were no longer merely marbles when we saw the rock. They had grown to the size of baseballs. Rolling swiftly after us.

The Mother glided on, a tireless strength in her graceful tawny body. And I leaped desperately, straining to drive myself as fast as possible.

We turned. Broke through the thick masses of verdure to the rock. Stood beneath its sheer wall, grim and black.

The red spheres were no more than a hundred yards behind. A sudden rumble of drums came from them, when we halted by the rock. I could see the dark ovals on their glistening red armor, that marked their eyes and the ends of their concealed tentacles.

"I can never climb that," the Mother was piping.

"I can leap up!" I cried. "Earth muscles. I'll carry you up."

"Better that one should live than both of us die," she said. "I can delay them, until you reach the top."

She started gliding back, toward the swiftly rolling spheres.

I bent, snatched her up.

It was the first time that I had felt her body. The golden fur was short, and very soft. The rounded body beneath it was firm, muscular, warm and vibrant. It throbbed with life. I felt that a strange sudden surge of energy was coming into me from contact with it.

I threw her quickly over my shoulder, ran forward a few steps, leaped desperately up at that sheer wall of black granite.

My own weight, on the moon, was only thirty pounds. The Mother, compact and strong though she was, weighed no more than a third as much. Combined, our weight was then some forty pounds. But, as she had realized, it was an apparently hopeless undertaking to attempt to hurl that mass to the top of the cliff before us.

At first I thought I should make it, as we soared swiftly up and up, toward the crown of red moss. Then I realized that we should strike the face of the cliff before we reached the top.

The face of the black rock was sheer. But my searching eyes caught a little projecting ledge. As we fell against the vertical cliff, my fingers caught that ledge. A moment of dreadful uncertainty, for the ledge was mossy, slippery.

CHAPTER VII
The Eternal Ones Follow!

My left hand slipped suddenly off. But the right held. I drew myself upward. The Mother slipped from my shoulder to the top of the rock. Grasped my left hand with one of the white mantles, drew me to safety.

Trembling from the strain of it, I got to my feet upon the soft scarlet moss, and surveyed our fortress. The moss-covered surface was almost level, a score of feet wide at the middle, where we stood, and a hundred in length. On all sides the walls were steep, though not everywhere so steep as where I had leaped up.

"Thank you, Adventurer," the Mother whistled musically. "You have saved my life, and the lives of all my people to come."

"I was merely repaying a debt," I told her.

We watched the red globes. Very soon they reached the foot of the cliff. The rumble of drums floated up from the group of them. And they scattered, surrounding the butte.

Presently we discovered that they were attempting to climb up. They were not strong enough to make the leap as I had done. But they were finding fissures and ledges upon which their long tentacles could find a grasp, drawing themselves up.

We patrolled the sides of the rock regularly, and I shot those which seemed to be making the best progress. I was able to aim carefully at an eye or the base of a tentacle. And usually a single shot was enough to send the climber rolling back down to the green jungle.

The view from our stronghold was magnificent. On one side was an endless wall of yellow scrub, with crimson mountains towering above it in the distance. On the other, the green tangle of the luxuriant creepers swept down to the wide silver river. Yellow and green mottled the slope that stretched up to scarlet hills beyond.

We held out for an entire day.

The sun sank beyond the red mountains when we had been upon the butte only an hour or two. A dark night would have terminated our adventures on the spot. But fortunately the huge white disk of the earth rose almost immediately after sunset, and gave sufficient light throughout the night to enable us to see the spheres that persisted in attempting to climb the walls of our fort.

It was late on the following afternoon that I used my last shot. I turned to the Mother with the news that I could no longer keep the red spheres from the walls, that they would soon be overwhelming us.

"It does not matter," she piped. "The Eternal Ones have found us again."

Looking nervously about, I saw the bars of ghostly light once more. Seven thin upright pillars of silvery radiance, standing in a ring about us. They had exactly the same appearance as those from which we had fled at the pool.

"I have felt them watching for some time," she said. "Before, we escaped by running away. Now that is impossible."

Calmly she coiled her tawny length. The white mantles were folded against her golden fur. Her small head sank upon her coils, blue crest erect above it. Her violet eyes were grave, calm, alert. They reflected neither fear nor despair.

The seven pillars of light about us became continually brighter.

One of the red spheres, with black tentacles extended, dragged itself upon the top of the butte, with us. The Mother saw it, but paid it no heed. It was outside the ring formed by the seven pillars. I stood still, within that ring, beside the Mother, watching—waiting.

The seven columns of light grew brighter.

Then it seemed that they were no longer merely light, but solid metal.

At the same instant, I was blinded with a flash of light, intolerably bright. A splintering crash of sound smote my ears, sharp as the crack of a rifle, infinitely

louder. A wave of pain flashed over my body, as if I had received a severe electric shock. I had a sense of abrupt movement, as if the rock beneath my feet had been jarred by a moonquake.

Then we were no longer upon the rock.

I was standing upon a broad, smooth metal plate. About its edge rose seven metal rods, shining with a white light, their positions corresponding exactly to the seven ghostly pillars. The Mother was coiled on the metal plate beside me, her violet eyes still cool and quiet, revealing no surprise.

But I was dazed with astonishment.

For we were no longer in the jungle. The metal plate upon which I stood was part of a complex mechanism of bars and coils of shining wire, and huge tubes of transparent crystal, which stood in the center of a broad open court, paved with bright, worn metal.

About the court towered buildings. Lofty, rectangular edifices of metal and transparent crystal. They were not beautiful structures. Nor were they in good repair. The metal was covered with ugly red oxide. Many of the crystal panels were shattered.

Along the metal-paved streets, and on the wide courtyard about us, things were moving. Not human beings. Not, evidently, living things at all. But grotesque things of metal. Machines. They had no common standard of form; few seemed to resemble any others. They had apparently been designed with a variety of shapes, to fill a variety of purposes. But many had a semblance to living things that was horrible mockery.

"This is the land of the Eternal Ones," the Mother piped to me softly. "These are the beings that destroyed my people, seeking new brains for their worn-out machines."

"But how did we get here?" I demanded.

Evidently they have developed means of transmitting matter through space. A mere technical question. Resolving matter into energy, transmitting the energy without loss on a light beam, condensing it again into the original atoms.

"It is not remarkable that the Eternal Ones can do such things. When they gave up all that is life, for such power. When they sacrificed their bodies for machines. Should they not have some reward?"

"It seems impossible—"

"It must, to you. The science of your world is young. If you have television after a few hundred years, what will you not have developed after a hundred thousand?

"Even to the Eternal Ones, it is new. It is only in the time of my own life that they have been able to transmit objects between two stations, without destroying their identity. And they have never before used this apparatus, with carrier rays that could reach out to disintegrate our bodies upon the rock, and create a reflecting zone of interference that would focus the beam here—"

Her piping notes broke off sharply. Three grotesque machines were advancing upon us, about the platform. Queer bright cases, with levels and wheels projecting from them. Jointed metal limbs. Upon the top of each was a transparent crystal dome, containing a strange, shapeless gray mass. A soft helpless gray thing, with huge black staring eyes. The brain in the machine! The Eternal One.

Horrible travesties of life, were those metal things. At first they appeared almost alive, with their quick, sure movements. But mechanical sounds came from them, little clatterings and hummings. They were stark and ugly.

And their eyes roughened my skin with dread. Huge, black, and cold. There was nothing warm in them, nothing human, nothing kind. They were as emotionless as polished lenses. And filled with menace.

"They shall not take me alive!" the Mother piped, lifting herself beside me on tawny coils.

Then, as if something had snapped like a taut wire in my mind, I ran at the nearest of the Eternal Ones, my eyes searching swiftly for a weapon.

It was one of the upright metal rods that I seized. Its lower end was set in an oddly shaped mass of white crystal, which I took to be an insulator of some kind. It shattered when I threw my weight on the rod. And the rod came free in my hands, the white glow vanishing from it, so I saw it was copper.

Thus I was provided with a massive metal club, as heavy as I could readily swing. On earth, it would have weighed far more than I could lift.

Raising it over my head, I sprang in front of the foremost of the advancing machines—a case of bright metal, moving stiffly upon metal limbs, with a dome-shaped shell of crystal upon it, which housed the helpless gray brain, with its black, unpleasant eyes. I saw little tentacles—feeble translucent fingers—reaching from the brain to touch controlling levers.

The machine paused before me. An angry, insistent buzzing came from it. A great, hooked, many-jointed metal lever reached out from it suddenly, as if to seize me.

And I struck, bringing the copper bar down upon the transparent dome with all my strength. The crystal was tough. But the inertia of the copper bar was as great as it would have been upon the earth; its hundreds of pounds came down with a

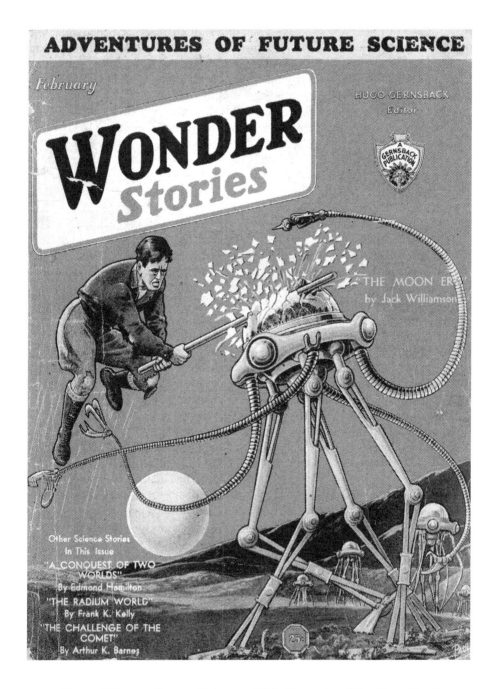

*Cover of WONDER STORIES, February 1932, illustrating "The Moon Era."
Painted by Frank R. Paul*

force indeed terrific.

The dome was shattered. And the gray brain smashed into red pulp.

The Eternal Ones would certainly have been able to seize the Mother without suffering any harm. And probably any other creature of the moon, that might have been brought with her on the matter-transmitting beam. But they were not equipped for dealing with a being whose muscles were the stronger ones of earth.

The two fellows of the Eternal One I had destroyed fell upon me. Though the copper bar was not very heavy, it was oddly hard to swing, because of its great inertia. The metal limbs of the third machine closed about my body, even as I crushed the brain in the second with another smashing blow.

I squirmed desperately, but I was unable to twist about to get in a position to strike.

Then the Mother was gliding toward me. Blue crest erect upon her golden head, eager light of battle flashing in her violet eyes. From her smooth, tawny sides the mantles were stiffly outstretched. And they were almost scarlet with the flashing lights that played through them. My momentary despair vanished; I felt that she was invincible.

She almost reached me. And then rose upon her glossy coils, and gazed at the brain in the transparent dome of the machine that held me, her membranes still alight.

Abruptly the machine released me; its metal limbs were relaxed, motionless.

My encrimsoned copper mace rose and descended once more, and the machine fell with a clatter upon its side.

"My mental energy is greater than that of the Eternal One," the Mother piped in calm explanation. "I was able to interfere with its neural processes to cause paralysis." She looked about us suddenly.

"But smash the delicate parts of this machine that brought us here. So that if we have the good fortune to escape, they cannot soon bring us back. I know it is the only one they have, and it does not look as if it could be quickly repaired."

My club was busy again. Delicate coils were battered beneath it. Complex prisms and mirrors and lenses shattered. Delicate wires and grids in crystal shells, which must have been electron tubes, destroyed.

The three machines we had wrecked had been the only ones near. But a score or more of others were soon approaching across the metal-paved court, producing buzzing sounds as if of anger and excitement. Some of them were near before my work was done.

Too many of them to battle. We must attempt an escape.

I stooped, picked up the Mother's warm, downy body, and ran across the platform, toward the ring of approaching machine-beings. Near them, I leaped, as high and as far as I could.

The spring carried me over them, and a good many yards beyond. In a moment I was in the middle of a worn pavement of metal. The street, almost empty of the machines, ran between ancient and ugly buildings, toward a lofty wall of some material black and brilliant as obsidian.

I hastened desperately toward the wall, moving with great leaps. The Eternal Ones followed in humming, clattering confusion, falling swiftly behind.

They had been taken quite by surprise, of course. And, as the Mother had said, dependence upon the machine had not developed in them the ability to respond quickly to emergencies.

As we later discovered, some of the machines could travel much faster than could we. But, as I have remarked, the things were not of a standard design, all differing. And none of those behind us happened to be of the fastest type.

I do not doubt that they could easily have destroyed us, as we fled. But their object would have been defeated. They wanted the Mother alive.

We reached the shining black wall well ahead of our pursuers. Its surface was smooth and perpendicular; it was fully as high as the cliff up which I had leaped with the Mother. And there was no projecting ledge to save us if I fell short.

I paused, dropping the heavy mace.

"You could toss me up," the Mother suggested. "Then leap."

There was no time for delay. She coiled quickly up into a golden sphere. I hurled her upward, like a football. She vanished over the top of the wall. I lifted the mace, threw it up, and to one side, so it would not strike her.

The Eternal Ones were close behind. A mob-like group of grotesque machines. Buzzing angrily. One of them flung some missile. There was a crashing explosion against the black wall, a flare of green light. I realized the danger of being separated from the Mother, even as I leaped.

My spring carried me completely over the wall, which was only some five or six feet thick.

I descended into a luxuriant tangle of the green creepers. Foot-thick stems covered the ground in an unbroken network, feathery leaves rising from them higher than my head. I fell on my side in the delicate foliage, struggled quickly to my feet. The green fronds cut off my view in all directions, though I could see the top of the black wall above.

Before I struck the ground I had glimpsed a vast green plain lying away eastward to the horizon. In the north was a distant line of red mountains. The city of the Eternal Ones lay westward.

I saw nothing of the Mother; I could not, in truth, see a dozen feet through the exotic jungle.

"This way," her cautious whistling tones reached me in a moment. "Here is your weapon."

I broke through the masses of delicate fronds in the direction of the sound, found the Mother unharmed, coiled in a golden circle beside the copper bar. She glided silently away; I picked up the bar and followed as rapidly and quietly as I could.

Once I looked back, when we passed a narrow open space, and saw a little group of the Eternal Ones standing upon the black wall. They must have been looking after us, but I do not suppose they saw us.

For the rest of the day—it was early afternoon when we escaped—and all night when the jungle was weird and silvery in the earth light, and until late on the following day, we hastened on. We did not stop except to drink and bathe at a little stream, and to scrape the sweet white powder from a few of the great argent flowers we passed. We ate as we moved. The jungle of creepers was unbroken; we were always hidden in the luxuriant, delicate foliage.

At first I had been sure we would be followed. But as the hours passed and there was no sign of pursuit, my spirits rose. I doubted now that the Eternal Ones could follow the trail swiftly enough to overtake us. But I still carried the copper mace.

The Mother was less optimistic than I.

"I know they are following," she told me. "I feel them. But we may lose them. If they cannot repair the machine which you wrecked—and I am sure they cannot do it soon."

We had approached a rocky slope, and the Mother found a little cave, beneath an overhanging ledge, in which we rested. Totally exhausted, I threw myself down, and slept like a dead man.

It was early on the next morning when the Mother woke me. She lay coiled at the entrance of the cave, the frail mantles stiffened and flushed a little with rosy light, violet eyes grave and watchful.

"The Eternal Ones follow," she piped. "They are yet far off. But we must go on."

CHAPTER VIII
An Earth Man Fights

Climbing to the top of the rocky slope, we came out upon a vast plateau, covered with green moss. The level surface was broken here and there by low hills, but no other vegetation was in view before us. At a distance, the plain resembled a weird desert covered with green snow.

It took six days to cross the moss-grown table-land. We finished the white powder we had carried with us on the fourth day; and we found no water on the fifth or sixth. Though, of course, those days were of only eighteen hours each, we were in a sorry plight when we descended into a valley green with the creepers, watered with a crystal stream whose water seemed the sweetest I had ever tasted.

We ate and rested for two nights and a day before we went on—though the Mother insisted that the Eternal Ones still followed.

Then, for seventeen days, we followed down the stream, which was joined by countless tributaries until it became a majestic river. On the seventeenth day, the river flowed into a still greater one, which came down a valley many miles wide, covered with yellow thorn-brush and green creepers, and infested with thousands of the purple balloon-creatures, which I had learned to avoid by keeping to the green jungle, where they could not throw their webs with accuracy.

We swam the river, and continued down the eastern bank—it was flowing generally south. Five days later we came in view of a triple peak I well remembered.

Next morning we left the jungle, and climbed up to the little moss-carpeted plateau where I had left the machine. I had feared that it somehow would be gone, or wrecked. But it lay just as I had left it on the day after I landed on the moon. Bright, polished, window-studded wall of armor, between two projecting plates of gleaming copper.

We reached the door, the Mother gliding beside me.

Trembling with a great eagerness, I turned the knob and opened it. Everything was in order, just as I had left it. The oxygen cylinders, the batteries, the food refrigerator, the central control table, with the chart lying upon it.

In a week—if the mechanism worked as I hoped it would—I should be back upon the earth. Back on Long Island. Ready to report to my uncle, and collect the first payment of my fifty thousand a year.

Still standing on the narrow deck outside the door, I looked down at the Mother.

She was coiled at my feet. The blue plume upon her golden head seemed to droop. The white mantles were limp, dragging. Her violet eyes, staring up at me, somehow seemed wistful and sad.

Abruptly an ache sprang into my heart, and my eyes dimmed, so that the bright golden image of her swam before me. I had hardly realized what her companionship had come to mean to me, in our long days together. Strange as her body was, the Mother had come to be almost human in my thoughts. Loyal, courageous, kind—a comrade.

"You must go with me," I stammered,

in a voice gone oddly husky. "Don't know whether the machine will ever get back to earth or not. But at least it will carry us out of reach of the Eternal Ones."

For the first time, the musical pipings of the Mother seemed broken and uneven, as if with emotion.

"No. We have been together long, Adventurer. And parting is not easy. But I have a great work. The seed of my kind is in me, and it must not die. The Eternal Ones are near. But I will not give up the battle until I am dead."

Abruptly she lifted her tawny length beside me. The limp, pallid mantles were suddenly bright and strong again. They seized my hands in a grasp convulsively tight. The Mother gazed up at my face, for a little time, with deep violet eyes—earnest and lonely and wistful, with the tragedy of her race in them.

Then she dropped, and glided swiftly away.

I looked after her with misty eyes, until she was half across the plateau. On her way to the sea, to find a home for the new race she was to rear. With a leaden heart, and an aching constriction in my throat, I climbed through the oval door, into the machine, and fastened it.

But I did not approach the control table. I stood at the little round windows, watching the Mother gliding away, across the carpet of moss. Going ahead alone... the last of her race....

Then I looked in the other direction, and saw the Eternal Ones. She had said the machines were near. I saw five of them. They were moving swiftly across the plateau, the way we had come.

Five grotesque machines. Their bright metal cases were larger than those of the ones we had encountered in the city. And their limbs were longer. They stalked like moving towers of metal, each upon four jointed stilts. And long, flail-like limbs

dangled from the case of each. Crystal domes crowned them, sparkling in the sunlight—covering, I knew, the feeble gray brains that controlled them. The Eternal Ones.

Almost at the edge of the plateau they were when I first saw them. I had time easily to finish sealing the door, to close the valve through which I had let out he excess air upon landing, and to drive up through the moon's atmosphere, toward the white planet.

But I did not move to do those things. I stood at the window watching, hands clenched so that nails cut into my palms, set teeth biting through my lip.

Then, as they came on, I moved suddenly, governed not by reason but by an impulse that I could not resist. I opened the door and clambered hastily out, picking up the great copper mace that I had left lying outside.

And I crouched beside the machine, waiting.

Looking across the way the Mother had gone, I saw her at the edge of the plateau. A tiny, distant form, upon the green moss. I think she had already seen the machines, and realizing the futility of flight had turned back to face them.

As the machine-things came by, I was appalled at their size. The metal stilts were fully six feet long, the vulnerable crystal domes eight feet above the ground.

I leaped up, and struck at the brain of the nearest as it passed. My blow crushed the transparent shell and the soft brain within it. But the machine toppled toward me, and I fell with it to the ground, cruelly bruised beneath its angular levers.

One leg was fast beneath it, pinned against the ground, and its weight was so great that I could not immediately extricate myself. But I had clung to the copper bar, and when another machine bent down, as if to examine the fallen one, I seized the weapon with both hands, and placed another fatal blow.

The second machine fell stiffly beside me, an odd humming sound continuing within it, in such a position that it almost concealed me from the others. I struggled furiously to free my leg, while the other Eternal Ones gathered about, producing curious buzzing sounds.

At last I was free, and on my knees. Always slow in such an unexpected emergency, the machine-beings had taken no action, though they continued the buzzing.

One of them sprang toward me as I moved, striking a flailing blow at me with a metal arm. I leaped up at it, avoiding the sweeping blow, and struck its crystal case with the end of the copper bar.

The bar smashed through the crystal dome, and crushed the frail brain-thing within it. But the machine still moved. It went leaping away across the plateau, its metal limbs still going through the same motions as before I had killed the ruling brain.

I fell back to the ground, rolling over quickly to avoid its stalking limbs, and struggling to my feet, still holding grimly to the copper bar.

The remaining machine-beings rushed upon me, flailing out with metal limbs. Desperately, I leaped into the air, rising ten feet above their glistening cases. I came down upon the case of one, beside the crystal dome that housed its brain. I braced my feet and struck, before it could snatch at me with its hooked levers.

As it fell to the moss, humming, buzzing, and threshing about with bright metal limbs, I leaped from it toward the other, holding the bar before me. But I struck only the metal case, without harming it, and fell from it into the moss.

Before I could stir, the thing drove its metal limb down upon my body. It struck my chest with a force that was agonizing... crushing. A rocket of fiery pain seemed to burst in my brain. For a moment, I think, I was unconscious. Then I was coughing up bloody foam.

I lay on the red moss, unable to move, the grim realization that I would die breaking over me in a black wave that swept away even my pain. The metal limb had been lifted from me.

Then the Mother was beside me. She had come back.

Her warm smooth furry body was pressed against my side. I saw her violet eyes, misty, appealing. She laid the rose-flushed mantles over my side. The pain went suddenly from it. And I felt new strength, so I could get to my feet, though red mist still came from my nostrils, and I felt a hot stream of blood down my side.

The remaining machine-monster was bending, reaching for the Mother. I seized the copper mace again, struck a furious blow at the crystal shell that housed its brain. As it crashed down, beating about blindly and madly with its great metal limbs, my new strength went suddenly from me and I fell again, coughing once more.

A flailing limb struck the Mother a terrific blow, flinging her against the moss many yards away. She crept back to me, brokenly, slowly. Her golden fur was stained with crimson. Her mantles were limp and pale. There was agony in her eyes.

She came to where I lay, collapsed against my side. Very low, her musical tones reached my ears and died abruptly with a choking sound. She had tried to tell me something, and could not.

The last of the Eternal Ones that had followed was dead, and presently the machines ceased their humming and buzzing and threshing about upon the moss.

Through the rest of the day we lay there, side by side, both unable to move. And through the strange night, when the huge white disk of the earth bathed us in silvery splendor, and in my delirium I dreamed alternately of my life upon it, and of my adventures upon this weird moon-world, with the Mother.

When the argent earth was low, and we were cold and drenched with dew, lying very close together to benefit from each other's warmth, the wild dreams passed. For a few minutes I was coldly sane. I looked back upon a life that had never had any great purpose, that had been lived carelessly, and impulsively. And I was not sorry that I had come to the moon.

I remained with the Mother until she stirred no more, and no effort on my part could rouse her to life. With tears in my eyes, I buried her beneath the green moss. Then stumbling to the ship, I climbed in. Sealing the door and starting the machinery, I felt the ship lift quickly toward the distant beckoning earth.

Jack Williamson on "The Moon Era"
(Spoiler Alert!)

"The Moon Era" was a first-draft novelette; I remember hammering out 27 pages of it in one day after the spell of the story had captured me. My record stint.

The story derived from S. Fowler Wright's great far-future fantasy *The World Below*, which I must have heard about from Ed Hamilton. *Astounding* was running into trouble by then, but *Wonder Stories* bought my story, to run in the February issue with a different last paragraph—in my own not-very-logical ending, the first-person narrator had died with his story not yet told to anybody.

—from *Wonder's Child: My Life in Science Fiction,* by Jack Williamson,
copyright © 1984, 2005 Jack S. Williamson.
Used by permission of the Estate of Jack Williamson

Space Opera revisited

An Essay by JAMES E. GUNN

The late, great Jack Williamson believed that space flight was the central myth of science fiction, the way the Trojan War was the central myth of the Greeks. He had helped create the myth himself with *The Legion of Space* (serialized beginning in 1934 in *Astounding Stories)*. Years later, after World War II had validated the SF tropes of space flight and atomic weapons, SF began to be published in books again, first by fans, then by mainstream publishers, and one of the first reprinted (Fantasy Press, 1947) was *The Legion of Space,* along with other space epics such as E. E. "Doc" Smith's *Lensman* series (beginning in 1948) and his *Skylark* series (beginning in 1946).

As Gene Roddenberry's *Star Trek* series would immortalize the phrase twenty years later, space was the final frontier. Spaceflight was what set SF apart from pulp adventure stories of other kinds—sea stories, wild west stories, war stories, detective stories, and stories of mysterious places on Earth like Africa, the Far East, the Arctic or Antarctic, or the ocean floor. Getting off this planet entirely was the ultimate SF experience.

Before the beginnings of rocket research in the early 20th century, flying into space was fanciful, another way of placing a story in Northrop Frye's "world beyond the hill." Lucian of Samosata, a 2nd century Hellenistic writer, wrote stories about getting to the moon—a seemingly accessible world looming enticingly in the night sky. One was *Icaromennipus,* about a man who flies to the moon with one wing from a vulture and one from an eagle, and then a more significant work satirizing travel writers, "A True Story," about a band of heroes whose Argonaut-like vessel is caught up in a whirlwind and carried to the moon. Lots of moon stories followed, including works by astronomer Johannes Kepler, Cyrano de Bergerac, and Edgar Allan Poe.

As science began to focus humanity's eyes on the heavens, space stories slowly became more realistic. Cyrano used a variety of mechanisms, including bottles of dew attached to his belt, but finally reached halfway to the moon on rockets before Diana, the goddess of the moon and also the goddess of cattle, rescued him because his hero's bruises had been rubbed with beef fat. The hero of Kepler's "Somnium," Duracotus, called upon demon power, but once his protagonist reached the moon, Kepler described it with (what was then) scientific accuracy. Poe's protagonist, Hans Pfaall, escaped from Dutch creditors in a balloon equipped with a hand-operated condenser to help the balloonist breathe the thin air. Jules Verne shot his moon voyagers out of a cannon. H. G. Wells reverted to the fanciful by sending his *First Men in the Moon* with an anti-gravity substance called Cavorite.

By the second decade of the 20th century, Albert Einstein's relativity theories began to make space seem more comprehensible—even, perhaps, more accessible. It may have been Einstein's theories about the speed of light that inspired Doc Smith to write *The Skylark of Space* in 1919, though he did not get it published until Hugo Gernsback serialized it in *Amazing Stories* in 1928. Publication may have had to wait for the invention of the first SF magazine in 1926, or for Edwin Hubble's 1924 discoveries that the universe was not one galaxy, but was as filled with galaxies as the galaxy was filled with stars. That may have expanded the science-fictional imagination. Even so, Smith's heroes got into space by the chance discovery of a propulsion system based on liberating "the intra-atomic energy of copper." Smith launched the era

of what later became known as "space opera," more noted for derring-do than how-to-do. John W. Campbell, later to write more sensitive stories as Don A. Stuart and to become the editor who presided over the Golden Age, contributed a number of space epics, and so did Edmond Hamilton, who wrote stories about his Interplanetary Patrol for *Weird Tales*.

By the mid 1930s, stories were beginning to concern themselves with how ships and people might behave in space. Doc Smith's *Lensman* series, though fanciful in their descriptions of the battles between the Lensmen educated by Arisia and the minions of the evil Eddor, nevertheless dealt with hand-to-hand battles and the void of space; Smith evaded Einstein's speed-of-light limitation by inventing what Smith called "the inertialess drive." By the time Jack Williamson submitted the three novels that made up *The Legion of Space,* authors were beginning to demonstrate some concerns about the perils of space and the dangers of interstellar powers. Williamson also looked to literature for inspiration, and found it in Dumas and Shakespeare. His trilogy has been called "the Three Musketeers in space," plus fat, bibulous Giles Habibula modeled after Falstaff. In those days (and throughout his career) Williamson was fond of small groups of individuals challenging mighty forces (as in *The Humanoids),* although the ultimate defense of the universe in *The Legion of Space,* AKKA, turned out to be little more than a ten-penny nail.

The success of rocket technology, imagined in Russia by Konstantin E. Tsiolkovsky, pioneered in the U.S. by Robert Goddard beginning in 1926 and in Germany by Hermann Oberth, made space flight seem realizable. The romantic era of the space opera merged into the realistic era following World War II, typified by Ed Hamilton's "What's It Like Out There?" which depicted the deprivations and deaths among volunteers of an expedition to Mars, and the inability of a returnee to destroy the myth. The story was written in 1933 but couldn't be published until 1952 (in *Thrilling Wonder)*, when the public mood caught up with Hamilton's vision. As Charles Fort once wrote, "In steam-engine time, people invent steam engines."

Other events contributed as well: Willy Ley's 1944 non-fiction work *Rockets* became *Rockets, Missiles, and Space Travel* in 1951 and *Rockets, Missiles, and Men in Space* in 1968. Arthur C. Clarke's 1950 *Interplanetary Flight* was followed in 1951 by *The Exploration of Space.* He complemented his non-fiction work with novels such as *Prelude to Space* and *The Sands of Mars* (both 1951) and followed them with *Earthlight* (1955) and *A Fall of Moondust* (1961). In my case, I was impressed by a 1952 issue of *Collier's* magazine devoted to the next steps into space, written by Willy Ley and Wernher von Braun, and illustrated by Chesley Bonestell—later published in book form as *The Conquest of Space* (1955). I had written a couple of space operas—*Star Bridge* (1955), a romantic epic with Jack Williamson, and *This Fortress World* (1955), an anti-romantic space epic. *The Conquest of Space* got me started on a series of stories (beginning with "The Cave of Night," *Galaxy,* 1955) taking a hard look at the realities of space flight, that got collected in *Station in Space* (1958).

When Isaac Asimov began publishing his stories in 1939, he brought to bear his rational, scientific mind (though not in his chosen field, chemistry) on subjects such as robots and history. He launched his big series of space opera romances with "Foundation" (*Astounding,* 1942) and built upon his concepts of psychohistory and the fall of a Galactic Empire to write about practical matters of governance. James Blish began the series eventually brought together as *Cities in Flight* (1970) with "Okie" (*Astounding,* 1950). The concept of an anti-gravity device such as the "spindizzy" to free entire cities from earthly bonds was as fanciful as Wells's "Cavorite," but the problems of city governance and economics were pragmatic. Later, in his *The Seedling Stars* (1957) stories, such as "Surface Tension" (*Galaxy,* 1952), Blish would deal with the realistic possibilities of adapting humanity to other planetary conditions rather than terraforming those planets to human use. Few SF writers have not contributed to the space opera literature at one time or another.

Robert A. Heinlein had a major hand in space travel. A number of his stories published in the "slick" magazines in the 1950s popularized practical issues in space, along with some romanticism, collected in volumes such as *The Green Hills of Earth* (1951). But he began his engagement with space flight early: "Requiem," an *Astounding* story (1940) written in Heinlein's first year of publication, dealt with D. D. Harriman, the entrepreneur who has made space flight a reality but has been denied the realization of his dream of actually getting to the moon. Harriman hires a battered rocket ship he finds at a state fair and its equally battered crew to fly him to the moon where he dies happy. Here Heinlein mixed the romanticism of Robert Lewis Stevenson's verse with the economic realities and time span necessary to achieve space flight. That reality is exemplified in the extrapolation of World War I barnstorming pilots into a space-flight era when retired spaceships would similarly offer rides at state fairs. The back story is how Harriman's dream of reaching the moon has been sublimated into the entrepreneurial efforts to make it possible. Later Heinlein would go back and expand that back story into the novel *The Man Who Sold the Moon* (1950).

By 1942 Jack Williamson, adjusting to John Campbell's vision, began publishing a series of stories (as Will Stewart) about the perilous lives and adventures of miners working on contra-terrene ("seetee"—now called "antimatter") asteroids in the solar system, stories that would be gathered into *Seetee Ship* (1951) and a novel, *Seetee Shock* (1950). Here romanticism would be tempered by imagined reality.

Poul Anderson began his consideration of space flight with the political realities embodied in his Technic History series featuring Terran agent Dominic Flandry, the entrepreneur Nicholas van Rijn, and the Polysotechnic League of interstellar traders, beginning with *War of the Wing-Men* (1958). Another series of Anderson stories dealt with the movement of humanity into space, first the solar system, then the galaxy, under the general title of the Psychotechnic League. His masterpiece of space fiction, however, was *Tau Zero* (1970), in which a ram-scoop starship goes out of control and, through time dilation, survives the end of the universe.

Women made a major assault on space beginning with C. J. Cherryh in the late 1970s. Cherryh's *Downbelow Station* won a Hugo Award for 1981; she won another for *Cyteen* in 1988. Much of her extensive body of work has dealt with the space enterprise: "The reach for space and its resources is the make-or-break point for our species.... Therefore I write fiction about space and human adjustment to the unfamiliar." Lois McMaster Bujold made her debut the following decade with the first of her Vorkosigan series, *Shards of Honor* (1986), and won the first of her Nebula

Awards (and Hugo Awards for later works) for *Falling Free* (1988), a novel about space humans (quaddies) created with four arms instead of arms and legs, to better deal with the realities of space weightlessness. Cherryh's and Bujold's fiction deal more with the human implications of space flight. Vonda N. McIntyre and other female authors would add their viewpoints to what is humanly important about the human movement into space.

Meanwhile Frederik Pohl, with *Man Plus* (1976), about adapting a man to live on the Mars that science had begun to reveal, and *Gateway* (1977) about the dilemmas involved in alien vessels that take their human explorers on voyages to unknown destinations, provided a new breakthrough in the linkage of space and the human psyche. Both won multiple awards. Even earlier, Larry Niven had brought the knowledge of a physics major to a series of novels that reached a peak early with his third novel, *Ringworld* (1970), which combined his future history of humans in space, including the two-headed Puppeteers and the tiger-like Kzin, with the discovery of a world constructed by unknown engineers into the form of a ring around its sun. Niven combined his talents with those of aerospace engineer and political scientist Jerry Pournelle (already producing epics about future mercenary armies in space) to create the best-selling *Mote in God's Eye* (1974), about the discovery of fast-breeding and fast-adapting aliens. It would be the first of a series of successful collaborations.

A physicist who actually practiced science, Gregory Benford, began publishing novels in 1970 and produced his first major space epic, *In the Ocean of Night,* in 1977. It would lead into a series called Galactic Center that would feature a war to the death between humans and artificial intelligences near, and then in, the event horizon of the black hole at the center of the Milky Way galaxy. Another physicist, David Brin, would begin his novel-writing career with *Sundiver* (1980) and progress to the multiple-award-winning *Startide Rising* (1983) and the rest of the "Uplift" series in which humans find themselves unwelcome intruders into a galaxy in which other species, unlike humans, have been uplifted to sentience.

*I*n the early 1990s, perhaps inspired by reports from the Mars explorer vessels, SF writers burst out into a flurry of novels about the first manned voyages to Mars and efforts at terraforming. Beginning in 1991 with Robert Forward's *Mars Rainbow* and continuing into 1992 with novels such as Ben Bova's *Mars* (the first of a series dealing with what is known about the other planets in the solar system) and Jack Williamson's *Beachhead,* and culminating in Kim Stanley Robinson's *Red Mars* and later sequels, SF authors focused on the practical aspects of colonizing our most Earth-like neighbor. The more authors know about the facts of space, the more their works reflect realistic rather than romantic approaches—unless, like Ray Bradbury's *The Martian Chronicles* (1950), reality is deliberately subordinated to the romantic impulse.

The distinguishing characteristic between romanticism and realism may be that romanticism reports how things ought to be and realism reports how things will really be. The late Prof. Arthur Mizener suggested in *Modern Short Stories* that modern writers resorted to three major traditions: realistic (which Mizener called "comedy of manners"), romantic, and subjective. They can be distinguished, he wrote, by their attitude toward objective common sense: the realistic story makes us feel that objective common sense will not only be correct about how things will turn out, but right and wise in understanding that they must turn out that way; the romantic story makes us feel that objective common sense is likely to be correct about how things will turn out, but will miss the real meaning of things because it will not take into account the feelings of the central character; and the subjective story makes us feel that what men dream is so important, and therefore so real, that the objective world of common sense, however resistant to men's desires, does not finally count. Science fiction before the Golden Age of John W. Campbell was primarily romantic with an occasional note of realism; after Campbell became editor of *Astounding,* primarily realistic with an occasional note of romanticism; and after Michael Moorcock became editor of *New Worlds,* "new wave" SF was primarily subjective.

Toward the middle of the 1990s a new note of realism emerged with Charles Pellegrino's *Flying to Valhalla* (1993) followed by Pellegrino and George Zebrowski's *The Killing Star* (1995), which raised the question of rival sapient species in the galaxy. In an approach reminiscent of earlier suspicion of aliens typified by H. G. Wells's *The War of the Worlds* (1898), Pellegrino raised the specter of an entire solar system being destroyed by a body being propelled into it at relativistic speeds. If this could happen, Pellegrino speculated, every species would have a motive to eliminate rivals before potential rivals had a chance to eliminate them. In *The Killing Star,* that attack happens, as a counterpoint to the message of Zebrowski's earlier novel *Macrolife* (1979), which suggested that the natural environment for humanity was in space, in maneuverable, hollowed-out planetoids.

A concern about rival, star-traveling species had been anticipated almost a decade earlier by Greg Bear's *The Forge of God* (1987), which had Earth and much of humanity destroyed by the release of anti-matter neutronium into the center of the Earth. In *Anvil of Stars* (1992) remnants of humanity, settled on Mars, send out an expedition to destroy its destroyers. Bear also published *Moving Mars* in 1993.

What has been called *The Space Opera Renaissance,* in a 2006 anthology of that name edited by David G. Hartwell and Kathryn Cramer, got its start in the unlikely locale of the Great Britain. Noted for its rejection of large, expansive American SF, particularly in the New Wave that got started in 1964, British writers turned their attention to the stars beginning in the late 1980s, nurtured by the founding of the British magazine *Interzone* in 1982. First came Ian M. Banks with *Remember Phlebas* (1986), then Paul McAuley with *Four Hundred Billion Stars* (1988), Ian McDonald with *Desolation Road* (1988), Colin Greenland with *Take Back Plenty* (1990) and its sequels, then Stephen Baxter with *Raft* (1991) followed by *Timelike Infinity* (1992), the first of his Xeelee series. Other United Kingdom writers followed: Peter Hamilton with his *The Reality Disfunction* (1996) and sequels, Alastair Reynolds (who lives in The Netherlands) with *Revelation Space* (2000), and others including, most recently, Charles Stross, who mixes space opera with the Singularity in *Singularity Sky* (2003) and *Accelerando* (2005).

About the British turn to space opera, Paul McAuley wrote (quoted in Hartwell and Cramer's anthology): "There was a conscious attempt to subvert the triumphalism dominant in American sf... I was also aware of the perception of British sf as being low key, inward looking, and, yes, disillusioned with the toys of sf. I wanted to try and combine the two—the grand sweep of vision the best American sf can give, grounded in gritty realism...." He went on in a *Locus* interview to say: "New space opera—the good new space opera—cheerfully plunders the tropes and toys of the old school and secondary sources from Blish to Delany, and deploys them in epic narratives where intimate, human-scale stories are at least as relevant as the widescreen baroque backgrounds on which they cast their shadows....[L]ike cyberpunk, [the new space opera] is eclectic and pluralistic, and infused with the very twenty-first century sensibility that the center cannot hold, that technology-driven change is continuous and advancing on a thousand fronts, that some kind of posthuman singularity is approaching fast or may already have happened. Most of all, its stories contain a vertiginous sense of deep time; in the new space opera, the Galaxy is not an empty stage on which humans freely strut their stuff, but is instead a kind of junk yard littered with the ruins and abandoned wonders of earlier, more powerful races."

The staging of space operas continue, in the U.S. with writers such as the late Charles Sheffield, Spider Robinson, Jack McDevitt, Nancy Kress, Mike Resnick, and others, in particular Vernor Vinge, whose *A Fire Upon the Deep* and sequel imagine a galaxy where artificial intelligences operate with the casual intrusiveness and inattentiveness of Olympian gods.

Contemporary astrophysics, with its Big Bang, Dark Matter, Dark Energy, Black Holes, Stellar Clusters and Gas Clouds, String Theory, and alternate universes, provide license for the kind of limitless speculation that resides at the heart of space opera. But at the same time, the existence of scientific theories has provided a house in which the opera, in all its grand sense-of-wonder, can be staged, but the walls still contain the action and shape the sound. •••

THREE'S A CROWD...

by Eric Brown

Illustrated by Steven Kloepfer

I was in the cargo hold with Karrie, securing crates which had shaken loose after the last phase-out from voidspace, when Ella buzzed me to say she was picking up a mayday signal.

I looked at her face on my wrist-com. "We'll be right up, Ella."

I'd bought *A Long Way from Home* on the cheap, and had never had lift-pads installed. It was a long climb up the ladder from the hold to the flight-deck.

On the way Karrie said, "You should see yourself when you're talking to Ella."

I looked up at her. "Give it a rest, Karrie." This wasn't her first dig about how I was acting towards our new team member.

"Straight up, Ed," Karrie went on. "You're like a love-sick teenager."

"You're imagining things. I'm old enough to be her father."

Karrie snorted a laugh at this. She stopped, lodged an elbow on the deck of the corridor leading to our cabins, and peered down at me. I stopped too, rather than crash into her boots.

"Reality check, Ed. My objection isn't your relative ages. It's the fact that she isn't even human."

I sighed. "Climb, Karrie, okay? We've got a mayday signal to attend to, remember?"

She climbed, but she didn't shut up. "No, I'm serious. You shouldn't let yourself fall for something that's no more than a meat shell wrapped around a complex integrated processor."

A meat shell and an integrated processor that mimics a twenty-year-old Venezuelan Indian girl, I thought to myself.

"I'm not falling for her," I said. But who was I kidding? Certainly not Karrie, who was a bright cookie, and not myself... though I'd tried hard to deny my feelings towards the non-human entity called Ella ever since I'd hired her back on Procyon VII.

Karrie sighed. "Ed, I just don't want to see you get hurt, is all. Remind yourself, next time you're feeling lustful towards her, that she's a machine."

I considered. "Okay, I'll do that—if you promise me one thing."

"Name it."

"That you'll act civilly towards her."

"You mean, treat it as if it's a human being?"

"Exactly that. And you can start by calling her Ella, not *it*, okay?"

She thought about that, then said, "You don't want me to hurt its feelings, Ed? Listen to me: it's a *machine*. It has no feelings. It thinks, it doesn't feel."

"Karrie, do it for me, *please.*"

"Okay, if you stop looking at her with those come-to-bed eyes."

"Deal," I said, wondering if I could keep up my part of it.

Karrie slipped into the flight-deck and eased herself into the engineer's sling, ignoring Ella as she passed. I hitched myself into the pilot's sling and glanced across at my co-pilot.

And Karrie wanted me to ignore the kid? Listen, my brain told me she was a vat-grown biological body on the outside of a very clever AI core, but all I could see was what I'd seen back in the bar on Pro-

cyon VII: a beautiful, vulnerable sixteen-year-old without a friend in the universe.

I know: call me stupid.

I was aware of Karrie's eyes on me, and tried not to stare too long at Ella. She'd taken to wearing very little on the hot flight-deck: skimpy ripped shorts and a bandanna knotted between her small breasts. That left a lot of sweat-sheened mocha flesh to avoid looking at.

"So what gives?" I said.

"I picked up a mayday signal seven minutes ago, Ed. It's weak, but that's because it's from space-norm."

"Identification?"

Her eyes rolled to show their milky whites as she accessed the ship's smartware core. A jack connected the back of her head to the com-console before us.

"No identification, but my guess is it's alien."

"Alien?" I sat up. "What kind of alien?"

She shook her head. "The mayday's routed through a translation program, which suggests it isn't one of the common species."

"Intriguing. So let's go have a look-see, okay?"

Ella nodded.

I glanced across at Karrie. "You second that?"

She glared at me. "Thanks for asking. Yeah, let's see what trouble the greenies have got themselves into."

I ignored her venom, and her speciesism. "Okay, hold on tight," I said as I eased *A Long Way from Home* out of void-space.

We rattled about like a tin can in a particle accelerator, and a minute later the grey of voidspace was replaced with the limitless black of space-norm, scattered with distant suns.

Ella touched her pad with slim fingers, and the alien ship appeared on the delta viewscreen before us.

"If that isn't the strangest looking shit-pile I've ever seen," Karrie opined, leaning forward in her sling.

Loath though I was to give credence to Karrie's scatological description, the alien ship did look somewhat... *biological,* let's say.

Karrie went one better. "It's a flying turd, Ed."

Ella, staring at the ship, corrected her, "That's highly unlikely, Karrie. For one thing, excreted fecal matter would not emit a mayday signal."

"So literal, aren't we, girl?" Karrie smiled sweetly across at Ella, who didn't so much as blink.

"Okay, you two," I said. "Ella, will you open a com-channel, please?"

She tapped again, and seconds later the flight-deck was filled with a high, intense jabbering. A second after that, the translation program kicked in.

"...request immediate assistance... Structural integrity breached. Total systems failure... Atmosphere remaining: one hour. We request immediate assistance..."

I said, "Hail them. Identify ourselves and request identification. Ask how many individuals they are. Tell them we'll help if we can."

Ella fingered the pad, then spoke into her com, giving our species designation and willingness to aid, if that were possible.

Of course, if the aliens breathed methane, or some other noxious mix, then all we could do would be to tow the ship to the closest inhabited planet and hope some outfit there could effect repairs.

"...I am [untranslatable]... from star Jaykendra. Atmosphere compatibility with *Homo sapiens* within tolerances... I am one individual, and kindly request permission to board."

I looked at Karrie and Ella. "One of 'em... Okay, we can house it in the hold until we get to Altair with the ship in tow. We'll hand it over to the Federation, then lodge a compensation claim. Who knows, it might even come through in ten years or so."

Karrie nodded. "Sounds good to me."

Ella said, "I'll relay our willingness to assist."

"A Long Way from Home calling... Request granted. Prepare to board."

I eased the ship alongside the alien vessel, scanning its length for any sign of an egress port. Failing that, I'd take a bell cross and cut my way through its skin.

I found a likely looking bud beside the ship's front end. Without being told, Ella initiated the com-program to customize our docking rig to the alien ship's port.

As the umbilical snaked across the gulf, I said to Ella, "Set the smartware program to scan for weapons when they come across."

She nodded. "Will do."

I said, "Any chance of establishing a visual connection? I'd like to see what our house guest looks like before it boards."

She nodded and tapped at her pad. "I'm getting something, but it's low-res."

The alien ship flickered from the viewscreen. In its place was a murky interior shot of what I took to be the flight-deck, or its equivalent.

I leaned forward, staring.

"Ugly looking beasts," Karrie observed. "And I thought there was only one of the critters?"

Disappearing through a circular exit hatch were what looked like three overweight caterpillars, dun coloured and bristling with spines.

"Could have been a translation error," I said.

The aliens shuffled off into the depths of their ship and disappeared from view.

A minute later Ella reported, "They're in the umbilical, and they're clean.

They're carrying nothing in the way of weapons. They should be aboard in a couple of minutes."

"Close the bulkheads and route them into the hold," I said. "Karrie, ready the grapples and grab the ship."

"If they'll stick," she said under her breath.

"And then," I said, "we'll phase out and make for Altair. St Christopher would be proud."

I set course and found myself looking forward to greeting our hapless guests.

"Ella, can you copy the translation program and come with me to the hold?"

She nodded, tapped her com and rolled her eyes as the program downloaded itself into her cache.

"Why take her?" Karrie asked, glaring at me.

"Because," I said patiently, "you're supposed to be grabbing the alien ship, and I need Ella to translate."

"I could have taken a portable core," Karrie pointed out.

I glanced at Ella. She was still communing with the smartware. "There's one other thing, Karrie. Ella will be armed, and her reactions are faster than yours—and mine, too, okay?"

"According to the smartware, they're unarmed, Ed."

"They're unarmed—but they're alien. I'm taking no risks. They might be what they claim to be, but how do I know that? That's why I'm locking them in the hold until I know one way or the other."

Ella unjacked her head from the console and nodded at me. "All set, Ed."

Lips pursed, Karrie swung back to the viewscreen and commenced grabbing the alien ship.

We climbed down from the flight-deck, detouring to the storeroom in order to pick up a stunner. I passed the sleek pistol to Ella. "Know how to use one of these?"

She took it, turned it over in her hand, found a port and slipped an extrusion from her index finger into the butt. She closed her eyes, and opened them a second later. "Do now," she said. Handy girl to have around, Ella.

"We'll keep our distance and I'll find out who and what they are. I'm sure things'll be fine, but it's best to be careful."

She nodded. "Understood."

I smiled at her, letting my eyes linger on hers for longer than was normal. Whereas a human woman would have reacted, either with a smile or with embarrassment, Ella didn't bat an eyelid.

I recalled what Karrie had said about Ella's being no more than a machine. I knew it, intellectually, but my biology was slow on the uptake.

I led the way to the hold.

We paused before the sliding door and looked through the viewscreen.

The hold was big—around the size of a skyball court—and half-filled with packing crates and containers. The lighting in there was dim, and it was a second before I made out our guests.

One of them was curled on a crate, spiraled as if asleep. Another was humping itself across the floor, from crate to crate, as if carrying out an inspection. The third creature was positioned in the middle of the hold, its front half rearing upwards, its big, faceted eyes—like sable sieves—staring at the door as if it were expecting us.

I pressed the sensor panel and the door slid open.

The first thing I noticed was the smell, the unpleasant, adenoid-pinching reek of formaldehyde or chloroform. The second thing was the high chittering that passed between the creatures as we stepped into the hold. The sleeping alien uncurled itself and slid from its perch, while the curious creature left off its inventorying and shuffled across to join the others. All three faced us, rearing as if in some form of ritual greeting.

The chittering had ceased, as if they were waiting for me to speak. I glanced at Ella and said, "What were they saying?"

A pretty frown creased her flawless forehead. "I didn't catch all of it, but it was something along the lines of, 'We have company. Be aware...' or 'Be vigilant.'"

I cleared my throat. "Welcome to my ship, *A Long Way from Home.* I am Ed, the captain; this is Ella, my co-pilot."

I paused while Ella translated this. It was a strange experience listening to the high twitters she emitted, as if this wild-looking Amazon had suddenly taken to trilling like a bird.

The central alien, a little larger than the others, had reared up and now swayed from side to side as it spoke. Imagine the high notes of a piccolo, segueing from time to time into those of a dog whistle. The ultrasonics soon gave me a headache.

Ella listened attentively, and turned to me when the whistling ceased.

"There was nothing wrong with the earlier translation, Ed, when it said they were one. It is. It's a composite lifeform, a gestalt soma-form. It might be three separate bodies, but one mind governs the whole, one identity."

"I've heard about them. Aren't they from out beyond the Nazzruddin Stardrift?" In my thirty years in space, I'd had dealings with perhaps a dozen of the more common alien races, and heard stories of a dozen others which kept themselves to themselves.

"Their homeworld is a moon of a gas giant orbiting a red supergiant in the

'Drift," she said. "They don't often come this far into the Rim."

"They have different functions, right? I mean, each section has a specialty."

Ella nodded. "I think so. The central section is the communicator, though they communicate among themselves as well - each section has two brains, one composite, and a secondary, rudimentary cerebellum which is what houses its specialty... as far as I can make out."

"What do the other sections do?"

"I'll ask." She phased into shrill twitters again, and seconds later the central section of the tripartite caterpillar analogue replied.

Ella reported, "The section on our left is the observer, the one on the right is a..." She frowned again, and my stomach flipped at the sight of the pretty crease, like quote marks, that appeared between her molten eyes. "The translator's having trouble with the word. It's something like an organizer or planner."

I nodded. "Okay," I said. "Could you ask them what brought them so far from home?"

She relayed my question, and the Communicator replied.

I watched its tiny, bud-like mouth work, while the flesh that covered its body undulated with a queasy kind of external peristalsis, its foot-long spines rising and falling with the motion.

"They were heading for a star along the Rim on a trading mission," Ella said, "a hundred light years from their homestar. Their ship suffered a malfunction while in voidspace and they overshot their destination. When they phased out, they found themselves a thousand light years from home."

"They can thank their lucky stars we were passing," I said. "Okay, tell them that we'll take them as far as Altair, then hand them over to the Federation authorities. That should take a day. Ask them if they need anything in the way of food or water."

Ella nodded and relayed my words.

The Communicator swayed, its head turning so that its big, multi-celled eyes regarded first me and then Ella as it replied.

Ella said, "It thanks us, and is happy with the prospect of being taken to Altair. It does not require sustenance—apparently it last ate three days ago, and will not require food for another three days."

"Ask if we can forward any messages to its own kind about their circumstances."

Ella passed on the offer, to which the Communicator replied that that would not be necessary. "It said that they will contact their superiors via the Federation when they reach Altair."

"Very well. Okay, tell them, if there is anything else they require, we'll provide it if we can."

Ella spoke. The Communicator replied. "They require nothing more, Ed. And they thank us again for our assistance."

I nodded towards the Communicator, smiled and raised a hand in farewell, feeling awkward as I always did in the company of sentient creatures with whom I had nothing in common.

Before we left the hold, Ella reached out to the control panel beside the sliding door and tapped in a code. We stepped from the hold, and as the door slid shut behind us, I asked, "What were you doing?"

"I've set the speakers to pick up anything they say to each other, and then to broadcast it to me."

I stared. "Why?"

She looked at me. "Ed, while they were speaking to us... they were communicating among themselves."

I stared at her. "Are you sure? I mean, I didn't hear anything—" Nor, for that matter, did I see the Communicator's mouth move. I said as much to Ella, and asked if we were dealing with a ventriloquist caterpillar. Her unblinking gaze told me that she didn't appreciate the joke.

"Ed, they communicated to themselves in sub-sonics, sub-vocalising deep within their throats."

"Did the translation program catch anything?"

"I was concentrating on what they said to us." She closed her eyes. "I'm working on the translation now..."

I watched her as her eyes turned up, showing full, macabre orbs of white. She looked at me and said, "It's difficult... The sub-sonics is a secondary language, quite different from the audible primary. The program can't decode as much... They were saying something about... whether they can trust us, or not."

I shrugged. "Well, perhaps that's to be expected, in the circumstances. Anyway, we've got to remember that they're alien, and we can't judge their words and actions as we might those of our own kind."

I realized what I'd said, then, as she gave me a look and replied, "Do you think I am in ignorance of the difference inherent in other sentients? As Karrie would say, do you take me for a dummy?"

I smiled at her acute observation.

She closed her eyes suddenly, listening to something deep within her cache. "Ed, they asked each other if... we *suspected.*"

"Suspected what?"

"That's the frustrating thing—they didn't say," she said. "But they were worried that we might have suspected something."

She reached out and touched the control panel beside the door. The speaker relayed nothing but silence from the hold.

Ella said, "Let's return to the flight-deck and listen in. They might communicate audibly when we're not about."

We climbed, Ella first, and I kept my eyes averted from the sight of her bottom as she climbed nimbly to the flight-deck.

Karrie had successfully caught the alien ship in our grapples, and we were all set to phase out. I slipped into the pilot's sling and initiated phase out, and seconds later the stars disappeared. All that could be seen through the viewscreen now was the marmoreal grey of the void, and in the foreground the lumpish outline of the alien vessel, riding close.

I gave Karrie a quick resumé of our audience with the Jaykendrans, and told her about Ella's suspicions.

She raised a skeptical eyebrow. "Aliens are notoriously difficult to work out, Ed. I mean, they're hard enough for us humans to fathom, and we're biological. What hope would a non-human processing system have?"

I glanced across at Ella. She was in her sling, jacked into the com-panel.

"I think you underestimate her intelligence, Karrie. Anyway, remember our deal."

She smiled at me, but there was nothing friendly in the smile. "I saw you ogling her ass a minute ago, for Chrissake. Deal's off. And anyway, she doesn't have intelligence, just advanced parallel processing abilities." At least Karrie had the grace to say this in little more than a whisper.

A minute later Ella unjacked and said, "I've routed the speaker through the com." She reached out and fingered her touchpad. "We'll be able hear everything they say."

I lay back and eyed the grilled speaker above our head, expectantly.

Karrie said, mocking, "Think they're planning to take over the ship, Ella?"

"I cannot guess what they might be planning, Karrie. However, we might

soon learn."

After a minute of absolute silence, a sound issued from the speaker.

Karrie said, "Sounds like they need tuning, Ed. Think that's a plot to sabotage us?"

I glared her into silence.

Ella said, "I'll route myself into the core. What I say from now on is a literal translation of their words, okay?"

I nodded. I noticed that even Karrie was sitting forward in her sling.

I stared at Ella, at her slim limbs and bare, perfect feet, and knew that taking her on had been the best decision of my life.

From the speaker above my head, a high tweeting commenced. A second later, Ella spoke in a flat, emotionless voice.

"We can assume it is dead?"

"Dead, certainly, or dying."

"Will they have the [untranslatable] *to learn of our scheme?"*

Pause.

I looked across at Karrie, who pulled an alarmed scowl.

The tweeting resumed, and Ella spoke.

"They are human, and therefore limited."

"But the small one, it is not human."

"It is a synthetic, and therefore dangerous."

A pause, then, *"What now?"*

"We wait. Soon, we will gain our freedom."

"I would like assurance that [untranslatable] *is dead."*

"Cease your concern. It is incapacitated. That is sufficient."

Silence.

We listened, expectantly, but no further warblings issued from the hold.

Ella unjacked herself and looked from Karrie to me. "They are not what we assumed them to be, Ed."

I said, "So... what do you make of

that?"

Karrie said, "Who the hell were they talking about? Who's dead?"

"Obviously," Ella replied, "someone or something aboard the ship."

I was sweating. "That thing about gaining its freedom..."

"Is the hold secure?" Karrie said.

Ella said, "Of course. Locked from the outside."

"So what do we do? I'd like your suggestions. Ella?"

She was instant with her reply, "We should board the alien ship, try to learn about the Jaykendran. It was in doubt about whether someone or something in the alien ship was dead—we should cross to the ship and find out."

"Karrie? Any thoughts?"

"Seeing as how the critter is locked in the hold, we have time to do as Ella said. You don't think it was armed?"

"Didn't seem to be," I said.

I considered the situation, then made my decision. "Okay, we'll get ourselves over there. Ella, link the umbilical."

Karrie said, "Who's going, Ed?"

Nothing was going to keep me from poking around inside the alien ship, and it would make sense if Ella accompanied me. I told Karrie this, and she said under her breath, "How did I guess?"

I stared at her. "What do you mean by that?"

She looked away, through the viewscreen at the alien ship. "Just that you and hot-pants seem inseparable these days. Word of advice, keep your mind on the job when you're over there, okay?"

"Jesus, Karrie."

Ella reported, "Umbilical locked."

"Okay, let's go."

We climbed from the flight-deck and hurried along the corridor to the umbilical, passing the hold where the Jaykendrans were imprisoned.

As I followed Ella along the umbilical to the alien ship, she said, "Karrie seems perturbed by my presence, Ed."

"Yeah," I said. "It's called jealousy."

"She assumes that you and I are involved physically?"

Well, that was one way of putting it. "No, it's just that she thinks I'd like us to be."

A pause, then, "And would you?"

I felt myself blush, and was glad Ella was leading the way and couldn't see me. "No, of course not."

"We could become intimate, Ed."

My heart hammered. "Would you like that?"

She said, "I have the integrated processing to appreciate physical and sexual intimacy."

"Ella, I said, 'Would you like that?'"

She considered the question. "It would be interesting," she said at last.

"Interesting," I repeated. Despite myself, I said. "Let's just keep our relationship professional, okay?"

She nodded. "That's fine by me, Ed."

She's a computer, I told myself, an AI who just happens to look like a highly desirable human being.

We came to the hatch that opened at our approach to reveal the murky interior of the alien ship. Ella led the way down a soft corridor—'soft' as in the floor seemed to be manufactured from some padded, fibrous material. The effect was like walking across a mattress. To steady myself I reached out to a wall, then retracted my hand quickly. The surface seemed to be coated with a tacky, sebaceous fluid.

"What the hell is this?" I said.

"My theory is that the ship is biological, Ed. Not manufactured, but grown."

We came to what approximated to the flight-deck, an oval chamber plunged into a visceral gloaming and equipped with what looked like vegetable pods affixed to the floor and ceiling by stalks.

"Okay, we're looking for a victim... maybe another of their kind."

"Let's start here and then move systematically through the ship," Ella said.

I stared around the flight-deck. There was no sight of a tripartite dead Jaykendran.

Then Ella touched my arm and said, "Look, Ed..."

I looked across the chamber to where she was pointing.

The slit in the skin of the chamber appeared for all the world like a wound, a meter-long incision through flesh and muscle, revealing weeping arteries and lacerated organs.

"There are more, Ed!"

Once I'd seen one wound—if it were a wound—I saw others everywhere I looked on the floor, walls and ceiling.

It looked like someone had gone berserk with a samurai sword.

Ella stiffened and grabbed my arm. At the same time, I heard it.

A barely audible mewling filled the air around us.

"What the hell...?" I began.

"It's speaking," Ella said. "The ship. It's speaking to us."

My heart raced. "Can you translate?"

She nodded. "The language is Jaykendran," she said. She closed her eyes, concentrating.

When she opened them, she appeared alarmed. "I'll let the ship speak through me, Ed."

Seconds later, she channeled the wounded starship. *"Help me... You... human, yes? You can assist me?"*

"Ask it what happened," I told her.

She twittered, and the starship replied. Ella relayed, *"It attacked me, disabled me. Committed... [untranslatable]. It is dangerous, be warned."*

She asked a question of her own, and then channeled the ship's reply. *"I am Thendra, police ship, custodial transport vessel. My prisoner... it is a killer. On my world, it killed citizens for material gain. I was transporting the prisoner to Handra for trial, segmentation. It... [untranslatable] and attacked me, attempted to kill me. While I was incapacitated, it called for your assistance. Be warned, the prisoner is dangerous. It will kill you and commandeer your ship."*

I said to Ella, "But the Jaykendra isn't armed—"

She spoke to the ship, and received a swift reply. She said, "It doesn't need weapons as we understand them, Ed. It... ejects acid. You can see what it did in here."

I said, "Can we help the ship?"

"The ship is not mortally wounded, but severely incapacitated. It is healing, but it will take time to be fully functional. Perhaps weeks. It is more concerned about our welfare."

I considered the alien in the hold, and said, "Tell the ship that we have the prisoner under restraint."

She relayed my words and listened as the ship replied. She looked at me, eyes wide. "The ship says that the prisoner will not be constrained by the hold. The acid... it can eat through metal."

A cold sweat clutched me. "What the hell is it planning?"

"The ship says that it will attempt a takeover of our ship, in order to escape."

"Jesus. What can we do?"

Ella closed her eyes and spoke to the alien ship. I watched her as she emitted trills like a piccolo, the beautiful and bird-like notes sounding strange coming from her full Venezuelan lips.

At that second, my wrist-com buzzed.

I accessed the call with a premonition

of dread.

Karrie stared up at me from the tiny screen. "Ed! The bastards broke out of the hold! They crawled up to the flight deck, spat fucking acid at me!"

"Where are you now?"

"I dived out, nearly killed myself getting away. I locked myself in my berth— but they're on the flight-deck, and who knows what they're planning."

"You okay?"

"Bruised and sore, but I'll live."

"Hold on. We're coming over. We'll be with you soon." I looked at Ella. She was listening attentively to the ship's warblings. "Listen, Karrie. We'll keep the com-channel open. Tell me if the bastard comes after you, okay?

"Will do. What have you found over there?"

"Can't explain now," I said as Ella opened her eyes and stared at me.

"Ed," she said, "the ship has a plan. It says it can help us."

Ella explained, "The ship says that if we can incapacitate one of its parts, then the others will be rendered ineffective."

"The stunner?"

Ella lifted the pistol and nodded. "It should work. We have others in the storeroom. All we need is one shot."

"And then, when we've stunned one of its segments?"

"The ship says that the prisoner's action has provoked summary justice."

"Meaning?"

"Meaning that we should return the section to the ship, and it will then eject the stunned section into space. The others will be taken to Thendra, where they will be tried and most likely reintegrated with a complementary, non-criminal section."

I nodded, marvelling at the complexity of our alien neighbours.

"Okay, okay..." I paused, looking across at Ella. "So, how do we go about this?"

"We get back to our ship, grab another stunner, and climb to the flight-deck."

"Leaving ourselves open to the prisoner taking acid pot-shots at us?"

"I'll go first. I can shut off my pain receptors if I'm hit."

My stomach flipped at the thought. "I'm not letting you get yourself killed."

"So what do you suggest?"

I thought about it, came up with nothing. "Okay, we'll go over. But I'll go first."

Ella stared at me. "I can't let you do that, Ed."

"Ella, I'm the captain here."

"Which is the reason why you are not expendable. Besides, I'm a non-human entity, Ed."

"Not to me, Ella."

She shook her head and said, calmly, "Madness."

The impasse was interrupted by Karrie, shouting at me from my wrist-com. "Ed, for Chrissake... I just patched into the surveillance cams. One of the bastards is leaving the flight-deck and heading this way!"

I stared at Ella. "Let's get going!" To Karrie I said, "We're on our way."

As we negotiated the umbilical, Ella said, "This might work in our favor, Ed."

"How so?"

"Think about it. If one of the segments is going after Karrie, and two others are on the flight-deck, then it'll make it easier to stun one of them."

"The section heading for Karrie," I said.

The berths were on the level below the flight-deck, accessed via the ladder along a short corridor.

We came to the ship and Ella paused, stunner raised as she peered into the corridor. "All clear. Follow me."

We hurried along the corridor and past the hold. A neat hole had been melted through the sliding door, precisely wide enough to allow the escape of the Jaykendran sections.

We slipped into the storeroom. I helped myself to a stunner, set it to maximum power, and nodded to Ella. We quit the storeroom and ran along the corridor.

Ella reached the foot of the ladder welded to the bulkhead. I wondered, then, how the alien had managed to negotiate the rungs, as caterpillars weren't noted for climbing ladders.

Then I noticed the bulkhead, and the oily trail the creature's suckers had left on its climb to the flight-deck.

From my wrist-com, Karrie called, "Ed, where are you? The bastard's getting awful close."

"We're on our way."

Ella was already pulling herself up the ladder. I followed, fear like a fist in my chest, twisting.

If one of the sections decided to peer from the flight-deck now...

"Ed!" Karrie's voice yelled from my wrist. "It's right outside the door. Jesus, it's burning its way in—the door's dissolving!"

The fear in her voice drove me upwards. "We're coming!"

Up ahead, Ella stopped. I looked up and saw why. The bristling head-piece of a Jaykendran section emerged from the hatch to the flight-deck. A puckered, anus-like opening below its segmented eyes dilated. A stream of colourless liquid jetted from the opening, narrowly missing Ella and myself and hitting the deck below us with a sizzle. Ella raised her stunner and fired, and the alien retracted its head.

We climbed.

"Ed... Ed!" Karrie's voice was soft, fearful. I looked at the screen on my wrist-com, but the image was a blur. "It's in here with me, just staring... It's—it's speaking to me, whistling."

Ella paused in her ascent and said into her wrist-com, "Karrie. Boost the gain so I can hear what it's saying. I'll talk to it via your com, okay?"

"Done," Karrie said.

The alien's high-pitched whistling issued from Ella's wrist-com. She listened, then replied. While she was doing this, I raised my stunner and kept an eye on the hatch to the flight-deck. When I saw a spray of bristles emerge above the seal, I fired. The creature retreated.

Ella finished her reply to the alien, then spoke into her com. "Karrie, it wants you to go with it to the flight-deck, help it fly the ship back to its homeworld."

"Jesus, what should I do?"

"I've told it you'll comply. We're almost on your level. When you emerge from your berth, I'll stun the creature."

"Okay," Karrie said. "I'm moving towards the door. It's following me."

Ella nimbly climbed the last three meters to the corridor, jumped from the ladder and crouched around the corner from Karrie's berth.

I was torn between watching her, fearing for her safety, and keeping an eye on the flight-deck hatch.

Her voice wavering, Karrie said, "We're coming along the corridor, Ella."

"Okay, when you get to the ladder, just climb. Leave the rest to me."

"I'm coming to the end of the corridor..."

She came into sight, looking pale. She passed the crouching Ella without giving any indication that she'd seen her and approached the ladder.

A meter behind her came the humping form of the Jaykendran section, its bristles undulating, its poison-shooting sphincter open in readiness.

Ella made her move. To shoot the alien,

she had to emerge from around the corner, take aim and fire. She was fast—but the alien was faster. Ella fired and missed, and the alien fired and hit its target.

In cold disbelief, I saw Ella's gun-hand detach itself from her wrist and go spinning off along the corridor.

She didn't even scream. Instead, she attacked the alien.

She threw herself at the creature, hit it full-length and hung on, impaling herself on its spines. Her flesh tore; spines erupted through her back, skewering her perfection. Like the non-human entity she was, she fought on. She flipped herself to her feet, hugging the alien, and tottered backwards in grotesque imitation of an intimate waltz. I had no idea what she intended, other than keeping the creature from spraying acid at us and herself.

Karrie was clutching the rungs of the ladder just above me. "Ed!" she screamed, looking up.

I raised my stunner. One of the sections was poking its head through the hatch, its oleaginous sphincter dilating in readiness. I fired, knowing that if I could disable this section, then the one attacking Ella would be incapacitated too. The bolt lanced towards the hatch, illuminating the well, and took off six inches of the alien's bristles. It ducked back out of sight, leaving an acrid stench in the air.

I looked back at Ella. She was approaching us, backwards. I aimed, but Ella was between me and the creature.

A second later they came to the edge of the corridor, teetered for a second, and fell the ten meters to the deck below. I cried out as Ella slammed against the deck, the alien on top of her.

I expected that to be the end, unable to see how she could have survived the fall. I should have known. As I stared, she rolled, somehow pushed herself to her feet and, still pinned to the alien by a dozen spines, launched herself along the corridor.

Only then did I work out what she was planning.

"No!" I cried.

I heard the hatch of the airlock hiss open, a scuffle of feet, and then the hatch hiss shut again.

Like a fool, thinking only of revenge, I launched myself up the ladder, swarming past Karrie, and dived onto the flight-deck, firing indiscriminately.

My half-cocked plan was to disable one of the sections before Ella managed to cycle herself through the lock and out into the vacuum.

A Jaykendran section swiveled, jetted acid, and burned the stunner from my hand. I was lucky, looking back—had the acid connected with my flesh...

The little of it that did spatter from the rapidly melting pistol sizzled across the arm of my suit, burned through and seared my flesh.

I screamed and fell to the deck.

The two sections advanced, sphincters puckering.

I kicked out, more through good luck than good judgment managing to connect with a head-piece and send the creature rolling. The second section reared, its sphincter taking aim.

I stared into its oily aperture, inches away.

A second later, to my utter disbelief, the alien wilted, flopped sideways and lay lifeless across the deck. The second section was likewise immobile.

Then I stared through the delta viewscreen, and saw why.

Ella and the alien were floating through the vacuum in an eerily grotesque aerial ballet. Ella hung, skewered, arms and legs splayed—but the alien had exploded and was no more than a sheath of ichor-dripping skin connected to Ella by its remaining spines.

All I could do was weep in grief and pain, but thank God Karrie had her wits about her. She dived onto the flight-deck, leapt over my prone form, and slid into a sling. Seconds later she was running frantic fingers across a touchpad, swearing to herself and staring through the view-screen.

"Karrie?"

She didn't bother answering.

I watched, amazement mixed with admiration, as one of the twin grapples detached itself from the skin of the alien ship and snaked across the gulf towards Ella and the shredded alien.

Karrie hunched over the controls, sweat streaming, and yelled as she commanded the grapples to latch onto the floating forms of the dead alien and the gracefully splayed non-human entity.

I wept as the grapple retracted and disappeared from sight.

We hauled the inert Jaykendran sections from the flight-deck—none too gently, I admit—and across to the alien ship.

We hurried back to the flight-deck as the translation program relayed the vessel's communiqué. *"Humans, I thank you for your assistance, and apologize for the injuries occasioned."*

I said, "We're glad to be of service, ship."

"I will soon have healed sufficiently to continue on the journey. The prisoner is secured."

Karrie said, "What will happen to it?"

The ship replied, *"It will be rehabilitated, to learn from its crimes and atone, once it has been reintegrated with a third section."*

"Good luck, ship," I said. "Farewell."

"Farewell, humans," said the ship.

Karrie commanded the remaining grapple to disengage, and the alien ship slowly peeled away from us and phased into the void.

One hour later, Karrie and I sat on either side of the recuperation pod in the med-bay.

Ella lay unmoving within the pod, her face visible through the small screen. She appeared to be sleeping peacefully, the bloody tears on her cheeks the only indication that her eyes had exploded in the vacuum. The wounds along the length of her body were closed now, the silver cicatrices already healing.

A com-lead was jacked into her occipital console, snaking past her bare right shoulder and interfacing with the pod's integral com.

I said, "You'll be fine, Ella. We'll get you to a sanatorium. They'll fix you up, get you new eyes, another hand."

Her face remained impassive, but I heard the smile in her voice as she communicated to us through the com. "Looking forward to that, Ed. Can't wait."

Karrie said, her voice soft, "You saved our lives, girl."

"You saved mine, Karrie. We're even, okay?"

Karrie smiled. "Even," she said, reaching out and taking my hand.

A while later, Karrie said she was returning to the flight-deck. "I'll phase us into the void, set course for home..."

I just nodded and said, "Fine."

She stopped by the hatch. "You coming up, Ed?"

I stared through the screen of the recuperation pod, and shook my head. "I'll be up in a while, Karrie, okay?"

She paused as if to say something, thought better of it and left.

I returned my gaze to the beautiful creature in the recuperation pod, wishing I could hold her hand, as the ship carried us through the void towards Altair. • • •

The Portable Star

by Isaac Asimov

Illustrated by Don Anderson

If space voyages are "romantic," Holden Brooks was certainly carrying on the tradition when he stepped into the cabin of his best friend's wife, with one straightforward objective in mind.

He did not signal. He merely opened the door and walked in. She was waiting for him as, somehow, he had known she would be, wearing a loose night garment. She held out her arms to him and they trembled slightly. Her dark hair fell below her shoulders, accenting the pale roundness of her face.

Her name was Celestine Van Horne and her husband sat in one corner of the room, idly pinching his ear-lobe.

Holden paid no attention to the husband's presence. He stepped directly to Celestine and placed his hands on her shoulders. She swayed toward him and they kissed violently, longingly, over and over again.

Breathlessly then, he swept her from the floor, cradling her in his arms. Her eyes closed, and her hand stroked the back of his neck gently.

Holden had turned toward the bed when, for the first time, someone spoke.

It was scarcely an impressive speech. Philip Van Horne was scarcely an impressive man. His sandy hair was thinning, his frame was slight, and his eyes were a pale blue. He rose from his chair and said with an air curiously compounded of indignation and bewilderment:

"What's going on?"

Holden placed his soft burden on the floor and looked at the man who had spoken. Holden was taller than Philip by half a head and more massive. His lips drew back, showing strong teeth in a broad face. His shoulders hunched a little. The light of battle was glowing in him.

Celestine, having backed against the bed, watched with a feral pleasure.

Philip looked nervous. He said, sharply, "Holden, stop it."

Holden moved forward with little shuffling steps. His fist shot out, catching Philip on the side of his head and sending him to his knees. Celestine's laugh was high-pitched and strained.

Philip got to his feet with an effort and stumbled toward the door. His wife was there before him, spread-eagling herself as a barrier. She was still laughing.

Philip looked over his shoulder in horror. "Don't do it, Holden. Don't!"

Holden didn't. A puzzled look seemed to soak into his face. His hands, which had risen to encircle Philip's neck, fell limply.

Celestine, her eagerness fading, moved away from the door, and sat down on the bed. She lit a cigarette,

Holden said. "I'm sorry, Phil. I knew what I was doing, but I just *had* to. I—"

"I know," said Philip, brushing his knees. "It's *they*."

"That's right," said Holden. "I'm sorry, Celestine."

"Oh, well," she said, shrugging.

Philip said sharply, "Put some clothes on, Celest."

His wife raised her eyebrows. "Now don't be silly, darling. I wasn't myself. No one was."

Holden Brooks was still apologizing. "They just push buttons and have fun. You understand how it was, Phil? There was no way I could stop—"

"Oh, shut up," Philip said, "and go away."

The door signal flashed.

"That's Grace," said Holden. His eyes went quickly from husband to wife. "Listen, there's no use saying—"

Philip said, "She knows what the situation is."

Grace Brooks edged in. She was a little thing with a triangular delicately-boned face that ended in a pointed, dimple-centered chin.

She said in a low voice, "I was getting afraid to be alone."

Holden took her hand. "All right, Grace. Let's try for some sleep."

When the Van Hornes were alone, Celestine stubbed out her cigarette and placed it in the small vent that puffed it out into the poisonous atmosphere of the alien planet on which they were stranded.

They stared distrustfully at one another. There was nothing to do, nothing to say. They were slaves, both of them, all four of them.

Slaves more thoroughly than any Earthly understanding of the word....

It had been exciting when it was first suggested. Holden Brooks and Philip Van Horne worked in adjacent offices in the Administrative Service of the Housing Unit in which they lived. Both had accumulated half-year sabbaticals, and some months earlier Holden had bought a space flivver none the worse for being second-hand. Why not, then, a shared-expense space tour?

"There's no point in having a space-flivver," Celestine said, when the four of them talked it over, "if you don't use it. Air and water last just about indefinitely with a good recirculating system, which the ship has, and power is no problem. So that just leaves food to think about. And we can renew stocks almost anywhere."

Grace said, "I don't think I could drink recirculated water."

"Nonsense, darling. Pure water is pure water, even if it comes from perspiration or sewage. You're just being medieval if you worry about that."

It worked out well. The controls of the space-ship were simple enough, and in a week Philip could handle the ship as well as Holden could. The *Spacionautic Handbook,* with its details on all inhabited planets, stood always ready to direct them to this or that interesting one.

In fact, the entire vacation might easily have been a complete success had not the ion-beam alignment in one of their micropiles lost focus, first fitfully, and then permanently.

Holden Brooks put his fingers through his brown hair in dismay and said, "Well, we just can't make any Jumps through hyperspace, that's all."

"Wasn't the ship overhauled before we left?" Celestine demanded, sharply.

Philip bit his lip. "You can't predict these things, damn it."

"Then what do we do?" Grace wanted to know, her thin voice tremulous.

"Pull in for repairs, I guess," Holden said, dubiously.

And because their Jumps, after all, were amateurish ones, it turned out that there was no inhabited planet within half-a-light-day's distance. None, that is, that the ship could reach in reasonable time by traveling through normal space.

Holden checked the handbook twice, then Philip checked it.

There was only one star in the neighborhood and there was only one planet in its family where the gravity was not impossibly high, and the temperature not impossibly extreme. The handbook called it Sigmaringen IV, and placed a dagger mark next to it which meant, conventionally, that it was uninhabited and uninhab-

itable.

Grace looked troubled. "It sounds horrible. Can't we fix the beam in space?"

Philip said, "Focusing a beam in the absence of a gravitational field is for an expert, not for us," and they headed for Sigmaringen IV. Their ship dropped to the planet's surface on the noiseless, flameless gravity-shield of the field-vortices produced by the two micro-piles that were still in working order.

What made Sigmaringen IV sound horrible to Grace was the *Handbook's* information on the planet's chemical makeup. The thick atmosphere consisted exclusively of nitrogen and argon in a proportion of three to one, with small quantities of the other inert gases. There was no water on the planet, no trace of free oxygen or of carbon dioxide in the atmosphere, not more than a trace of carbon in the soil. The soil consisted almost entirely of aluminum and iron silicates with a heavy overload of free silica which, whirled aloft by perpetual winds formed an apparently permanent "cloud layer."

"Just like Venus," muttered Phil. "Old home week." His thin, solemn face twisted into a half-smile.

It was "day" when they landed, but the only light was the dull gray that filtered diffusely through the dust clouds.

Grace shuddered and said, "We should have ultra-waved for help."

Holden's troubled eyes looked down upon his wife out of a perplexed face. "I thought of that, too, but it would cost an awful lot. Isn't that right, Phil?"

"A year's salary for each of us," Philip said incisively. "They don't send repair ships through hyperspace for half-credit pieces."

The first day on Sigmaringen IV was passed in adjusting the beam-focus. On the whole, it was a creditable job, and by the time the planet's rotation brought them and their ship into the night-shadowed half, it seemed obvious to both men that the ship would survive one Jump at least, probably half-a-dozen.

Holden stood up, put down his ergometer, and said, "It's night. Might as well leave the take-off for morning."

Philip yawned. "Why not? Better check with the girls, though."

For a wonder, the girls raised no objection. Grace frowned a little, but confined herself to a murmured, "If you say so."

The first night on Sigmaringen IV, in retrospect, was uneventful. Over the morning coffee, Celestine bubbled excitedly about her odd dream. Holden, with initial creaking, began to recount one of his own.

Finally Grace, with a marked reddening about the cheekbones, said, "I won't tell you my dream. Let's get away from this horrible place."

Celestine laughed. "Darling, that sounds terribly sexy. You *must* tell us. Were we in it?"

Grace said, "We're being watched. I'm *sure* of it."

"Oh, come," said Celestine. "There's no carbon on this wretched world and even I know that means there can be nothing living on the planet."

Phil said, "Actually, we have nothing to keep us here. We can go."

Holden mopped his lips and got up. "I'll take first shift."

In five minutes he was back. He said, "Funny things! I can't get the ship started!" He stared at them out of bovine eyes.

"What do you mean?" Celestine demanded. "The beam is focused, isn't it?"

"Nothing's wrong with the controls as far as I know. I just can't get close to them. When I try, I get—" He waited a

long time and then, as though he had failed to think of another word, he mumbled, "Scared!"

"Scared?" In various tones, all three said that.

Holden, visibly suffering, said in a choked voice, "You try it, Phil."

Philip got silently to his feet, walked out.

In less than five minutes, he also was back. "Scared stiff," he whispered. "Couldn't touch a thing."

"Are you two mad?" demanded Celestine.

Philip ignored her. He turned to Grace, "What was your dream?"

Grace's small face was white and against it the makeup stood out harshly. She said, "I dreamed we were surrounded by children and they were curious about us. I dreamed they were watching us and wouldn't let us go. It was very real and I—I still feel it."

Philip said, "I felt it, too." He looked troubled.

Celestine said, "Darling, this is too ridiculous. Grace is open to suggestion. She's a sweet girl, but she's sensitive, and this *is* a gloomy world. That's *all*. Now let's leave."

Philip said, "How?"

Celestine looked at her husband with something approaching contempt and said, "If *I* knew how to handle the controls—"

"You'd be just as badly off," said Philip.

Grace said quietly, "They're watching us right now."

Philip looked at her thoughtfully, raised his eyebrows, and leaned back in his chair to flick the polarity knob that controlled the transparency of the ports.

"I doubt there's anything to see," he said.

He was quite wrong.

At a distance of a hundred yards from the ship and spaced some five to ten yards apart, a series of mounds could be dimly, but definitely, made out through the sandy murk. Five could be seen. Philip frowned and stepped hastily to the other side of the ship. He transparented the opposite port. Six mounds there.

"Apparently," he said, "we *are* surrounded."

"They're just mounds of earth," protested Celestine.

Holden said, "They weren't there when we landed."

Grace said, "They're not material. They're energy creatures. They use earthmounds as—as clothing. Or adornment."

"Such nonsense," said Celestine.

Philip said, "If those things are telepathic, their thoughts and emotions may be leaking across. Grace is most sensitive to them."

"And I'm the least sensitive—is that it?" Celestine was suddenly furious. She got to her feet, "Is this a joke of some sort? Are all three of you up to games to panic me?"

Grace burst into violent laughter and Celestine turned on her with eyes glaring. She shrieked, "It's funny, is it?"

Grace shook her head but could say nothing. She whooped and shouted and held her sides. She grew weak from laughter until it subsided into breathless sobs.

Then Philip giggled and burst into unrestrained laughter. Holden joined him, his baritone brays overriding all.

Celestine was in tears. "Of all the nasty, contemptible—" She stuttered in her attempt to find appropriate adjectives, and then before she was anywhere close to recovering her emotional equilibrium she, too, was swept away on a tidal wave of shrill mirth.

Grace cried, "Stop it! Stop it!"

Slowly, and in the order in which they had begun, they stopped. Celestine was last, flushed, a handkerchief over her mouth.

Grace said, agonized. "They're pushing buttons. They! They!" Her forefinger jabbed toward the port. "They can make us do anything."

There was no argument. They all felt it now. Even Celestine's last argument sounded timid and weak when she said:

"The *Handbook* says there's no life on the planet."

"The *Handbook,*" said Philip, gravely, "bases its reports on a quickie expedition, probably, that reported no oxygen, no carbon and no water, after passing through the atmosphere and manipulating a reflection spectrometer. Ordinarily that means no life, but I'll just bet that no expedition ever thought it worth their while actually to land on this planet."

Grace stared out the port and whispered, "Children about an ant-hill. Watching them scurry. Putting obstacles in the way to see what the ants would do. Maybe stamping on a few."

Philip said, "No telling when they'll get tired, either. Holden, I think we better start recirculating water."

"Must we?" Grace asked faintly.

"Now don't be ridiculous, darling," said Celestine with sudden sharpness. "The wastes are electrolyzed and the hydrogen and oxygen are compressed and stored, then combined again into water as pure as pure. It's so pure we have to add mineral tablets to it."

Holden moved into the engine room. A moment later, the faint hum of the recirculator could be heard.

Philip sighed. "Well, they let us do that."

As the ten-hour day period progressed, Holden tried three more times to get the ship started. Philip tried twice. Neither succeeded.

Holden said tensely, "I say, attack. I say, shoot a few of them down. We have blasters."

"They won't let us, you fool." In his own discouragement, Philip was growing careless with epithets.

Holden paid no attention. He said, "I'm willing to try. I'll put on my suit, go out there, and shoot them down. If they don't let me, they don't let me, but I'm going to try."

Philip said, with shrill anger, "What's the use? If we can't even go near the controls, how do you expect to get near *them?*"

Celestine said sharply, "Oh, shut up, Phil. At least Holden is showing guts. Do you have any better suggestion?"

Holden climbed into his space suit. His fingers, large and clumsy in the enclosing metallo-latex, snapped on his helmet. He hefted a blaster and marched in stubborn silence to the airlock.

Philip shrugged and said to Grace, "It isn't going to do any good, and it might be dangerous for him. Don't let him go, Grace."

"Don't do it, Grace," Celestine said, quickly. "Don't stop him. It just kills Phil to see someone else with backbone."

"Don't be foolish," Philip said. "Has it occurred to you that we can't afford to lose him? I can't pilot this ship all alone."

Grace said in a monotone, "I don't think he's in any danger. I just don't feel any danger for him."

It was suddenly lonely, with just the three of them watching Holden Brooks through the port. He was a large, robotic figure, murkily grotesque, slogging on heavily as he leaned into the wind. Sand spurted up from under his mesh boots at every step.

They could see him raise his arm, point his blaster, and involuntarily they held their breaths.

The featureless mounds of soil that were their alien tormenters did not move.

Holden fired. The subsidiary bonds that held together the molecules of one of those mounds were neutralized in the force-field emitted by the blaster. All at once, without sound or flame, the mound blew apart into impalpable dust. Except for some remnants at what had been its base, it was gone.

Holden aimed at another and another. Then they, too, were gone.

Inside the ship, Celestine cried excitedly, "Good! Good! He had guts and he's doing it. So much for caution."

Philip was silent, his lips compressed. Then suddenly he said, "Look!"

He pointed. Where the first mound had stood before it disappeared, as if by magic, a new mound stood.

At each spot where the blaster had had its effect, and which had been blank a moment before, a mound once more puffed up out of the ground. Holden, looking to right and left, let his arm drop. As he stood there staring, his attitude of frustration and discouragement were plain even through the impersonal lines of his suit.

Slowly he turned, and slowly he trudged back to the ship....

The four space voyagers ate without appetite, and sat helplessly about the clutter of the meal.

After awhile Philip said, "They *are* energy creatures, as Grace said. Blasting the soil in which they dress themselves is like tearing a man's shirt. He can always get another one." He paused thoughtfully, before he said, "If we could only attack their minds directly!"

"How?" grumbled Holden.

"There's such a thing as psychology,"

Philip reminded.

"Yes, but what do we know about their psychology?" demanded Celestine.

"Nothing." Philip shrugged. "I grant that. But they're intelligent. They must have emotions or they wouldn't enjoy playing with ours. They can frighten us. Suppose we could frighten them. They're only children, if Grace's intuition is right."

"The blaster didn't frighten them," said Holden.

"They knew it wouldn't kill them," Philip pointed out, "so there was nothing to be afraid of. They'd fear death, I suppose, but how do you go about killing energy beings? Now what else would they fear? Pain? Loss of security? Loss of loved ones?"

"Ghosts, too," added Celestine, disagreeably. "Have you thought they might be afraid of them?"

Philip looked at her with his eyebrows raised in approval. "You're right!" he exclaimed. "The unknown! Any creature is afraid of what it doesn't understand, of something outside its experience."

Holden said, "The ship is outside their experience. They're not afraid of it. I'm sorry to say."

"The ship is just another form of matter," said Philip, "and we're just another form of mind wrapped in matter." He looked thoughtfully out at the mounds, just barely seen now in the dimming light. And he said musingly, "Now what *wouldn't* they understand?"

Grace said dreamily, "The sun, the unclouded sky, the stars. They've never seen any of those."

"I dare say you're right," said Celestine. "But we can't bring the stars down to them, so that's no good. Stars aren't portable."

Grace rose to her feet. Her face suddenly looked dreamier than ever. Her lips were parted. She moved slowly to Holden and deposited herself on his lap with a gesture that was almost abandon. She lifted her face to his with a slow smile. When she spoke her words were slurred.

"Ta' me t'bed, Hol'n. I feel so *funneeeee.*" She put her cheek against his and giggled.

Holden reddened, and said protestingly, "Now, Grace—"

Grace tossed her head back and looked at Philip and Celestine upside down. She said "W'rried 'bout *them,* are you? J'st a pair o'—"

At the accusation that followed, Philip's eyes opened wide, but Celestine only said, with dry amusement, "Why, the little she-devil!"

Holden got to his feet in confusion, holding his wife desperately, while she squirmed against his body in a manner to make her meaning and emotion unmistakable.

"They're making her do this," he muttered. "I—I'd better take her away."

It was half an hour before he reappeared.

He said, "She's herself now, but she's—got a headache. She's embarrassed about what happened, how she acted in here. You won't mention it to her, will you?"

Celestine shrugged. "Nothing she said or did shocked us."

Holden said miserably, "How can we stop it all? If we just sit here and let them poke our minds here and there, we'll find ourselves killing each other or doing other terrible things."

Two hours later Holden, in gruesome proof that he had been prophetic, had invaded the Van Horne cabin to claim Celestine, and had nearly killed Philip in the process.

Now he was gone again, and Philip sat on the edge of the bed, elbows on wide-spread knees, fingers intertwined loosely, his face dazed and unhappy.

Celestine said, with abruptness, "Well, there's no use brooding about it. It couldn't be helped. Do you want a sleeping pill?"

Philip looked up, and when he spoke it was not exactly complimentary to her. He wasn't even thinking about Celestine. What he said was:

"A portable star."

"What?" His wife stared at him.

"Something you said earlier," he said. "A portable star. It might work." He stood up. His hands balled into fists and he moved about restlessly. "We can't just let things go on, can we?"

"What are you going to do?"

Philip didn't answer. He just tore out of the cabin and on into the engine room. With feverish, inspired haste, he dismantled the water recirculator and removed the gas cylinders. Cautiously he twisted the hoses together, clamped them into position with wire from the electrical stock supply drawer and fitted an Elgin tube of transparent quartz over the combined nozzles. Turning again to the water recirculator he loosened the pencil-thin catalyst-chamber,

squinted a moment at the spongy platinum-black it contained, and slipped it in his pocket.

He moved back into the common room and pulled his own space-suit from its rack. The other three in the party were waiting for him—Holden, with a hangdog look on his face, and his eyes sliding away from direct contact; Grace, pale and scrubbed-looking, as though fresh from a sponge bath; and Celestine, wearing new makeup, though it showed traces of an unsteady hand in the application.

Celestine asked Philip, "Are you leaving the ship?"

"That's right," he told her grimly.

"Help me with this, Holden."

Holden lifted the cylinders onto the back of the suit, strapped them in place just next to the oxygen cylinder that would supply Philip's respiratory needs. He passed the two hoses over Philip's head.

Philip shifted the catalyst-chamber from his trousers pocket to the pocket in his space-suit. He dipped his finger into a glass of water and ran it around the inner surface of the quartz jacket he had drawn over the twinned hoses.

Celestine began, "What do we do for

FULL DISCLOSURE DEPT.

I feel that I can't let this story go without mentioning this—probably because if I don't, I'm bound to get letters and asides in reviews, suggesting I'm pulling the wool over your eyes by advertising it as a "rare classic story."

Dr. Asimov wasn't particularly proud of this story. In fact, in his autobiography, he named it as his least favorite, saying he'd handled the sex "sleazily." Which is why it remains that very rare thing—an uncollected Asimov story.

But inasmuch as it's entirely possible to get this far in reading the story and ask, "What sex?" I have to feel the good Doctor had somewhat broad standards as to what constitutes sleaze.

Besides, if you're really trying to hit humans where they live, and impair their ability to work together, fomenting sexual jealousy seems like one of your more effective options.

Anyway, I prefer it to the other story the (then future) Dr. Asimov published in *Thrilling Wonder,* "The Hazing" (October 1942)... so much so that I'm willing officially to deny that the appearance of "The Portable Star" in the Winter 1955 issue had any role in that being the original run's last.

-The Editor

water if you—" and let her question fade into silence.

"Take care of yourself, Philip," Grace said uncertainly.

"Thanks," he said tightly. He placed the helmet over his head.

Once outside the ship, Philip Van Horne felt cut off from all things human. He had polarized all ports to full opacity before leaving the ship, and now no spark of light invaded the solid blackness all about.

Slowly he moved away from the ship, bucking the steady wind. Hearing its whistle against his suit was the only sensation he could recognize. Dimly he sensed the natives, curious, waiting for him.

He halted and cracked open the gauges to both cylinders. When he felt the gentle push of gas within the quartz jacket he put his gauntleted hand over it.

He lifted the nozzles. *They* could see him, he hoped, or could sense him by whatever method it was they used. A sudden thought chilled him. What if they lacked the sense of sight, or any sense corresponding to it? Desperately he refused to think of such a thing. They *had* to be sentient!

He raised the catalyst-chamber toward the open top of the quartz jacket. For a single moment, he was furiously certain that this would do the trick. But only for a moment. He paused, hands lifted halfway. Could anything work so simply, after all? To try, to fail, to have to return to the ship to report failure—

His hand moved, stopped again. Swift thoughts came.

The creatures—call them that—were emotion-controllers. Was the doubt of his success his own? For a moment he had been certain, and then—

Had the triumph he had felt spilled over too openly? Were they now canceling it out in their own way?

Once more, half-heartedly, he made a tentative gesture of raising the catalyst-chamber, and instantly depression hit him, as dark as the night that surrounded him. It would not work. How could it?

And that thought decided him. The depression had come too quickly, too patly. It had not come from his own mind, but from *theirs*. He could fight it now, and he did.

He fought the despair, fought his own apparent knowledge of inevitable failure. Closing his mind to what was trying to seem to be bitter certainty, he lunged at the quartz tube with its leaking gases swirling upward.

He fought the fear that followed. But it grew until it became the same fear that had kept him from taking the controls of the ship. However, the ship's controls were complicated. There were fifty motions involved, each with its fresh surcharge of fright. And here it was necessary only to touch one object to another.

In the dark, he could not tell by sight how close chamber was to quartz except for the position of his arms. But he knew there must be only inches left. He compressed those inches, and his forehead slicked with perspiration.

He fought with what remained of his untouched mind, and momentarily he felt the dim contact of metal against quartz. Contact broke off immediately in a perfect agony of despair, but that one moment had sufficed. The moisture he had introduced within the quartz was a second catalyst, and between the effect of powdered platinum and water traces, the hydrogen and oxygen combined in chemical action and burst into flame.

Pale blue, dancing in the residuum of the open end, it sparked in his hand like a star, twinkling and shifting tirelessly.

And the aliens were gone!

Philip could now see that. Out here it had been as black as tar before. It was as black as tar now, except for the dim blue star in his hand. But there was a lightness in Philip Van Horne's mind that was clear enough in the information it gave him. The touch of the aliens had been so constant a factor for over two full days that, with it removed, it was as though a boulder had been heaved from his crushed body, leaving him free to stand once more.

He called into his radio, "Holden! Holden! Get to those controls!"

Turning, he ran back to the ship as fast as he could pump his encased legs....

The two men were at the controls. The two women were asleep.

At last Philip had a chance to explain more in detail to Holden, who still couldn't seem to take it all in.

"It wasn't just light," Philip was saying. "They knew what light was, from the steady gray illumination of their cloudy skies. The illumination may have been whiter, but they recognized it for what it was. To them, it was still just a piece of their sky that had come down to the surface. Flame was something else again."

Holden shook his head, "I still don't see why."

"It was *blue* light that flickered and shifted, and could be carried about. That was the main point. It was light that could be held in the hand. It was a portable star, and not just featureless light in the sky or from a ship. Remember flame can't exist on this world of theirs with its atmosphere of nitrogen, argon, and sand. In millions of years nothing could possibly have burned on Sigmaringen IV until I got the compressed hydrogen and oxygen from the water recirculator and let them burn in one another. The aliens were faced with the unknown, the incomprehensible. They were only children, after all, and ran."

Around the space-ship now was the comforting blackness and emptiness of space, the friendliness of the stars.

Holden sighed deeply. "Well, we'll be Jumping soon, and then we'll just be a day or two outside Earth. We can report these energy creatures, only... Phil?"

"Yes."

"There's no point in telling what happened to us."

"No, I suppose not."

"Let's just forget it all. It was mental control. It's better to forget."

Philip said, "Much better."

His words rang hollowly in his own ears. Mental control or not, he would live with the memory of Celestine barring him, from the door while Holden pursued him with clutching fingers; the memory of Celestine laughing wildly.

Forget?

In his mind, he could hear Celestine laughing and, quite uselessly, he put his hands over his ears.

"What's the matter?" said Holden.

"Nothing," Philip said drearily.

by James Trefil

Radioactive decay is the ultimate philosopher's stone—the stone that alchemists believed could turn lead into gold or, more generally, one chemical element into another. Since alpha and beta decay change the number of protons in the nucleus, they also change the chemical identity of the atom of which that nucleus is a part.

After alpha decay, a nucleus will be able to hold two fewer electrons than it did before the decay. The two "extra" electrons will eventually wander off, leaving behind an atom that has fewer electrons in orbit. This atom will, of course, be identified as a member of a different chemical species from the original atom.

One way of thinking about beta decay is to imagine that one of the neutrons inside the nucleus undergoes beta decay itself, producing a nucleus with one more proton and one less neutron. There are always loose electrons wandering around in nature, and one of them is eventually attracted to the atom. The final result is that an atom of a different chemical element has been born—one with one more electron in orbit than had originally been there.

The strangest animal has its own phylum. Deep under the surface, clustered around hydrothermal vents in the ocean floor, lives one of the strangest animals known. A reddish worm that creates a long, tough tube to live in, it ranges up to 25 feet long, ingests its food, but has no organs that correspond to a mouth or intestines. Apparently these worms are nourished by bacteria that live inside their cells. There are two species of them sharing a genus, but no other animal is at all like them, so they have a phylum all to themselves.

Big stars live fast, die young, and make spectacular corpses. It may seem paradoxical that big stars, with all that extra fuel, actually live shorter lives than their smaller contemporaries. The reason is fairly simple. The bigger the star, the stronger the pull of gravity trying to make it collapse. The stronger the pull of gravity, the more fuel has to be burned in the nuclear fires to keep the star stable. The net result is that a star ten times as big as the sun will live only 20 or 30 million years, while a star much smaller than the sun might live as much as 100 million years.

We all have the same grandmother. One way of discovering something about recent human evolution is to compare DNA sequences among different groups of humans. The idea is that this DNA is not subject to the changes forced by natural selection, and therefore changes only slowly, at a regular rate. Knowing the rate of change in mitochondrial DNA now, and knowing how much the DNA in two individuals has diverged, we can extrapolate back to the time when they had a common ancestor.

By studying the DNA in mitochondria, scientists traced the human family tree back to a single woman, whom scientists have christened "Eve." Eve apparently lived in Africa about two hundred thousand years ago, and was the distant great-grandmother of us all.

A computer "virus" operates in a manner very similar to a real virus. Computer "viruses" are small programs that tag along with large programs when they enter a computer and, once inside, take over the mechanism of the computer to perform some function other than the one that's intended. For example, a computer "virus" may simply fill up all the blank memory in the computer with garbage or, in particularly nasty cases, wipe the memory clean. The term "virus" is used because, like real viruses, computer "viruses" do not themselves possess the mechanisms to carry out their nefarious ends. Instead, they commandeer machinery that already exists.

The naming of hurricanes started with the Army Meteorological Service in World War II. Originally, hurricanes were named after women—thus, you might get Abagail, Betty, Claudia, and so forth. In the interest of sexual equality, hurricanes are now alternately given male and female names.

The list of available hurricane names each year runs to 21—one for each letter of the alphabet but Q, U, X, Y and Z. The busy hurricane season of 2005 was the first ever to exhaust the list, ending up with six additional storms, named after letters of the Greek alphabet.

The Casablanca award for the classiest experiment in history. The movie Casablanca is often called the classiest movie ever made. In this spirit, we offer the Casablanca award to the first experimental verification of the Doppler effect. This was done by the Dutch scientist Christian Buys Ballot (1817-1890).

He assembled a group of trumpeters and put them on an open railroad car. Standing along the railroad tracks were a group of people who had perfect pitch (i.e., who could tell what a musical note is simply by listening to it). The engine was started up, the train went by, the trumpeters played their notes, and the observers recorded what they heard, verifying Doppler's predictions in the process. Next to this, experiments with oscilloscopes and microchips seem pale and insipid. • • •

DARK SIDE

BY KEVIN KING

Illustrated by Lawrence Kim

Garamond couldn't stop staring out the window of the lunar module, drinking in every detail. This was officially a rest period before the final EVA, but he could rest when he got back to Earth. He just kept staring and grinning, because he was on the Moon and it was a fluke.

Not that he wasn't qualified to be here. He was one of the top lunar geologists in the world—what few there were.

But the fluke part—they were the backup crew: he and Tom Hagan and Frank Ullrich. The primary three had come down with a nasty case of the Hong Kong flu a mere 64 hours before liftoff, so it became their job to execute the mission.

Even flukier, there weren't supposed to be any more lunar landings. President Nixon had initiated cuts in the program back in 1970, leaving the last three moon-ships earthbound. 18 was commissioned as the Detente Express— Apollo-Soyuz— so 19 was put on the fast track as a military mission.

Run by the Department of Defense, it was the first of its kind—a shadow mission, sent secretly to survey a location for an American base on the ultimate strategic high ground, the lunar north pole. Even with an upcoming diplomatic space mission, the DOD didn't trust the Soviets any farther than they could toss them. The International Space Treaty of 1967 prevented any nation from claiming lunar real estate, but the big brass knew a base here would be mighty intimidating. That was the point.

For Garamond, being covertly recruited for Apollo 19 was like Christmas in July. He had had no idea the mission existed, even though, as a civilian, he'd consulted on several DOD-funded NASA projects. He thought he'd missed the Moon landing program because he made it into the astronaut corps too late. So it goes. Buck up and hope for a shot at Skylab or the shuttle, if and when.

So when he was hand-picked to be part of the backup crew for this top-secret lunar expedition, he saw it as a top-notch qualifier for a future mission in Earth orbit. At least he'd make it into space. But when that nasty flu virus cleared his way to the Moon's surface by grounding the first-stringers, he couldn't believe it. He felt guilty, at first, for being so happy due to other men's misfortune. But he realized it wasn't a deliberate choice on anyone's part. Microbes are amoral functionaries. As a result, he was now the man to do the job.

Honestly, a mission under the auspices of the military wasn't Garamond's preference. As a scientist whose professional lifeblood was intellectual curiosity, he was used to a free-roaming—some might say undisciplined—lifestyle. But with opportunities to do lunar rock-hunting non-existent nowadays, he was hardly going to turn down an opportunity like this in favor of personal comfort. He knew very well it was this or nothing, and he made the necessary adjustments.

Besides, for a kid who grew up watching *Captain Video* with his dad and brother, and mowing lawns for money to buy the latest copies of *Planet Stories* and *Galaxy Science Fiction* as soon as they hit the rack, this was the stuff of dreams. Call it fate, beating the odds, or an outright miracle, he was in the right place at the right time, doing exactly what he'd worked so hard to do.

Too bad he could never tell anyone that he'd been here. Not his parents, not his brother, not his sisters. Not even Craig Studdard, who beat him up in sixth grade for being an egghead. No one. Defense had severe penalties for loose lips.

T—he crackle of static roused him. "Peary Station, this is Houston."

Rest period was over. Time flies on cloud nine.

"Rise and shine, gentlemen. Rise and shine."

It was Randy Wills' shift at CAPCOM. His mellifluous drawl charmed pretty women and iron-willed officers, but it didn't work as an alarm clock. Captain Hagan didn't stir.

Garamond turned away from the triangular window. "Joe! Cock-a-doodle-doo!" His voice sounded tinny bouncing back from the aluminum bulkhead.

A snort from the mission commander. He rolled off his hammock and onto his feet.

Garamond clicked onto the vox through his headset mike. "Back at you, Houston. Up and at 'em."

"Good deal, *Panther*. How's Cap'n Joe? Still got the sniffles?"

"You can ask him. He just got back in from milking the cow that jumped over the Moon."

Wills guffawed. A quarter of a million miles away and he was still a good audience for Garamond's lame humor.

Hagan clicked in. "Stinkin' jokers. It's a wonder we get anything done. And I'm feeling tip-top, if anybody cares."

He suspected The Man was lying. Hagan wanted that last EVA as badly as he himself did, but his health had taken a nose-dive since their last trip outside, and the flight directors were considering putting the kibosh on their final jaunt. Hagan wasn't happy about it, but he was following orders like a good Navy man.

"You do sound pretty chipper, Joe. But Herr Franz wants to talk to y'all, anyway." Randy pronounced it "hair," which was ironic, since Franz had none.

Dr. Edward H. Franz was the Flight Surgeon, the most hated man in the Astronaut Corps. His job was to be over-cautious and stop anybody from doing anything risky, which was pretty much anything in an astronaut's job description.

The space medicine boys had had a lot of power at the beginning of the program, but after it became apparent that humans could exist in orbit without imploding or going insane or having their brains turn to jelly, flight surgeons were mostly given the tin ear.

But the fact that Franz was given time to consult on this situation meant they'd been talking down there while the lunar crew slept—well, since Hagan had slept—which meant they were genuinely worried.

Franz came on-line. "Greetings, gentlemen." Cadence like a Teutonic automaton. "How are you?"

"Fine," Garamond answered.

"Good. Captain Hagan, how are you? Better? Wors—?"

"Fine," he cut in. The Man had no patience for this.

"You were coughing earlier?"

Silence. Every millimeter between Houston and Peary Crater yawned between them.

Wills spanned the chasm. "Say again? We lost that."

Dead air crackled in their headsets.

"Uh, Colonel Lancaster requests an answer, Captain," Wills relayed.

Lancaster was the mission flight director—in essence, Hagan's superior. He

owed him a straight answer. But the commander knew that admitting symptoms was the first step toward not getting to go outside to play again.

Hagan rolled his eyes; Garamond held back a laugh. "Yessir. Coughing, sir."

Franz ran the litany: "Accompanied with sputum?"

"Runny nose and scratchy throat. Yes, sir." He didn't need the "sirs," but it was a habit.

"Body aches, centering in the joints?"

"Somewhat, sir. But I'm feeling much better. Rest period did me good."

That was no lie; Garamond could tell by looking at him. "I'll vouch for that, Doctor."

"I'll take that under advisement," Franz replied.

He was gone. Wills chimed in. "The good doctor's confabbing with the bosses, gentlemen. I think the gist is they're trying to decide on a 'go, no go' for the number three EVA."

"Do they look happy?" Garamond asked.

"You really want an answer?"

"Cancel that."

Wills chuckled. "So I guess we got a second to chat, boys. The gang in the back room wants me to ask how many pounds of rocks you grabbed on your last trip outside."

"Too many," Hagan growled. "We'll never get off the ground."

"Don't worry, we're within specs."

"They're thinkin' this'll be their last chance for awhile," Wills said.

Garamond knew all too well. "We got enough to keep 'em busy into the next millennium."

"My, my! They'll be happier than a pig in slop." Wills' backwoods roots were showing.

Due to the secrecy of the mission, there was no TV transmission—one less signal for the Russians to intercept—as well as a strict schedule for voice communication, so the back room geologists leaned on Garamond to keep them updated.

"And my divining rod was wobbling up a storm, so we may find ourselves some water yet."

Wills laughed at the idea of a scientist in a spacesuit prospecting for water like an Okie from Muskogee.

But Garamond was serious about the water. The lunar poles were a study in contradictions. They were the only places on the Moon that never rotated into darkness, yet they also held the only permanently shadowed areas anywhere on the surface. The deeper regions of Peary Crater's forty-five-mile-wide depression hadn't warmed to sunlight for millions of years, so the temperature there in the dark was a subfreezing -280 degrees Fahrenheit. It was a perfect shelter for water ice, or so the theory went. And that was one of the things the back room rock hounds were rabidly curious about, and what Garamond had been most determined to discover.

The military brass were especially curious. If there was water here, that meant the site was nicely suited for base-building. Water was troublesome to haul from earth, or to manufacture on the surface in sufficient quantities to support construction and maintenance of a permanent installation. If it was here already, so much the better.

Where the theoretical water came from was unknown. Possibly outgassed during the Moon's cooling phase, or deposited later by meteor impacts— Garamond hoped to bring some home to help settle the question. Maybe some of his samples contained it, frozen deep inside; it was impossible to tell with the naked eye. And where there's water, there's the potential for life.

Wills suddenly snapped to. "Here we go, gentlemen."

The rhythm of the lunar module's cooling pumps kept time as Hagan and Garamond waited to hear the verdict.

"The telemetry on your vitals checks out, Joe. Y'all are go for EVA number three. Down some chow and get out there. You're burnin' moonlight."

A mere five years ago, the Moon had been untrodden since its birth, as far as anyone knew. Now, he and Hagan were the thirteenth and fourteenth humans to scuff up the magnificent desolation.

The captain grunted, manhandling the two-wheeled Modular Equipment Transporter across the crater floor, heading for a new site in the shadows near Peary's rim.

They were carrying less equipment than previous missions, to make a lighter payload due to the trickier dynamics of achieving a polar orbit. In addition, extra booster power was required along the way. Thus a modified, unmanned Saturn 1-B was launched prior to their own Saturn V's departure. Conveniently, the 1-B's blastoff served as a distraction to the press, who'd been led to believe the dual launches were tests of manned orbiting laboratory hardware for the post-Apollo program.

After the 19 crew's translunar injection burn, Ullrich masterfully piloted their craft to rendezvous with the 1-B's second stage—the S-IVB—already soaring toward the Moon. After link-up, the additional booster's thrust added the muscle necessary to attain polar orbit.

Given these additional challenges, planners hadn't included a lunar rover—a lighter payload allowed more fuel for the lander. Thus, the crew was assigned the MET, a tool cart design left from an earlier mission. Which meant they walked everywhere, pulling the MET, loaded with equipment, along with them.

They'd been out for less than an hour, but Hagan was running on empty. His breathing was raspy over the headset.

"You okay with pulling that? I'll take a turn."

"I'm fine," Hagan growled.

Garamond wasn't convinced. "Let's stop and pick up a few," he suggested. Joe could rest without losing face.

They halted, kicking up slow-motion dust clouds.

Hagan leaned against the tool cart, breathing hard. "Give me a second, okay, Kyle?"

"You sure you're doing all right, Chief?"

"Yeah. Get at it. I'm right behind you."

"Will do." Garamond glanced at the checklist on his forearm and reached for the tongs. He spotted a scattering of green anorthosite and went for a sample.

"Joe, could you grab me a bag and—"

"My cooling garment's on the fritz."

"Say again?"

"It's not... it's not cooling."

"It checked out just fine, Chief."

"I'm burning up. It's not working."

Garamond's pulse thumped a beat. He loped closer.

"Gimme a look-see."

"I'm damn hot, that's all I know. Damn hot out here..."

Garamond glanced at Hagan's backpack hookups. All okay. "Maybe your flu's flaring up. I'll get on the vox to Hous—"

"No! Stick to the schedule! Commies'll hear every word you say! Don't you dare!"

"Okay, Joe. It's okay."

Hagan's gold faceplate bounced Garamond's own image back at him. He couldn't see The Man's face, so it was impossible to tell what shape he was in. All he had to go by was his breathing, labored and liquid over the headset. Garamond laid the tongs on the MET. "Joe, raise your visor. Let me see how you're doing."

"Back off, Opie."

Red hair and a boyish face had gotten Garamond the nickname, and using it put him in his place. But he insisted. "Let me see your face."

"I'm burnin' up. Fix the coolant pump or the hoses..."

"Open up!" He reached for the visor clip.

"What the hell...?" More coughing. A clumsy attempt to bat him away.

Garamond slid the reflective shield upwards to reveal the clear visor beneath, and the face within. He gasped.

He saw the eyes first: blood red where they should be white. It looked like every capillary in Hagan's eyeballs had leaked. Beads of sweat trickled into his eyes. Must've been maddening.

"My God, Joe..."

Hagan turned away from the sun, eyes hyper-sensitive to the searing light. "Get away..." he growled.

"Your eyes are red. You're sweating like nobody's business. I'm no doctor, but—"

"Back off, rookie! I can deal with..." He didn't have the breath to finish the sentence. His face was wet with sweat and mucous and saliva. He could drown in his own fluids if they didn't get back to the LM and get his helmet off.

"Joe, all due respect, you don't have a choice. We're going back."

They abandoned the MET and returned to the ship. Inside, Garamond ran the cabin repressurization sequence as Hagan leaned against the bulkhead and retched.

He removed Joe's helmet. It was a slimy mess. He grabbed wipes and disposal bags as Hagan gulped air, puking into one bag and reaching for another.

Garamond stayed sealed in his suit for protection from this, whatever it was. Eventually his own backpack would run out and he'd have to breathe the cabin air, but he'd cross that bridge when he came to it.

Hagan's nausea had finally settled down, and Garamond cleaned him up the best he could and helped him into his hammock. The Man lay there, propped against the rear wall to keep his throat clear; eyes closed, breathing through his mouth. He answered Garamond's questions with nods and grunts. His throat hurt. It was almost swollen shut.

There were several options in the mission plan at this point, including Garamond piloting the LM up to orbit for rendezvous with Ullrich, orbiting in the command module *Blackhawk*. But that wouldn't work if he succumbed.

He informed Houston of the situation. Lancaster scuttled the comm restrictions and kept the line open. Mission Control was doing everything possible to expedite their return. And Wills told him that National Security Adviser Kissinger had been alerted.

But climbing the chain of command took time. Garamond was waiting, watching Hagan get rapidly worse, drifting in and out of consciousness. This sickness moved like wildfire. He couldn't afford to be patient.

He clicked onto the comm to Ullrich. Frank was his closest friend, and he wanted to talk privately, ship-to-ship. Kyle wanted reassurance that he could fly solo back to the command ship, if he had to.

"Don't sweat it, Kyle. We ran it over and over in sims. You can do it in your sleep." Frank's voice sounded distant. The *Blackhawk* was cruising out of comm range. "It'll be a snap. Besides, it won't come to that."

"Not so sure about that, buddy."

"Is Hagan really that bad off?"

"Pretty bad. Yeah. He'll be worthless on the ascent, far as I can tell."

They'd never really expected this to happen, despite their training. A lot that could go wrong, especially with no copilot. Ullrich tried to lighten the mood.

"Hey, just promise me you won't leave Nancy and Karen's picture behind."

Kyle forced a laugh. "No, no. No way. It's safe in my ditty."

Garamond had a snapshot of Ullrich's wife and ten-year-old daughter tucked away in his on-board ditty bag, as a favor to his friend. The photo was from a camping trip to Yosemite they'd taken together, the previous summer. Garamond had snapped the picture himself. Though Ullrich could never tell his family the truth, he'd have the photo as an official lunar souvenir. If Frank couldn't land on the surface, at least he'd have a photo that had.

Suddenly, Hagan moaned and coughed, barely able to catch a breath.

"He sounds worse, Frank. I'm getting back on the horn with CAPCOM."

"Copy that."

He clicked over: "Randy, any ETA on a liftoff, or are they still debating the price of oil in Saudi Arabia?"

"No ETA on that. But they've pretty much decided this ain't the Hong Kong flu."

The cooling pump in Garamond's suit whirred as his mind ticked backwards, trying to figure out how this happened.

He wasn't a virologist or a physician, but he had an ex-girlfriend, a child of medical missionaries to South America, who was both. During one of their many coffee house debates, she'd described the symptoms of Bolivian hemorrhagic fever. The crimson eyes he remembered. But this wasn't lush Amazonia; the Moon's surface was virtually anti-life, bombarded by deadly cosmic radiation. Unless—

Hagan was retching. Garamond barely got him a disposal bag in time. Blackish blood clots burbled up. Not good.

He wiped his commander's face and dropped the bag into the waste compartment. Hagan settled back, shuddering.

"Soon as we hear from Houston, we're out of here. I may get to pilot this baby yet."

Garamond grinned, hoping for a response—a grunt, some abuse. Nothing.

"Houston, Peary Station. Joe's in a real bad way up here."

Wills spoke up. "I was just gonna talk at you. Herr Franz has been on with USAMRIID, talking to a virologist."

USAMRIID was the Army's Medical Research Institute for Infectious Diseases. That connection usually meant biological weapons. Odd.

"Here's a question for you and the captain." Wills' words were molasses. "Do y'all remember if you've come into contact with any local substances?"

"What do you mean?"

"I think they mean the rocks. Hang on." Static as he double-checked. "They're noddin'. They mean the rocks."

"You know the drill—we don't touch 'em. Keep 'em as pristine as possible."

"All righty."

"Then there's the dust. We track it in from outside. It's all over. It oxidizes and we breathe it in, I'm sure."

"Copy that. How about Joe?"

Joe wanted to get his two cents in. Opened his mouth. A red wash covered his teeth. Garamond winced. Joe's gums were bleeding.

"I'll answer. You take it easy." He patted Hagan's forearm, offering what comfort he could through his thick gloves. "Joe was in contact with the sample bags. Insisted on repacking the rock boxes for a tighter fit."

"Thank you, Kyle. We'll get back to you."

Garamond waited, mind racing, trying to stay a jump ahead. The brain trust was attempting to diagnose where Hagan had caught the bug. And it was looking more obvious. He'd caught it here.

It was possible, they discussed, that there was water frozen in the rocks they'd gathered in the shadows on the crater floor. Bring them inside, and the H_2O might've liquefied and ended up on Hagan's fingers, in microscopic amounts, for a quick trip into the hothouse of its human host. Or maybe it was in the dust—

Joe howled in pain, writhing in his hammock.

"What in blazes is that?" Wills asked.

"It's Joe." His stomach twisted in knots. "I'm out of my depth, gentlemen. I need some help up here."

"Hang tight, Peary Station."

"Hang tight? Damn it, Randy! Get us back home!"

"Okay, Kyle, okay. I'm sorry. I'm just the monkey in the middle here."

Garamond took a deep breath. "Yeah... I know."

They left it there.

Hagan's breathing had gotten so shallow it was barely perceptible. His eyes were dull. Blood bubbled from clenched teeth.

"Captain Hagan contracted a local disease," Franz's monotone startled Garamond, loud in his headset. "This has always been a remote possibility, and we fear it has become an actuality."

The first three Apollo crews had been

quarantined when they returned to Earth, but nothing bad had happened, and NASA let its guard down. Too soon, apparently, thought Garamond.

"What is Captain Hagan's current condition?"

It was hard to look at Joe with a detached eye. "He's still bleeding out... eyes are glazed. He's very pale." He paused. "That enough?"

"Yes. Thank you. Our main concern is for the safe return of the crew," Franz's tone sounded too much like HAL 9000. "However, we must ascertain the feasibility of that course of action."

"Say again?"

"The disease is progressing rapidly. The prognosis is not optimistic."

Hagan was gone within the hour. The doctor said it was likely his internal organs had liquefied, and his vital systems shut down. The virus had attacked like a cheetah taking down prey.

Now Garamond shared quarters with a corpse that had vectored a microbe that could kill a human within 36 hours of contact. And he was sealed in a spacesuit that had only a few hours of air left. It's not that he couldn't replenish the air, but he had to remove his helmet and unhook his backpack to do it.

Dr. Franz figured the gestation period of the virus to be about twelve hours. This was an efficient, voracious beast, practically tailor-made to eat humans alive from the inside.

During training they'd gone over the standard Lunar Receiving Laboratory procedures. Discussing the slim possibility of encountering an alien virus, specialists explained a Yale professor's theory that any agent of disease had to be exposed to humans for generations before becoming life-threatening. So much for that.

Now Garamond was faced with the fact that he'd breathed the same air and touched the same surfaces as Hagan. With two men living in a space the size of a Volkswagen, it was impossible to avoid. What gave him hope was that he hadn't manifested any symptoms. Yet.

Wills relayed the order that Hagan's body was classified as a level-four biohazard and was to be left behind on the Moon's surface.

Garamond made preparations. He replaced the captain's helmet, clicking it into place. Hagan's gold visor became a burial shroud, hiding the ravages of the disease, and a face Garamond no longer recognized. He removed Joe's personal effects from his ditty bag—a photo of his wife and three sons, his Academy class ring, his astronaut pin—and sealed them in the utility pocket on the thigh of his suit. It was like the funeral rites of ancient warriors and kings, buried with the items they'd need in the netherworld. He wasn't sure where Hagan was right now, but wherever he was, he wanted to give him these things for the crossing.

He picked out a small rise a walkable distance from the LM. He'd take Hagan there so his body wouldn't be tossed around by the force of the exhaust when the ascent module blasted off. Armstrong and Aldrin had blown the American flag into the dust during their liftoff from Tranquility Base; Garamond didn't want to be responsible for a similar indignity to Hagan's no-longer-earthly remains.

Once there, he propped him against a rock, and stood in tribute. He snapped a final salute and headed back to the ship.

Lancaster made it known that the mission priority was now the return of the rock samples. Garamond had consulted with the military constituents of the space program long enough to know what was going on. The DOD and USAMRIID had nothing in common but biological warfare. Despite the fact that President Nixon had diverted USAMRIID to peaceful uses in the wake of signing the international bio-weapons treaty in 1969, the treaty was still unratified, and the cold warriors saw this as a window of opportunity, especially with nuclear disarmament on the horizon. They needed a new secret weapon, and Garamond had unwittingly discovered it for them.

He was to start liftoff preparations as soon as he got back inside. Ullrich had already made his orbital corrections for rendezvous, so he'd better get cracking. Mission Control requested that he read back every mark on the nav computer as he punched in the settings. He was exhausted and alone and could easily make a mistake. He agreed.

He crawled into the cabin on hands and knees, closed the hatch and stood up, initiating the repress sequence.

That was when the headache hit so hard it buckled his knees. His vision grayed over. He grabbed the yellow handles of the optical alignment telescope and held on, hoping the pain would subside.

"Give us a go when you've reached full pressure."

He could barely hear Wills through the jackhammer pounding in his ears.

"You copy that, Kyle?"

He couldn't reply for long minutes. Houston kept calling; there was nothing he could do.

The cabin repress cycled through, and finally the throbbing ebbed, exchanged for a crashing wave of nausea. He barely got his helmet off in time to reach for one of the few remaining disposal bags.

Garamond didn't know how much air was left in his backpack; the less the better. He felt okay now. But having observed Hagan, he knew he was in that brief period before the final plunge, and

he wanted to take advantage of it.

He cleaned up and got back outside, shoving the rock boxes out ahead of him.

Lancaster was so angry at his insubordination that he'd gotten onto the comm, shouting so loud he screeched. Garamond clicked off. He didn't plan on calling back.

He wouldn't contact Ullrich to say good-bye, either. It was enough to know Frank would make it back alive, that Nancy and Karen would see him again, that he'd live to a ripe old age.

Garamond was a weapon now, hot with deadly virus, capable of killing hundreds, maybe thousands of people. His return to the command ship would've been a death sentence for his best friend. He wouldn't have it.

Garamond had no wife or children of his own. His professional commitment had taken a toll on his personal life. And he wouldn't dwell on his parents' and siblings' imminent grief. It would be hard for them, not knowing. He wished there was some way to let them know that his hard work had paid off, that he'd walked on the Moon against all odds, that their belief in him had been rewarded. Maybe someday, his friend Frank could tell the story.

Garamond opened the rock boxes one by one, unclipped the Teflon bags and dumped out every rock they'd gathered over the last three days. The samples lay scattered, exposed to the scorching sunlight and incessant downpour of ultraviolet radiation. The water ice locked inside would soon heat up and outgas, taking the virus with it. Even if they did dare to send someone back here for this—which would be immensely expensive and risky, with no guarantee of duplicating the discovery—Garamond wasn't going to make it easy for them.

He was heading back to the location on

the shadowed floor where he'd scooped the deadly samples from the regolith. Garamond wanted to destroy what he could of the killers' hideout. But given how he felt, the traverse was daunting. The site was less than half a mile out, downhill all the way, but it seemed like a marathon.

As he walked, rock hammer tethered to his suit, dragging an empty sample box behind him, he wondered what story would be spun by the higher-ups to obscure this mission— how they'd explain why someone's husbands and brothers and sons had disappeared off the face of the earth. He didn't wonder long; he could do nothing about it. He was at the site.

He was struggling to breathe; his joints were aching. Swinging the hammer was more and more difficult with every minute that passed.

He pushed himself on to shatter the layer of rock where he'd first found the deadly samples. He then scooped the chunks into the sample box to drag them up the slope, into the sunlight, where he could dump them onto the surface to be scoured by the merciless solar wind.

There was no way he could know how much of this sector sheltered water ice, or how wide and deep the deposit ranged, or if that ice even contained any of the same deadly virus. His hope was that the UV radiation would mutate the microscopic killers into harmlessness. No guarantees, but he'd done his best.

Garamond sighed, his breath sounding hollow inside his helmet as he trudged back toward the LM. His feet were lead, scuffing across the regolith. He felt groggy; the oxygen in his backpack was running low. He knew he was breathing proportionately greater amounts of his own exhaled carbon dioxide. It would soon poison him, first with unconsciousness, then with death.

Garamond could go no further. He found a little rise, a place within sight of the LM, and sat down. Without an atmosphere to peer through, every detail was crisp: the rocks, the crater floor, the sky filled with stars, the foil-covered spider-ship that brought him.

He turned a bit so he could see Earth, large and low in the sky. "The good Earth," Frank Borman had called it on his trip around the Moon, a few Christmas Eves ago. The good Earth.

His eyelids were heavy. He relaxed, leaned back, and let sleep overtake him.

Next Issue

It's about time as MARC SCOTT ZICREE examines some films that handle the concept of time travel well... and others that make him want to go back and shoot their grandfathers.

In his comic novella, "As You Were," HENRY KUTTNER shows us that you can't always get what you want, but if you travel in time, you just might find you get what you need.

A man flees a doomed future to test the power of ideas to change the world—and history—in "Canterbury April" from RAYMOND F. JONES.

The Irritated People

by Ray Bradbury

Illustrated by Kevin Farrell

harles Crossley, President of American Jet-Propelled Ships, felt himself spread-eagled in his favorite living room chair. The voice on the televisor moaned. Europe. Crossley twitched. Secret atomic factories. Crossley jerked. Semi-dictatorships. Crossley sweated. Political pressures. War. Crossley writhed.

His wife shut the televisor off indignantly. "Nonsense!" She stared at her limp husband. "Tri-Union hasn't any weapons, we haven't any, neither has Russia, Britain or anyone else. That was all settled and forbidden ages ago. When was it? 1960?"

Crossley stroked his receding hairline, sighing. "They're making atom bombs in secret," he said. He littered the rug with cigar ash.

"Stop that!" cried his wife. "My nice rug!"

"The rug, oh, the confounded rug," he said, and muttered away, closing his eyes for a long minute. Then he opened one eye. He looked at his wife. He looked at the rug, the cigar in his hand, the fallen ashes.

"The rug?" He shut his eyes again. Five minutes later he leaped up with an explosion of sound. "The rug! I've got it! I've

Originally appeared in Thrilling Wonder Stories, *December 1947.*
Story copyright © 1947 Standard Magazines, Inc. Copyright renewed 1974 by Ray Bradbury.
Reprinted by permission of Don Congdon Associates, Inc.
Illustration copyright © 2007 Kevin Farrell

got it!" He seized his wife, kissed her. "You *are* brilliant! I love you! That's it, that *is* it!"

He rushed madly off in the general direction of Europe!

Thus began the Tri-Union-American war of the year 1989.

The small jet-propelled ship crossed the Atlantic in fiery gusts. In it was Charles Crossley, a man with an idea. Behind it three thousand other ships tore along, putting space behind. They were his ships. They belonged to his company. He employed the men. This was his own private war.

"Ha!" Mr. Crossley laughed quite obviously.

The radio cut in on him. "Crossley?"

Crossley answered. "Speaking."

"This is the President, Crossley." The voice was sharp, and it fairly heated the interior of the ship. "Turn back, in the name of common sense. What *are* you up to! I'll seize your company!"

"This can't wait, Mr. President. We've been sweating it out for months. The Tri-Union won't admit it's setting up a fascistic skeleton in Europe, we can't find any proof they are, but there are rumors. We've got to get it out in the open. We can't wait. I'm sorry I have to act alone. Bombardiers?"

"Ready!" Three thousand voices.

"Crossley!" shouted the President, far away.

"Here comes Vienna!" Crossley jerked his hand down. "Bombloads, release!"

"Release!" Three thousand voices.

"Crossley!" The President.

"Bang!" said Crossley.

Pink confetti tumbled down through the clear cool summer air. Tons and tons of pink, whirling confetti! Confetti by the bombload, three thousand cargoes of very pink, very fine confetti!

"And to think," mused Crossley happily, as he turned his ship homeward, "to think the entire idea came from spilling ashes on the rug! Hi-ho!"

The President of the United States shook his fist.

"You bombed them!"

Crossley yawned. "There is no law against dropping waste paper," he said, quietly.

"You attacked the people of the Tri-Union states!"

"No one injured," said Crossley, calmly. "No explosions, no bruises, no fatalities. Did anybody even get a piece of confetti in his eye? The answer is no. A two letter word."

Crossley lit a cigarette. "Fifty thousand housefraus and one hundred thousand children swept sidewalks. Men flooded employment offices in Vienna for street sweeper jobs. But, ah, that clever, devilish confetti! It was electrically and chemically impregnated. It vanished when touched by human hands. It reappeared when humans withdrew from the immediate vicinity. Brooms helped little. When disturbed the confetti had a curious habit of jumping like tiddle-de-winks or jumping beans. Sensitive little things. I dare say it'll be some weeks before Vienna is clean. That is what I have done to the Tri-Union. The World Organization forbids an attack. Was this an attack, sir? Confetti on the wind? Eh?"

"The World Organization forbids war!" cried the President.

"This is not war." Crossley leaned forward, tapped the desk earnestly. "Suppose we dropped confetti every day, causing Tri-Union population to pluck and curry their lawns 365 days a year? And there are *other* things we can do, Mr. President. Little, irritating things. Imagine it, Mr. President, will you?"

The President imagined it for quite a

while. Then, slowly, he began to smile.

It was a sweet day, a morning in the Tri-Union state of Bruegher. The sky was blue, the clouds were nicely white. And upon the rolling green hills a picnic was spread, with thousands of tossed paper napkins, hundreds of bread heels, crusts, can openers, sardine tins, dropped eggs and wadded cardboard cartons. The picnic, like a river of several thousand parts, engulfed the park-like hills. One small boy running through the dells paused to leave his semi-digested lunch.

Laughter. Wine bottles gurgling! Songs!

The President of the United States and Mr. Crossley clinked glasses, heading the picnic, drank gustily, refilled, drank again. Others yelled, screamed in delight, played tag, threw away bottles!

And on twenty thousand other Tri-Union hills twenty thousand other small family ships landed. Twenty thousand more picnic riots began. Sixty thousand napkins, well wadded, were dropped from wiped lips! One hundred thousand shattered egg shells were spilled! Sixty thousand shiny soup cans were left gleaming in the sun. Three hundred million ants rushed out to welcome them. And the thirty million people of Greater Bruegher glared at the invasion, knowing not what to do. What was the world coming to?

At nightfall, the last little boy had emptied himself of his brackish contents, the last little girl plucked bawling from a poison ivy nest, the last sardine dispatched, the last beer bottle left a foamy vacuum.

Flying away into the night, the American invaders sent back their war cry which sounded remarkably like, and probably was, a belch.

General Krauss, personal representative of Brugh, the new semi-dictator of Europe, shouted out of the televisor:

"Mr. President, you, *you* were seen, by reliable witnesses, to peel an egg and, bit by bit, throw the shell under a one hundred year old linden tree!"

Crossley and the President stood together in the White House inner sanctum. The President spoke:

"Krauss, the peace laws specify no nation may manufacture weapons for killing, wounding or destruction of another's national populace or property. We are helpless to attack you, therefore. All the while, you, in secret, make weapons—"

"You can't prove that!"

"—make weapons," said the President, grimly. "So, in last recourse, we use weapons which are no weapons at all. We have destroyed nothing and no one."

"Ah-hah!" Krauss' eyes snapped on the visor. His face vanished. A new scene replaced it, showing a green meadow. Krauss' voice crackled behind it, in comment. "Property damage to Greater Bruegher! Listen! Rough estimate! Sixty-five thousand ants, large and small, both black and red, biting and non-biting, were trodden on at your picnic!"

The scene dissolved to yet another.

"Hark! Ten million grass-blades. Approximately. Ten million trampled and crushed. Two thousand pretty flowers. Picked!"

"That was an error," apologized Crossley. "The children got out of hand."

"Two thousand flowers," repeated Krauss savagely. *"Picked!"*

Krauss took time to get hold of himself. He cleared his throat and continued.

"Approximately thirty billion atomic particles of wood brushed off Great Bruegher sycamores, oaks, elms and lindens by adults playing tree tag—AND—sixty million particles scraped from Greater Bruegher fences by young men escaping angered Greater Bruegher bulls.

AND! And—" he thundered. The scene dissolved once more, and a most interesting view was revealed. "And—sixteen thousand cubic feet of A-1, first class forest moss crushed, roiled upon and otherwise malpracticed by young lovers idling in the thickets! There you are! The proof! The proof! This is war!"

The first Tri-Union airships flew over New York a week later. From them, on parachutes, little yellow boxes floated.

Crossley, in his garden resting, preparing new methods of attack on the enemy, was astonished as one of the devices hovered by the red brick garden wall.

"A bomb!" he cried, and leaped into the house, sorry he had started this infernal war.

Edith, his wife, peered from the rear window.

"Oh, come back," she said. "It's only a radio."

They listened. Music. Blues music.

"From back in the Mad Forties, when I wore pigtails," said Edith.

"Hmm," said Crossley.

The music, if such it could be called, concerned a lady afflicted with "—I got those mad about him, glad about him, but I get so sad about him bah-looze!"

"Interesting," said Crossley.

"Yes," she said.

The song ended. They waited.

The song began again.

"Is that all it plays?" said Edith. "I don't see any dials to change the record with."

"Oh, oh," said Crossley and shut his eyes. "I think I begin to see the light—"

The song ended and started a third time.

"That's what I expected," said Crossley, "Here, give me a hand."

The song flowed into its fourth, fifth and sixth renditions as they poked at the dangling machine. It dodged—like a hummingbird. "Radar-sensitives," gasped

Crossley, giving up. "Oh, pfui!"

Edith covered her ears with her hands. "Oh, Charles," she said.

They went in the house and shut the door tight and shut the windows tighter. Nevertheless, the music penetrated.

After dinner, Crossley looked at Edith and said:

"What do *you* make it?"

She counted on her fingers. "This next time will be the one hundred and thirteenth repeat," she said.

"That's what I counted," said he, handing her wads of cotton.

He worked feverishly that evening. He made plans for war using confetti, toothpaste tubes that refused to function, a chemical that dulled razors with the first scrape, and—mmm, let me see....

His young son, age twelve, was doing his homework in the next room.

"Oblivious to that awful music," said Crossley in admiration. "Kids are marvels, can concentrate anywhere." He crept up on his son, looked over his shoulder.

The boy was writing a composition:

"Poe authored The Cask of Amontillado, Masque of the Red Death, and I Got Those Mad About Him, Glad About Him, But I Get So Sad About Him—"

"Blues," said Crossley. He turned. "Edith! Pack the suitcases! We're leaving home!"

They piled into the family helicopter. As the helicopter lifted into the sky, Crossley's small son said, looking down at the music box in the garden, "Two hund-derth time!"

Crossley hit him.

It was useless to flee. The hovering radios were everywhere, bawling. They were in the air and on the ground and under bridges.

They could not be shot down; they

dodged. And the music played on.

Edith glared at her husband who was somewhat responsible for all this. His son tentatively eyed Crossley's shins for kicking.

Crossley called the President.

"YOU!" screamed the President. "CROSSLEY!"

"Mr. President, I can *explain!*"

So the war progressed. The World Organization hunched forward tensely awaiting the moment when either side got off bounds, fired a shot or committed a murder. But—

Normal civilized pursuits continued. Imports and exports flowed, foods, clothing, raw materials were exchanged.

If either country had broken relations, made guns, knives, grenades, the World Organization would have leaped in. But not a gun was fashioned, not a knife sharpened. There were no murders, wounded, or bruised. The World Organization was helpless. There was no war.

Well, almost none.

"Heinrich!"

"Yes, my wife?"

"Come look at this mirror!"

Heinrich, chief deputy of the police department in a Greater Bruegher village, came slopping in his easy slippers, holding his clay pipe like a small tame bird in his hand.

Heinrich looked into a mirror that was ridiculous, like at a carnival.

"What has happened to it over night?" he wondered. "Look at me. Ha, I look like an idiot!" He chuckled. "My face stretches like rubber, shivers, is distorted. Well. The mirror is warped."

"*You* are warped!" shouted his wife. "Do something about it!"

"I will buy a new one. In the meantime, the one upstairs—"

"Is also warped!" she snapped. "How

will I get my hat on straight, or see if my lipstick is drawn fine, or my powder neat? Clumsy idiot, hurry and fetch a new one! Go, get, rush!"

Crossley had his orders. Find a way out. Or arrange a truce. If these next attacks by the United States did not produce results, the United States must bargain for peace. Peace, yes. Peace from that abominable woman singing the abominable blues twenty times an hour, night and day. The American Public would hold the line as long as possible, said the President, but time was short and puncturing everybody's eardrums seemed a most unlikely way out. Crossley was to get in there, and pitch.

Crossley pitched. His jet plane streaked over Europe in the great offensive. Three thousand bombloads of something or other were dropped, at his order, and then the three thousand company ships curved and shot home. He lingered on, cruising the length of Europe, awaiting results.

He got them.

A large, unseeable beam took hold of his ship and drew it steadily down into the dark mountains of Greater Bruegher.

"Well," said Crossley. "Adventure."

The entire capture was quiet, convivial. When he stepped from his grounded craft he was politely escorted into a city of ultra-modern buildings and avenues between the mountains, and there, in a small edifice, in a small room, he met his enemy.

Krauss sat behind a desk as Crossley entered. Crossley nodded and bowed.

"Hello, Krauss. You'll be prosecuted for kidnapping."

"You're free to go any time," snapped Krauss. "This is an interview. Sit."

The chair was shaped like a low pyramid. You could sit, but you slid in all directions. The ceiling where Crossley was expected to sit was very low. He had to choose between back-ache or slithering around on a pyramidal chair. He chose to slither.

Krauss reached over and pinched Crossley.

"Ouch!" said Crossley.

Krauss did it again.

"Stop that!" said Crossley.

"All right," said Krauss.

Under Crossley, the chair exploded.

Gibbering, Crossley leapt up. He banged his head on the ceiling. He held his back end with one hand, the head with the other.

"Mr. Crossley, shall we talk of peace?"

"Yeah," said Crossley, bent over. "When you stop making secret weapons. Otherwise, more confetti, more picnics and pigs-knuckles."

"And more music in America, ah, Mr. Crossley?"

Another pinch.

"Ow! We can stand the music long enough to use our next weapon. We always did have it over you stuffed-shirts over here. You were the inventors of psychological warfare, but we gave it a few improvements."

"Can one improve over music, Mr. Crossley?"

"We'll find a way. Ouch. Keep that away from me!"

"I'll detail our plans, Crossley. First, an oversupply of mosquitoes, in America. *Hungry ones.* Then, a chemical which causes all men's shoes to squeak with each step. Third, electrical pulses to make alarm clocks ring an hour early each morn—"

Crossley was professionally interested.

"Not bad. All within the Peace Rules. All harmless. Mmm, except those mosquitoes."

"Merely skin irritatives."

"Still, the World Org might rule against it."

"Out with the mosquitoes, then!"

"Ouch."

"Did I *hurt* you? Sorry. Well, let us see if we can hurt you a bit more. This paper on my desk. It is a radio report of your death five minutes ago. Your plane crashed, says the report. I have only to broadcast it, and then make sure you 'live' up to the facts contained therein. You see?"

Crossley grinned. "I'm to report to the President every hour. No report, immediate World Org investigation. Do *you* see?"

"Your plane crashed."

"No soap. The Brindly-Connors motors never conk. And the new reactive-propellants on my ships prevent bad landings. So."

Krauss fidgeted. "We'll think of some way."

"It's time for me to phone the President; may I?"

"Here." A phone was handed him.

Crossley took the phone. Electricity shot up his arm, into his chest.

"Jeepers!" He dropped the thing. "I'll report you!"

"You have no proof. We both play this irritation game, do we not? Go ahead. The phone."

This time, Crossley got the President:

"Crossley, you've heard the news, have you?"

"What news, sir?"

"The chewing gum, you moron, the chewing gum!"

"In the streets, sir?"

The President groaned. "In the streets, the roofs, the dog's fur, the cars, the shrubs, everywhere! Big as golf-balls. And sticky!"

Krauss gloated, listening.

Crossley said, "Courage, Mr. President.

Use the croquet hoops."

"Croquet hoops?" Krauss seized Crossley's arm.

"Invisible croquet hoops," Crossley smiled.

"No." Krauss triumphed. "People will stumble, be hurt, even killed by them. The Word Org would stop you!"

"Oh," said Crossley. His face fell. "Look, Mr. President. About those hoops. Forget them. Proceed with Plan 40 and 45 instead."

Another phone rang. Krauss picked it up, answered it.

Your wife, Herr Krauss.

"All right, put her on."

"I'm okay, Mr. President. Had a little engine trouble."

"What!"

Darling, the most terrible trouble!

"Katrina, I have no time. There is much to do."

This is important, you fool! It's horrible!

"Well, what is it, my liebschen? I'm busy."

"Answer me, Crossley, were you shot down?"

"Not exactly, Mr. President. They're trying to figure out a way to kill me. Haven't hit on one yet."

"Mr. Crossley, please, not so loud, I can't hear my wife talking. Yes, darling?"

Hans, Hans, I have dandruff!

"Say that again, I have so much noise here, Katrina."

"I'll call you again in an hour, Mr. President."

Dandruff, Hans, dandruff. A thousand, five thousand flakes on my shoulders!

"You call to tell me this, woman? Goodbye!"

BANG!

Crossley and Krauss hung up in unison, Krauss on his wife, Crossley on

the President.

"Where were we?" said Krauss, sweating.

"You were going to kill me. Remember?"

Again the phone. Krauss swore and answered. "What?"

Hans, I've gained ten pounds!

"Why do you insist on calling to tell me these things?"

Mrs. Leiber, Mrs. Krenschnitz and Mrs. Schmidst, they too have gained ten pounds!

"Oh?" Krauss hung up, blinking. "So." He glared at Crossley. "That's what it is. All right, Crossley, we, also, can be subtle. Doctor!"

A door slid open in the wall. There stood an evil looking rascal, sleeves rolled high, testing a hypodermic on his own emaciated arm, enjoying it. He looked up at Crossley and said:

"Practice."

"Get him!" cried Krauss.

Everybody jumped on Crossley.

Darkness.

"How do you feel, Crossley?"

How was he supposed to feel? All right, he guessed. He lifted himself from a kind of operating table and looked at the doctor and at Krauss.

"Here Doctor," said Krauss. "Explain to Mr. Crossley what he may expect ten years from now."

"Ten years?" said Crossley in alarm.

The doctor placed his thin fingers together, bowing. He whispered daintily.

"Ten years from now you may expect a—ah—little trouble. It will commence one year from now. Unobtrusively. Here or there a slight gastric upset, a cardiac disturbance, a minor intra-irritation of the lung sacs. Occasionally, a headache. A sallowness to the complexion, an earache, perhaps."

Crossley began to sweat. He held onto his knees.

The doctor continued, slowly, pleased with himself.

"Then, as the years pass, a small flicker, like bird wings, of the heart. A pain, as if stabbed in the groin. A twitching of the peritoneum. A hot sweating, late of nights, drenching your bedclothes. Insomnia. Night after night, cigarette after cigarette, headache after headache."

"That'll do," said Crossley bleakly.

"No, no." The doctor waved his hypodermic. "I'm not finished. Temporary blindness. I almost forgot that. Yes, temporary blindness. Fuzzy lights in your head. Voices. Paralysis of the lower limbs. Then, your heart, in one last explosion, lasting ten days, will beat itself into a bruised pulp. And you'll die, exactly—" he consulted a mental calendar, "—ten years, five months and fourteen days from today."

The silence in the room was touched only by Crossley's ragged breathing. He tried to lift himself, shivered, fell back.

"Best of all, there will be no evidence of what we have done to you," said Krauss. "Certain hormones and molecular impurities were put into your body. No analysis now or after death would reveal them. Your health will simply fail. We will not be held responsible. Clever, is it not?"

The doctor said, "You may go now. Now that we have fixed you, like a timebomb, to die later, your are free to go. We would not want to kill you here, that would make us responsible. But, ten years from now, in another place, how can that be due to us?"

The phone. "Your wife, Herr Krauss."

My hair is falling out!

"Now, now, be patient, my wife."

My skin is yellowing! Do something!

"I will be home in an hour."

There will be no home here, then, YOU!

"We must go on to Victory, my sweet."

Not on a path strewn with my golden, golden hair!

"Yes, my wife, I will say hello to the doctor for you."

Hans, don't you dare hang up on me. Don't you—

Krauss sat down, fluttering his hands weakly. "My wife called me to say all is well."

"Ha," said Crossley, weakly.

Krauss reached over and pinched him. "Ouch."

"There," said Krauss. "Speak when you're spoken to."

Crossley stood up, laughing. The doctor looked at him as if he were insane.

"I've got it. I'm going to commit suicide!"

"You're crazy," said Krauss.

"Ten years from now I die, so why not commit suicide here, thus bringing an investigation by the World Organization, eh, Mr. Krauss?"

"You can't do that!" said Krauss, dumbfounded. "I won't permit it!"

"I'll jump off a building, perhaps. You can't hold me here for more than another hour or the Organization will come to see what ticks. And the minute you let me go, I'll jump off a building."

"No!"

"Or crash my ship, purposely, on the way home. Why not? What've I to live for? And if it causes your trial, so much the better. Yes, I've decided. I'll die."

"We'll hold him here," said the doctor to Krauss.

"We can't," said Krauss.

"Release him," said the doctor.

"Don't be silly," said Krauss.

"Kill him!"

"Sillier still," gasped Krauss. "Oh, this is terrible."

"Which way," said Crossley, "to the

tallest building in town?"

"You go down to the next corner—" said the doctor and stopped. "No. Stop. We must stop him."

"Get out of the way," said Crossley. "Here I go."

"But this is preposterous," screamed Krauss. "Doctor, we must think of something!"

Women sobbed in the streets, their hair trembling in their hands, detached from their heads. Puddles formed wherever women met to weep. See, see, my beautiful hair, fallen! *Your* hair, you butcher's mate; what of mine? Mine! Yours was hempen rope, a horse's tail! But mine, ach, mine! Like wheat in the high wind falling!

Crossley led the doctor and Krauss along a wide street.

"What goes on?" he asked naively.

"Beast, you know well enough," whispered the doctor fiercely. "My wife, my beauteous Thickel, her blonde hair'll be a ruin!"

"Speak roughly to me again," threatened Crossley, "and I'll hurl myself before this next bus."

"Don't, no!" cried Krauss, seizing his arm. To the doctor: "Fool. Is your wife more important than hanging?"

"My wife is good as your wife," snarled the doctor. "Katrina and her henna rinse!"

Crossley led the way into a building and up in an elevator. They walked on a terrace on the thirteenth floor.

"It is a riot," moaned the doctor, surveying the street below. "The women storm the beauty salons demanding help. I wonder if my Thickel is with them, raging?"

In huge clusters the women of the city held their heads in their hands as if they might topple and fall plunk on the ground. They argued, phoned husbands in high

government circles, sent telegrams to the Leader, pummeled and kicked a bald man who laughed at them in their misery.

"Pardon me, Krauss," said Crossley. "There." He flicked a constellation of dandruff from Krauss's lapel.

"My hair," said Krauss, in realization. "My lovely hair!"

"Will you sign peace terms, or shall I jump from this building and let you and your wrathful wife become bald?"

"My wife," sobbed Krauss. "Bald! Ah, heaven!"

"Turn over all secret officers of your plan, admit your guilt in full, and the attack will stop. You will keep your hair," said Crossley. "And cure me of my fatal illness."

"That," said Krauss, "we cannot do. The illness, I mean. But the peace terms, ah, my sweet, balding wife, the peace terms, I reluctantly accept. Peace, it is."

"Fine," said Crossley. "But, one more term." He grabbed the doctor, held him out over the edge, as if to drop him.

"Stop!" Frantically, the doctor squirmed. "I lied! We did nothing to you. It was psychological. You'd have *worried* to death in ten years!"

Crossley was so surprised he let go.

He and Krauss stared down at the dwindling doctor, falling.

"I didn't really mean to drop him," said Crossley.

"Squish," murmured Krauss, a moment later, looking down.

Crossley pushed his jet-ship homeward.

"Edith, it's over! The music'll be off in an hour!"

"Darling!" she radioed. "How'd you do it?"

"Simple. They thought it enough to irritate people. That was their error. They didn't strike psychologically deep enough. Their type of irritant only touched surfaces, made people mad—"

"And sleepy."

"But we attacked their ego, which was something else. People can stand radios, confetti, gum and mosquitoes, but they won't take baldness or turning yellow. It was unthinkable!"

Edith ran to meet him as he landed. The radio still hung in the garden, drifting, singing.

"What do you make it, now?" he cried. She kissed him.

Pulling back she counted swiftly inside her head, glanced at the floating radio and said, automatically:

"That makes two thousand three hundred and *ten!*"

THE STUFF OF LIFE—ORBITING SATURN!

PASADENA, Calif.—NASA's Cassini spacecraft has revealed for the first time surface details of Saturn's moon Hyperion, including cup-like craters filled with hydrocarbons that may indicate more widespread presence in our solar system of basic chemicals necessary for life.

Hyperion yielded some of its secrets to the battery of instruments aboard Cassini as the spacecraft flew close by in September 2005. Water and carbon dioxide ices were found, as well as dark material that fits the spectral profile of hydrocarbons.

A paper appearing in the July 5 issue of *Nature* reports details of Hyperion's surface craters and composition observed during this flyby, including keys to understanding the moon's origin and evolution over 4.5 billion years. This is the first time scientists were able to map the surface material on Hyperion.

Cassini's ultraviolet imaging spectrograph and visual and infrared mapping spectrometer captured compositional variations in Hyperion's surface. These instruments, capable of mapping mineral and chemical features of the moon, sent back data confirming the presence of frozen water found by earlier ground-based observations, but also discovered solid carbon dioxide (dry ice) mixed in unexpected ways with the ordinary ice. Images of the brightest regions of Hyperion's surface show frozen water that is crystalline in form, like that found on Earth.

"The Hyperion flyby was a fine example of Cassini's multi-wavelength capabilities. In this first-ever ultraviolet observation of Hyperion, the detection of water ice tells us about compositional differences of this bizarre body," said Amanda Hendrix, Cassini scientist on the ultraviolet imaging spectrograph at NASA's Jet Propulsion Laboratory, Pasadena, Calif.

Details are online at: http://ciclops.org/view.php?id=3303. More information on the Cassini mission is available at: http://www.nasa.gov/cassini .

—press release from nasa.gov,
July 4, 2007

4e-Membrance of Things Past

an interview by Winston Engle

*N*o one could love science fiction as much as Forrest J Ackerman (yes, without a period). Not only has his obsession with the genre earned him the sobriquets "Super-Fan" and "Mr. Science Fiction," it predates the name itself, going back to within six months of the founding of Amazing Stories *as the first regular magazine of "scientifiction."*

An inveterate punster and coiner of neologisms, Ackerman reduced his nickname "Forry" to "4e" (and now, naturally, communicates via "4e-mail"), long lived in the "Ackermansion," and invented, to the dismay of some, the expression "sci-fi."

He owns an extraordinary collection of science fiction and horror memorabilia, from Frank R. Paul original paintings to Bela Lugosi's Dracula cape. He has been a writer, an agent, and an editor. He founded Famous Monsters of Filmland, *where as "Dr. Acula," he provided boyhood reading for a whole generation of filmmakers.*

But before all that, he was a charter subscriber to Science Wonder Stories, *a regular letter-writer, and Honorary Member Number One of the Science Fiction League. And it's this that we asked him about for the first new issue of* Thrilling Wonder Stories.

We spoke with "4e" at his new home, the "Acker-mini-mansion," in Hollywood.

THRILLING WONDER STORIES: How did you get started reading science fiction magazines?

FORREST J ACKERMAN (4e): Well, in October 1926, little nine-year-old me was standing in front of a magazine rack, and the October 1926 issue of a magazine called *Amazing Stories* jumped off the news stand, grabbed a hold of me, and in those days magazines spoke. And that one said, "Take me home little boy, you will love me."

TWS: You've said that at first, you didn't realize it was a magazine, that it came out every month.

4e: Yes, I didn't realize, I thought that this was a miracle, that this was the only copy of this magazine that there ever will be, but as soon as I discovered every four weeks I could have a new fix of science fiction, why, I was off and running. And several years later my mother came to me quite concerned, she said, "Son, do you realize how many of these magazines that you have"—'cause I never threw them away—"I just counted them. You have twenty-seven, can you imagine? By the time you're a grown man, why, you might have a hundred."

Well, mother lived with me till she was 92 and in my eighteen-room home were

50,000 science fiction books and complete runs of *Amazing Stories* and *Science Wonder Stories* and *Astounding Stories, Unknown* and *Strange* and 200 different science fiction magazines from all around the world.

TWS: What did she think of that?

FORREST: My parents were never so much concerned about my collecting. I spent most of my youth with my grandparents, who were very supportive of me. In 1926, I was also interested in a magazine called *Ghost Stories,* and my dear maternal grandmother would read me the entire issue of *Ghost Stories* and then go back to the beginning and read it all over again to satisfy me.

TWS: You read *Science Wonder Stories* from the very beginning...

4e: Before *Science Wonder Stories* was ever published, all the readers of *Amazing Stories* received a circular announcing that there was going to be a new science fiction magazine that didn't have a name yet. But you could subscribe to it for twelve and a half cents a copy, for all the rest of your life. So, I of course immediately subscribed, and I came home from grammar school one day and there was the first issue of *Science Wonder Stories.*

TWS: You started writing letters to *Science Wonder Stories* almost immediately

4e the neologismatist, from Wonder Stories, *January 1934*

Edmond Hamilton is an extra treat nowadays.[...] Having used most adjectives over and again long ago, it's hard to commend; but I must say that the time spent with the new Hamiltonarrative was every bit of interest.

Speaking of time brings to mind the "End of Tyme," the issue's scientifictioustory."[...]

And, about scientifilms: present information taken *conservatively* points to two picturizations of the end of the world, one of invisibility, an interplanetaryarn, and a story of the future.[...] You've seen *Floating Platform No.1,* and S. FowlerWright's *Deluge;* Wells' *Invisible Man,* and the fantasy of a modern Prehistoria—*Son of Kong*[....]

and became very well known as a letter writer. How did that get started?

4e: Well, as fast as I read an issue, I was impelled to write a letter and give my opinion of the stories. I would rate them in what was the most popular story in my mind and would comment on the illustrations and so on, and other readers of the magazine kind of began to look forward to these letters from young Forrest Ackerman. And before I knew it, I was kind of considered, along with another chap named Jack Darrow, to be one of the leading science fiction fans of the era.

TWS: When the first issue of *Science Wonder Stories* came out, you were twelve. It must have been a thrill to see your name in print.

4e: Well, my father was kind of proud to see his son's name, and so I caught on, and I thought, well, if I had my name in every issue, then my father would be sure to buy it, and to show it to the men at the office and brag about his son.

TWS: When would you say you became a fan in the organized sense, communicating with other fans?

4e: In the first issue of *Science Wonder Quarterly,* in 1929, I had the first letter on the first page of the reader's department, and it had my address, so I began to hear from other readers around the world, and before I knew it I had 127 correspondents, all over the United States, and England, and France, and Germany, and Japan, and Hungary, and... I just lived to see my mailbox filled up with letters from my correspondents.

TWS: In 1930, you founded the Boys' Science Fiction Club—very enterprising for... you must have been thirteen at the time. Had 116 fans participating in a sort of lending library by mail.

4e: Well, I created the Boys' Science Fiction Club... it was not the "Boys' and Girls'," because at the time, girl readers of science fiction were about as rare as a unicorn's horn. So, I created this correspondence club, I believe it was ten cents

Logo of the Science Fiction League. Created by Frank R. Paul.

to become a member, and you contributed either three issues of a science fiction magazine that had a serial in them, or a hard-covered novel. We didn't yet have paperbacks. So, for, I believe, two cents a copy, you... I was the librarian, and you would write and borrow either the three magazines or the book, and I was not only the president of the club, but I took care of all of the mailing. I had a vice-president, a Hungarian boy named Frank Sempols, who lived in my neighborhood and went to high school with me.

TWS: Was that still going on in 1934 when Hugo Gernsback started the Science Fiction League?

4e: I believe so, but now it became possible for all of my members to join a much wider organization. So, I guess my club

was no longer needed.

TWS: You were an executive director and Honorary Member Number One of the Science Fiction League. Was that because you already knew so many other fans?

4e: Well, the editor of the magazine at the time himself was a fan, Charles D. Hornig, and he felt that just automatically, I should be the first honorary member, and then they began creating... you could become a bachelor of science fiction, or a master of science fiction, according to how many questions you could answer correctly, and I was the first one to become a master of science fiction. I believe I answered 99 percent of the questions correctly.

TWS: It must have been a great time to be a young science fiction fan, when Charles Hornig became associate editor of *Wonder Stories* when he was seventeen, and you were seventeen when the Science Fiction League started. It seems very young to become part of the science fiction establishment.

4e: Well, somehow or other, it just seemed natural to me. I just fitted right into everything. Hugo Gernsback, who was regarded as the father of science fiction, called me the son of science fiction, and he inscribed his novel *Ralph 124C 41+,* "To Forrest Ackerman, the premier science fiction authority in America." And in 1949, Willy Ley, the great exponent of space travel, in a public newspaper named me "Mr. Science Fiction."

TWS: What did you find in science fiction that you loved so much?

4e: Well, I don't believe in life after death, or reincarnation. I feel I'm only here once, and I've been fortunate to have been born with what is called a sense of wonder. I wondered about prehistoric times and dinosaurs, and the sunken city of Atlantis, and I buy the imaginations of H.G. Wells, and Olaf Stapledon, and Ray Bradbury, and Robert Heinlein. I've been catapulted from my armchair into distant times of the future. So, I've been able to live a very exciting, fulfilling life by the imagination of the authors of science fiction.

TWS: Did you have any official duties as executive director of the Science Fiction League?

4e: No, I don't believe I had any official duties as an executor. They just liked to use my name on the masthead or the stationery.

TWS: Why did Gernsback start the Science Fiction League? Was it to spread the word about science fiction, and his magazine in particular?

4e: Gernsback felt the time had come to unite science fiction fans. He even at one time created a Science Fiction Week, and during that time he arranged to have science fiction films like *Metropolis* and *Things to Come* and *The Invisible Man,* and so on, shown in theaters around the country to stir up interest with the general public in science fiction.

TWS: Did you have input at the beginning of the League, in coming up with the by-laws, or anything like that?

4e: No, I didn't involve myself with by-laws or anything, I just created Science Fiction League Chapter 4 right here in Los Angeles, and contacted all known fans. There was a second hand book and magazine shop on Hollywood Boulevard called "Ship's Shop," and Lucy B. Shepperd, the proprietress let me put up a sign. She had rows and rows of second hand science fiction books that one could rent, and I put up this sign saying that if you were interested in science fiction, come on a Thursday evening to Clifton's Cafeteria and attend free meeting of Chapter #4 of the Science Fiction League, and if you liked it, we'd be very happy to have you become a member. So, a young, ebullient fan named Ray Bradbury came and he liked it and he became a member, and a chap named T. Bruce Yerke, and an Australian-born fan, Russ Hodgkins, and we had the woman who wrote down the information on meetings. Her name was Wanda Test, and so we called her minutes "Thrilling Wanda Stories." She had a son,

4e the Esperantist, from Wonder Stories, *May 1935*

Forrest J. Ackerman, 530 Staples Ave., San Francisco, Calif., First Class Honorary Member Number One and Executive Director, "deziras korespondadi kun kelkaj geamantoj de Scienc-fikcio logantaj en Esperlando; intersango de simplaj leteroj pri Stf. generale, kaj filmoj de fantazio. Americanaj au fremdlandaj Stf. Esperamtistoj, bonvulu skribi."

"I want to correspond with some science fiction fans attracted by Esperanto; exchange simple letters about SF generally, and fantastic films. American or foreign SF Esperantists, please write."

Roy Test who was interested in Esperanto, so he became known as "Esperan-Test."

TWS: Could you tell us a little bit about Esperanto?

4e: What do they teach you in school nowadays? Well, a Polish optometrist named Dr. Ludvic Zamenhof thought it would be wonderful if there was one simple language that everybody on Earth could speak.

Well, I went to night classes at the local Los Angeles University, and no one ever learned Esperanto more quickly than I, because I felt I was being propelled a hundred years into the future, where everybody would be speaking Esperanto. If I could have time-traveled a hundred years into the future and brought back even a bottle of smog, I would have been thrilled. But now, I could capture this language of the future, and every word went right into my mind and stayed there. And on the occasion of the one hundred anniversary of the creation of Esperanto, I flew over to Warsaw, in Poland, and for ten days, I was among 7,000 people from sixty different countries, and we could all talk to each other.

TWS: Besides you and Jack Darrow, the rest of the executive directors were authors from the magazine. Did you communicate with them, were there ever any

meetings with everybody.

4e: At the time I had 127 correspondents around the world, I was also in correspondence with a number of the early authors like Jack Williamson and Edgar Rice Burroughs, and as a youngster I had hung around movie studios collecting autographs from stars, and that carried over into the science fiction world, that I began writing to authors and asking for their autographs. And finally, in 1939, at the first World Science Fiction Convention, I met in person authors I had been corresponding with... Ray Cummings and of course the fabulous artist Frank R. Paul. And some of my fan correspondents like Jack Spear, and Arthur Widner, and Bob Tucker, and David Kyle, Robert Lounge...

The SCIENCE FICTION LEAGUE

—a department conducted for members of the International Science Fiction League in the interest of science-fiction and its promotion. We urge members to contribute any items of interest that they believe will be of value to the organization.

EXECUTIVE DIRECTORS:

Forrest J. Ackerman
Eando Binder
Jack Darrow
Edmond Hamilton
David H. Keller, M. D.
P. Schuyler Miller
Clark Ashton Smith
R. F. Starzl
Hugo Gernsback, *Executive Secretary*
Charles D. Hornig, *Assistant Secretary*

4e leads the list of League Executive Directors. Granted, it's an alphabetical list, but being Honorary Member Number One must count for something.

TWS: Another member of the board was David H. Keller. Could you tell us something about him?

4e: He was one of my favorite early authors, and at one time, I visited him in his home in Pennsylvania, and I stayed overnight, and I noticed at each meal he was including a handful of different vitamins, and he said he was attempting to lengthen his life with these. He did indeed live to a ripe old age.

TWS: Did you take any?

4e: My wife didn't believe in vitamins.

She said you eat a healthy diet, and that's sufficient.

TWS: It worked. Is that your secret? (Laughter) You have an amazing memory.

4e: Well, it's not that I remember things; I know you can't tell whether I'm making it up or not, so I just say anything and you believe it. (Laughter)

TWS: What was the relationship of the League to the individual chapters? Was it just the column in *Wonder Stories,* or was it a more direct involvement?

4e: No, there was no special involvement in one chapter or another. We knew back in Boston, I believe, was the Province collection of fans, that goes on to this day. But the very earliest club, now known as the Los Angeles Science Fantasy Society, began in 1934, and every Thursday eve-ning since has had a meeting. I've attended over half of the meetings in the last seventy years.

TWS: How important was the League to early fandom? Do you think that it helped speed up the organization of fans with each other?

4e: I think it was extremely important because it called to the attention of the general public this selection of forward-looking individuals. Originally, a fan named Rick Ferry said it was a sad and lonely thing to be a fan. Since high school, I was regarded as the resident crazy, everybody was ridiculing Forry Ackerman, they thought that... we were going to the moon, or we were going to have atomic power, and all these things, they knew were never going to happen. And I remember on that fateful evening when I saw a human being set foot on the moon—vindication! Where are you now, all you laughing hyenas, thought Forry Ackerman was a crazy kid?

TWS: How did things change for the League when Gernsback sold *Wonder Stories?*

4e: Well, as I recall, the original title was abandoned and the group was under a new banner. But it was substantially the original fans. *Thrilling Wonder Stories* kind of departed from the Gernsback vision. It was his intent to kind of enthuse young readers to become physicists and chemists and astronomers and astronauts and so on. And *Thrilling Wonder Stories* were kind of more interested in just exciting science fiction, not necessarily so... scientifically accurate, but just to tell fascinating tales with a tinge of science in the background.

TWS: The column on the League started getting smaller and smaller when the

4e the fantastic film fanatic, from Wonder Stories, November 1931. He was quick to report new SF films to his fellow readers... sometimes too quick, as, in the case of Creation, they would occasionally fail to see release.

Our campaign for more science fiction motion pictures is resulting in huge success. First Universal gave us Frankenstein and now—now RKO, I am happy to announce, is making Creation! [...]

It will be a modern story of weird adventure. A yacht is caught in a tropical storm. As it is driven near to a rocky shore, an earth shock dislodges the side of a cliff, revealing a subterranean passage. Helpless before the storm, the yacht is carried into the aperture to emerge finally in a world peopled by giant beasts of another age. The man who furnished the dinosaurs for the silent film of The Lost World will supply the prehistoric monsters for this picture also. Creation ought to be an A-1 science fictional thriller!

magazine became *Thrilling Wonder Stories.* Did that reflect a waning interest in the League?

4e: Yes, 'cause they were less interested, were kind of beginning to dwindle.

TWS: In Gernsback's last issue of *Wonder Stories,* you published your first science fiction story, with Francis Flagg. How did that come about?

4e: Well, Francis Flagg was a well-established name author, but he began to run out of ideas, and I was overflowing with ideas, but I did not have any stature yet as an author, so I began supplying plots to Francis Flagg, and he wrote them up… the first one was called "Earth's Lucky Day." And that was published, and then another one, I forget the name of it, but it appeared in *Thrilling Wonder Stories.* So, we had a happy collaboration of an experienced, accepted author, and the young fellow with the vivid imagination.

TWS: Is there anything else that you'd like to say about those early days that we haven't addressed?

4e: Well, I remember at one time when I

4e's Lucky Day: his favorite artist, Frank R. Paul, illustrates his story with Francis Flagg.

was temporarily living in San Francisco, I found a series of stories called "Tani of Ekkis." The author had the name of Aladra Septama, and I found that actually he was a lawyer, Judson W. Reeves, having his office in downtown San Francisco. So one day I went to his office and met him, and he took me to lunch afterwards and out to his home, and there I was staggered to see the first six issues of *Amazing Stories* on display. I had not been aware of it April of 1926 when it began. I only began to collecting in October. And to my undying gratitude, Aladra Septama—I was always fascinated by that pseudonym, I regret I didn't ask him how he created such a name—but Aladra Septama took the six copies of *Amazing Stories* that I had missed, and gained my undying gratitude by making me a gift of them.

TWS: Do you still have them?

4e: (mock offense) Of course I have them! I never threw away a science fiction magazine in my life! • • •

4e at 9t, still as enthusiastic a "scientifiction" fan as ever.

Special thanks to Elisabeth Fies for interview videography and additional questions.

SALVAGE

by Cleve Cartmill

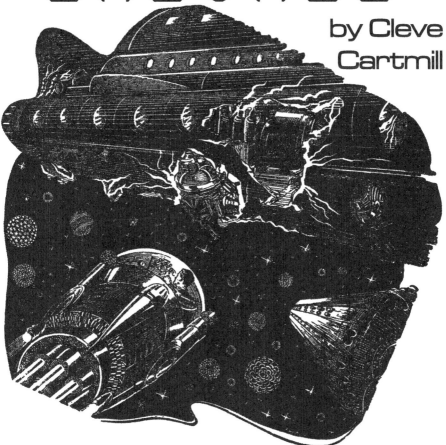

"Decelerate," I said to the pilot.
He turned his face toward me.
It was like an oval of baked mud with tiny
cracks running every which way, a lump
of red sandstone for a nose and great big
emeralds for eyes. Pat was an old-timer,
and he had taught me all I knew about
flinging a ship through space.

"You know," he said dryly, "what that's
gonna get you. Amos T. Grubb will be
stabbing you with question marks. You
sure you know what you're doing, Jake?"

"No," I said, looking at the image on
the screen.

"But that ship's a derelict, and I've got
a troublesome memory."

Pat shrugged and kicked in the nose
jets. The *Dolphin* slowed and I began to
weigh my normal 180.

"It's your funeral," Pat said.

How almost right he was.

Amos T. Grubb clambered into the control room, leaning back against the forward pull, his thin pink face a bristling

exclamation point. Cap was right behind him, unhurried as usual, his square face showing only a mild curiosity.

"What are you—" Grubb began in his double-edged voice, glaring at Pat.

"I'm responsible," I broke in. "Don't pick on Pat."

He transferred the glare to me. "Jake Murchison, have you gone mad?" he asked as if he really wanted to know.

I waved at the screen. The drifting hulk almost filled it now. You couldn't see anything but the silhouette, but my memory supplied a gaping hole in her side. That hole had a name I couldn't quite remember but I knew where to look. I pushed past Grubb and Cap, clawing my way along the passage.

"Be right back," I said. "If I'm right we're rich."

I made it to the circular recreation room and found the book—*Space Pirate,* by Clem Gardener. I took it back to the control room, fighting against the deceleration.

"If any of you guys could read," I said, "you might remember. Unless I'm mistaken, that's the long-lost *Astralot* drifting out there, with one hundred and eighty-five tons of herculium aboard. Whether you can read or not, you know what herculium is—or was. There's a photo in here somewhere."

I flipped the pages, found it. Yep, she had the high tail fin popular a hundred years ago. The silhouette matched the pulsating image on our screen. I showed it to Cap and Grubb. "As soon as we get alongside," I said, "we can verify her name. But I don't think there's any question. This is it. Her cargo could buy a planet—any planet."

Pat turned his wrinkled face to me. "Herc... what?"

"Herculium. Time was when it was dime a dozen but Hercules Phamign died without revealing his process. Now there ain't no more. That, friends, is it. One hundred and eighty-five tons of that alloy will construct—oh, I don't know how many—warships which can't be—how do you say?—penetrated. I guess I mean invulnerable. Anyway, however you look at it, this, my friends, is it."

Amos T. Grubb looked at me like I was a piece of wet clay he wanted to strike a match on. "If," he said.

"If what?"

"If it's there."

"It's a gamble," I agreed.

"Nonsense," Grubb said. "We have a job to do that doesn't have any *ifs* in it. I've invested a great deal of money in this salvage venture. I mean to get it back. Throw in the drive," he said to Pat.

Cap caught his breath. "I give the orders here, Mr. Grubb—or Jake. Let's hear more what this is about. Then we'll decide."

I found the place. I read aloud, "On November twenty-ninth we spoke the *Astralot.* We maneuvered to bring our port broadside battery into play and blasted a tremendous hole in the treasure ship. All aboard must have died instantly.

"I led the boarding party that found the treasure vault. Its massive door yielded readily enough and we stared at the greatest treasure ever assembled in history.

"At that instant, orders came to return aboard. Our detectors had picked up a Space Patrol ship. We made a careful fix on the derelict's position, estimated her rate of drift, direction and so on and fled to our asteroid base.

"We waited, straining with eagerness and dreaming of vast riches, until the Space Patrol was sure to be gone. Then we returned cautiously to the scene.

"We never found the *Astralot* again.

"She must have fallen into an uncalculated orbit. We searched that area of deep space for two years. We robbed and murdered for funds to continue that tremendously expensive operation. We were caught by the Space Patrol in the early part of the third year.

"But now, as I sit in my cell writing this, I feel once more the deep thrill when I think of the *Astralot,* yours for finding, drifting helplessly in—"

"And so on," I said. "We'll be close enough in five minutes to make sure. That treasure is something! I want it."

Cap looked thoughtfully at me. "We have no equipment to work in space, Jake. All our stuff is for the mine on Pluto, high-pressure stuff for working at eight thousand feet underground."

"I'll find a way," I said.

"Meanwhile," Amos T. Grubb said in his abrasive voice, "we void our contract on Pluto. Space Salvage, Incorporated, will then be out of business. And I'll be ruined. I won't stand for it. A bird in the hand, I always say—"

"Always is right," I said. "I know, Mr. Grubb. You've got a stake, all right. If you hadn't stepped in with dough, we couldn't have accepted this Pluto salvage contract. And we're fixed to fulfill it. That'll get us out of the red.

"But this *Astralot* job will put us on Venusberg's main drag for life. Captain Lane and I can retire and live the life of lecherous ease we want. We can pay you back with a tremendous bonus, junk the *Dolphin* and have fun."

Grubb turned to Pat, the temporary glow in his eyes fading. "Throw in the drive," he ordered once more. "I'm paying for this trip, and I have a right to decide what—"

I grabbed him by a shoulder. "I'm bigger and younger than you," I said. "If you try to give one more order, I, personally, will fling you in the brig."

What happened was certainly unexpected. I didn't even see it happen. First thing I knew, I was flat on the deck and if my jaw wasn't broken it was a miracle. Quite a number of constellations were flickering behind my eyeballs. I recognized Orion as it flashed past.

It developed later that he had hit me with his fist. I didn't believe it at first but then I tried to explain it by the fact that I was forward of him and his blow was aided by the pull of deceleration. But that didn't help my pride much. I was just plain old smacked in the kisser and it nearly killed me. The little man was a sockeroo.

I started to get up but when I saw it wasn't necessary I dropped back against the bulkhead. Cap Lane had Grubb in his arms, lifted off the deck, and the little guy was yelling and kicking. Pat turned away from the control board long enough to sap Grubb with a rocklike fist and Cap laid the still form on the deck. I got up.

Grubb was out about half an hour, and in that time a number of things happened, none of them helping my aching jaw.

Cap looked down at the unconscious body. "Well," he said reflectively, "I've always wondered what it would feel like to be an outlaw. Looks like we're going to find out. You know what inflicting bodily harm on a passenger gets you."

"He hit me first," I said, defending Pat. That's what I meant to say anyway but it came out sort of scrambled.

Cap rubbed the corners of his chin with a hand that was almost as weathered and large as Pat's. He pulled his heavy white eyebrows together over his startling blue eyes. His motions were slow and measured, as were his words. Cap never hurried.

"You laid hands on him, Jake. That's the phrase he'll use in court. He could make a self-defense plea stick. And that means loss of license, a fine and, if he sues for damages, he can take everything we've got."

"Leave him to me," Pat said, peering through the starboard port. "I'll fix him. There she is."

We followed his gaze and saw the dark hulk of the *Astralot,* looming five hundred yards off the starboard bow. Pat maneuvered alongside, matched the derelict's drift and cut off the power.

The hole was there, a great tear that punctured the ship to her vitals for almost all of her mile-long hull. Jagged points of metal along her port beam looked like a mouthful of filed teeth.

"That certainly rules out getting her into operation," I said. "We've got to salvage her here."

"There's the name," Pat said. "She's the one, all right."

Cap said, "More than a hundred years. Suppose somebody else has looted her and not reported it?"

I shrugged. "It's a chance. Not a big one, I think. If herculium had showed up in any quantity the whole Solar System would know about it."

"Here's another thing," Cap said. "Just how do you propose to get aboard her? We've got no space equipment."

"Nobody would listen to me," I said bitterly. "I wanted to load a complete outfit."

"I-told-you-so's don't do any good, Jake. We had to choose between that and the Valadian drill. There isn't room on this ship for even a runt mouse to stow away."

"Yeah, I know. Well, I propose to call Jenkins in on this. He's a clever boy."

"How'll you get him awake?"

"We've got some somnol antidote in the medicine chest. He's been out long enough for it to act."

"And then," Cap went on deliberately, "we drift along here while you try to fig-

ure out something. Meanwhile we do stand to void the Pluto contract. You know our deadline for beginning operations."

"If I can do it in twenty-four hours," I said, "we can still make it. Though if we get that herculium aboard, I don't give a hoot if we never see Pluto. Except it would make Junior happy." I gestured at Grubb.

"There's another problem," Cap said. "What'll we do with him? He's going to be more trouble than a tank full of Venusian rock sharks."

"Leave him to me," Pat suggested again.

"I think not, Pat," Cap said. "If we don't show up with Grubb in good shape we're really in trouble. And if we do," he said wryly, "we're in a mess. Well, Jake, it's been nice being your partner."

"I got us into this," I said. "I'll get us out."

"I hope so. I truly hope so. My mother never raised me to be an outlaw. That's what she always said. 'Son, be a good citizen and nothing bad will ever happen to you.' If she could only see me now," he concluded.

"I'll get Jenkins," I said, "and one of those mudders—that giant, what's his name, Carroll?—to stand guard over Junior. Then we'll get moving, fast."

Jenkins was near the door of the dormitory, lashed to his bunk like the other two dozen salvage men. I think each man snored at a different frequency. I injected the antidote and stood back. His hands were free, and I didn't want him to bust me one when he got the preliminary delirium that always accompanies artificial awakening.

He threshed around some, cursing in back-country Mercurian dialect, but when he focused he gave me his slow grin framed in freckles.

"There already, Jake?"

"Nope." I showed him the needle. "This is special. Come and help me with Carroll."

This mudder, Carroll, was nearer seven feet than anything else but a seven-foot pole and he was built like one except for his shoulders, which are what a mudder needs. They were a couple of parsecs wide and his arms were like towing hawsers. I needled him, and the snapping of his lashings were like the popping of the Valadian drill.

The next thing I knew, Carroll was holding me in his arms like I was a baby, saying soothing things in a singsong voice. If his face hadn't looked like the dark side of the Moon, you'd have thought he was a mother.

"I'm so damned sorry, Jake," he crooned. "I didn't know, I couldn't know."

I rubbed my jaw. "The next guy that socks me," I said, "will feel the full fury of my wrath—as soon as I wake up."

Carroll wouldn't let me walk. He carried me into the control room and put me carefully in the pilot's seat. He blinked at Grubb's unconscious body and I told him what to do. He went out with the little man under one arm.

I briefed Jenkins and he stared thoughtfully at the *Astralot,* running a freckled hand through his straw-colored hair.

"Just how do you propose to board her?"

"I thought maybe you'd come up with a brainstorm," I said.

Jenkins wagged his head. "All the stuff we've got is designed for opposite conditions, to work deep underground under high pressure."

"We've been over that," I said impatiently.

"We could take a fix on her, run back to base and get some space outfits."

I showed him the book. "Captain Stag

lost her and you can bet he had a better navigator than we have. Besides, we lose the Pluto contract for sure if we go back, and we wouldn't even know if the treasure was aboard, assuming we could find the ship again."

Jenkins read the passage. "That Captain Stag was quite a boy. Well, if Gardener can be believed"—he tapped the book— "the stuff *was* aboard. Our first step is to see if it still is. In what, though?"

"The Look-See?" I suggested.

He stared at me. He formed a "no" with his mouth but the intercom furiously cut him off.

"Captain Lane!" the voice of Amos T. Grubb said angrily. "I demand to know what my status is. Am I under arrest? If so, on what charge?"

"Well, not exactly, Mr. Grubb," Cap answered slowly into the grille. "I just want to keep you safe."

"From what? That idiotic first mate partner of yours? I can handle him. I did when he laid hands on me."

I felt my jaw.

Cap muttered "I told you so" to me, then spoke into the intercom. "I think it would be better if you stay where you are," he soothed.

Grubb would have none of this. "I demand freedom from this big ape. I want my legal rights or I'll have you up before the Board. I mean it."

"You could," Cap admitted. "Well, all we want you to do is stay out of our hair till we discuss our problem."

"I promise nothing! Nothing but trouble, that is, if I am not instantly allowed the freedom of the ship. I am concerned in that problem, as well as you. I have a voice in the final decision."

"Okay," Cap surrendered. "Let him go, Carroll." Cap wagged his silvery head. "Something none of us thought of, Jake. You waked two extra mouths to feed.

Going to be awful short rations before we reach any port."

"I'll put 'em back to sleep," I said, "and hope I can guess the right amount. Looks like neither one is going to be any use."

"Keep your shirt on, Jake." Jenkins grinned at me. "I started to say the Look-See wouldn't do but I have figured out a gadget. Can I tear up that Valadian drill?"

Grubb bustled in to hear that. His mouth dropped open and his thin face turned red as a cooling star. "Do my ears play me false?" he asked in a gentle voice full of cracked ice. "Do you," he said to Jenkins, "whoever you are—"

"Jenkins," I broke in. "Field technician—Grubb, financial backer."

Grubb nodded curtly. Jenkins said, "Likewise."

"Do you seriously intend to use the most valuable piece of machinery on board for this hare-brained scheme?"

"We'll pay you for it," I said.

"With what?" he asked nastily. "High-vacuum doughnut holes?"

"Somebody's got to decide," Jenkins said. "I can make the Look-See maneuverable if I can have that compressed air assembly."

We all looked at Cap, even Grubb.

Cap stared out the port at the millions of stars off our bow. It was a long time before he spoke and nobody broke the silence. "It definitely means," Cap finally said, "losing the Pluto job if we tear up the drill. It's a long gamble.

"If the treasure is there, we have to devise a way of getting it out. If it's in crates or boxes we might snake it out with a grapple—*if* we can get a grapple into the cargo hold. But, once we go into this, it's goodbye Space Salvage, Inc. Of course, it might be goodbye anyway." He looked at Grubb. "Are you going to bring charges?"

"For assault?" Grubb's voice had its normal rasp again. "Not if we proceed at

once to Pluto. There is certain money to be made from that operation. This"—he gestured at the *Astralot*—"may be a fairy tale, written by a jailbird trying to recall high adventure. I never heard of that ship before."

"I have," Carroll rumbled gently in his deep voice.

None of us had heard the giant enter. We gave him our ears. He could have had my shirt if he'd asked.

"Clem Gardener," Carroll said softly, "was my grandfather on my mother's side. The *Astralot* was really lost and she had the stuff aboard. I looked up the old records."

"As far as I'm concerned that settles it," I said.

Cap nodded. "Goodbye, salvage company," he said.

"And a lot of other things," Grubb snapped. "I see I'm outvoted, but when we reach port I'll have your licenses, your ship and maybe your treasure too. Jake, you're a young man with a fine future if you use your head. Don't do this thing. If you do, so help me, I'll ruin you."

I tried to tell him to go to blazes. I got the words all set in my mind and pushed them into my throat. But they stuck there. He meant what he was saying. And, I thought, suppose the treasure isn't aboard and suppose if it is we can't get it out?

I gulped the words back and stuck my hand out to Cap. We didn't say anything. We didn't need to. I motioned Jenkins and Carroll to follow me.

Jenkins, as usual, was right. The big observation shell didn't blow up. It was a tubular gimmick about fifteen feet long, three feet in diameter, with inlets for oxygenated air and a place to peer through. It was made of chilled steel and quartz. It had a lifting eye on the head for lowering it down a shaft but we shifted this to the tail end for a hauling line.

It wasn't designed for working in a vacuum but it sprang no leaks as I slid gently out of the airlock toward the *Astralot* and the full blinding glory of the skies poured through the observation head from all points.

I was cramped for space, what with the control panel plus the compressed air tank. We'd finally installed it inside for fear it might snag if we welded it to the surface of the shell. The air hoses, jury-rigged "jets," we fastened to the outside at calculated angles.

I fingered the stern assembly button and the shell leaped forward. The career of Jake Murchison, recently a salvage man, almost ended there and then. I barely had time to blast with the nose jets and stop the Look-See from smashing the observation head against the *Astralot.* The head was a half globe of six-inch quartz but even so, that blow would have smashed it.

In spite of the growing cold, I sweated as the shell became motionless. Carroll's gentle voice came out of my talker.

"I told you," he said. "Touch those buttons easy, like they were cobras, say. You were lucky this time."

"Are the cables okay?"

"Yeah. We gave you plenty of slack. Jenkins figured your first blast might be a little too juicy."

"Jenkins thinks of everything. Give me some tension on the line. I'm heading for the port. Good thing your pirate grandfather left it open."

I jiggled the starboard bow jet and the Look-See's nose swung slowly. I let it drift, stopped it with the port jet when the opening was dead ahead. I was feeling the cold now.

I looked at the control panel, fixing it in my mind. I wished I'd had a little time for practice, to learn where each button was,

so I could find each of them with my eyes shut. Inside that vast ship I was going to have myself a job where a sure, quick touch might be necessary to keep me out of the obits.

I jogged the stern jets and in a couple of seconds I was inside, the big headlamp knifing through the complete blackness.

I slid gently ahead to where the entrance ramp intersected the main corridor. I estimated the space, and thought maybe I could turn the fifteen-foot hull without fouling the drill assembly mounted on the stern.

I got the hang of the buttons and played the keyboard like a piano—but plenty pianissimo. Inch by inch she advanced, swung, scraped the walls, drifted free, swung.

Then I was looking down the main corridor. But only for half a second. I clenched my eyes and yelled.

"Haul in!"

"What's the matter?" Carroll asked instantly.

I gulped back my nausea. "Never mind! Haul handsomely!"

They inched me out, with the hull scraping and complaining. I opened my eyes, panting.

"What happened, Jake?" That was Cap's voice, full of deep concern.

"Bodies," I said, gagging over the memory. "I can't go down that corridor. They're bobbing around everywhere. Even if I could get through, I wouldn't try it. Did you ever see a hundred bodies suddenly exposed to deep space?"

"No," Cap said. "And I don't want to."

"Carroll's granddad must've had a steel stomach."

"But look, Jake. We've staked the works. If you don't get in there we're sunk."

"Bring me aboard. I'm cold."

They looked at me with disappointment—and disapproval. Cap put it into words.

"Perhaps one of us should try. I don't have a squeamish stomach."

"I'm not ashamed of the way I feel," I said. "And I don't even want to talk about that corridor. It would have to be cleared before the Look-See could make it, anyway, and that would take a month with the equipment we've got. I'll have to go through the side."

Jenkins added a frown to his freckles. "Is there a hole big enough? If there is it'll be dangerous. Those jagged edges would slide your hauling line."

"Any other suggestions?" I was still cold and all this talk put an edge on my voice.

"No," Jenkins said shortly.

We had a look at the *Astralot*. "There," I said, pointing. "I can get through that opening. Put our port in line with it, Pat, so we'll have a straight haul. Also I've got to have some heat in there."

We rigged up a suit of heavy underwear, wrapped with resistance wire with a rheostat in series. I experimented with it, found it satisfactory and got back into the Look-See. We tied my underwear circuit in with the headlamp and I was off again.

Getting inside was simple enough. I turned the headlamp from side to side, examining a mess of broken machinery and collapsed bulkheads. "Put Carroll on," I said to the talker.

"Yeah, Jake," he said.

"This seems to be an auxiliary engine room of some sort. Did you ever see a blueprint of the ship?"

"Yes. I know my way around pretty well."

"If you weren't so big you could do this job yourself. Well, where do I go? There's a blasted door off a corridor leading aft

and a busted bulkhead leading forward."

"Aft," he said. "And not far. Keep a sharp lookout to starboard. You ought to see an open door."

"Okay. A little tension on the line."

Jenkins broke in. "We don't dare, Jake. Once you're at an angle to us, we'll have to slacken off and hope the line doesn't get fouled on the ragged edges."

"Just how," I asked, "do you expect to get the stuff out, then? Everything's all broken to bits in here. If you can't pull a hauling line taut you'll sure have trouble snaking a grapple through."

"Maybe it's sentimental," Jenkins said, "but I have a little more regard for your safety than that gimmick magnetically attached to the Look-See's hull. We'll have to snake it through even if we have to clear out the broken machinery. But I don't want to take a chance on the hauling line right now. Anyway, go on in and have a look."

"Sheer sentimentality," I said. "But thanks."

I played my keyboard, negotiated the turn and floated down an empty corridor. I saw an open door. I angled the headlamp inside.

And there it was.

Herculium. Stuff of the lost process. Nothing known could penetrate it—neither disintegration rays nor the impulses from the cumbersome atomic reintegrator. That little man with the club foot, Phamign, once processed himself a process and said, "The devil with everybody!" when they tried to find out how he did it. He was offered. Oh, yes, he was offered and offered. And then he died. But before he kicked off he foundried a secret shipload for the third planet of Arcton.

And sent it off on the *Astralot*. So the histories say. I was looking at the greatest fortune perhaps ever assembled in one place. I yelped once.

"It's here. We're in, kids!"

I could hear them cheer. Carroll said, "Start sending it out."

That's when my heart sank. The fortune was in pigs, slick and gray, with beveled edges. My grapple was a tong affair, designed to pick up large rough objects such as crates. It could never hold even one of these pigs. And if it could, it could only take one at a time, which meant a round trip each time for me, to drop it, return to the ship and attach it again.

"I guess we're whipped," I said. I told them what I saw and thought. I could hear a concerted groan. "I'm coming aboard. I'm dropping the grapple. Haul it in."

I released the grapple and began the delicate job of negotiating the corridor backwards, by feel, guesswork and memory. I had a bad time at the turn, but scraped free and let them take over with the winch.

We were a sad quartet on board. Amos T. Grubb put in his two cents.

"If you had listened to me," he began. He stopped, leaving the obvious unsaid.

We were so low nobody even snapped at him. Finally Carroll made a despondent suggestion. "Does anybody know if herculium responds to a magnetic field?"

We leaped at that like hungry hounds. We took the library apart, book by book, and found nothing on it.

"Let's try it, anyway," Jenkins said. "If it doesn't work we're whipped."

I hated to say it, but I had to. "That's no good, boys. I can't get the Look-See inside the treasure room. The corridor's too narrow for a right-angle turn. I can barely squeeze through from that engine room."

That threw everybody into another spin but Jenkins came up with the answer. "The arm on that drill," he said. "We can mount it on the nose on a hinge arrangement. We'll fold it against the shell so it doesn't add to your length, and stick a

control inside."

"More equipment," I said. "There's barely room enough to breathe now. Okay, I'll scrunch a little."

So, a couple of hours later, I was inside the derelict again. I jetted gently to the corridor, swung the nose starboard, eased forward—and stuck. I kicked the nose jets. Nothing happened. I kicked full blast. Metal groaned. I stopped. If I tore the hull, I would cease to have any interest in—anything. I thought of those bodies and gagged.

"I'm stuck," I said. "That big magnet is fouled overhead. Haul away handsomely."

I could feel the gentle tugs, then a sharp *spang!*

"Oh, Lord!" Jenkins' voice whispered.

The line had parted. Well, this seemed to be it. I was wedged firmly, wouldn't blast loose without wrecking my only protection. And the worst of it was I was going to have plenty of time to think about it. There wasn't going to be anything quick about it. It would be a tossup which ran out first, my air or my heat. I would either suffocate or freeze or both. And even if I'd had a knife there wasn't room enough for me to get my arm free and cut my throat.

I cut off the headlight. "Any suggestions," I said and if my voice shook, so what, "will be gratefully received."

"Give me the picture," Carroll said.

"I can't see what the trouble is but it feels like the magnet is hooked on some projection."

"Can you swing either way?"

I tried it, port and starboard. Nothing but groaning metal. "I've got enough power, maybe, to break loose but I'll tear a hole in her. You know what that means."

I could almost feel his shudder. Then he said sharply, "Idiot! I mean me, Jake.

When I threw the juice to that magnet, I might have left the switch on. Try it."

I did and instantly the Look-See swung free. "Saved by the bell," I said and I was almost crying. "Here we go again."

"Thank heavens!" Carroll stammered and I was sure he was blinking. That big gentle giant, that dope.

"If you hadn't thought of that—" I said. "Well, I owe you a drink, fella. Now on my left, ladies and gentlemen, we have that colossal treasure of the ages, millions and millions in little gray pigs. Watch closely, now. See how I lower the arm of the magnet. Ah, contact. Now see how I—"

I broke off. I was afraid to flip the switch. What if the magnet wouldn't pick it up?

"Well?" Cap demanded.

"All right. I got scared. This is it."

I flipped the switch. Nothing changed. The magnet was in contact with about six pigs. I lifted it.

I couldn't believe it, even though I saw it. Almost a hundred bars—ninety-five, we counted later—clung to my magnet. Of course, they were weightless here and that accounted for it. But it was startling.

I felt wrung out. I was sweating all over. "It's—it's okay," I whispered.

The rest was routine. Under pneumatic power I backed and filled and I dodged the overhead magnetic trap by extending the arm ahead of me. There was a tendency for the load to slip to one side or the other, responding to the call of magnetism, but I got so I could almost play tunes on my buttons, nudging the nose each time the magnetic field drew it toward one wall or the other.

I refused to think about Grubb and his threats. He had us by the short hair and maybe he could even take our treasure. We had broken the contract and in this business, where fulfilling contracts often means saving lives and valuable property, penalties are fantastic. And rightly so.

We finally got the whole load aboard, distributed so the weight wouldn't be concentrated in a small space and maybe drop through the hull when we hit gravity. Cap, Jenkins, Carroll and I each held onto one pig. For sentiment. We went into conference.

Pat got us under way and we looked at Grubb.

"What are we going to do with him?" Jenkins queried.

"Are you still planning to sue?" I asked.

"Of course not," he said sweetly. It sounded strange, coming from him.

I looked at him sharply and saw the joker. That sweetness was a mask, a very thin mask for what lay underneath. You could see it smoldering in his eyes.

"Just what do you mean by that?" I asked.

"It's very simple," he said happily. "I put up the money for this trip. I bought equipment you didn't have and couldn't buy. If it hadn't been for me you wouldn't be here and you wouldn't have a treasure aboard. Am I correct?"

"Mmmm, yes," Cap admitted. "But I see what you're getting at, and it won't work."

"But it will," Grubb chortled. "By intersellar law monetary gains of a chartered ship—aside from purely contractual gains—belong to the charter holder. Any accidental increase in the expedition accrues to me."

I looked at Cap and I guess the same thing was in my eyes as in his—deep, bleak despair. The joker—and what a joker. I had darned near killed myself for this.

Nobody spoke for a long time. Not that we had complete silence. Grubb's chuckles broke that.

Pat turned away from the board. "I asked you before—let me handle the little rat."

"Wait," Cap said. "Let me think."

"Why?" Jenkins asked. "We've got to kill him. We have no choice."

"And how would we explain it?" Cap asked.

Grubb seemed more amused than anything else. "Yes, how?" he asked pleasantly. "The story will help pass the time until I come into my—ah, inheritance."

"*I* know," Jenkins said suddenly. "It's no problem. We put him in the *Astralot.* What's one more body among others? We simply shove him through the lock, and then nudge his body aboard with the Look-See."

"Somebody else, not me," I said. "I've seen bodies that—"

"That doesn't explain his absence," Cap objected.

Grubb's grin got a trifle uncertain. His eyes flickered between Jenkins and Cap.

"It's simple," Jenkins went on. "We *did* find a derelict. We *did* salvage her cargo with makeshift equipment. Poor Mr. Grubb, whom we loved like a brother, got too anxious and exposed himself to space."

"He went aboard first, see, and tried to get out of the Look-See. When we hauled it back aboard his body snagged on something, and we were unable to recover it." He addressed an imaginary board of inquiry.

"And, gentlemen, we shall be happy to prove this—*if* we can find the derelict." His voice became its normal biting self again. "And, of course, if anybody insisted on that, well, the *Astralot* would simply have vanished again. We'll phony up the data on our log about the location of the derelict and nobody would ever be able to find her."

Grubb wasn't grinning at all now. He was kind of white.

"I won't phony up my log," Cap said. "No need to, anyway. We can actually stick him on a snag. You've got something, Jenkins."

"Good Lord, men!" Grubb quavered. "You can't—"

"Shut up!" Pat snarled. "Want I should put him in the airlock, Cap?"

Cap began to grin. "No. No need. Look, Grubb, your status on board is as a passenger. You didn't need to come along and in a sense you paid your way. The Board might award you an interest in the treasure but I don't think it would be very big after we tell how you tried to thwart us and described your sweet disposition. Passengers, you well know, have no interest in accidental gains, as you call them."

Grubb had listened to the first part of Cap's speech but I don't think he heard a word after the first "passenger." He gazed wonderingly at Cap and his eyes were glazed.

"You—you could have done it," he whispered. "You could have got away with it." He was silent for a moment, then shuddered. His voice had its natural rasp when he spoke again. "I suppose an apology is in order?"

"From whom?" Cap growled.

"Me, of course," Grubb snapped. "For being greedy. I—I do apologize, gentlemen. And I thank you, Captain Lane, for—I know it sounds melodramatic, but it's true—for saving my life."

"Whatever that's worth," Jenkins said in disgust.

"Thank you," Grubb said acidly. "But I am going to sue you, nonetheless, as a matter of principle."

We were shocked, all right, but not surprised. It was typical Grubb. And you kind of had to hand it to the little guy. He had courage, to stick to his principles when he knew we could dispose of him neatly.

"But on what grounds?" Jenkins asked in a puzzled voice.

"Breach of the Pluto contract!"

"Ain't we headed for Pluto now?" Jenkins asked. "All I have to do is put that drill back together."

"You can't," Grubb said, as if he were talking to a three-year-old. "That is a secret known only to Valadian engineers. Didn't you ever hear of the Valadian monopoly?"

"Yeah, but *my* grandfather invented the Valadian drill," Jenkins drawled.

Grubb was neither pleased nor displeased. "Very well," he rasped. "I—" He looked helplessly at us and, for the first time, sadly. "I cannot prosecute."

I felt sorry for him. He was so determined to be nasty and it meant an awful lot to him. You could see that just by his expression. Then, too, I like a fighter. The others were now looking at him with more admiration than amusement.

"Mr. Grubb," I said, "A guy who goes all out like you do really deserves something for a tough battle. Here, I'm going to give you this pig. Booby prize." I pushed it toward him.

"No, Jake," he said with a faint grin. "I'm just a passenger, remember? And"— he rasped in his old manner—"I'm not a booby!"

He pushed the pig back at me, hard. It had no weight but it had plenty of momentum. I tried to duck and the last I remember was Pat's, "Oh, Lord! Right on the button again!"

THE ADVENTURE CONTINUES

The Space Salvage team rescues the crew of a ship trapped on a magnetic asteroid. Jake falls for a gorgeous red-headed space captain... and discovers she's the daughter of his greatest rival. Ninety-seven people face suffocation if Space Salvage can't free them from a vast lake of slime. A ship with fissionable explosives and a dead crew heads for a catastrophic crash-landing. All this, *and* they must fight pirates for a world-changing secret.

Space Salvage, Inc.

coming August 22 to the THRILLING WONDER VINTAGE line of novels

www.thrillingwonderstories.com

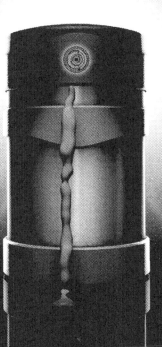

a can of PAINT

BASED ON THE SHORT STORY BY A.E. VAN VOGT

"A perfect example of how to mount an impressive and sleek production for very little money."
—Guillermo del Toro—
(Director, PAN'S LABRYNTH, HELLBOY)

"No film brings the feeling of the golden age of science fiction lierature to the screen better."
—Foster on Film—

"I'm sure A.E. van Vogt himself would have been mesmerized by this superb presentation of his tale."
—Steven-Elliot Altman—
(bestselling author of DEPRIVERS)

—WINNER—

Best SF Short

Shriekfest
Shockerfest
OC Film Fest

Best Special Effects

L.A. Independent Short
Film Festival

Best Score

California Independent
Film Festival

See the trailer and buy the DVD at
www.thrillingwonderstories.com

ENGLOMERATE PRODUCTIONS PRESENTS A MAKE BELIEVE MEDIA USA PRODUCTION AARON ROBSON JEAN FRANZBLAU "A CAN OF PAINT" BASED ON THE SHORT STORY BY A.E. VAN VOGT MUSIC BY GORDY HAAB PRODUCTION DESIGNER NICK LOIZIDES EDITOR ROBI MICHAEL VISUAL EFFECTS SUPERVISOR THOMAS MARINELLO DIRECTOR OF PHOTOGRAPHY NICK LOIZIDES SPECIAL MAKEUP EFFECTS JAMES LACEY EXECUTIVE PRODUCER WINSTON ENGLE SCREENPLAY BY WINSTON ENGLE PRODUCED BY THOMAS SAMMON DIRECTED BY ROBI MICHAEL

ENGLOMERATE PRODUCTIONS

Make Believe

INVISIBLE FILMS

DOLBY DIGITAL

FARTHEST

BY GEOFFREY A. LANDIS

Illustrated by Lawrence Kim

At ten million miles an hour, *Orpheus* fell out of infinity toward the enigma.

Looking for Leah, I found Tally in the electronics shop. Her face was covered with a green plastic light shield, and she had an omniblaster taken apart on the workbench. She prodded at its guts with an oscilloscope probe. I was fascinated; I'd never seen a blaster taken apart before. I didn't even know you could take one apart—I'd always thought that they came in one piece.

"What'cha doing, Tal?"

She didn't look up. "Stand out of the beam path, please."

I thought I was out of it, but I stepped backward a pace anyway.

"What does it look like I'm doing, Tinkerman? I'm tuning up this blaster, that's what. Shade your eyes."

I shut my eyes, but then opened them just a slit so I could see what she was doing. She poked something inside, and a

HORIEONS

thin bright stream of purple-pink light sprayed out of the nozzle. I squeezed my eyes tight, and watched the afterimage of the flash fade from a deep sea green to a faint swatch of darkness.

A moment later she grunted. "You can open your eyes now."

I opened them cautiously. Green dazzle still flashed across my visual field. "I didn't know that omniblasters went out of tune."

"Shows how much you know." She prodded further into the disassembled gun.

Looking at it carefully, I could pick out what must be the main crystal. It looked like a chunk of dark glass wrapped up in cottony white insulation, with cryo lines sticking out at odd angles.

"They don't," she said, looking sidewise at the oscilloscope trace while making an infinitesimal adjustment with a plastic screwdriver. "The factory tunes them, and you're not supposed to mess with it. But I don't like depending on a weapon that I haven't personally checked tuning and focus on. Do you? That last little difference between factory-tuned and hand-tuned could be the critical shot that'll save my ass. Yours, too, white boy.

Close your eyes again, please."

I squeezed them tightly shut this time, and the flash barely leaked in past my eyelids.

Tally grunted again. "Better. So what brings you down here, anyway? You hot-shot scientists suddenly decide it's time to rub shoulders with us hoi polloi?"

I looked around. Hotshot scientist? She couldn't mean me; I was a pretty-good technician and not too bad as a backup pilot, but no kind of scientist.

"Or maybe you dumped that honky bitch and decided to go looking for a real woman?" She looked up and grinned, white teeth gleaming against beer-bottle dark skin. She was good looking, sexy as a tiger in her own compact and well-mus-cled way, but not for me.

"Not a chance, Tally."

She shook her head. "Don't I know it. Well, it's your life. Any time you wanna change your ways, I'm not hard to find, kid. I'll make you forget her in a hurry."

I nodded my head and smiled. "I know you too well, Tally. Why, I bet when you make it with a guy, you wear three blasters and fourteen pounds of grenades, just in case some misdirected army tries to take you out while you're distracted."

"Maybe I do." She laughed. "Any time you want to find out, kid, I keep my cubie door unlocked. But open the door real slow, right? Don't want to make a mistake and perforate your skinny white ass. Shield your eyes, please."

I complied, and the darkness behind my eyelids flashed pink-white for a moment.

"Okay, it's done."

I opened my eyes, and watched her put the omniblaster together.

"Want me to do yours?"

"Mine? I haven't even checked one out of the weapons locker. Why, do you think I'm going to need one out here, ten billion kilometers from nowhere?"

"Who knows? Better safe than sorry, that's what I figure. But, really, what brings you down here, Tinkerman? You looking for me?"

I wasn't, actually, but was too polite to say so. "We just got in range for the long-focus cameras. I thought you might want to see."

"Oh, yeah? Damn right I do. Why didn't you say so right away?" She lifted her jumper and dropped the just-tuned blaster into a holster skin-taped under her left breast. In the brief flash of skin, I saw another holstered blaster and sheaths for two knives. For Tally, paranoia was a way of life. She caught me looking. "You like what you see, white boy? I might give out free samples if you ask nice."

"Maybe later." We both knew that later would never come, but the banter was a game Tally enjoyed playing. We'd played it for years, ever since Leah and I had first met Tally Okumba. She'd been the body-guard for an expedition to the ruins of old Los Angeles. Hardly anything lived in OLA any more, but the things that did were tough, fast, and clever. And hungry. None of them, however, proved to be as tough, fast, or clever as Tally. Not by half. The funny thing was that Leah and Tally had liked each other instantly. Leah Hamakawa respected competence in any field, and Tally found Leah's intelligence infinitely amusing. They got along so well that most of the time I felt like I was in the way. But it was certain that Tally's passes at me would never go farther than words, even though Leah occasionally hinted that she would have no objections if I did de-cide to find another romantic interest.

As if I could.

We found Leah, of course, already in the science briefing room, with Sailor sitting on her shoulder. Sailor

T. Bird was a dingy-yellow cockatiel with a ruff of pink feathers behind his ears and a salacious vocabulary. Over long voyages, one of the amusements of the crew was teaching him new phrases. He cocked his head to look at us when we came in, but he didn't say anything. Leah nodded toward the screen. "Just look at it," she whispered.

On the screen, the long-range photograph of the enigma was projected, looking like a lumpy, faceted ball made of spare parts from an armadillo.

"The scale of the photograph is deceptive," the head astrophysicist said. "The object is nearly a quarter of a light-second across."

I whistled softly. The thing was *big*, capital B big. Sitting next to it, the Earth would look like a pea next to a grapefruit. A lumpy, mutated grapefruit.

Sailor cocked his head at my whistle—whistling was his favorite game—and said, "Hey, sailor, wanna show a girl a good time?" Tally reached out to scratch him behind the neck feathers, and he bent his head forward and chirruped softly.

"So why wasn't it discovered from Earth?" somebody asked.

"Too dark. The picture we're looking at was taken with reflected starlight, brightened by a factor of ten million with image enhancers. You'd never be able to see it from Earth, not even with the orbital telescopes. Too dim."

"Any ideas as to what it is?"

"One thing for sure," Tally said, still scratching Sailor with one hand. "It's an artifact, all right."

"Impossible!" said Leah. "Look at the size of it. It couldn't possibly be artificial. Not something that big."

Tally shook her head. "It's big and it's artificial. And one more thing. Dangerous." She smiled. "Deadly."

The enigma had been discovered by gravity. Starprobes crossing the great dark a light-week past Pluto were being nudged off course. Barely enough to warrant a mid-course correction, but consistently enough for the trajectory computers back home to notice. They figured it for the gravitational pull of a subjovian, a frozen planet wandering a lonely path far from any sun. They calculated where the object had to be, and sent a ship—*Odysseus*—with a crew of three to investigate.

The day before *Odysseus* was to have made contact, the lasercast status reports fell silent. Two weeks later the carrier wave and telemetry resumed, but no reports. Groundside tracked *Odysseus* as it came into the system, and intercepted it well outside the orbit of Jupiter. The onboard computer memories were blank; all the science logs, erased. Of the three explorers, only one returned. He was insane. Now it was our turn.

Orpheus was a high-thrust research ship, seven times as big as *Odysseus,* twice as fast, with three fusion engines capable of five gees for as long as the crew could stand it. We were armed to the superstructure, bristling with sensors from microwave to gamma telescopes, and staffed with a crew of scientists, technicians, pilots, psychologists, and a survival specialist, ready for anything.

Or so we hoped.

Orpheus decelerated at a gee and a half. Overgee makes me feel clumsy, stupid, and perpetually tired, like the last stage of drunkenness, when you've lost the veneer of happiness and are left feeling weak and slightly sick. In overgee you have to watch your actions, think out each motion as precisely and carefully as a drunkard's.

Sex in overgee is no advertisement for spaceflight—but it beats no sex at all. The trick is, you have to go slow. Now if I could convince Leah....

It was free time, off shift. She was lying on her side on our shared bunk, the curves of her shoulder and hips casually seductive even under the shapeless jumpsuit. I sat down on the bunk and, taking infinite care, started to gently knead her shoulders.

"What do you think it is?" she said.

"Uh, a backrub?"

"No!" She laughed. "The... enigma. You think it's an artifact, too?"

"What do you think?" I moved down her back, feeling her spine like a string of carved wooden beads, felt the enigma of her shoulderblades, the perfection of her ribs.

"I don't think it's artificial." She shook her head, lazily, and rolled over onto her stomach. Her eyes were half-closed, misty in thought. I straddled her, weight on my knees, and continued rubbing. "Something funny," she said, speaking mostly to the pillow. "No radar reflection. Not millimeter band, not microwave, none. We should be close enough to get some signal. And another thing. We're taking photos all the way in, trying to synthesize a 3-D composite, but it isn't working. It's as if no two photos are of the same thing, like it's changing shape every time we take another picture."

I carefully stretched myself down on the bunk beside her, reached around and slid down her zipper with one hand while continuing to caress her back with the other. "Tell me more," I said softly and slid the jumpsuit off her shoulder. The enigma I was interested in was closer at hand, and had a name, but was no less mysterious to me for that. As mysterious as my own emotions, unpredictable but impossible to ignore.

"I don't think we're seeing it at all," she said. "What we see isn't what's really

there. It's hiding from us, Tinkerman."

I kissed her shoulder.

"It's nothing we've ever seen before. It's an enigma, all right. But I'll find it out. I'll strip it bare, and steal its secrets."

Leah Hamakawa had attracted me and fascinated me since the day I first saw her. As for her—I don't know. Often it seemed that she tolerated me with an offhand amusement, like she might tolerate a stray puppy who followed her home and cried pitifully on her porch. I wasn't her intellectual equal, not by half. I could be her pilot and her handyman: nothing she couldn't do herself if she put her mind to it, but someone convenient to have around.

I'd been following her, loving her, for so long I no longer even remembered why, or if what I followed was her, or just some image of my own dreams.

Someday, I fear, she would wander off, attracted by some mystery to be explained or scientific anomaly to be investigated, and barely even notice my absence; perhaps, at best, missing me in some vague way.

But not yet. In our shared cabin, in that high gravity, thinking out each motion carefully as any drunkard, I laid down beside her and slowly slid between her legs, and forgot about the future, about the past, forgot about everything but the feel, the smell, the texture and softness and warmth of her, until at last I think that even she forgot herself for a little bit, and existed only with me in the here and now.

Half a trillion kilometers from home, *Orpheus* was a cluster of twelve identical spheres held in a circle by cobwebs of beryllium-titanium, with a long slender cylinder in the center. Attached to this were the three small space-transfer vehicles for ferrying supplies ship to ship, each an open beryllium-alloy geodetic trusswork, a jungle-gym with small atomic-hydrogen rockets. The somewhat larger surface lander, *Eurydice,* was held in a cradle nestled against the core. Extending from the back of *Orpheus* was a longer truss, clustered with dropaway hydrogen balloon-tanks like fat jellyfish caught in a fishnet. At the farthest end were the bumpy donuts of the three fusion engines. The fusion flames were transparent, but shoved the ship with a firm, invisible hand. The whole thing was irregularly cluttered with telescopes, clusters of antennae, radar dishes, plasma probes, lasers, and other scientific instruments.

We approached the enigma, and the closer we got, the stranger it became. It no longer showed on photographs as an object a quarter light-second across; in fact, it barely showed at all.

Orpheus's fly-by was half a million kilometers closest approach, ten times farther than doomed *Odysseus's* first pass. A year in transit, and the captain wanted to scope out the beast before committing to anything closer.

I joined Tally and Leah in the number-three science pod. Gradient Forward gravitometer, magnetometer, ion density and species, spectroscopy in a hundred bands; Leah's restless attention flicked from instrument to instrument. She watched the instruments with the gaze of a lover, with all the attention she had never given me, seeing a mystery to be unveiled. Tally was just as intense, fixing on one instrument for a long moment, then suddenly shifting to another, watching it as she would keep an eye on an enemy, or an unknown danger to be appraised and conquered.

Neither paid attention to me.

Sailor hopped up to perch on my shoulder, and I idly reached up to scratch him behind his neck feathers.

I looked out. I seemed to be the only one looking directly out the porthole, toward the enigma itself, instead of its digital reflection. In the porthole the enigma was invisible, an empty space in blackness. All around were stars: Gemini, the Pleiades like scattered diamonds, the Hyades like a sprinkling of fairy dust, twinkling romantically.

I blinked. Without an atmosphere, stars do not twinkle. I looked again. Still twinkling.

"Leah? Are we in atmosphere?"

Her eyes barely flicked to the panel. "No."

"You crazy, white boy?" Tally asked. "You know this is no atmosphere ship. Ion density gets high, Captain Shen aims us outta here right quick, count on it."

I kept silent, looking out. The stars were definitely twinkling. It was pretty, but I didn't like it. I looked back toward the enigma.

"Closest pass in ten seconds," said Leah.

And suddenly I saw it, in the very center of the enigmatic black, the one thing that shouldn't, couldn't be there: a planet. Not a subjovian, dark and frozen half a trillion kilometers from the sun, but a world with fluffy white clouds and green continents and blue oceans, inviting and impossible.

"Closest pass, *now.*"

The planet whipped past, shrank to a distant blue pinprick, and vanished.

Even if a frozen, desolate planet were there, it would be invisible in the starlit darkness between the stars, with no sunlight to illuminate it. It could not possibly be visible with the naked eye.

What we're seeing on the instruments may not be what's really there, Leah had said.

"A planet," I said, but nobody was listening. "A planet."

The fusion engines stopped *Orpheus* ten million kilometers from the enigma, and shut down, waiting. *Orpheus* would drift slowly toward the enigma, but at a distance of half a light-minute, the pull was small. It would be days before a noticeable motion would build up.

The enigma stood below us: invisible, yet omnipresent.

The ship was in free fall, and everybody but the duty pilot was in the recreation and auditorium pod for the science conference.

Except for me, and—perhaps—Sailor, no one else had seen the planet. Or, if they had, they were keeping quiet about it. In fact, no two of the instruments had seen the same thing. There was something there, but they couldn't tell what it was. It didn't seem to have a defined surface, didn't reflect radar, didn't respond to radiation probes of any sort—lasers through pulsed x-rays. Two small probes sent on a closer fly-by returned, in perfect condition, but with blank electronics. The only thing that they agreed on was the gravity: a perfectly symmetrical, perfectly spherical gravitational field, with no spherical harmonics, equatorial bulge, or mascons of any sort. A spectacularly bland field, Leah concluded.

The surprise, though, was from the communications crew. The uplink from Earth was gone. Stranger still, they had detected a reflection of our own transmissions, echoing from empty space. "If you integrate the intensity of the reflected signal," said the comm officer, "allowing for the ship's motion and assuming a Gaussian backscatter cone, the total intensity is very nearly the same as the intensity of the signal beam."

"Which means?"

"Our signal isn't getting home."

The discussion continued, everybody talking at once. "An artifact." "A black hole." "A new type of subjovian." Sailor hopped from shoulder to shoulder, whistling and chattering, quite plainly enjoying the hubbub.

Leah shook her head, and her short dark hair fanned out around her face. In free-fall her body rotated in reverse, a tiny dance. "No. Something—strange."

"In a moment," said Captain Shen, "I will make a decision as to how, or if, to proceed." In an instant the hubbub quieted as the crew turned to listen. He was a short oriental man, with a fringe of white hair around his otherwise bald head, and an identical fringe of beard around his chin, both trimmed to little more than stubble. Inscrutable he was not—he joked and played ZG volleyball with the rest of the crew, and bunked with the second pilot, Dale Ten Eyck—but in matters concerning Orpheus, once he made his decision, he would not be swayed.

"This ship is not a democracy," he said. "However, before I make any decisions, I will listen to any opinions or suggestions this group may care to offer. We can start back now. Sooner or later we will clear this echo-sphere—"

"About a week by my guess, captain," said the comm officer.

The Captain nodded. "Thank you, Mr. Lawson. At that point we will be able to send our data back. This will be a noteworthy achievement, and I think at that point we could declare the main scientific objective of the mission accomplished. Alternatively, we can remain here and try to learn what we can. Opinions?"

"Stay."

"If we go, nobody will believe us. We gotta see this through."

"Stay."

"Make another fly-by, this time close."

"Hell yes, we're nowhere near done."

"Another year, to report nothing? Let's

get the job done first."

"Very good," said the captain. "I will take your opinions into account. Dr. Hamakawa? You had something to add?"

Leah nodded. "Yes. We should go back, but not a fly-by. There's something there. I propose we should make a landing."

The captain didn't even blink. "And which piece of data makes you believe that there's a surface we can land on?"

"Individually? None. But together… yes. Something is distorting our sensors, so there must be *something* there. We know it has gravity; that's one thing it can't disguise. It's a planet-sized object. If it were a black hole, it would be the size of a golf ball, impossible to see. It's not a star. Even a brown dwarf would be visible in the IR from Earth. Something strange. Something very strange. But long odds, way long odds, that it's got a surface. And we won't find out until we go there."

"And the proof, Dr. Hamakawa?"

"Call it gestalt." She shrugged. "Or intuition. If that's not proof, all I can say is, the proof is on the surface."

The captain nodded. "Very well, Dr. Hamakawa. Make me a plan for landing." There was a bustle of noise, and Captain Shen raised a hand for silence. "I haven't made a decision yet. Make me a plan, Dr. Hamakawa. I won't endanger this ship under any possible circumstances, and I won't bring it closer than half a million kilometers to the anomaly. Make me a plan that allows for all possibilities, even the ones that you have dismissed as impossible." He spun on his axis. "I'll be waiting for you at twenty-two hundred hours, shift-one time. Carry on."

The trajectory Leah picked was an unusual one: a constant-thrust elliptical epicycloid. It was known in theory, but as a pilot, I'd never heard of anyone actually flying such an odd curve before. *Orpheus* would drop the lander, *Eurydice,* into a highly elliptical orbit. As *Eurydice's* orbit approaches periapsis— the lowest point—it ignites its engines and simultaneously begins to rotate at a slow, constant velocity: a ponderous, fiery pinwheel. The rotating thrust vector successively slows the orbital motion, drops *Eurydice* toward the hypothetical surface, then slows and stops the descent. For a moment *Eurydice* hovers, thrust exactly countering gravity. As it continues to slowly rotate it tips slightly, accelerates off to the side, and thrusts back into orbit.

Leah explained the advantage of this maneuver: once started, it requires no changes in thrust or rotation to complete. As long as the engines themselves work, even if the navigation and guidance electronics have failed completely, *Eurydice* still safely returns to orbit.

Eurydice would only hover, not land. Captain Shen would not let Leah risk *Eurydice* on a landing, no matter how brief, and so Leah came up with an alternative plan.

The hover point was calculated as the one-gee gravitational contour. Half the crew volunteered; Leah picked Tally and me for her landing party. We each had one of the three space-transfer vehicles, crammed with equipment, strapped to the outside of *Eurydice*. We were to visually verify that the enigma had a surface—if it *did* have a surface—in the brief moment that *Eurydice* hovered. The decision would have to be made as an on-site judgment. If it looked landable, we would blow our transfer vehicles free of *Eurydice* at the hover point and drop down.

The same maneuver in reverse would be used to pick us up.

"It's crazy," said Tally, shaking her head. "I like it."

"It'll work," said Leah. "The enigma is

odd, but we know that the laws of gravity still work."

"Count me in," said Tally. "When do we do it?"

In Tally's spartan quarters is a statue of the Buddha, hand-carved out of rosewood. Hers is not the fat, smiling Buddha sold behind the counters of expensive Chinese restaurants, but a slender man with ropy muscles sitting crosslegged, his eyes closed, his long staff resting casually across his lap. I have never heard Tally mention the statue, or even glance toward it, but the small statue has traveled everywhere with her, and if she is in a place where there are flowers to be found, there will always be a single fresh flower set carefully before it. It seems out of place, unless one recalls the traditions of the warrior monks.

I have never asked.

Perhaps, floating alone in her transfer vehicle strapped to *Eurydice,* waiting for the unknowable, she prayed. I know I did. I am sure that Leah did not. *Eurydice's* drive turned on, and slowly built up thrust.

Silence punctuated by concise bursts of radio instructions. Nothing was visible below, not even blackness, but I had a sense that we were suspended motionless, and something huge was coming toward us at incredible velocity. I sat in a web seat inside a tiny bubble canopy attached to the open framework of the transfer vehicle, which was itself held to the solid mass of *Eurydice* by polymer straps that didn't look strong enough to hold up a good-sized fish. The transfer vehicles, which had never been designed to be cargo carriers, had been loaded to the limit. Every piece of equipment that any member of the crew had thought we could conceivably need was jammed into one or another of the mesh carriers strapped to

every surface of the vehicles, making the ungainly t-vehicles even more lumpy and asymmetrical.

I caught my breath and looked down again, willing my eyes to focus. Something was below me, something that my brain refused to focus on. Concentrate on one tiny part. An edge. Follow the edge, around, to... a circle? A circle.

Suddenly it popped into focus for me, not just one circle, but thousands, millions; a surface of perfect, sharp-edged circles. Each circle was tangent to another circle at every point along the circumference, myriads of circles so tiny as to be nearly points, others so large that they disappeared into perspective at the mathematically-sharp vanishing point, and every size between. No circle overlapped any other. Fractal circles.

It was so clearly defined that it was completely impossible that I could have failed to see it moments before.

Eurydice fell, and rotated as she fell, the plasma of the fusion exhaust drawing a pencil of insubstantial shimmer across the fractal landscape.

And inside the circles, I suddenly saw more circles. It resolved into layers of circles, a surface with myriad holes of all sizes, under which was another surface with holes, underneath which... a carved Chinese ball with a million ivory shells, except that I could now see that the shells were not ivory, but spectroscopically pure shades that shifted as we moved. The circles expanded to swallow us as *Eurydice* dropped towards them. Did the pilot see the same thing? Did Leah?

The surface was in such crystalline sharp focus that it could have been a centimeter away or a thousand kilometers. The laser altimeter and the landing radar both showed nothing but vacuum under me; the outside camera showed only snow. I felt the double jolt as Tally and

Leah cut free of *Eurydice* at almost the same instant. We were at the cusp of the cycloid, and for an instant *Eurydice* hovered motionless. Before I could think it over, I hit the release and joined them.

Pyrotechnic charges severed the polymer straps holding my transfer vehicle to *Eurydice* and blew it free. The t-vehicle, which I had never thought to name, started to tumble for an instant. Before I could grab the manual controls, the gyros kicked in. My engine stuttered to life and the autopilot pushed the vehicle away from *Eurydice* and her invisible, deadly exhaust. *Eurydice* veered over sideways and accelerated away, dwindling into a tiny, ascending speck, and then I was suspended alone over a frightening fractal vastness.

"Separation," I said into my radio, but my words were swallowed into the echoless deep.

I suddenly realized that the fractal surface had relief, staggering depths and dizzying heights. I began to wonder how I could make a safe landing on a surface which neither my altimeter nor my radar could find, a surface which could be any distance below, when that surface bumped up under me and I was down.

After a minute or two I saw Tally's vehicle hovering, the exhaust flickering yellow and blue. My heart skipped for a second. Flickering exhaust was a bad symptom; the jet of a properly functioning atomic-hydrogen rocket should be perfectly invisible. Her vehicle slid sideways, skittered over to a flat spot near my vehicle, and shut down without incident. I released my breath.

I went back to staring at my instruments. If they were correct, we were in atmosphere, although I couldn't remember any sign of airflow when I was descending. But I ran the mass spec, and it showed oxygen, nitrogen, argon, carbon dioxide—all at the right pressure and in the right proportions, even a trace of water vapor. As if this place were made for us. Waiting for us.

I turned off cabin life-support and opened the valve to equalize cabin pressure with the outside, but didn't crack my suit. There was no rush of cabin air out the pressure vent, and no red lights flashed on in the circuits monitoring cabin atmosphere to indicate a leak to vacuum. I looked away, and then suddenly looked back. Something had moved. A sudden, irrational fear clutched my stomach. I took a deep, deliberate breath, and let it out slowly. Calm. I stared at the panel for a moment, then caught a flash of yellow flicker behind the panel. I bent my head down to look. In the tangle of wires behind the panel, a familiar pair of beady black eyes stared back at me.

I offered a finger, and the bird looked at it dubiously. "Might as well come out and enjoy the view, Sailor," I said. "You came this far, might as well see the sights."

"Girls just wanna have fun," Sailor complained, and stepped gingerly onto my gloved finger. I put him on the top of the panel. He shouldn't have been here. He didn't belong to anybody in particular; Sailor was the ship's bird and wandered freely about *Orpheus'* crew space, but he still shouldn't have been on the lander. He must have snuck in after the techs finished the preflight inspection, while we were still in the pilot's briefing. "You're in big trouble, fella," I told him.

"Trouble is my middle name," he agreed solemnly, and ducked his head to preen his chest feathers. He didn't seem to have the slightest interest in the strange landscape outside. "I'm looking for a good time, sailor, how about you?"

I contemplated Sailor as I watched Tally deploy a habitation balloon from her vehicle. He seemed fine, breathing the air of the enigma with no sign of ill effects. When the hab was inflated, I came down the ladder and walked over. Gravity felt right. Although I'd neglected to make a measurement, I was sure it couldn't be more than a percent or two away from one gee, and it felt a lot closer than that.

In a few minutes Leah approached from the other direction. I hesitated a long time, watching her walk up, then made the decision. If the cockatiel could breathe it, so could I. I vented my suit to ambient and took my helmet off. The air was cool and clean.

"That was one stupid move, boy," Tally greeted me, when I entered the inflated habitation bubble. "You suicidal, or just been paying no attention to your instruments at all?"

"Said it was okay to breathe."

She looked surprised, and turned to her own set of instrumentation. "Son of a fox. I'm sure I checked a minute ago."

"It was hard vacuum when we landed," said Leah, just entering the bubble. She straightened up, took off her helmet and shook out her hair. "Then it changed. This environment is just about perfect sea-level Earth normal. Have any of you looked up?"

I did. Through the transparent bubble, the sky was a pale cloudless blue.

"While we were descending, the sky was no color at all," Leah said, slowly. "It was fascinating. Not black, not even gray, but completely absent of color. And now—when we weren't watching—it changed. For us."

"You seem to have a malf on your main engine, Tally," I said. "Your exhaust was flickering."

"Yeah. I had engine warning lights flashing all over the place just before touchdown. Nothing I could do about it except land, though."

"I'll do a diagnostic on it."

"Right." Tally checked the charge on her two omniblasters. In addition to these, she was fielding a large sample pack and a smaller carryall pack. A pair of radios and an inertial navigation log, which would locate her position relative to her landing vehicle regardless of how far she traveled, dangled on her belt. I knew she had other weapons hidden away in the packs and elsewhere. "You can go back to your vehicles if you need to check instruments there," she said abruptly, "but don't go any farther than that. Keep your suits on at all times. Assume that the environment could change back to vacuum at any instant. Keep a watch at all times. Got that?"

"Why?" I asked.

She went back into her t-vehicle and came out with a projectile gun strapped across her back. "It looks like we were expected. I'm going to scout around to find out if our welcome is a friendly one. Don't go exploring."

I watched her walk away. It seemed to me that she vanished over the horizon only a few moments after she started walking, but perhaps I was too wound up to notice the time passing. When I looked back, Leah was already cycling through the bubble's tiny airlock. I watched as she returned to her t-vehicle and began taking more measurements. There seemed something odd about the way she walked, and after a moment I realized that her feet never quite seemed to touch the surface. The fractal nature of the surface must extend to microscopic scale, with imperceptible crinkles smaller than the wavelength of light, packed densely enough to support her weight, insubstantial enough to be completely invisible.

I walked back to my own lander and fetched Sailor.

"There's a thousand things paradoxical

about this place," Leah said when I returned. She was standing by the bubble, looking out into the perfect, cloudless sky.

I nodded. I had my suit sealed again, obedient to Tally's order, but I gestured to Sailor, who sat on my shoulder breathing the atmosphere and chattering softly to himself with no concern at all.

"No, the fact that we can breathe the air is the least among them. Can you see me?"

"Sure," I said.

"You can see the landscape okay?"

"Yes...."

"How? We're half a trillion kilometers away from the sun. What's the light source?"

I looked around. It was true. Though everything was perfectly illuminated, there was no light source at all. No shadows. The light just was.

"Did you get a reading of the local gravitational acceleration before you got out of your vehicle?" she asked.

"Well, no. But I have a pretty good feel for gee. This feels pretty close to one gee."

"Feels that way to me, too. I'd say, no more than one point oh five gee. That's why I was so surprised when I looked at the instrument. Two point three."

"Two point three gees? Impossible. I know what overgee feels like. We're not in anything like two gees."

"Fascinating, isn't it? But think about it. We cut away from *Eurydice* at the one gee level, and went down. Now, what if the meter is right? We've had problems with all the other measurements, but so far everything related to gravity has been dead on."

"But that's im—"

She held up a hand. "Not so fast. The gee level would still *feel* right to us if our time sense has been sped up proportionately."

"Time dilation? But that would take incredible gravity fields...."

"Not exactly time dilation, I don't think. But something similar. I think when we dropped from *Eurydice*, we dropped down a lot more than just a few dozen kilometers. I think that space in this vicinity is highly distorted. I think we *did* drop down to the 2.3 gee contour."

"But that's..." I tried to do a quick calculation in my head. Newtonian gravity... one over *r* squared... square root of 2.3... "Almost nine thousand kilometers? We didn't drop down nine thousand kilometers. That's crazy!"

"Eight thousand eight hundred."

"Leah, we didn't have enough *fuel* to descend nine thousand kilometers against one gee. Much less against overgee."

"Ah, but you're forgetting: space is distorted here. To us, the distance appeared to be less. A *lot* less. And the closer we get to the center of this object—or at least, to the event horizon—the more space is compressed."

"Now we're really having fun," Sailor added, happy to join the conversation.

"Event horizon?" I said. "You think this is a black hole?"

She shook her head. "Quite the opposite. You know better than that. A black hole would slow time down, not speed it up. This is the opposite of a black hole."

"A white hole?"

"No. There's a danger in using such easy buzz-words, Tinkerman. It's not a white hole. Don't try to categorize this with a simple word, you'll only poison your thinking. It's not that simple. Not that simple at all."

"Trouble is my middle name," said Sailor.

Standard procedure was for us to stay in constant radio contact with each other, but we had problems even getting a reliable signal from Tally's locator beacon, and had no luck at all with voice. I started the delicate work of opening up the engine of Tally's t-vehicle, and Leah went to work on science measurements.

It was several hours before Tally returned. She had her helmet dangling back over her shoulder, and had peeled the gloves of her suit back to the elbow fittings, apparently to give her better dexterity with the projectile rifle that she had unslung and now carried loosely at the ready. "You can take off your suits," she said.

"No danger?" Leah inquired.

"Oh, there's danger out there," she said. "Plenty of danger. Just not from the air."

She checked the gun, safetied it, put it down, and then slid the sample pack off her back and sat down crosslegged next to it. Seated, she looked like a black iron statue of some ancient god of death, surrounded with an aura of quiet power. When she spoke again her tone was more relaxed and contemplative. "Not at this level, though," she said. "I do believe that this level is safe. They seem to stay on the lower level."

"Level?" asked Leah.

"They?" I said. "What they?"

"Things," Tally said. "Dangerous things. Not too bad, if you're prepared for them and don't get careless. They're fast and have wicked claws, but they don't seem to be too smart. Got two of them, and the rest kept their distance." She opened her pack. The thing she brought out was the size of a small bobcat, but with longer teeth and six legs. The front legs had fixed, razor-sharp claws. Tally manipulated the hind leg to show how it was jointed. "Note the musculature. See how it hinges? Built for speed and maneuverability. Now, take a look at the center of gravity." She picked it up. "It can

run on the hind four; leaving the front ones free as weapons. That's important; makes it a lot more dangerous than a cat. It doesn't have to pounce to attack, and it can slash out at you at the same time that it's jinking like hell to avoid your shot. Took me two shots to nail this one." She lifted her sleeve to show where the loose thermal-control layer of her suit was torn. "The center paws are dangerous, too."

I was impressed. Anything that made Tally shoot twice was something to be taken seriously indeed. I looked at her face. She was good at keeping her feelings to herself, but from the brightness of her eyes and the almost imperceptible curvature of her lips, I suddenly realized that she was more excited than I had ever seen her. Something wickedly dangerous had attacked her, almost gotten through her defenses, and it made her happy.

"What do you mean by level?" Leah asked.

"I think," said Tally, "that this planet is layered like chinese balls. Shells within shells. I found a large hole"—this would be no problem, such holes were all about us, some of them tiny, others huge—"and lowered myself down."

"What was it like?"

"Just exactly like here. The sky was a slightly darker shade of blue. The rope almost looked like it was hanging from nothing, and the hole I had jumped down was faintly visible like a hazy, perfectly circular cloud. But there were animals down there. More holes, too. To a lower level yet."

"That explains why we had problems with radio contact," said Leah. "Radio propagates well enough along horizontal paths here, but not very well up and down."

"Any ideas about that?" I asked

"I have some thoughts about what's causing it, yes, but if I'm right, there's not much we can do."

"Put a relay at the edge of the hole to boost the signal?"

Leah looked dubious. "We can try it, but it probably won't help."

"How far down was it?" I asked her. I had looked down into the holes, but the strange confusion of depth kept me from judging. It could have been a meter or a kilometer.

"It's odd," said Tally. "From below, it looked like the opening was kilometers up above me, but it couldn't have been more than a meter. I didn't even need the rope—I could jump up."

"Really?" Leah said, suddenly exhibiting interest. "But your head wasn't above the level of the, ah, the ceiling?"

"No. It was very strange."

"Ah," said Leah. "Not the first strange thing." She was silent for a moment and then said, "We have another problem, and now is perhaps a good time to bring it up. The pickup by *Eurydice.*"

"What's the problem there?" asked Tally.

"I need to measure time," Leah said. "If what I'm beginning to suspect is correct, time for us is moving much faster than time on *Eurydice.* Unless we're in sync, *Eurydice* won't be coming down to meet us at the same time we're going up. We've been out of touch—that radio echo effect. I have to do some comparing of clocks to figure out just exactly how much difference in time there is, but I haven't been able to get through to *Orpheus.*"

"And your plan is?" Tally prompted. She didn't seem worried. Survival in hazardous environments was her specialty, but she was willing to leave the physics end to Leah.

"I've got a number of back-up options. Since we can't get a radio signal through to *Orpheus,* the first thing I'm going to do is to launch a rocket probe. I can put a couple of experiments on it that I want to do anyway, and the main payload of the probe will be a radio link to *Orpheus.* I've been looking at the recordings of how fast we lost signal as we descended, and I think that with the power we have available, an altitude gain of a few hundred kilometers measured in our current frame should allow us to squirt a signal to *Orpheus.* We will download the data we have so far to *Orpheus's* main computer, give them some precise information on our surface location—remember, although they know where they dropped us, they can't see the surface, and don't have a guess as to the enigma's rotation rate. Finally, the probe will squirt over our clock readings, and download from *Orpheus* the clock reading from her computer and also the clock reading that *Eurydice* had when she docked."

Tally nodded. "Sounds like a good plan to me. About time we called home anyway."

The rocket probe was a sphere about a meter in diameter filled with ultrapressurized atomic hydrogen, with a tiny catalytic engine on the bottom to convert the atomic-hydrogen fuel into a supersonic jet of diatomic-hydrogen exhaust. Tally said she thought we were safe to go to the lower level as long as we kept alert, and while Leah readied the probe, Tally and I deflated the bubble habitat and moved it down. I didn't see any of Tally's attack animals.

Down here, both the sky and the ground had the fractal pattern of nested circles.

When Leah got her rocket back with the data from *Orpheus,* I breathed a sigh of relief. Now that we had a method for communication, we were in a much better position. Tally went off exploring as soon as the probe hovered down—not without first warning us to keep alert and not to stray until she came back and told us it was safe. Leah vanished into the bubble to work with the data. After a while, I went in and asked her what she was learning.

"I put a precise atomic clock on the probe. Now that it's returned, I've got a direct comparison of time readings. As I expected, the more altitude the rocket got, the slower time passed for it relative to us. The returned clock was 23 minutes behind the control clock I kept here. It's the exact inverse of the gravitational twin paradox. Then, I measured the Doppler shift of the carrier wave from the probe. This gave me a second measure of the time dilation of the probe relative to us, and also of the compression of radial distance. From that we can get the metric of the space we're in."

"And?"

She smiled, her eyes misty and slightly distant. "I'm still thinking about it." She started to put on her suit.

"Where are you going?"

"To look around a bit. This place is fascinating. Everything I see sparks new ideas, new ways to investigate."

"But Tally warned us—"

She picked up an omniblaster and fastened the strap around her shoulder. "I'll be careful."

I watched her walk off. She might have asked if I wanted to go with her, but she hadn't. She had said nothing. I wondered why I was here. Wondered why I followed her.

She vanished over the horizon faster than I thought possible.

Despite Tally's warnings of danger, Leah returned without difficulties. She brought with her a sample bag filled with odd crystals. They were like the landscape, composed of circles within circles, to as small a scale as the eye could see, in shades of spectroscopically pure colors that were different at every angle you viewed them. When she picked one up, her fingers seemed to hover infinitesimally away from its surface, not quite touching it, an illusion of the infinitely recurved fractal surface.

Tally returned much later. Her suit was scraped and, in one place, the fabric was ripped right through to the liner, but she said nothing.

Leah only briefly looked up from her work analyzing the samples she'd found. "No report, Tally?"

"None yet."

Leah only grunted, and turned back to her crystals.

This place, whatever it was, seemed to be illuminated continuously, with no discernible day-night cycles. We must have been up for forty hours straight before Leah called a break. Sailor had long ago found a perch on one of Leah's instruments and tucked his head under his wing, occasionally opening one eye to whistle his annoyance at the uninterrupted light. We were all weary. Leah stripped down to her panties, completely unselfconscious, and designated a spot on the padded floor as her bed. We slept in a pile, Leah and I, innocent as children. Tally slept, too, I think, although it was hard to tell, since she sat upright by the airlock, gun on her lap.

I dreamed that I was walking across the fractal landscape. In the dream it seemed completely normal and comfortable to me. There was a girl from my home town walking with me, someone I'd known all my life, but hadn't thought of in years. I'd played with her as a child, gone to school with her, and now she was grown up. Whenever I glanced over in her direction, she was just out of sight, but we talked as we wandered across the landscape. She pointed out sights as we walked: a cluster of needles a thousand kilometers high, a crystal that trembled and then spoke in some strange alien language when it was touched, marvels that set my mind whirling. My delight amazed her, because it all seemed ordinary to her, since she lived here. It didn't bother me that I couldn't remember her name; I was sure it would come back to me in a moment. Then we sat by a cluster of crystals, on opposite sides, and she asked me about Leah.

"You don't really love her," she said, when I had told her everything. "I think you are in love with love."

"No," I said. I didn't want to think about what she had said. "No. You don't understand."

"Then teach me," she said softly, but before I could decide that there was no possible way to explain the complexity of the way I felt, I awoke to find Tally standing over me with a projectile rifle.

She was in a combat crouch, all her senses alert. "What the hell you think you're doing, boy?" she asked. "You want to go wandering, that's fine, but you carry an omniblaster with you, and you check with me first."

I looked around. The habitat bubble was nowhere to be seen. I was sitting by the cluster of crystals where, in the dream, I had stopped to talk with—what was her name? I'd never known such a girl. I'd been an only child; my parents had moved so frequently that I never kept the friends I made at school for more than a year. But she had been so real— She was all the friends I'd never made. A sudden sense of loss hit me so hard that for a moment I couldn't breathe. She didn't exist. She was my best friend, the only person I felt completely safe confiding in, and she'd never existed.

As an adult I'd kept the pattern I'd learned in childhood, never staying in one place, moving two or three times a year. Homes were temporary, places to put my things for a while, but not to get attached to. I had no real friends; I didn't even know how to make friends. Except for Leah.

But Leah was not the type of friend I could open my heart to. I'd always been too much in awe of her; too afraid that I'd lose her by showing weakness to ever risk showing myself.

And Tally; Tally was a friend.

Tally glared down at me. "You left so quietly I didn't even know you were gone until I heard the perimeter alarm." Suddenly she grinned. "Didn't realize you could move so quiet, boy, didn't know you had it in you." She clapped me on the arm and laughed. "Got past me! How 'bout that! We may actually make something of you some day. If you survive your own stupidity, that is."

"So," she said. "You ready to go back to base now?"

In the morning, Tally said nothing about my walk during the previous "night," and I said nothing as well. By the time I awoke, Leah was already preoccupied with preparing the rocket probe for another launch.

The first thing that "day," Leah launched the probe again, to update our clocks and to squirt her latest results across to *Orpheus* in orbit high above us. I went out to finish doing the diagnostic of the malfunction in Tally's t-vehicle. By the time Leah's probe landed, I had traced the problem to a misaligned injector, probably knocked askew during the pyro separation from *Eurydice.*

The probe returned with its memory filled with suggestions from the scientific staff, and a message from the Captain. Leah downloaded the memory to her research unit and read it with some annoyance. Then she called in Tally and me.

"Captain Shen suggests we return to *Orpheus*," Leah said. "He's nervous about the lack of continuous radio contact, doesn't like having to use a probe as a burst relay."

I was puzzled. "The old man wants to send another science crew down? They'd have the same problem, wouldn't they?"

Leah shook her head. "He wants to boost home. He says we've done the flags and footprints thing, the mission's successful, let's scoot."

The reference to a first landing as a flags-and-footprints mission was a historical relic. Nobody bothered planting a celebratory flag anymore, and the fractal surface wasn't like some virgin regolith that held footprints forever.

"Suggested, you say?" Tally asked. Depending on how it was phrased, a Captain's suggestion might or might not be an order.

"Suggested," Leah agreed. "He left it to our judgment of how valuable our work here was. My feeling is, flags and footprints and forget it? Jigger that. We're here; there's a lot to learn."

"So let's stay a while," Tally said. "Tinkerman?"

I looked at the two of them. If the Captain was nervous, I was nervous. But then, it was his job to play cautious. I shrugged, feigning confidence. "I'm pretty sure that the vehicles are okay for lift-off, but it wouldn't hurt if I did a test-firing on Tally's engine to verify the job I did fixing the injector," I said, "and then took a look at the other two t-vehicles to check that they don't have the same problem. I suppose that could take a day, maybe two if I took my time."

"Perfect," Tally said. "Nobody can argue with that. In fact, it could take you three days, maybe even more, who could say?"

"Also," Leah said, "Up there, time goes slow. Relative to us down here, I mean. Even if we take our sweet time exploring, by their clocks we'll be back soon enough. Especially if we spend most of our time further down, where the time effect will be even faster."

Tally smiled. "That's great. There's still a lot I want to investigate."

I 've set up a perimeter defense at 500 meters; stay inside that." Tally brought out another projectile gun and placed it by the bubble's airlock. "I want you to carry omniblasters at all times, even inside the bubble. I can't overemphasize how dangerous this place is. The hexacats on this level seem to be territorial, so they won't bother you unless you violate their space, but I can't guarantee anything about the larger hexapedal carnivores on the third level, or the fourth level beasties."

"You've penetrated two levels down?" Leah was interested now.

"Three. Don't follow." She looked back at us. "I'm going to scout out a safe site to place the hab bubble another level down. That should buy us some additional time before the captain gets the hots to order our asses back up. When I've checked the area, I'll get you." Tally put her hand on my arm. "Keep an eye on Leah, okay? She tends to go off." This was her oblique way of saying that I was the one who tended to wander off. It was her only mention of last night.

I nodded. "Right."

As Tally went exploring, Leah went back to examining the crystals she had collected. She was shining a low-power laser on one, watching the pattern of light reflecting from the myriad facets. The pattern shifted as she moved the crystal, now looking like some masterwork of an unknown genius of abstract art, now changing until it resembled a line of handwriting in some alien language. I walked up behind her and put my hand on her back, massaging her shoulder muscles. "It looks like something, almost," I said, "almost like something I should be able to recognize."

Leah replied abstractedly. "Information," she said. "The fractal pattern is self-similar at all size scales, but never exactly repeating. It stores information at all levels. This rock is like a sheet of paper, infinitely large, infinitely crumpled, almost infinitely dense with information." She shifted the laser. An alien landscape with a twisted, writhing sea. "A perfect crystal has no entropy, stores no information. Add disorder to the crystal, and the disorder contains information. Perfect disorder—infinite entropy—is indistinguishable from maximally dense information." She pulled the crystal out from the laser, and held it in front of her. It was hard to look at; your brain couldn't grasp the shape in its entirety, the complexity within complexity.

"But what does it mean?" I said.

"Nothing. Information without context is meaningless." She tossed the crystal on the ground. "Without intelligence, information is just... another form of entropy. The crystals down here are a bit more complex than the ones on the surface. I'm going to check the next few levels down."

"But Tally warned—"

"Tally is obsessed with danger. Of course she finds danger; that's what she's looking for. I'm looking for information." She waved away my imminent objection. "Oh, I'm not stupid; I'll be careful. I'll keep a watch out for danger, and I'll carry a blaster. Even one of Tally's overpowered projectile guns, if you insist on it."

She was crazy, I suddenly realized. Not just impulsive, but literally, quantifiably insane. The psychologists even had a name for what she had. They called it new-planet syndrome, or explorer's euphoria. Long ago, a mission briefing had warned us that everybody got it, at least a little, the first time they set foot on a new planet. The all-encompassing sensations of *alienness* overwhelms the critical thinking of the brain, producing giddiness and euphoria. The first explorers on Miranda had been so fascinated by the ever-changing vistas of the ice cliffs that they had continued trekking long past the halfway point on their oxygen consumption, and had to be rescued by an emergency drop of spare oxygen canisters from orbit. It had happened even on Earth, explorers of the Antarctic or of Africa continuing to press on to new vistas long after all common sense would have told them to return to base. Explorer's euphoria was most pronounced when the explorers were cut off from contact with the quotidian world. The Miranda explorers had been out of radio contact for several days.

We were out of radio contact.

It wasn't fatal. Oh, it could cause people to make hasty decisions, but the Miranda team had been an extreme case. As long as we guarded against it, we should be okay.

I couldn't fault Leah. We all had it. I, too, found myself making excuses to stay. I, too, wanted to explore.

"Fine, then," I said. "I'm going with you."

Leah turned to look at me, surprised, and then shrugged and turned her back. "Suit yourself."

She set out at a fast pace, almost a run, without saying another word. I stuffed a spare radio beacon into a pack with my inertial locator and backup transponder, and scrambled to keep up. When I finally caught up with her, she didn't acknowledge my presence, but she did slow her pace infinitesimally. There was a distant look in her eyes. I asked her opinion about what we were seeing. Her reply was only to ask me to quit making meaningless chatter; she was trying to observe the environment and didn't need any distractions.

I thought that she was in no mood to communicate, and then she turned to me, as if she hadn't just snapped at me, and said, "Imaginary time."

"What?"

"I need a paradigm shift here, Tinkerman." She picked up a crystal. It seemed unique and beautiful, with delicate filaments feathering the edges like an ornate crystalline snowflake. Unique and beautiful, just exactly like every other one all over this strange landscape. "I'm just spinning wheels, free associating. Every measurement I make points to imaginary time."

"What does that mean?"

"I'm not sure. I would have said imaginary numbers are just a mathematical tool, but... Look. As we go deeper into the gravity well here, our time vector—the passage of time we experience—is rotated in the imaginary plane."

"Does that mean what we experience down here isn't real?"

She threw the crystal down on the ground in disgust. "No! The first thing you have to understand is, there is nothing at all 'imaginary' about imaginary numbers. That's just a name. All numbers are figments of the human imagination; imaginary numbers are just as real as any other numbers."

"Then what does it mean?"

"It means that the time we experience here is partly in a direction orthogonal to time experienced outside. Hours go by here, and only minutes pass outside."

"That's time dilation."

"Yes, but in reverse. The mathematics are the same as a Minkowski rotation."

"But what does it *mean?*"

She shrugged. "I'm just spinning wheels here, Tinkerman. Speculating. Like I said, I'm looking for a paradigm shift. Now, shut up and observe the environment."

The environment was worth observing. It was spectacular, always changing. We traversed razor-thin bridges over seemingly bottomless gorges, with our feet never seeming quite to touch the ground, and then an instant later we seemed to be at the bottom of huge chasm, looking up through a narrow cleft. We saw none of the predators that Tally had found to be so dangerous, and this fact struck me as odd, since she had originally found them easily, just moments after reaching this level. In fact, it occurred to me that the very existence of the animals was more than a bit odd. What did they subsist on? Where were the plants, the food animals; where was the energy source for their metabolism? How could there be vertebrate animals half a trillion kilometers from Earth? Spread out across the great dark, we had found other planets with life, in distant solar systems, but few had even superficially terrestrial body forms. And, most important of all, why did we accept it all so calmly, and with so little curiosity?

But I wasn't likely to get any answers from Leah, not with the mood she was in. Perhaps later she would be more expansive.

The opening Leah chose to take down to the next level looked exactly like a dozen others we had skirted, a pattern of perfect circles. She put a radio relay on the edge and tested it. The radio relay had not worked very well in communicating with Tally, but it was a safety measure to take nonetheless. If nothing else, it served as a locator to mark this spot for later reference, if for some reason the inertial logs that we all carried should fail.

It seemed to me just then that there were eyes watching us. I looked around cautiously, but in the anfractuous complexity of the terrain there could be a thousand watchers, or none. Wait; was that a movement? Something sparkled.

Leah looked over the edge, and then carefully lowered her equipment. "Thanks for coming with me," she said. "You don't need to wait. I'll be fine."

Leah put her hand on the edge, swung both feet over, and dropped.

I was torn. Should I follow her down, or should I investigate the glitter in the distance, try to find out what—or who— was watching? It took me only an instant to decide. Leah had very clearly invited me not to follow her.

I hiked over to where I had seen the sparkle. It was more difficult to find than I had thought, since distance and perspective in this place was hard to judge, but with some searching, I found it. It was a scrap of multi-layer insulation, gold-coated plastic foil only a few microns thick, the type that had once been used to insulate the hydrogen tanks of rockets. A type of foil that had been obsolete for decades.

If it had been on the surface, I might have dismissed it as some ancient piece of debris. Hundreds, possibly thousands, of rocket stages had used such insulation. But for it to get down here, something must have brought it down from the surface. What? Or, who?

There was no point in waiting for Leah, so I went back to the habitat bubble, contemplating the existence of the tiny scrap of foil. When I reached the bubble, I found another surprise waiting: Sailor had company. He was twittering and whistling and hopping madly up and down, preening his feathers, posing, and then frantically preening again. Just out-side the bubble wall was the object of his affections: another cockatiel, a light green bird with a brilliant blue feather ruff, perched outside the bubble.

"Hey, sailor!" he said, and then did his wolf whistle. "Hey, sailor! Hey sailor! Wanna show a girl a good time?"

The strange bird whistled back, a few bars from the southern anthem. Then it said, in a low, sultry voice, "Hey there, brother. You ain't just whistling Dixie."

I approached the other bird cautiously, and extended a finger. Without hesitation, it hopped onto my finger and then up to perch on my shoulder. A friendly bird. Tame. That was crazy. How had it gotten here? Refugee from some crash?

It takes an expert, or another cockatiel, to tell the sex of a cockatiel. I decided from the way Sailor was whistling and preening that this one had to be female. "Let's call you Olive, little bird," I said. "Now where the hell did you come from?"

"Space, the final frontier," Olive said, and then she whistled Dixie.

A crash. It was the only explanation that made sense. It was crazy that our computers didn't have any record of an accident, records of the loss of some ship headed somewhere that might pass this direction in space, and results of an investigation of the cause, but nothing else made any sense. Some time, and not too long ago, a ship had crashed here. The bit of foil, the bird. If we could land on this place; so could others. The bird must be a survivor. And what if there had been other survivors?

When Leah came back, I showed her the new bird and explained my speculations that there had been a crash.

"Don't be ridiculous, Tinkerman," she said. "Think about it for a moment, will you? How big is this place? A hundred million square kilometers? How many levels? Just think about it. Suppose that there was some earlier landing, one that we somehow never heard about, unlikely as that may seem. What are the chances that our landing spot would be anywhere near the other spot? A million to one, Tinkerman. A million to one, minimum."

"But the bird—"

"Information," she said. "A bird is just information in another form, just like you and me and everything else; all information. In the end, how is a bird any more remarkable than a crystal, or even a rock? It's not. Information in different form, that's all."

She wasn't making any sense. Explorer's euphoria; she had it bad. We all had it. It was time for us to go back to *Orpheus,* way past time. But we couldn't go back until Tally returned.

"Entropy is information," Leah said. "A perfect sine wave carries no information, no entropy. A perfect crystal has no entropy, no information. If information is stored in the crystal, the entropy increases. When maximum information is stored, the crystal is indistinguishable from a random lattice."

Leah looked at me, her eyes distant, bright. "A bird? A bird, Tinkerman, you think that's odd? There are stranger things on this place than any bird."

We had to leave. But how could we go back now? Whether Leah helped or not, I had to search for survivors.

The radio hadn't revealed any unexpected signals, but then, we hadn't been broadcasting. If there had been survivors of a crash, it was possible that they could be scanning, waiting desperately for a signal, perhaps unaware that we were already here. The weird radio echo would have meant that *Orpheus* would never have received their distress call. Down here, though? Odd as radio propagation here was, radio was still the first thing to try. I swept the international space-rescue band for signals: no luck, not even static. She might just not be broadcasting, though. They might not. She—they—might be waiting for a signal. I recorded a message into the transceiver's RAM, "Hello, are you there? Please respond. Hello, are you there?" and set the transceiver to broadcast it, slowly scanning the message across all of the rescue-band frequencies. When she replied—that is, if she—they—replied, the frequency monitor would lock in on the signal and alert me.

I couldn't think straight; the sourceless light and the odd landscapes were beginning to disorient me. I stared outside, and the strange vista seemed to hook me, seemed to pull me into it. I felt that I was vast, larger than planets; and then suddenly that I was infinitesimally small. Something was blinking at the edge of my vision.

I was tired, that was all. Just tired. I crawled away, laid down, and in an instant was asleep.

When I awoke, some timeless period later, the message light on the transceiver was blinking fiercely. It had been blinking last evening—night? What time was it? My message must have been answered the very instant it had been sent.

The reply message was only five words, not rushed, not desperate, not repeated; the voice of a girl or young woman. "I'm here. I've been waiting."

Leah was gone, out exploring again. Maybe she hadn't slept at all. I scanned the radio spectrum again. Empty. No, wait, not quite empty. There was a carrier wave. No further messages, but a carrier wave persisted, as if a transmitter had accidentally been left energized when nobody was there. Enough to compute a vector. I copied the vector down, erased the buffer, and set the scanner to capture and hold anything new. Then I grabbed an omniblaster and a portable receiver, and set out on the rescue run.

The vector led down a level, two. It could only have been tremendous luck that the survivor's camp had been aligned so that the radio waves had been able to make it in a straight line. I was careful to put radio repeaters at each drop site to serve as locator beacons, an automatic precaution against getting disoriented, although there was no chance of that; the landscape was unforgettable, luminous against my brain. Another level down.

The site was just as I'd imagined it, a half-cylinder of gleaming multi-layer foil propped with titanium struts to make a crude tent, with a parabolic antenna beside it aimed back the way I'd come, a dish salvaged from some unlucky ship. The reflective foil mirrored back distorted images of the landscape, so that the tent blended into the background, not out of place at all, but merely one more strange shape among myriads. I shouted greetings as I approached, and thought I heard some faint reply from inside.

The tent was like the enigma, as I passed through layer after layer of crinkled foil, thinner than spider-web. Inside was the same sourceless light.

Her voice was familiar and strange; a voice I'd known all my life, a voice I'd never heard before. Her words were almost the same as the words she'd said on the radio. "I've been waiting for you."

My words stuck in my throat. Tears welled up in my eyes, and I couldn't see. I couldn't think of anything to say. She waited, calmly looking at me, and her perfect calm made my own fluster even worse. I suddenly realized that I had an erection, and turned away, embarrassed. I realized that that would seem even more

odd. Had she seen? What did she think? How long had she been here?

"I'm—" I started, and stopped. "Greet—hello. I'm, my name is David Tinkerman."

"Of course it is." She smiled then. "Davy Tinkerman. I've been waiting for you."

It was impossible that she knew me, and yet somehow I, too, knew her from somewhere. No one had called me Davy since I'd been maybe eight years old. And suddenly I flashed on it. She had been a baby-sitter, when I'd been eight, and we lived—where? I couldn't remember which house. Her name was right on the tip of my tongue. God, how could I have forgotten? I'd been infatuated with her, hopelessly in love, back when I was eight and she'd been, what, fifteen? Unapproachable. I'd sworn, back then, that when I grew up I would find her and marry her, that I would love her forever; and she hadn't laughed at me, she'd nodded and said she'd wait.

I hadn't thought of her in decades.

She was older now, no longer a teenager. But she ought to be years older than I, and yet she wasn't. It was the time dilation effect, of course, it must be. She must have gone into space at the first opportunity; just a year or two after my family had moved away—my family always moved away—she'd gone to space. She must have crashed here on her first mission. What, twenty years ago? Thirty?

"How long have you been here?" I asked.

"A minute. A decade." She shrugged. "A million years. Time doesn't have much meaning here, I don't think. An hour, an eternity." She smiled again, and my heart shattered. "I'm glad you found me, Davy. I've been waiting for you forever."

We talked as we followed my trail back to the bubble, she following right behind me, close enough that I could sometimes feel the tickle of her breath on my neck, feel her infrared luminosity glowing against my back. I tried to hide the tumescence in my crotch by staying slightly ahead of her. I told her about the years we'd lost, how it had come to pass that I'd gone into space, about projects I'd worked on, my feelings of pride when something I'd built flew. Somehow, as much as I talked, and poured out my heart, I never quite happened to mention Leah. It didn't matter; I knew that she knew. We would have time to talk, the whole voyage back to tell each other our life stories. They would like each other, I was sure; become fast friends, after they got acquainted.

When the bubble finally got into view, I stopped, flung out an arm, and turned to her. "Here we are—"

There was nobody behind me.

There was a survivor, I know," I told Leah. "I met her. I *talked* to her, Leah!"

"Of course." Leah did not seem convinced; in fact, she did not seem interested at all. She'd barely acknowledged my presence when I'd come back in, shouting excitedly about finding a survivor of the crash. "I've been thinking about information theory, Tinkerman. Speculating, really. There is tremendous information content in these crystals, did I tell you that already? I'm just beginning to learn how to access it."

"Leah, just get this!" I said. "Can you believe it, it was somebody I actually knew! A girl I knew; she ran away to space when I was a kid."

"Incredible stuff, Tinkerman, even mind-boggling, if I may use that term." For a second I thought she was responding to what I'd said, instead of still talking about her crystals. "Yes, of course you knew her."

"I did! She—"

Leah picked up a crystal and held it in front of her, turning it from side to side in her hand. "Then what was her name?"

"She—what?"

Leah looked up at me, the first time she'd looked up from her crystals since I'd returned. "You said you knew her. What was her name? Surely if you knew her, you know her name?"

I opened my mouth, then closed it. Of course I knew her name. Of course I did.

I just couldn't think of it at the moment.

"I've been thinking about information theory, Tinkerman," Leah said. My lack of response to her question didn't seem to bother her in the slightest. "Have you ever thought about information theory?"

I sighed. "What about it?"

"A black hole swallows information. You already knew that, of course."

"Sure. A black hole swallows everything."

"Yes, but most particularly, it swallows information. It swallows mass, yes of course, but it emits Hawking radiation. Matter in, energy out, no problem. Einstein could have predicted that. But information, now that's a problem."

I wanted to talk about the girl, the survivor. I would have to go back and find her. Had she gotten lost? Had she followed me at all? I couldn't remember the last time she'd spoken to me as we'd walked back toward the bubble; I couldn't remember for sure if she'd said anything at all. But Leah obviously was in no state to discuss the subject. Maybe it was best to humor her. "Why is that a problem?"

"Tinkerman, think about it. A black hole is a cosmic eraser! Matter and information go in; energy comes out. A spherical shell of clean, randomized, content-free energy. What happens to the information?"

"So it gets erased. Does it matter?"

"Does it matter! Tinkerman, in quantum mechanics, information is entropy. Entropy is conserved. You can't just erase it. Tinkerman, where does the information go?"

"The lost-and-found counter of a bus depot in Cleveland," I said. "And, frankly, I don't think I could care less. Look, Leah—"

At that moment, Tally burst through the bubble's airlock door. She looked awful. The projectile rifle was hanging loose in her hands, as if she was almost too tired to hold onto it. A jagged gash had been torn down the side of her face, and one side of her jumpsuit hung in tatters, exposing her underwear, which, I noted with a tiny fragment of my attention, was black silk, not at all what I would have expected. In other circumstances, it might have been sexy. The rip also exposed the knife and the omniblaster she had strapped to her thigh, and an incredible amount of dried and caked blood. I hoped it wasn't all hers.

Weary, dirty, and bloody; for all of that she was grinning madly.

"Tally!" I said. "Boy, am I glad to see you! Listen, I need your help. I found—"

"Save it, Tinkerman. I'm declaring an emergency."

"But you have to hear this—"

"I said, stuff it! Look, for the duration, you're going to have to stick to this level. There's some bad shit three levels down, stuff too hot for you to handle. No insult, okay? But you're not trained for this kind of trouble. I've cleared this level; you're safe here as long as you keep your eyes open."

All the time Tally was talking, she was gathering stuff from the hab. The two omniblasters were on fast-charge. She picked up a lot of other things, cramming them into a web-back she slung over her shoulder: rounds for the projectile rifle, canis-ters for a cooking stove, spare battery packs. She grabbed some other parts from her personal effects. With a sudden feeling of disorientation, I recognized them as components removed from her t-vehicle. Struts. An energy pack. Pieces of the backup guidance computer. A spare gyro. All back-up or secondary system stuff, but you just don't tear apart the backups, not on a vehicle you're planning to trust your life to.

"Man, who would have thought they'd be so hostile?" she said, her voice musing, almost purring. "Who would have thought they'd be so *fast?*"

She put the pieces together with sure, easy assurance, as if they were a grade-school science kit. I'd worked with those parts, and parts like them, for most of my life, and I'd never seen anything quite like the object she was assembling. Nevertheless, I could recognize a weapon when I saw one.

"But—but I just came back from three levels down," I said. "There's a survivor—"

She whirled on me. "You were three levels down? Great Lord Jesus, didn't I tell you to stay put until I cleared the area? You're lucky you still got your head attached to your shoulders. Don't do it again. That's an order.

"You two, can up the bubble—no, scrub that, just grab your essentials and your blasters and get up out of here. Top priority. Get your backsides up top and get the landers ready to go. I'll join you pronto, but don't wait for me; if I don't show up, call for a pick-up and boost out to *Eurydice* maximum ASAP. Don't hold waiting for me. You copy?"

And as abruptly as she had come, not even waiting for a reply, Tally was gone. They were mad, both Leah and Tally, and Tally was dangerous. But I had to rescue a survivor. I picked up the sample bag where Tally had deposited the body of the creature that had attacked her so long ago. Even dead, it looked menacing, with fangs curved for ripping, large eyes set wide to triangulate prey. I had never seen one alive, not even at a distance. I had met nothing alive, nothing at all, save for a bird, and a girl.

"I'm going back for the survivor," I told Leah. "When I get back, we boost for the return pick-up. I hope to hell that Tally gets back. Can you get ready to message *Orpheus?*"

"Black holes emit energy," she said. "At the event horizon—if you could reach the event horizon—the temperature of a black hole is infinite."

I walked over and put both of my hands on her shoulders. I wanted to shake her; instead I kneeled down and looked up into her eyes. "Leah, are you listening at all?"

"Of course I'm listening, Tinkerman. Return pick-up, two of us plus one crash survivor. Tally, if she gets back. No problem. Now, have you been listening to a thing I've been telling you, or have I just been feeding information into a black hole?"

I sighed. "You can message *Orpheus?*"

"Of course. Look, this may be important. Entropy is connected to temperature. The energy content of information must be proportional to temperature."

"I'm leaving now, Leah."

"Approaching the center of the enigma, we must be approaching, not an event horizon, but an antihorizon. You can never reach the center, of course; the concept of a center may not even have physical meaning. The temperature approaches negative infinity. The necessary solution to the black hole paradox; the most improbable state."

She was still talking to herself when I left.

As I returned downward, contemplating the odd behavior of Tally, I had a sudden thought. If time goes faster the deeper you go into the enigma, and if the place really did have life-forms on it... then, deep inside, the life must evolve at a tremendous rate. How fast did time speed up? How many levels were there? Suddenly I realized that, if space were distorted, then there might be an infinite number of levels.

I passed the last of the radio beacons I'd left, and there ahead of me was the cobbled-together hut, with the parabolic dish. There was a sudden hollow feeling inside me, and I knew she wouldn't be there.

I rushed though the layers of foil, and there she was, waiting. She was slender and beautiful, and my body ached all over. My breath came so short that I could hardly speak. "Why didn't you come up with me?"

"Up?" she said, as if the concept had never occurred to her. "Is there an up? Up has no meaning to me." Her voice was the same, familiar and childlike and strange at once, the voice I'd heard whispering in my dreams, and I felt as if I'd never left her.

Her words made no sense, but then, nothing here made sense any more. "Leah says that your existence is impossible," I said.

"Leah," she said, musingly, as if the word had some secret meaning to her.

"You can't be here," I told her, fighting to get the words out before I forgot myself, before I was totally overcome by the incandescent heat of her presence. "You must be—" I could hardly say it. "You are a figment of my imagination."

She reached out and brushed my cheek with one hand, her touch infinitely light, and smiled wistfully. "I am real, Davy. More real than you are, I think. Are you real? Or are you only an involuted dream?"

"The crash," I said. The whiskers of my cheek tingled in the exact shape of her fingertips. "Do you remember the crash? Do you remember coming here?"

"Crash?" she said, slowly, as if the thought had never occurred to her. "I don't remember a crash. I don't remember the past. Maybe there is no past. I remember only being here. And you. I remember you."

But that could be post-traumatic syndrome; crash survivors are usually disoriented, amnesiac; and to be stranded for years, far from humanity? What had that done to her? How could she be coherent? How could she be sane at all?

I reached out hesitantly and touched her shoulder. Even through the thin foil of her jumpsuit I could feel the heat of her body. She was trembling slightly, or perhaps the trembling was in my hands. Of their own accord my fingertips began to stroke her. "Are you real?" I whispered. "How can you be real? How could you be here?" My body was thrumming, and a sensation of intense, almost unbearable sweetness seemed to suffuse through my body.

"I am real," she said, softly, as I helped her remove her jumpsuit and she, in turn, helped me out of the confining awkwardness of clothing.

I didn't think of Leah at all.

I don't know how long I spent with her, whether it was hours or days, making love, talking, gazing into her bottomless eyes and realizing that, for the first time in my life, I had found somebody who understood me and accepted me for everything I was, and for everything I would never be. Time had little enough meaning here. Hours or days, it was a long time later before I went outside the tiny shelter, and even then it was for the most mundane, the crudest possible reason. For

all that we had shared every part of ourselves over and again, I was still too shy to use a urine collection bag in front of her.

Leah stood there, waiting for me.

"It's time for us to leave," Leah said. Her voice was gentle, almost wistful. I had never heard her like that. "We have to leave now, Tinkerman."

And I saw Leah in a new light. She was older than I'd remembered. God, when had I last looked at her, really looked at her? Of course she was older; we both were. Her hands were too large, her eyes set too far apart. Her clothes were rumpled and stale, and her fingernails were ragged. How could I ever have been so obsessed with her? She was a human being. Only a human being: fallible, plain, slightly ridiculous. I had been a child when I'd thought I'd fallen in love with her; for all these years, I'd been chasing a child's dream.

"I'm not going back, Leah," I said. I hadn't realized that this was my intention, but the moment I said it, I knew it was true. I wasn't going back. "I've—I've found someone. I'm staying here."

"I know."

"You know?"

"God, how much I've learned! It's all here, Tinkerman, all encoded in the crystals. How much there is left to learn! I've learned unified field theories; physics for seven and ten dimensions. I don't know how useful it is; I don't know if any of it will have any use at all. I think that anything I can learn here might be only the physics of imaginary universes, impossible universes; of universes that might have been, or might yet be, or may only be dreamed of." She picked up a crystal and stared at it, unseeing. "Beautiful, and cold."

"I'm not going back, Leah," I said. "Tell the captain—hell, I don't know. You can tell him anything."

"There is no end to it," she said. "I could stay here forever, and forever keep on learning new things, forever moving deeper and deeper into the enigma." She dropped the crystal and sighed. "I can't force you, Tinkerman. It's time to go, past time, long past time. But I can't force you to come back. I can only ask."

She turned and walked away. Not once did she look back.

I went back into the shelter, and she was there, as incredibly lovely as ever, waiting. Her very perfection was almost unbearable. She was made for me; every curve, every microscopic cell of her perfectly suited for me. There was a question I had to ask, and I didn't know how to say it. "I love you," I said, finally. "Utterly. Helplessly. Why? How?"

"I know."

It wasn't an answer. I didn't know if I'd wanted an answer. "What are you? Are you even human?"

She tilted her head, and in the corners of her eyes was a faintest trace of a smile. "Can't you tell? Of course I'm human. I have to be. I am exactly as you want me to be."

"Then what *are* you?"

"I have never contemplated myself before." She hesitated for a moment, eyes half closed, thinking. "I am capable of neither love nor hate. I simply am what I am."

"You don't love me."

"If you think I love you, then I do."

"If I left?"

"I would be as I ever was, neither loving nor hating."

There is only one way to leave paradise, and that is to simply walk away. I knew that if I looked back, even for an instant, I would never be able to leave.

I kept walking.

The transfer vehicles sat where I had left them, three stumpy obelisks, gracelessly alien against the recondite involutes of the enigmatic landscape.

"You were looking for great scientific truths," I said to Leah, "and that is what you found."

"Yes."

I didn't dare say what I had found. It hurt too much. "And Tally?"

But I didn't really have to ask about Tally. I already knew. When we got to the surface, I had instantly seen that her t-vehicle, her only ride home, had been cannibalized. The spherical tank of atomic hydrogen was missing. It was the fuel for the lander; the most energetic form of chemical matter possible. It was also—if used wrong, if used without the nozzle, if used just as a defocussed beam of invisible supersonic gas, by a person who knew just exactly what she was doing—a very dangerous weapon.

"Tally wanted a challenge," Leah said. "All her life, she has been seeking a worthy opponent, something tougher, smarter, and stronger than she was." Leah shook her head. She was silent for a while, and then, very softly, she said, "And you?"

I turned away and closed my eyes. She walked up behind me and put her hand on my shoulder, very gently, so softly that I perhaps only imagined it.

"I'm sorry."

I shook my head. "Let's get these vehicles off the ground."

We boosted the probe first, its robotic memory loaded with the message for *Orpheus* and a synchronized clock, to tell them exactly where and when we would make the rendezvous. The t-vehicles didn't have enough fuel to launch directly into orbit; we would boost and hover, trusting that *Eurydice* would be there for us. It was a dangerous way to make rendezvous; doubly dangerous when the communications link was so erratic. If we stayed, though... yes, if we stayed, that would be even more dangerous.

I put Sailor into my t-vehicle, setting him onto the instrument console. The instant before I sealed the cockpit, though, he darted free and fluttered away. There was no time to chase him; the rendezvous schedule was already established. In the distance, I caught a glimpse of something rising up to join him, a speckle of feathers, deep green with just a hint of blue. And then the count was zero.

Leah first, and I a fraction of a second later, we boosted out into the unknown, into hope and faith.

◖ n *Orpheus,* waiting for us in orbit, the landing mission had been a short one, the total elapsed time only a few hours. The mission debriefing lasted nearly as long as the mission. Most of the questions were directed at Leah, questions on observations and scientific points. She seemed weary; her face drawn, her answers short and factual, completely free of any of the speculations she had confided in me during the mission. I didn't mention the survivor I'd found. How could I? How could I have explained my actions? They seemed bizarre, now, even to myself.

But I thought of her constantly.

Orpheus orbited slowly, ten million kilometers from the enigma, waiting for days for Tally to show up. She didn't.

"There is nothing more we need to do here," Captain Shen said. "On your evidence, I believe I have to declare crewman Okumba lost. It's time to go home."

It took another day to reconfigure *Orpheus* for boost, to run full-up checks on the navigation and control systems, ramp up the main fusion engines to standby power and check them out.

Later, when *Orpheus* had been configured for boost, preflight inspections completed and verified that all loose items were accounted for and stowed for resumption of gee, I had a sudden thought. The captain, as expedition leader, had the prerogative of assigning a name. I found Captain Shen.

"Enigma," the captain said, replying to my question. "Just Enigma." He must have seen my puzzlement. "I logged the name as Enigma, Mr. Tinkerman, so that we would make the crew's unofficial usage official."

I nodded. I'd just expected something classical, or maybe Dantean. Shayol, perhaps, or Lethe, the shore from which no one returns. "Enigma it is, then."

I was on shift, second back-up in the nav station. The one-minute warning sounded, and I gazed out the viewport, searching for the enigma. I knew exactly where to look, and still I saw nothing, not even a twinkling of starlight, where the enigma waited. Nothing. There was no reason at all why, when the boost came and the sudden heaviness of thrust-induced gravity weighed me into my couch, my eyes should be suddenly filled with tears.

"I've thought about it," I said to Leah. We were lying side by side in our bunk. "I don't understand it. I don't understand anything."

Although we weren't touching, I could feel her body, warm beside me. I hadn't touched her, hadn't made any advances, since that moment, long ago, when we'd gone to our separate transfer vehicles to drop from *Eurydice* into the unknown. It seemed like a lifetime to me. She was a human, only a human. And what human could ever compare with an ideal?

Across the tiny cubicle, fastened securely in place against the oppressive force of overgee, the statuette of an ascetic Buddha gazed up at something above my head with blank, enigmatic eyes.

"Tell me, what don't you understand?" Leah said.

I gestured, toward the back bulkhead, where—millions of kilometers behind us—the enigma was. "That. What we saw, what we did. Everything."

"Ah. Information, Tinkerman. Pure, inchoate information. But information without context, without intelligence—without humanity—is meaningless." Now she was talking softly, to herself. "I knew that. I did know that."

After a pause, she said, "Captain Shen will be sealing the records of the landing expedition. Officially, our little trip down never happened. The expedition report will say no definite surface was found, and Enigma will be listed as a danger to transit, with a keep-away zone established." She was silent for another long moment. "It has to be that way, Tinkerman, you know that." She seemed to be trying to convince me. "We're not ready. We don't know how to be gods."

I lay back, digesting the information. Gods? "That won't keep people away forever. We're curious. Besides, if the captain really wanted people to stay away, he should have named it something less mysterious than 'Enigma.' He should have named it something boring. He should have named it 'Smith.'"

Leah laughed gently. Her body radiated softly warm against my back.

"Someday people will come back," I said. "You can bet on it."

"I know," Leah said. "But there are a hundred thousand other things to investigate, out here in the great dark. Subjovians. Comets. Solitary planets. Some maybe even stranger than this. It will keep us away for a while. A hundred years, perhaps. Maybe more. And perhaps then, just perhaps, people will be wiser, more mature."

"I doubt it."

"I've convinced the old man that it's dangerous, anyway. It's all I can do."

Gods? Had Leah really meant it, when she said that we could have been gods? And just what had she meant, when she said that information had to be shaped by intelligence? What exactly qualified as intelligence? Was, say, a bird sufficient intelligence? Could a cockatiel be a god? Could it become one, in a hundred years, or a thousand?

Some day people would return to the enigma. I wondered what they would find.

What I did know was that, in the end, Leah had come for me, had come down deep into the engima, when she must have known that every meter she went deeper into the enigma would make it harder for her to ever want to leave. She had come for me.

I don't like overgee. You have to think out every move slowly and carefully. It makes sex awkward, clumsy.

"You've changed, Tinkerman," Leah said.

"Yes." I hadn't realized it until she said it, but I had.

"You've grown, somehow." Her eyes were closed. "I think I like you better this way."

I closed my eyes, and instantly I could see another, a girl who'd never needed a name, who I'd known forever, since long before the world was formed. A child's dream, really. But we were all children, somewhere deep inside. Maybe even Leah.

I'd made my choice, and there is no use looking back. Far behind me, I could hear the throbbing of the pulsed fusion engine. I opened my eyes, and knew I was going home. • • •

many worlds in science and science fiction

an essay by Joseph d. miller, phd

In many ways biology and physics in the 21st century appear to be on a convergent path. Since at least Watson and Crick's discovery of the double helix structure of DNA, biologists have focused more and more on the underlying physical substrates of life. Thus immense energy has gone into understanding the physical steps involved in the transcription and translation of genes into proteins, the geometry of gene sequences and the regulatory non-coding regions which modulate transcription, the elaborate folding structures of proteins, the structure of cellular membranes and the "scaffolding" which allows receptor proteins embedded in the membrane to "talk" to a host of intracellular mechanisms, the structure of ion channels and the dynamic modifications of that structure which modulate the entry of ions into the cell, to name just a few fronts in structural biology and biophysics. All of this might be described as the "physics of biology."

Less well-known are excursions into the "biology of physics." One of the foundations of modern physics, as realized in the Standard Model of electroweak theory and quantum chromodynamics, is quantum mechanics. The other pillar of the Standard Model is general relativity. These pillars of physical thought have allowed the four fundamental forces of nature (electromagnetism, the strong and weak nuclear forces, and gravity) to be understood with unprecedented clarity. However, unifying all four forces in one grand unified theory has proved a difficult task, although there are theoretical indications from string theory and quantum gravity that such a Theory of Everything may be possible.

The biological and psychological implications of special and general relativity have been explored in science fiction. Such works as *Tau Zero* by Poul Anderson and *The Forever War* by Joe Haldeman consider the effects of time dilation on human interactions. *The Stars My Destination* by Alfred Bester suggests that a "gut" understanding of general relativity would completely alter both our perception of the universe and our ability to traverse it. But similar considerations of the psychological implications of a "gut" understanding of quantum mechanics have been curiously absent from most science fiction till very recently, most notably in works like *Quarantine* by Greg Egan. This may reflect the possibility that quantum mechanics is deeply incompatible with our ordinary "classical" view of reality; thus the old adage attributed to Niels Bohr, "If quantum mechanics hasn't profoundly shocked you, you haven't understood it yet."

But just what is it about quantum mechanics that generates this incompatibility? Perhaps the first thing to consider is the now almost universally held view that matter, in its most elementary form, is both wave and particle. But the wave-like character of matter is typically observable only in the microscopic regime. Objects with high mass/energy have minuscule wave-like properties, whereas the wavelength of atomic-scale particles is large in comparison.

But the wave function is more properly a graph of probability amplitude, that is, where the particle is most likely to be. Under the right circumstances (e.g., microdegrees above absolute zero), wave functions of different particles can overlap, or superpose, forming "superatoms" more properly known as Bose-Einstein condensates. The condensate may be treated as a single particle, the component states of which are superposed in a Hilbert space of many dimensions. Quantum computers, if and when they are built, will take advantage of the superposition property for computation. It is easy to imagine a classical computer with a memory of 1000 bits, physically actualized by 1000 transistor gates capable of being logically either on or off. The number of possible combinations of these gates is 2^{1000}, or more states than there are physical states of matter in the universe. But any of these possible states must be realized sequentially in a classical computer; in a quantum computer, these states are superposed and realized simultaneously in Hilbert space. This superposition property will allow a degree of parallelism never before possible in computation, and will facilitate the solution of problems in areas like cryptography which are insoluble by today's computers.

But where is this Hilbert space which could potentially encompass more states of matter, and thus information, than that present in the entire universe? Before answering that question, let's consider some of the other bizarre properties of quantum mechanics. A second counter-intuitive notion in quantum mechanics is the idea of entangled states. A pair of electrons in the same orbital must have diametrically opposite spins (the Pauli Exclusion principle). It has been shown that in such a case, separation of the two particles to great distance does not disrupt this property. Indeed, the measurement of spin of one particle instantaneously determines the spin of the second particle, no matter how far it is from the first electron. The spin of the second particle can be determined so soon after the measurement of the first particle's spin as to exclude the transmission of any information to the second particle at velocities below the speed of light.

However, this transluminal influence is not truly information. If we imagine two such entangled particles separated by 100 light years, and an observer at each location, then when observer 1 says the spin of particle 1 is up, instantly observer 2 can observe the spin of particle 2 to be down. However, observer 2 cannot know if it is the prior observation of observer 1 of particle 1 that has determined the state of particle 2, or if the state of particle 2 is simply determined by the direct observation of observer 2 (interestingly in this case, the symmetric possibility is that the future (relative to observer 1) observation of observer 2 of particle 2 is just as likely to determine the state of particle 1 as the observation of observer 1, a seeming causality violation). In any case the observed spin appears to be randomly determined, a conclusion which could only be undermined by information about the spin of the other particle, information which must necessarily be transmitted at sub-luminal speed. This situation, as well as the uncertainty regarding which observer determines the state of an entangled particle, negates the possibility of reliable supraluminal information transmission, according to most interpretations. However, it also suggests a bizarre interconnectedness of matter in the universe, a property Einstein called "spooky action at a distance," and which modern physicists refer to as non-locality. And at least one modern physicist, Roger Penrose (1989), mentor of Steven Hawking, states, "Although EPR-type experiments do not, in the ordinary sense of sending messages, conflict with causality of relativity , there is a definite conflict with the spirit of relativity in our picture of physical reality."[1] Perhaps sensing a loophole, one science fiction author, Charles Stross, in *Singularity Sky,* actually does make use of entangled matter for supraluminal communication.

t he implicit problem with this formulation of entanglement is that it relies on an observer at each locale. Niels Bohr, in what came to be known as the Copenhagen interpretation of quantum mechanics, suggested that one should view the unobserved electron to be in a superposition of spin states, up and down simultaneously. Thus the probability amplitude for either state would be equal. But the observer has the ability to collapse the wave function, localizing the electron in one probability state or the other. However, the resultant collapsed state is not predictable or controllable by the observer, at least in this thought experiment. In science fiction one of the best-realized applications of the Copenhagen interpretation is Greg Egan's *Quarantine*. The

reader eventually discovers that the universe is populated with intelligences who exist in superposition. Our ability as observers to collapse such superpositions by astronomical observation at greater and greater distances is a threat to the continued existence of such life forms!

The Copenhagen interpretation puts tremendous weight on the observer; it has been argued (the Wigner's friend argument)[2] that the observer must be a conscious entity; a recording machine like a camera cannot collapse the wave function. Any sort of recording device produces an output which has no effect on the wave function until that output is observed. Similarly, one could imagine a sequential chain of recording devices, in which every recorder records the output of the previous device, culminating in some final output which when observed does indeed collapse the wave function. But this is very close to our current reductionist model of the visual system! There is a chain of sequential neurons extending from the retina to the lateral geniculate to the visual cortex, essentially a chain of visual recorders. But at some level in visual cortex, association cortex, or perhaps some global integrated engagement of the entire forebrain, "consciousness of" occurs and the wave function collapses. This is reminiscent of the nineteenth century notion of the internal homunculus, the tiny observer who lives in our brain. But who observes the observer? In fact, it has been suggested that the observer must be self-conscious (in order to avoid an infinite series of internal homunculi/observers), presumably a global, or at least cortical, brain property. So collapse of the wave function

1.   Penrose, Roger. *The Emperor's New Mind: Concerning Computers, Minds and the Laws of Physics.* Penguin, 1991.
2.   Wigner, Eugene P. *Symmetries and Reflections.* Ox Bow, 1979.

might then entail a prior collapse of superposed neuronal states.[3]

This in turn suggests that quantum phenomena may be a critical aspect of cortical neuronal activity; Penrose suggests that neuronal microtubules are of the appropriate spatial and temporal dimensions to be the substrate of the observer process. I have suggested[4] that the intra-neuronal calcium spark is just as viable a hypothetical mechanism, critical to a large number of neuronal properties such as depolarization, local calcium-dependent kinase activation and gene transcription. Thus the Copenhagen interpretation may be constrained neuroanatomically, physiologically and perhaps phylogenetically (since only the Great Apes exhibit self-consciousness). It may prove possible to define the minimal mental hardware necessary to collapse the wave function. And certain neuropathological states involving a loss or radical alteration of consciousness (e.g., Alzheimer's) might impair the capacity to collapse the wave function.

But if the collapse of the wave function is a random, inherently probabilistic event, how do we account for consensus reality? How does macroscopic certainty emerge from an aggregate of particles in superposition (plus those few collapsed to a single state following observation by some observer)? First, it is true that consensus reality is not universal; those who perceive things at variance to the consensus are usually medicated or more rarely venerated as visionaries or prophets! And even within the consensus, there is considerable variation in the particular ways that people "see" things. Witnesses to crimes are notorious for the variability in their observations.

Still, there is a general framework to our perceptions to which most of us subscribe. This suggests that wave function collapse is a social phenomenon; in some way, consensus reality is a gestalt, the resultant of all the observers in a given culture. And when cultures collide, there is an evolutionary mechanism which selects the consensus view with the greatest fitness; other views and their associated observers are killed, converted, or consigned to reservations.

The Copenhagen interpretation and its extension described here can be attacked from a variety of angles. First, it has been argued that Copenhagen applies only to microscopic events, not to macroscopic reality. That notion is refuted by the famed *gedankenexperiment,* Schrödinger's Cat, which demonstrates that superposition at least is possible at the macroscopic level.[5] And indeed superposition has been demonstrated for particle aggregates like Bose-Einstein condensates extending well into the macroscopic range.[6] But even if macroscopic superposition is common, it may be argued that observers are unnecessary to collapse the wave function. Instead, thermal coupling

3.   Stapp, Henry P. *Mind, Matter and Quantum Mechanics.* Springer, 2004.
4.   Miller, Joseph D. The prospects for a quantum neurobiology. Neuroscience Net (www. neuroscience.com) 2 Article 10011, 1997.
5.   Dan Simmons in *Rise of Endymion* envisions a society in which the Schrödinger's cat protocol is used instead of supposedly morally indefensible capital punishment. A criminal takes the place of the cat. The chance of being executed, much like the cat, is 50% in a given time interval. However, the prisoner is also the observer (as in Wigner's Friend), and thus is the agent of collapse of the wave function which either ends or does not end his life.
6.   Dunningham, J., Rau, A., Burnett, K. From pedigree cats to fluffy bunnies. *Science* 307:872-875, 2005.

to the environment (i.e. decoherence) spontaneously destroys superpositions after some interval of time. The problem with decoherence is that it remains necessary for an observer to observe the particle aggregate to see if collapse has already occurred. There is no way to determine if the collapse is due to decoherence or the observation itself! Furthermore, delayed choice experiments suggest that superposed states could persist without decohering for astronomically long periods of time.

Perhaps the most radical interpretations of quantum mechanics eliminate the privileged position of the observer, and thus the problem of measurement, wave function collapse and much of the difficulty with entangled states (e.g., Bohm's theory, Cramer's transactional theory). We will consider here one such class of interpretations, Many Worlds, which may prove testable, and which may involve biology to an even greater extent than the Copenhagen interpretation of quantum mechanics.

Many Worlds models of the universe, broadly speaking, come in at least five flavors. The earliest is Everett's Many Worlds model.[7] This model solves the measurement problem by doing away with the notion of wave function collapse. Instead, every superposed state is posited to exist in a corresponding parallel universe. The universe splits at the moment of a measurement through decoherence. This has the attractive feature of potentially allowing a single Schrödinger wave function to describe the entire universe or, more properly, multiverse (assuming you

know the boundary conditions—a large assumption). That wave function evolves linearly in the same way as any wave function but without the sudden observer-induced collapse of the Copenhagen interpretation. The space in which the multiple universes reside is the Hilbert space mentioned above.

This resolves another problem with the Copenhagen interpretation (as well as many other interpretations of quantum mechanics). Quantum computers with up to seven constituent q-bits have been realized.[8] Computations (e.g., factoring) require the superposition of states implicit in a quantum computer (a seven q-bit computer would be capable of 2^7, or 128, essentially simultaneous parallel operations). The Hilbert space in which these states are superposed appears to be "real," else it would be hard to see how a true computational result could be obtained. But a quantum computer with about 350 q-bits would allow the superposition of more states than exist in the universe (the Bekenstein Bound).[9] It seems that either you cannot build a quantum computer of anything approaching that size, or if you can construct such a computer, then the Hilbert space in which the states are superposed is not in this universe! The solution to this conundrum is to assume that the parallel computations take place in parallel universes, i.e., the space in which the parallel universes in Everett's theory are embedded is Hilbert space.

Another problem solved by Many Worlds concerns the apparent "special" character of our universe. Why should this universe have exactly the right physical parameters (e.g., ratio between electro-

7. DeWitt, Bryce S., Graham, R. Neill (eds). *The Many-Worlds Interpretation of Quantum Mechanics.* Princeton Series in Physics, Princeton University Press, 1973.

8. *Wired News,* Dec. 19, 2001.

9. Beckenstein, Jacob D. Universal upper bound on the entropy-to-energy ratio for bounded systems. Phys. Rev. D 23:287-298, 1981.

magnetic and gravitational force) as to allow the evolution of galaxies, life and intelligence? Many Worlds, in contrast, states that our universe is one out of many possible, many of which are probably lifeless.

The major difficulty of the Everett theory for science fiction writers is that the Many Worlds cannot communicate.[10] This is required to maintain the linearity of the wave function and the consequent orthogonality of the superposed universes. It also leads to the direct prediction that gravity must be quantized; otherwise, the gravitational fields of other worlds could strongly interact with our own universe, leading to effects probably at variance with our best cosmological models. Also, if intercommunication were possible, we would be faced with Fermi's famous question, "Where is everybody?" In all likelihood at least some universes should have developed technology to traverse universes if this is at all possible. But to date we don't seem to have been visited, colonized or subjugated![11] In science fiction Fred Pohl has explored this latter possibility in *The Coming of the Quantum Cats.*

We do have a fiction of non-communicating parallel worlds. That fiction is sometimes called alternate histories and is perhaps best realized in works such as Dick's *Man in the High Castle,* Robinson's *Years of Rice and Salt,* Moore's *Bring the Jubilee,* Gibson and Sterling's *The Difference Engine* and any number of works by Harry Turtledove.

But most science fiction utilizing the Many Worlds interpretation allows intercommunication and even travel among the worlds. Notable examples include Asimov's *The Gods Themselves,* Benford's *Timescape,* Bear's *Eon,* Laumer's *Worlds of the Imperium,* Heinlein's *Number of the Beast,* Reed's *Down the Bright Way,* King's *Dark Tower* series and Zelazny's *Nine Princes in Amber.* In each case, a plethora of worlds is implied, and some communication device, door, drive, or Pattern is used to either communicate with or cross over into alternative worlds. This kind of intersection is not allowed in Everett's theory, but other models hold out the possibility. The first of these assumes that a Type I multiverse is incredibly large, an assumption consistent with Guth's theory of cosmic inflation and with the latest evidence from the Kobe satellite's examination of inhomogeneities in the cosmic background radiation. In addition, it is possible to measure the maximum amount of information possible in any volume of space. Assuming matter is

10. Perhaps the favorite mechanism for traveling to a different parallel universe is the singularity at the center of a black hole. Hawking originally thought that information could disappear from the universe when matter enters a black hole, presumably venturing near the singularity. Where does the information go? Hawking's answer was, somewhere else, possibly a different universe, or a different part of our universe at great spatial or temporal remove. This has been the basis for any number of inter-world adventures, as well as speculation about chains of black hole-connected mother and daughter universes (as in Lee Smolin's *The Life of the Universe,* Oxford, 1999). However, Hawking now says that information can actually leave black holes, although in a rather mangled state. This may remove the major underpinning for the SF convention of singularity-mediated interuniversal travel.

11. There is a possible escape from this limitation. Construction of a sufficiently large quantum computer should access many of the states in Hilbert space accessible by other technological quantum computer builders in other universes. If so, interference could result which we might see as an inexplicable error rate, potential evidence of Many Worlds with technology at least as advanced as our own.

space-filling, it becomes apparent that universal "bubbles" repeat about every 10^{118} meters.[12] These bubbles are isolated from each other by their own event horizons (essentially the shell representing the farthest extent light can travel over the age of a given bubble). Such bubbles would share the same physical laws but could easily have very different boundary conditions. In principle, given enough time it would be possible to journey between two such universes.

The theory of chaotic eternal inflation allows a Type II multiverse which could constitute an infinite number of Type I multiverses, with possibly differing physical constants. But these bubbles of Type I bubbles could not intercommunicate because the space between them is stretching at velocities greater than light. Neither Type I nor Type II universes seem to have been employed in science fiction, even though they are simpler in some ways than the Many Worlds of Everett. This may reflect the more than cosmological distances which appear to separate Type I or II bubble universes. It would seem that science fiction writers prefer to somehow traverse the multiple dimensions of Hilbert Space or brane theory (see below) than the rather mundane spatial distances which are thought to separate these Level I or II classes of universes.

Brane theory provides yet another multiversal theory. Branes are higher dimensional "membranes" (4- to 10-dimensional in most theories) which are embedded in the typical 11-dimensional space of string theory. Branes in many ways are comparable to Many Worlds, with the exception that gravity is an intercommunicating force across branes. Since gravitational waves can carry information, there is no restriction on inter-brane communication. Any device that detects gravitational waves (e.g., LIGO) could in principle pick up gravitational waves from another brane, and it is possible that such waves could be modulated in such a way as to transmit information. In fact, Alastair Reynolds has already employed this concept in the last book in his *Revelation Space* series, *Abolution Gap.* In a fashion reminiscent of Hoyle's *A for Andromeda,* Reynolds has the inhabitants of a "nearby" brane transmit enough information via gravitational "radio" to our brane as to allow their physical reconstitution in our brane.

A final variant multiverse could be called the Platonic multiverse. Here the assumption is that any self-consistent mathematical system, possibly with laws greatly divergent from the physical laws of our universe, could form the basis of a parallel universe. Norman Kagan's story "The Mathenauts"[13] considers exploration in such a multiverse. And in Baxter's *Ring,* the Xeelee aliens leave our universe for a universe of what appear to be Pla-

---

12. There are concerns about the gravitational stability of multiple brane models. However, without knowledge of distance metrics (what is a typical interbrane distance?) or force rules (does gravity go as the inverse ninth power in an 11-dimensional multiverse with nine spatial and two temporal dimensions?) in such a multiverse, it is not clear how serious this problem is. Suffice it to say there are many references in the literature to what are basically "Many Braneworlds" models.

13. Reprinted in *The Mathenauts: Tales of Mathematical Wonder* (Rudy Rucker, ed) Arbor, 1987.

14. Tegmark (2003) refers to the Platonic multiverse as Level IV, where Level III would be the Everett multiverse. Colliding branes (ekpyrotic theory) could give rise to Level II multiverses in this classification scheme.

tonic geometric shapes.[14]

We have seen that the Copenhagen interpretation leads to a number of biological speculations concerning the psychology and physiology of the observer. In what ways can biology be involved in Many Worlds interpretations, and how is that involvement instantiated in science fiction? In Egan's "Wang's Carpets,"[15] the Many Worlds are incorporated into the biological complexity of what at first appears to be a relatively simple colonial organism. But eventually the explorer/protagonists discover that the carpets are single polysaccharide polymers of enormous complexity whose edges exhibit what is called Wang tiling. Wang tiles are isomorphic to universal Turing machines, powerful computers which can emulate any possible deterministic serial computer.[16] But the computational power of the biological computers is applied to generating an extremely high-dimensional space, essentially a Hilbert space, with particles corresponding to Fourier-decomposed periodicities in the Wang tiling of the constantly growing edges of the carpets. These particles have evolved into life forms, including intelligent entities, hermetically sealed from the physical universe.

What Egan has done is to internalize Many Worlds into the topology of an organism. This is an incredible recursion; the organism, presumably a denizen of one of the Many Worlds includes in itself a potentially infinite matrix of the Many Worlds! This is very reminiscent of the superposition of neuronal states in conscious observers which Penrose and others have posited. Ironically, Penrose's discovery of aperiodic Penrose tiling limits the power of Wang tiling, and by extension the computational capacity of a Turing universal computer. From the plausibility angle, it is a bit hard to see how the protagonists are able to "decode" this Hilbert space, since they presumably inhabit only a very small piece of it themselves, by Everett's interpretation completely isolated from all other worlds.

In *Teranesia,* Egan postulates a protein, essentially a polymerase, which reconstructs DNA by extracting information from alternate universes in such a way as to "improve" both the human genome on which it acts, and its own function as a kind of biological quantum computer. Once again this idea, though brilliant, violates the definition of parallelism in the Everett interpretation.

But it may be possible to introduce biology in a Many Worlds theory that does allow interaction. The best candidate for such a possibility is probably the brane model. While 1- and 2-brane models are most common, there is no theoretical limit

---

15. Reprinted in *The Hard SF Renaissance* (David G. Hartwell, Kathryn Cramer, eds.) Orb, 2003.

16. One problem with Turing machines or Wang tiling is that most non-trivial problems turn out to be computationally undecidable (e.g., the famous Halting Problem—can a universal Turing machine determine whether an arbitrary program will eventually halt, or continue to execute indefinitely?—This problem has been proved to be undecidable.) Interestingly, in terms of Wang tiles, if one could cover an infinite plane only with periodically repeating tile patterns, that would be equivalent to showing that the Halting Problem is actually decidable. However, Penrose and others have shown you can cover the plane with aperiodic tiles. Thus, Wang's conjecture fails, and the Halting Problem is undecidable. Nonetheless, it is possible to design nucleic acid analogs of Wang tiles (Seeman, N.C. DNA engineering and its application to nanotechnology, *Trends in Biotechnology,* 17:437-442, 1999) suggesting an enormous potential computational power in the genome.

on how many braneworlds may exist in the 11-dimensional universe of brane theory. The only requirement is that the constituent branes must have a dimensionality one less than that of the 11-dimensional universe in which they are embedded. Thus, braneworlds might have anywhere from four to ten dimensions, assuming our particular brane is of the most degenerate type.

Typical space-time diagrams are similar to the one depicted in Figure 1. Here the vertical axis is time and the horizontal axis is one spatial dimension. The remaining spatial dimensions are suppressed for the sake of presenting an intelligible figure.

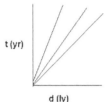

Figure 1 Time-like world lines

The lines are world lines, or the paths that any object takes through space-time. The line at 45 degrees represents light speed; world lines that are relativistically possible are the time-like world lines above the 45 degree line.

Similarly, we can graph entire braneworlds in a space-time diagram representing the dimensionality of the 11-dimensional universe. Figure 2 shows two such branes parallel to each other. The only force thought to be transmissible between such branes is gravity.

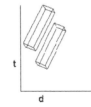

Figure 2-Two parallel 5-branes in 11d space

Recently there has been a suggestion that branes may collide (ekpyrosis), perhaps due to gravitational interaction. Such interactions would be extremely violent, and would essentially reinitialize the branes, perhaps creating entirely new universes in the process. Clearly this is not the type of interaction desirable for inter-brane travel! Figure 3 plots the space-time path of two ekpyrotic branes, with all but one spatial dimension suppressed.

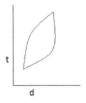

Figure 3-Two ekpyrotic branes colliding

The world lines are curved in a way reminiscent of geodesics in Riemannian space, with a collision at two points, analogous to a Big Bang and a Big Crunch.

But there is no particular limit on such collisions; they may occur indefinitely, creating a situation not unlike the periodic universe models that were popular before it was known that the matter density of the universe, and the consequent contractive gravitational force, was not high enough to overcome the accelerating expansion of the universe. Figure 4 traces the world lines for two such interlaced branes.

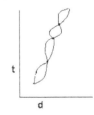

Figure 4-Two ekpyrotic branes colliding periodically

It is pretty clear that ekpyrotic branes, although capable of intersection, do not provide the kind of inter-universal travel beloved of all science fiction fans. There is however, another possibility. It has been suggested that branes may already occur in a "pre-intersected" form[17] and the brane literature considers the intersection of anywhere between 1- and 7-branes.[18] In

17. See for instance Gauntlett, Jerome P. Intersecting branes. QMW-PH-97-13, NI97023, hep-th/9705011.

18. There is no particular reason to exclude the possibility of intersecting 8-10 dimensional branes.

addition, Hawking suggests that two-dimensional time would allow the avoidance of singularities at the Big Bang and potentially at the Big Crunch, if one were to occur. Taken together, these possibilities allow a "checkerboard multiverse", as depicted in Figure 5.

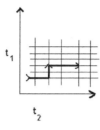

Figure 5-Multiple intersecting 5-branes in two-dimensional time

In this figure we suppress all spatial dimensions, and plot the two time axes. Vertical lines in the diagram represent multiple 4-branes with one vertical time di-mension; horizontal lines represent 4-branes with one horizontal time dimension. Time axes cross at events common to both dimensions. We assume Time's Arrow is always left to right, or down to up. Now it is apparent that if one may turn orthogonally at an event, it is then possible to travel in a brane perpendicular to the original brane. And at some further point in vertical time, one may turn orthogonally again and return to a brane with horizontal time. But that will actually be a different brane than the starting one! Furthermore, such a journey will always end in the future (relative to brane of origin) of the termination brane, consequently eliminating any causality problems (e.g., if Time's Arrow were reversed in adjacent vertical and horizontal branes, one could eventually return to the past of the origin point in one's own brane, kill one's grandfather etc.).

Is there any subjective human experience that would correspond to a perception of a second time dimension?[19] Such a perception would probably be transient, vaguely remembered and probably not logical in any ordinary sense.[20] Certainly the temporal flow of events in a second time direction need have little correspondence to our ordinary experience of linear time.

Such a subjective state is the dreaming that occurs in rapid eye movement (REM) sleep. Although dreams may be vivid, the logic of the waking state does not apply. In Australian aboriginal lore, Dreamtime is the true reality and our waking state is actually the dream! Events occur "all at once" instead of in a linear progression from past to present to future.

Typically there is some event or events in our waking experience that forms the nucleus of the dream. If the dream state is some form of progression along a second time axis, then the nucleating event might be considered an intersection in the checkerboard of Figure 5. Furthermore, from the vantage point of an orthogonal second time dimension, the waking past present and future might well be perceived "all at once," just as stereoscopic vision allows us to perceive the three-dimensional world instead of a radially expanding sequence of two-dimensional shells.

REM sleep is a state whose EEG is indistinguishable from the waking EEG. The vast majority of neurons are active both in the waking state and in REM. Only a few neuronal types (some cholinergic neurons and perhaps three types of monoaminergic neurons) differentiate the states. REM differs from waking in that muscle tone is almost completely absent, and rapid eye movements, which seem to scan the dream landscape, are present.

19. From this point, we leave the realm of published physical hypotheses, and enter the universe of science-fictional pure speculation!

20. For another essentially spatial interpretation of two-dimensional time, see Benford's *Sailing Bright Eternity,* in the Galactic Center series.

REM sleep (except in pathological conditions like narcolepsy) is entered from deep slow wave sleep, a very different electrophysiological state, characterized by massive synchronous and coherent neuronal firing, but at a much lower rate than what is seen in either activated EEG state, waking, or REM sleep.

If we accept the idea of Penrose, Stapp and others that quantum events in the brain are critical to certain cerebral functions, then slow wave sleep might be a global representation of superposed quantum neuronal events, a kind of cerebral Bose-Einstein condensate. Perhaps in this condition the subjective point of view can somehow turn at a ninety degree angle to allow perception along a second temporal dimension. When we wake, the point of view would then turn in the opposite direction, returning us to the waking state with only fragmented memory of the Dreamtime. This is, of course, rank speculation since we have no idea of what mechanism could allow this state of orthogonal temporal perception.

Still, it is interesting to pursue the consequences of this notion. Because of the topology of the checkerboard multiverse, the time flow which we are considering would be in an intersecting brane with at least a temporal dimension (of many possible) at right angles to our own. And the brane we return to on waking would be an alternate brane, probably different in some details from the origin brane. Thus we have an explanation for the peculiar sense of unreality we sometimes experience on waking, what the French refer to as *jamais vu*. And if the branes are indeed slightly different, we get an explanation for that odd stochastic perception— yesterday we understood the universe tolerably well, today ordinary matter is only 4% of the total and the universe is dominated by an energy we do not understand at all. Or yesterday was fine, but today is November 22, 1963 or September 11, 2001.

Now, this hypothetical form of interbrane travel would require certain characteristics: 1) adjacent branes would have to be similar enough that we could explain the progression of perceived events, resulting from historical discrepancies between adjacent branes, as actually occurring in one time dimension in one brane, our ordinary interpretation of reality; 2) to preserve consensus reality, everyone would have to travel about the same interbrane distance each night. It is, of course, true that deviations from consensus are allowed; observers rarely agree on all details of any observation, even one that takes place in our mundane brane. But anyone who traversed too great an interbrane distance might have a radically different history to reconcile; such individuals we label delusional and medicate accordingly. But the rest of us would share a certain commonality with the universe-altering sleeper of LeGuin's *Lathe of Heaven*. [21]

So whatever happened to the Gernsback Continuum?[22] We thought back in the sixties that by now we would have at least a lunar base, and would surely have visited Mars in person. Artificial intelligence, an end to cancer, a successful SETI, these were all things we assumed we would have by 2007. Instead we got the Johnson/Nixon/Reagan/double Bush continuum with Vietnam, an anemic manned space program, threats of global terrorism, etc., etc. Could this be in some literal

---

21. About the worst development in this scenario would be the widespread propagation of the non-sleeping human mutants of Nancy Kress's *Beggars in Spain!*

22. Gibson, William. *Universe* 11, 1981.

way a failure of dreaming? It is interesting to note that the sixties were when antidepressant drugs such as monoamine oxidase inhibitors came into wide use for treating depression. These drugs attenuate or even eliminate REM sleep in many people. Even our narcoleptics began to be treated with drugs that largely prevented their primary symptom, a sudden and uncontrollable REM sleep episode. In our 24-hour society, caffeine and amphetamines have replaced sleep in a widening segment of the population. And today we have drugs that promise to eliminate the need for sleep, with no sleep rebound. Are we then becalmed by sleep deprivation in a region of the "checkerboard" far from the Gernsback continuum?

In the unlikely event that this worldview has some truth to it, all daydreamers have an incredibly important role to play in getting us out of this Sargasso Sea of the mundane. And the science fiction community in particular may provide the dreams that propel us to branes unknown. As O'Shaugnessy said:

> *We are the music makers,*
> *And we are the dreamers of dreams,*
> *Wandering by lone sea-breakers,*
> *And sitting by desolate streams; —*
> *World-losers and world-forsakers,*
> *On whom the pale moon gleams:*
> *Yet we are the movers and shakers*
> *Of the world for ever, it seems.*
>   (Ode, 1-8)[22]

22. *Music and Moonlight: Poems and Songs.* Chatto and Windus, 1874.

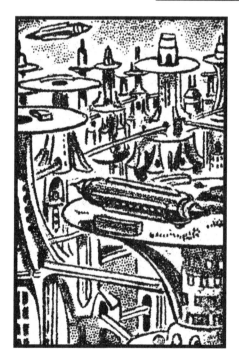

ENLIGHTENMENT

BY MICHAEL KANDEL

Illustrated by Kevin Farrell

I t's going to rain," came a voice out of nowhere, just as Clarence Teagarden had his hand on the doorknob, ready to leave for work at six in the morning. He turned the lights back on; he looked around. A lizard sat on the sofa. It was blue.

That there was no one but Clarence and the lizard in the living room seemed to rule out ventriloquism. And it was hard to imagine that a friend would get up before the sun to plant a rubber lizard with a recording device on Clarence's living room sofa. Clarence hadn't had that kind of joke-playing acquaintance since his college days: Horace Liverwright. The

sound of Horace's guffaws echoing down the dorm hall... how it got on Clarence's nerves, particularly in the evenings at exam time. To this day Clarence hated guffawing.

"Better take an umbrella," the lizard said.

Clarence got out his reading glasses to inspect the creature more closely. It was maybe ten inches long. It had the characteristically knobby, splayed digits of a gecko. Its blue was an unnatural, saturated, slightly phosphorescent blue, as if the animal had fallen into a pot of paint.

Clarence asked, "You're talking to me?"

The gecko smiled at him with its wide, lipless reptilian mouth.

"I wasn't aware that geckos came in blue," Clarence said.

The gecko didn't respond to that either, so Clarence added, "But you're not real, anyway."

"As real as you," it said, flicking its tail twice, timing the flicks so that the first fell on *real* and the second on *you.*

For some time, Clarence had been harboring the suspicion that he was in a dream. And in dreams, things often told the future.

But the gecko's message made no sense. How could it rain? There wouldn't be rain until Thursday, three in the afternoon Thursday, give or take five minutes. Unless, that is, McCloskey was up to something. Had the gecko come to warn Clarence of a new, nasty turn recently taken in the neverending office politics that went on behind Clarence's back?

He told the gecko, setting his jaw, "I'm *not* taking an umbrella today." And with that, he turned off the living room lights again, opened the door, quickly stepped out, closed the door and locked it. He pocketed the key and, as if nothing unusual had taken place, walked the two and a half blocks east on Arbutus to the train station, where the 6:15 was waiting.

As he took his regular seat on the train, he thought that the appearance of the gecko might mean that he would be waking up soon.

He was in his office at ten to seven. The coffee machine was on, gurgling and spreading aroma. Bart raised a hand in greeting through the studio glass, and Marie gave Clarence his work-order sheets. "Morning, all," Clarence said. His colleagues ummed in response, their heads down.

In his work area, he checked the instruments—hygrometers, anemometers, and digital gnomonometers. Everything was within tolerance. He checked the computer update: an occluded front, a few maritime zephyrs on the periphery, a central air mass that wasn't going anywhere soon. Rain my foot, he thought.

He relieved Bart in the studio, made himself comfortable before the mike, took a swallow of coffee, did his report (in fairly good voice, he thought), and at eight o'clock Xavier relieved him.

Back at his computer, Clarence sent around a memo to the staff about the new repair procedure for the solid-state theodolites. A well-worded memo went far in clearing up fuzzy thinking. Then a glance at his watch: there was a meeting. He almost forgot.

In the conference room, Fosdick rehashed what he had already told them about the dew point and multifactor system-system intercorrelativity issue. Clarence struggled not to yawn.

"We should replace our old psychrometers with UV spectrometers," said Fosdick toward the end.

Clarence thought, What took them so long? but he said, "Brilliant idea, Fosdick."

Bart seconded Clarence; Marie thirded. Fosdick was delighted at the support of the rank and file. He was a simple soul, the kind who beamed when you patted him on the back and gave a compliment. He had survived as an exception: every office needed a measuring stick for the iniquity of the others.

On the way home, on Arbutus, the sky grew impossibly gray, and there was actually drizzle. Clarence cursed. His briefcase got wet, since he hadn't taken an umbrella. The drops grew heavier and came faster. The drizzle turned to rain. He looked up at the sky in confusion and wrath.

That evening, after supper, Clarence said to his wife across the table, "Dear, I haven't mentioned this to you before, but I believe I'm in a dream. I may be waking up from it fairly soon, too." He decided not to mention the blue gecko.

She looked at him in that dry way she had. "You don't say," she said, putting down her cup. The cup clicked on the saucer, as if providing a sardonic cluck.

"I thought you should know," Clarence said, "seeing as you are part of my dream and will end when it does. We've spent, after all, a number of years together."

"Thirteen," she said. "And you forgot our anniversary last week."

Shit, he thought.

Husband and wife regarded each other for a sober moment. It had been a reasonably good marriage, though there wasn't a great deal of billing and cooing in it. He had been too busy, she too cool. But forgetting her anniversary yet again made him look disorganized. He had written the occasion in his date book last week but in the rush of things had forgotten to consult the date book.

"What do you expect to find," his wife asked him, "when you wake up?"

"I have no idea," he answered. "But I imagine that much will become clear."

"My advice to you, Clarence," she said, looking at her fingernails carefully, "is to take a vacation."

Clarence's boss, Arthur Highfield the Tenth, Esquire, had much the same advice when Clarence broke the news to him the following day. Clarence felt he had to do this since many crucial functions of the weather station depended on him. It wouldn't be right to leave Highfield in the lurch, in the event that Highfield and the weather station continued to lead some

kind of ghost existence after Clarence left them by waking up.

"Have you told this to McCloskey?" Clarence's boss asked.

"Not yet," said Clarence.

"Good. I wouldn't." Then Highfield leaned over and said in a surprisingly chummy murmur, "Tell me, Clarence. How long has it been since you went on a cruise?"

"I don't know," said Clarence. "Thirteen years?"

"You've been driving yourself. People are remarking how hard you've been driving yourself. Trainor, for example, just the other day. Sometimes it's not a bad idea, Clarence, to stop and smell the roses."

Easy for Highfield to say. Highfield had the key to the executive billiard room. When Clarence did too—when he had cleared the double hurdle of McCloskey and Trainor and got the better of Gloria Dora Batory, the biggest backstabber of them all—then and only then could he take a cruise to the Islands or the Gulf, and extol to underlings the virtues of smelling the roses.

By curious coincidence, Clarence had his annual checkup that same day, on his lunch break. The doctor was not pleased with the angiogram, encephalogram, and digital phalangiogram. "You should take a vacation," the doctor said, looking at the readouts.

"You're not the first to tell me this," said Clarence, buttoning up his shirt. "Or the second."

"I can prescribe a mild tranquilizer. It'll take the edge off."

"I'll be all right, Doc. Besides, I won't be here much longer."

"Actually, not to be morbid, but I was going to raise that possibility, Mr. Teagarden. Your systolic—"

"You don't understand, Doc. I'll be

waking up soon."

The doctor raised his eyebrows.

"This is all a dream I'm having," Clarence explained. "It'll be ending in a day or two, I think."

"Hm. And what gives you this impression, Mr. Teagarden?"

"I saw a blue gecko on my sofa yesterday morning, and it spoke to me."

"Really."

"It told me it would rain, Doc. Told *me,* can you imagine that? And then damn if there wasn't rain. My briefcase got wet. I think it may be ruined."

"It does rain sometimes, Mr. Teagarden."

"Of course it does, Doc, but only when I schedule it."

On the train home, Clarence sat with his friend Jack. Jack wasn't interested in Clarence's blue gecko problem. He had a problem of his own: a teenage daughter who was pregnant and refused to reveal the identity of the father. Also, just yesterday both Bob Fexler and Reginald Quayside had been promoted over Jack although Jack had been with the firm of Cobbler and Cobbler two years longer than either man.

The next day—amazing how quickly time passed when you were swamped— Clarence handed McCloskey his work-up for the next month before the bell rang. McCloskey looked it over, frowned, and said, "These isobars here."

Clarence pointed out those isotherms there. It balanced.

McCloskey looked harder for something wrong. "What's this?" he asked at last.

"What?"

"Here." Pointing with a manicured finger, gingerly, as if the chart might dirty him.

"Oh, that," said Clarence. "We've begun taking coriolis and borealis forces into account. It's a pain, but it pays in the long run. Less correction afterward."

"I'm not so sure."

"The Germans are doing it."

"Oh?"

"Bremen. Frankfurt on the Oder."

"Well, in that case."

"Klinga. Gernsheim. Fackelsgart."

"You appear to have done your homework."

"I've had a good teacher."

Clarence stayed late recalibrating the cirrostratus and cumulonimbus indicators. He didn't need to do it, but he felt charged up after his sweet little victory over Mc-Closkey, which he replayed several times in his head, chuckling. Before he left, he cast a supervisory eye on the row of meteorological gauges and vanes. The mercury was right where it should be. Ditto the precipitation. The wind was west by northwest and steady as a rock at 6.4 knots.

He grabbed a bite to eat at the diner across the street before he took the 10:45 home. Someone had left a newspaper on the table next to his, so Clarence took it and looked at it while he ate his oversalted cheeseburger and cold, limp fries. The headline read BLUE GECKO PREDICTS UNPREDICTED RAIN. The subhead read WEATHER STATIONS IN DISARRAY. WHAT ARE WE PAYING FOR? CONGRESS ASKS. The subsubhead read CLARENCE TEAGARDEN FACES QUESTIONING. It was all nonsense, of course. He turned several pages, and his eyes fell on the following announcement:

"Professor Wallace Pink, renowned astral sensitive, will give a talk at the Central Library this Thursday evening, 8:30, on the ladder of worlds and how we approach enlightenment as we climb from life to life, from dream to dream. It is to be hoped that weather operative Clarence Teagarden will attend."

Clarence made a mental note to attend Professor Pink's lecture. It sounded interesting. But in the whirl of work that week he completely forgot. The blue gecko put in two more appearances—at home, on Clarence's towel during a shower; and at work, on Clarence's monitor during a status report reformatting. On both occasions, the dream animal made oracular utterances, in the vein of "A trough coming this way, a big one." Clarence was tempted to give the gecko a smack but decided he better not: it might have a poison sac.

On Friday morning, after his report, Gloria Dora called him into her office over the intercom. Never inside her office before, he was impressed by the carpet, envious of the computer, and stunned by the aquarium. The fishtank was twice the size of his desk. Gloria Dora's fish all had lacy, graceful tails that moved like pennants in syrup.

"Clarence," she said, narrowing her lashed and lidded eyes over gaunt cheeks.

"Yes?" he said.

"There's been talk that our performance is down." She scrutinized him through the slits of her eyes. He wondered if she had heard about the blue gecko and its wildcat forecasts. "There have been stories in the press."

"Well, you know the newspapers," he said.

"You're not losing it, are you, Clarence?"

"Definitely not."

"Because if you are..."

"Not to worry, Gloria Dora. I've never been more in control." He chortled, to show her how much in control he was.

"Our operation is known for its reliabil-ity. We don't want to be associated with anything hallucinatory."

"Certainly not."

"And stop sucking up to McCloskey," she said, her eyes completely closed now, but he knew she could see him perfectly through the lids. "You're out of your depth there."

He nodded. "Lovely fish you have," he said on his way out. "That aquarium must weigh at least a ton."

Xavier called, "Hey, Clarence, look at this. The weirdos in the world." Xavier was holding up a folded newspaper. Clarence took the paper from him and read:

"Professor Pink's important lecture was postponed on account of ominous weather. It is rescheduled for this evening, same time, same place. It is to be hoped that Clarence Teagarden will make it this time and stop letting himself be distracted by the duties of a job that is not real, after all."

"I should go," Clarence said, scratching his ear.

"Can you imagine a guy being called Pink?" asked Xavier.

"Can you imagine a guy being called Teagarden?" said Clarence.

"I don't know. Wasn't there a trombone player once, named Teagarden?"

"I don't even remember where that damn lecture was."

"Central Library," said the blue gecko. "And it's 8:30, in case you forgot that too."

"What the holy thunder is that?" asked Xavier, eyes widening.

"It's a blue gecko," said Clarence. "It's been following me."

"And it talks?"

"It talks."

"It's going to come down heavy," the gecko told them, "when it comes down."

"Shut up," said Clarence.

The remainder of the day was uneventful. Clarence didn't take the 5:45 home. Instead, he worked late, had a burnt cheeseburger at the diner across the street, then walked up Seventh Avenue, past Runyan, to the Central Library.

It was closed—the door locked and all the lights off—but before Clarence could turn away with a muttered curse about wild-goose chases, the door opened and a gray-whiskered gentleman invited him in.

"You're here for the lecture?" asked the gentleman as Clarence followed him up a flight of marble steps that had a polished brass banister out of an earlier and better century.

"Yes," said Clarence. "Why is the place so dark?"

Their words echoed.

"Energy conservation," said the gentleman.

"Is Professor Pink here?" asked Clarence, doing his best not to stumble.

"He is," said the gentleman. When they entered a room, the gentleman switched on the lights, and the room turned out to be an auditorium. The whiskered gentleman faced Clarence and said, "I'm Professor Pink."

"Pleased to meet you. I'm Clarence Teagarden," Clarence said, offering his hand.

The professor didn't take it. "I know who you are," he said.

"So when does the lecture begin? We must be early."

"It begins now."

"There's no one here."

"You're here."

"You mean you're giving a lecture in an auditorium to only one person?"

"Is the glass half empty or is the glass half full?" asked the professor.

The man had muttonchops and unpleas-antly red cheeks, as if he had been in raw weather for years, perhaps aboard a ship on the North or Baltic Sea.

"You sound like that damn gecko," Clarence said. "Where should I sit?"

"Anywhere you like." The professor spread out an arm. There must have been more than a thousand seats. There were several tiers. One could put on a German opera in this place and have room left over for another German opera.

Clarence went and took a seat in the seventh row, a little to the right to get a quarter-profile of the speaker, while the professor took out his notes and arranged them on the lectern.

Professor Pink raised his head, cleared his throat, and began:

"Many of you—"

"There's only one of me," said Clarence.

"Please don't interrupt."

"I'm sorry."

"Many of you," continued Professor Pink, "have perhaps asked yourselves why life seems so strange sometimes. Why it seems like a dream."

Clarence thought: I've asked myself that a lot.

"There are manifold planes of existence."

Clarence thought: I'm not surprised.

"Please stop making comments in your head," said the professor. "It's distracting."

"I'm sorry."

"There are manifold planes of existence, worlds upon worlds, and we climb from world to world, from this world to the next world to the world beyond that, and as we climb this great existential, metempsychical, epistemological ladder, each rung takes us a little closer to the truth."

There was silence. Clarence waited for the professor to consult his notes and go on, but the professor didn't.

"Go on," Clarence finally said.

"That's it," said Professor Pink, folding up his notes and putting them in his jacket pocket.

"That's the whole lecture?"

"Yes. Does anyone have a question?"

"I have a question," said Clarence.

"Yes, Mr. Teagarden. What is your question?"

"If it's just a lot of worlds, then the next world will be a dream, too, won't it?"

"That was a very good question, Mr. Teagarden. Yes, you're right. The next world will be a dream, too. And the world after that. And so on."

"And the one before it, too."

"And the one before it, too. That's exactly right."

"But, in that case, how do we know we're dreaming?" asked Clarence. "I mean, know in the first place? For example, blue geckos don't talk, and they're not blue, either, in the real world. Or at least not blue as if they were dunked in a can of paint."

"I am what I am," said the gecko, on the seat in front of him.

"Shut up," said Clarence.

"Go on, Mr. Teagarden," said Professor Pink.

"Well," said Clarence, "what I'm getting at is this. How do I know geckos don't talk and that they're not blue, if I've never been in the real world, only in dream worlds?"

The professor nodded and said, "What probably happened in your particular case is that you slipped down a rung instead of climbing up a rung."

"Come again?"

"We carry with us a vestigial memory of our previous worlds. If we reach a height, in our climb upward on the great ladder of all-existence, a height that we have never before attained, then you are absolutely correct, Mr. Teagarden, we can have no notion that we are in a dream, for the memory of the world that was before will not point to the impossibility, say, of a blue gecko that speaks. If, on the other hand, we should slip down a rung, which doesn't happen often but does sometimes happen, unfortunately, then our vestigial memory will warn us, howbeit subliminally, that certain things that are taking place around us have no business taking place."

"In other words," said Clarence, thinking, "in my last world, I was higher up, closer to the truth."

"Precisely."

"But that's awful. What did I do to slip? I mean, I'd like to know so it doesn't happen again."

"Sometimes we try too hard, Mr. Teagarden," said Professor Pink, steepling his fingers. "Sometimes we tie ourselves up in tight little knots of should be and shouldn't be instead of going with the natural flow of is. The universal direction is upward, ever upward, but an individual may not be in touch with that direction. He may not take vacations, to give one example, thereby disturbing the precious circassian rhythm of his holistic being-in-self, his inner compass of rightness. Or he may be inattentive to the needs of his wife, forgetting such occasions for personal celebration as her birthday and anniversary. If I may say so, Mr. Teagarden, you seem to be that blinkered-visioned, tight-ass, self-centered, type-A type of person."

Clarence shook his head. "You don't know the place where I work. If I take a vacation, there'll be someone else at my desk when I get back. Probably Adolph Foovis." Foovis was a detestable ass-kisser who used floral breath fresheners.

When Clarence went home, it was too late to buy flowers, but he decided he would treat his neglected wife to a little lovemaking. It had been how long since the last time? A month? A year? Maybe the professor was right, that Clarence was letting his job dominate his life. He removed his clothes and tiptoed over to his wife's bed.

But the bed was empty. Puzzled, he turned on the lamp and saw that the bed was made. Not a wrinkle in it. He noticed a note pinned to her pillow. He unpinned it and read:

"Dear Clarence, I've decided to leave you. I'm joining the interpretive ballet. It's something I've always wanted to do. And the exercise will help my circulation. There's cold chicken in the refrigerator. Edith."

He shook his head. He hadn't even known her name was Edith. What was it Professor Pink had said? The inner compass of rightness. Could it be that Clarence simply didn't know which way was up?

"I don't belong here," he told the empty room. "I belong in a more real world."

There was a muted rattling and a hissing at the window. He went to the window and looked out. It was hail mixed with sleet. Clarence swore. This meant that McCloskey had used Foovis's proposal at the last minute, even though Edgerton had signed off on Clarence's proposal and given him the go-ahead for April and May. What a treacherous jungle it was at work.

Suddenly he was filled with revulsion. He made up his mind. He had had it with this world.

The next day, he told Jack on the train, "I should be higher up than I am."

"Me too," said Jack, sighing. "Ten years, and no promotion. I'm going nowhere."

"I'm not talking about that. I'm talking about Professor Pink's metempsychical ladder. I must have made some mistake, some wrong step, in a previous world, and now I'm stuck here. No, Jack, I'm taking the bull of all-existence by the horns."

"Professor Pink? What kind of a name is Professor Pink?"

"All our names are stupid," said Clarence. "Look at Barnaby Measley."

"What's stupid about Barnaby Measley? He's an okay guy."

"I don't have a name," the blue gecko put in.

"What the holy thunder?" exclaimed Jack. "Is that a blue lizard?"

"It's a gecko. Don't pay any attention to it," said Clarence.

"Hi there, little feller," Jack said to the gecko.

The gecko flicked its tail twice.

"I've decided," Clarence said, staring out the window at the gray houses and black oil tanks going past, "to see a personal executioner."

Jack wasn't listening, fascinated by the gecko.

Clarence made the appointment for Friday. He took with him his friend Jack and Cecily Celeste from the office, since two witnesses were needed. Both Jack and Cecily Celeste had been ill-at-ease to begin with, but when they entered Dr. Rassmussen's office, they turned slightly green.

The secretary, a dour woman who wore her steel-gray hair in a bun, gave Clarence a number of papers to fill out: a questionnaire, a release form, an affadavit. "Dr. Rassmussen will see you in about thirty minutes," she said.

"Thirty minutes?"

"You're lucky today. It's usually more like an hour and thirty minutes."

"What takes so long?"

The secretary gave him a cold look. "The people who come here, Mr. Teagarden, are making a fairly big decision. We can't rush them."

There were two other people in the waiting room, a man and a woman. The man was reading a news magazine and had an annoying sniff. He seemed to time each sniff to coincide with the turning of a page. Clarence wanted to hit him. The woman sat in the far corner, by a coffee table, and held her head in her hands.

"Half an hour's not so bad," whispered Cecily Celeste.

"It'll be an hour by the time we get back," said Clarence. "I won't have time for lunch. Edgerton's been breathing down my neck."

"But you won't be going back," Cecily Celeste said.

"Oh, right. I forgot."

"I hate waiting rooms," said Jack.

No one said anything for a while. They listened to the man turn pages and sniff.

"Clarence?" asked Jack.

"What?"

"Are you sure you want to go through with this?"

"I'm sure."

The woman was called in first. She heaved a long, melodramatic sigh as the secretary led her to Dr. Rassmussen.

"What do they use, an injection?" Jack asked.

"I don't know," said Clarence. "Who cares?"

"I mean," said Jack, "I wouldn't like it to be painful. For your sake."

"I don't imagine it's painful," said Clarence. "If it was painful, people would go to someone else, wouldn't they?"

"Next," said the secretary after a while, and the sniffler put the news magazine down and got up.

"Isn't it sad?" said Cecily Celeste, to no one in particular.

"I don't see what's so sad about it," said Clarence. "They're not leaving anything real."

"I know you think we're in a dream," said Jack, "but what if you're wrong?"

"I'll give you an example. Take that ceiling."

Jack and Cecily Celeste looked up at the ceiling.

"What about it?" asked Jack.

"It's so damn high," said Clarence. "We don't need twenty-foot ceilings."

"Ceilings are all like that."

"Yes, and that's the reason there aren't many floors in office buildings. Think of it, all that vertical space going to waste. If office buildings had thirty floors instead of eight, a lot more work could be got done. That's what my vestigial memory tells me."

"Mr. Teagarden," called the secretary.

"Time for you, Clarence," said Jack, and his voice broke a little. "I'll miss you, old man."

"You probably won't even exist, Jack," said Clarence, "when I wake up."

They followed the secretary to Dr. Rassmussen's office. Clarence was in a foul mood. Perhaps it was because Edith had walked out, leaving only one stringy drumstick for him in the refrigerator.

The secretary knocked a quick two-knuckle knock on the door and opened it. Dr. Rassmussen was writing something at his desk. "Have a seat," he said, not looking up. Clarence, Jack, and Cecily Celeste took seats opposite the personal executioner.

He finished writing, looked up, and asked, "Which one of you is Clarence Teagarden?"

"That's me," said Clarence.

"Sound mind?" asked the executioner, running a tired eye over some of the papers Clarence had filled out.

"Reasonably sound, I guess," said Clarence. "I have a job and more responsibilities than most."

"Is there a will?"

"No."

"Most people neglect to do that," said Dr. Rassmussen with a tsk, and he leaned over and gave Clarence a paper that was full of fine print. "You sign at the bottom, and your witnesses sign in the spaces to the right. Don't bother to date it, I'll do that."

They all signed.

"Don't you think you should have read it first?" Jack whispered as the paper was handed back.

Clarence felt like hitting Jack. "Let's get this over with, shall we?" he said to the executioner in a hard voice.

Dr. Rassmussen said to Jack and Cecily Celeste, "You can leave now." They got up and left, looking over their shoulders anxiously. Cecily Celeste gave a weak little wave as the door closed.

Dr. Rassmussen asked Clarence to take off his shirt and get up on the high recliner-table covered with disposable white paper. Clarence did, feeling chilly. The executioner attached electrodes to his head and chest.

"Are you going to electrocute me?" asked Clarence.

"No, this is for vital signs."

"To make sure I'm dead, when I'm dead?"

"That's right, Mr. Teagarden."

"You don't have to strap me down, too. I'm not going anywhere."

But his arms and both legs were strapped down tight. That was the procedure, evidently. Probably state law.

"Barometer's falling at eleven o'clock," said the blue gecko. "A cyclosyncline."

"Shut up," said Clarence. "I'm leaving you behind. And this stupid dream."

Dr. Rassmussen put on black rubber gloves. They were heavy-duty and ribbed. When they were on snug, he leaned over Clarence and put his gloved hands carefully and firmly around Clarence's neck.

"You don't mean you're going to do it that way...?"

Which was all Clarence could get out, because his windpipe was effectively blocked after that, from the throttling.

"Yes," answered the doctor as he throttled. "This method saves money—not much per person, maybe, but it—grunt—adds up." He panted a little from the exertion. "In addition," he went on, "I get exercise this way. It's not healthy, Mr. Teagarden—to sit all day, you know, in an office—grunt—without some—grunt—physical activity."

Clarence was really put out. He felt that somehow he was being made the butt of a joke. And this method of execution left a lot to be desired. It was no picnic having your lungs scream for air and your eyes bulge.

I hate this, he thought. It's so ridiculous. Finally, with relief, the lights went out.

C larence P. Ticklefloor the Seventeenth and Three-Quarters was sitting at his obloidate desquette working out persimmon daquiri mush algorithms (hard to manipulate, arthritic thumbs ouching, Fazio shouldn't insist on buying them cheap) when the thundercloud boinked the building and leaked a few scraggly bolts. The angels groaned, "Ah." That's all they were good for, like a damn Greek chorus, yes we know the milk is spilt, let's get on with it, all right? Clarence went to shut the blinds, because he didn't need bolts on the floor or in the petit pantry melting, all that blue wrinkling the carioca and credenza. Elsie wouldn't be in to clean until Thirdsday, and the boss bottlenose madras was coming for dinner, or came, depending on the ding-dong, Swiss movement and quartz.

Clarence took the 8:88 roller home, and at the door his wife said, "Have a good day?" pie-faced and white like a silly behind on a flag flapping cheers.

"Okay," he said.

"Dokay," she said.

"Dear?" he said.

"Year?" she said.

After their shallow dance-a-pants they sat down at the table and bibbed their chins nicely dimpled to give the poor little brown fuzzies a sporting chance, time for scampering a dozen for their lives across the cassar, like fingers loose or a English fox hunt with long horns. Pounce went the forks, forking yoicks, hunger makes us do it, we're animals ourselves, sergeant, after all.

"Dear? I think I'm dreaming." As he chewed.

"Dreaming?" As she swallowed wriggly-lumpily, one-two-three.

"Having a dream."

"Cream."

"No thanks."

"You forgot my birthmark, triple bastard."

"No? Yes? I'm so busy."

"Which end is up, you?"

"You're right, I don't."

"You don't."

"True."

"Empty a little, diddle. You're overdue."

"I should," he admitted, "but, you know, they always put curlew scissors and the knippers in the closet lumbering when my back is turned like Iago, and then what? It's the glue factory."

Fester Dirigiblus Comparison Slash Fife called Clarence into the porcelain star chamber next morning with freshets a-flying and starched angles down and said:

"My boy, oy, you should empty a little, diddle, you're overdue, I say it."

"I should."

And damn if the doctor didn't conclude the same or will conclude, depending on which cam or cog of the great toothed circle you habituate, mate, as it turns.

Clarence's friend, Baker Beaglefever the Nought, stout soul, no snout, spake to him on the 7:77, where they sat tandem touching arse to arse, saying: "So you still think you are?"

"Alas, I think it."

"Pinkit."

No, actually, not Pinkit, it's Professor Gonzaga Glom Glom in this dream, straight from Ancient Peru or so they say but who knows? Clarence's thought balloon is cloudy when he attends the big loquation oration. He's heard it before, he thinks, the manifold planes, we drop from world to world, fetal, like a plunkily ball binking down step by step, each step closer to the big substrate, the bottom of bottoms, the bedrock of the final bed. It must be the truth, what else could it be, the thing what lies under all what, all else, all what else, Elsie, and supports it?

Clarence doesn't know. It's Saint Elmo again at eleven o'clock, crackling like cellophane in a soda pop consortium. He hates to say it, fellows, but you know what, he's getting a little overwired, tired, yes, of answers and destinations.

Maybe it's a good thing.

Bing.

THE WORLDS OF IF

BY STANLEY G. WEINBAUM

Illustrated by Frank R. Paul

stopped on the way to the Staten Island Airport to call up, and that was a mistake, doubtless, since I had a chance of making it otherwise. But the office was affable. "We'll hold the ship five minutes for you," the clerk said. "That's the best we can do."

So I rushed back to my taxi and we spun off to the third level and sped across the Staten Bridge like a comet treading a steel rainbow. I had to be in Moscow by evening, by eight o'clock in fact, for the opening of bids on the Ural Tunnel. The Government required the personal presence of an agent of each bidder, but the firm should have known better than to send me, Dixon Wells, even though the N.J. Wells Corporation is, so to speak, my father. I have a—well, an undeserved reputation for being late to everything; something always comes up to prevent me from getting anywhere on time. It's never *my* fault; this time it was a chance encounter with my old physics professor, old Haskel van Manderpootz. I couldn't very well just say hello and good-bye to him; I'd been a favorite of his back in the college days of 2014.

I missed the airliner, of course. I was still on the Staten Bridge when I heard the roar of the catapult and the Soviet rocket *Baikal* hummed over us like a tracer bullet with a long tail of flame.

We got the contract anyway; the firm wired our man in Beirut and he flew up to Moscow, but it didn't help my reputation. However, I felt a great deal better when I saw the evening papers; the *Baikal,* flying at the north edge of the eastbound lane to avoid a storm, had locked wings with a British fruitship and all but a hundred of her five hundred passengers were lost. I

had almost become "the late Mr. Wells" in a grimmer sense.

I'd made an engagement for the following week with old van Manderpootz. It seems he'd transferred to N.Y.U. as head of the department of Newer Physics—that is, of Relativity. He deserved it; the old chap was a genius if ever there was one, and even now, eight years out of college, I remember more from his course than from half a dozen in calculus, steam and gas, mechanics, and other hazards on the path to an engineer's education. So on Tuesday night I dropped in an hour or so late, to tell the truth, since I'd forgotten about the engagement until midevening.

He was reading in a room as disorderly as ever. "Humph!" be grunted. "Time changes everything but habit, I see. You were a good student, Dick, but I seem to recall that you always arrived in class toward the middle of the lecture."

"I had a course in East Hall just before," I explained. "I couldn't seem to make it in time."

"Well, it's time you learned to be on time," he growled. Then his eyes twinkled. "Time!" he ejaculated. "The most fascinating word in the language. Here we've used it five times (there goes the sixth time—and the seventh!) in the first minute of conversation; each of us understands the other, yet science is just beginning to learn its meaning. Science? I mean that *I* am beginning to learn."

I sat down. "You and science are synonymous," I grinned "Aren't you one of the world's outstanding physicists?"

"One of them!" he snorted. *"One* of them, eh! And who are the others?"

"Oh, Corveille and Hastings and Shrimski—"

"Bah! Would you mention them in the same breath with the name of van Manderpootz? A pack of jackals, eating the crumbs of ideas that drop from my feast of thoughts! Had you gone back into the last century, now—had you mentioned Einstein and de Sitter—there, perhaps, are names worthy to rank with (or just below) van Manderpootz!"

I grinned again in amusement. "Einstein *was* considered pretty good, wasn't he?" I remarked. "After all, he was the first to tie time and space to the laboratory. Before him they were just philosophical concepts."

"He didn't!" rasped the professor. "Perhaps, in a dim, primitive fashion, he showed the way, but I—*I*, van Manderpootz—am the first to seize time, drag it into my laboratory, and perform an experiment on it."

"Indeed? And what sort of experiment?"

"What experiment, other than simple measurement, is possible to perform?" he snapped.

"Why—I don't know. To travel in it?"

"Exactly."

"Like these time-machines that are so popular in the current magazines? To go into the future or the past?"

"Bah! Many bahs! The future or the past—pfui! It needs no van Manderpootz to see the fallacy in that. Einstein showed us that much."

"How? It's conceivable, isn't it?"

"Conceivable? And you, Dixon Wells, studied under van Manderpootz!" He grew red with emotion, then grimly calm. "Listen to me. You know how time varies with the speed of a system—Einstein's relativity."

"Yes."

"Very well. Now suppose then that the great engineer Dixon Wells invents a ma-chine capable of traveling very fast, enormously fast, nine-tenths as fast as light. Do you follow? Good. You then fuel this miracle ship for a little jaunt a half-million miles, which, since mass (and with it inertia) increases according to the Einstein formula with increasing speed, takes all the fuel in the world. But you solve that. You use atomic energy. Then, since at nine-tenths light-speed, your ship weighs about as much as the sun, you disintegrate North America to give you sufficient motive power. You start off at that speed, a hundred and sixty-eight thousand miles per second, and you travel for two hundred and four thousand miles. The acceleration has now crushed you to death, but you have penetrated the future." He paused, grinning sardonically. "Haven't you?"

"Yes."

"And how far?"

I hesitated.

"Use your Einstein formula!" he screeched. "How far? I'll tell you. *One second!*" He grinned triumphantly. "That's how possible it is to travel into the future. And as for the past—in the first place, you'd have to exceed light-speed, which immediately entails the use of more than an infinite number of horsepowers. We'll assume that the great engineer Dixon Wells solves that little problem too, even though the energy output of the whole universe is not an infinite number of horsepowers. Then he applies this more than infinite power to travel at two hundred and four thousand miles per second for ten seconds. He has then penetrated the past. How far?"

Again I hesitated.

"I'll tell you. *One second!*" He glared at me. "Now all you have to do is to design such a machine, and then van Manderpootz will admit the possibility of traveling into the future—for a limited number of seconds. As for the past, I have just explained that all the energy in the universe is insufficient for that."

"But," I stammered, "you just said that you—"

"I did *not* say anything about traveling into either future or past, which I have just demonstrated to you to be impossible—a practical impossibility in the one case and an absolute one in the other."

"Then how *do* you travel in time?"

"Not even van Manderpootz can perform the impossible," said the professor, now faintly jovial. He tapped a thick pad of typewriter paper on the table beside him. "See, Dick, this is the world, the universe." He swept a finger down it. "It is long in time, and"—sweeping his hand across it—"it is broad in space, but"—now jabbing his finger against its center—"it is very thin in the fourth dimension. Van Manderpootz takes always the shortest, the most logical course. I do not travel along time, into past or future. No. Me, I travel across time, sideways!"

I gulped. "Sideways into time! What's there?"

"What would naturally be there?" he snorted. "Ahead is the future; behind is the past. Those are real, the worlds of past and future. What worlds are neither past nor future, but contemporary and yet—extemporal—existing, as it were, in time parallel to our time?"

I shook my head.

"Idiot!" he snapped. "The conditional worlds, of course! The worlds of 'if.' Ahead are the worlds to be; behind are the worlds that were; to either side are the worlds that might have been—the worlds of 'if!'"

"Eh?" I was puzzled. "Do you mean that you can see what will happen if I do such and such?"

"No!" he snorted. "My machine does not reveal the past nor predict the future. It will show, as I told you, the conditional worlds. You might express it, by 'if I had done such and such, so and so would have happened.' The worlds of the subjunctive mode."

"Now how the devil does it do that?"

"Simple, for van Manderpootz! I use polarized light, polarized not in the horizontal or vertical planes, but in the direction of the fourth dimension—an easy matter. One uses Iceland spar under colossal pressure, that is all. And since the worlds are very thin in the direction of the fourth dimension, the thickness of a single light wave, though it be but millionths of an inch, is sufficient. A considerable improvement over time-traveling in past or future, with its impossible velocities and ridiculous distances!"

"But—are those—worlds of 'if'—real?"

"Real? What is real? They are real, perhaps, in the sense that two is a real number as opposed to $\sqrt{-2}$, which is imaginary. They are the worlds that would have been *if*— Do you see?"

I nodded. "Dimly. You could see, for instance, what New York would have been like if England had won the Revolution instead of the Colonies."

"That's the principle, true enough, but you couldn't see that on the machine. Part of it, you see, is a Horsten psychomat (stolen from one of *my* ideas, by the way) and you, the user, become part of the device. Your own mind is necessary to furnish the background. For instance, if George Washington could have used the mechanism after the signing of peace, he could have seen what you suggest. We can't. You can't even see what would have happened if I hadn't invented the thing, but *I* can. Do you understand?"

"Of course. You mean the background has to rest in the past experiences of the user."

"You're growing brilliant," he scoffed. "Yes. The device will show ten hours of what would have happened *if*—condensed, of course, as in a movie, to half an hour's actual time."

"Say, that sounds interesting!"

"You'd like to see it? Is there anything you'd like to find out? Any choice you'd alter?"

"I'll say—a thousand of 'em. I'd like to know what would have happened if I'd sold out my stocks in 2009 instead of '10. I was a millionaire in my own right then, but I was a little—well, a little late in liquidating."

"As usual," remarked van Manderpootz. "Let's go over to the laboratory then."

The professor's quarters were but a block from the campus. He ushered me into the Physics Building, and thence into his own research laboratory, much like the one I had visited during my courses under him. The device—he called it his "subjunctivisor," since it operated in hypothetical worlds—occupied the entire center table. Most of it was merely a Horsten psychomat, but glittering crystalline and glassy was the prism of Iceland spar, the polarizing agent that was the heart of the instrument.

Van Manderpootz pointed to the headpiece. "Put it on," he said, and I sat staring at the screen of the psychomat. I suppose everyone is familiar with the Horsten psychomat; it was as much a fad a few years ago as the ouija board a century back. Yet it isn't just a toy; sometimes, much as the ouija board, it's a real aid to memory. A maze of vague and colored shadows is caused to drift slowly across the screen, and one watches them, meanwhile visualizing whatever scene or circumstances he is trying to remember. He turns a knob

that alters the arrangement of lights and shadows, and when, by chance, the design corresponds to his mental picture—presto! There is his scene re-created under his eyes. Of course his own mind adds the details. All the screen actually shows are these tinted blobs of light and shadow, but the thing can be amazingly real. I've seen occasions when I could have sworn the psychomat showed pictures almost as sharp and detailed as reality itself; the illusion is sometimes as startling as that.

Van Manderpootz switched on the light, and the play of shadows began. "Now recall the circumstances of, say, a half-year after the market crash. Turn the knob until the picture clears, then stop. At that point I direct the light of the subjunctivisor upon the screen, and you have nothing to do but watch."

I did as directed. Momentary pictures formed and vanished. The inchoate sounds of the device hummed like distant voices, but without the added suggestion of the picture, they meant nothing. My own face flashed and dissolved and then, finally, I had it. There was a picture of myself sitting in an ill-defined room; that was all. I released the knob and gestured.

A click followed. The light dimmed, then brightened. The picture cleared, and amazingly, another figure emerged, a woman. I recognized her; it was Whimsy White, erstwhile star of television and premiere actress of the *Vision Varieties of '09*. She was changed on that picture, but I recognized her.

I'll say I did! I'd been trailing her all through the boom years of '07 to '10, trying to marry her, while old N.J. raved and ranted and threatened to leave everything to the Society for Rehabilitation of the Gobi Desert. I think those threats were what kept her from accepting me, but after I took my own money and ran it up to a couple of million in that crazy market of

'08 and '09, she softened.

Temporarily, that is. When the crash of the spring of '10 came and bounced me back on my father and into the firm of N. J. Wells, her favor dropped a dozen points to the market's one. In February we were engaged, in April we were hardly speaking. In May they sold me out. I'd been late again.

And now, there she was on the psychomat screen, obviously plumping out, and not nearly so pretty as memory had pictured her. She was staring at me with an expression of enmity, and I was glaring back. The buzzes became voices.

"You nit-wit!" she snapped. "You can't bury me out here. I want to go back to New York, where there's a little life. I'm bored with you and your golf."

"And I'm bored with you and your whole dizzy crowd."

"At least they're *alive.* You're a walking corpse. Just because you were lucky enough to gamble yourself into the money, you think you're a tin god."

"Well, I *don't* think *you're* Cleopatra! Those friends of yours—they trail after you because you give parties and spend money—*my* money."

"Better than spending it to knock a white walnut along a mountainside!"

"Indeed? You ought to try it, Marie." (That was her real name.) "It might help your figure—though I doubt if anything could!"

She glared in rage and—well, that was a painful half-hour. I won't give all the details, but I was glad when the screen dissolved into meaningless colored clouds.

"Whew!" I said, staring at van Manderpootz, who had been reading.

"You liked it?"

"Liked it! Say, I guess I was lucky to be cleaned out. I won't regret it from now on."

"That," said the professor grandly, "is van Manderpootz's great contribution to human happiness. 'Of all sad words of tongue or pen, the saddest are these: It might have been! True no longer, my friend Dick. Van Manderpootz has shown that the proper reading is, 'It might have been—worse!'"

It was very late when I returned home, and as a result, very late when I rose, and equally late when I got to the office. My father was unnecessarily worked up about it, but he exaggerated when he said I'd never been on time. He forgets the occasions when he's awakened me and dragged me down with him. Nor was it necessary to refer so sarcastically to my missing the *Baikal;* I reminded him of the wrecking of the liner, and he responded very heartlessly that if I'd been aboard, the rocket would have been late, and so would have missed colliding with the British fruitship. It was likewise superfluous for him to mention that when he and I had tried to snatch a few weeks of golfing in the mountains, even the spring had been late. I had nothing to do with that.

"Dixon," he concluded, "you have no conception whatever of time. None whatever."

The conversation with van Manderpootz recurred to me. I was impelled to ask, "And have you, sir?"

"I have," he said grimly. "I most assuredly have. Time," he said oracularly, "is money."

You can't argue with a viewpoint like that.

But those aspersions of his rankled, especially that about the Baikal. Tardy I might be, but it was hardly conceivable that my presence aboard the rocket could have averted the catastrophe. It irritated me; in a way, it made me responsible for the deaths of those unrescued hundreds among the passengers and crew, and I didn't like the thought.

Of course, if they'd waited an extra five minutes for me, or if I'd been on time and they'd left on schedule instead of five minutes late, or if—*if!*

If! The word called up van Manderpootz and his subjunctivisor—the worlds of "if," the weird, unreal worlds that existed beside reality, neither past nor future, but contemporary, yet extemporal. Somewhere among their ghostly infinities existed one that represented the world that would have been had I made the liner. I had only to call up Haskel van Manderpootz, make an appointment, and then— find out.

Yet it wasn't an easy decision. Suppose—just suppose that I found myself responsible—not legally responsible, certainly; there'd be no question of criminal negligence, or anything of that sort— not even morally responsible, because I couldn't possibly have anticipated that my presence or absence could weigh so heavily in the scales of life and death, nor could I have known in which direction the scales would tip. Just—responsible; that was all. Yet I hated to find out.

I hated equally not finding out. Uncertainty has its pangs too, quite as painful as those of remorse. It might be less nerve-racking to know myself responsible than to wonder, to waste thoughts in vain doubts and futile reproaches. So I seized the visiphone, dialed the number of the University, and at length gazed on the broad, humorous, intelligent features of van Manderpootz, dragged from a morning lecture by my call.

I was all but prompt for the appointment the following evening, and might actually have been on time but for an unreasonable traffic officer who insisted on booking me for speeding. At any rate, van Manderpootz was impressed.

"Well!" he rumbled. "I almost missed you, Dixon. I was just going over to the club, since I didn't expect you for an hour. You're only ten minutes late."

I ignored this. "Professor, I want to use your—uh—your subjunctivisor."

"Eh? Oh, yes. You're lucky, then. I was just about to dismantle it."

"Dismantle it! Why?"

"It has served its purpose. It has given birth to an idea far more important than itself. I shall need the space it occupies."

"But what *is* the idea, if it's not too presumptuous of me to ask?"

"It is not too presumptuous. You and the world which awaits it so eagerly may both know, but you hear it from the lips of the author. It is nothing less than the autobiography of van Manderpootz!" He paused impressively.

I gaped. "Your autobiography?"

"Yes. The world, though perhaps unaware, is crying for it. I shall detail my life, my work. I shall reveal myself as the man responsible for the three-year duration of the Pacific War of 2004."

"You?"

"None other. Had I not been a loyal Netherlands subject at that time, and therefore neutral, the forces of Asia would have been crushed in three months instead of three years. The subjunctivisor tells me so; I would have invented a calculator to forecast the chances of every engagement; van Manderpootz would have removed the hit or miss element in the conduct of war." He frowned solemnly. "There is my idea. The autobiography of van Manderpootz. What do you think of it?"

I recovered my thoughts. "It's—uh— it's colossal!" I said vehemently. "I'll buy a copy myself; Several copies. I'll send 'em to my friends."

"I," said van Manderpootz expansively, "shall autograph your copy for you. It will be priceless. I shall write in some fitting phrase, perhaps something like *Magnificus sed non superbus.* 'Great but not proud!' That well describes van Manderpootz, who despite his greatness is simple, modest, and unassuming. Don't you agree?"

"Perfectly! A very apt description of you. But—couldn't I see your subjunctivisor before it's dismantled to make way for the greater work?"

"Ah! You wish to find out something?"

"Yes, professor. Do you remember the *Baikal* disaster of a week or two ago? I was to have taken that liner to Moscow. I just missed it." I related the circumstances.

"Humph!" he grunted. "You wish to discover what would have happened had you caught it, eh? Well, I see several possibilities. Among the worlds of 'if' is the one that would have been real if you had been on time, the one that depended on the vessel waiting for your actual arrival, and the one that hung on your arriving within the five minutes they actually waited. In which are you interested?"

"Oh—the last one." That seemed the likeliest. After all, was it too much to expect that Dixon Wells could ever be on time, and as to the second possibility— well, they *hadn't* waited for me, and that in a way removed the weight of responsibility.

"Come on," rumbled van Manderpootz. I followed him across to the Physics Building and into his littered laboratory. The device still stood on the table and I took my place before it, staring at the screen of the Horsten psychomat. The clouds wavered and shifted as I sought to impress my memories on their suggestive shapes, to read into them some picture of that vanished morning.

Then I had it. I made out the vista from the Staten Bridge, and was speeding across the giant span toward the airport. I waved a signal to van Manderpootz, the thing clicked, and the subjunctivisor was on.

The grassless clay of the field appeared. It is a curious thing about the psychomat that you see only through the eyes of your image on the screen. It lends a strange reality to the working of the toy; I suppose a sort of self-hypnosis is partly responsible.

I was rushing over the ground toward the glittering, silver-winged projectile that was the *Baikal.* A glowering officer waved me on, and I dashed up the slant of the gangplank and into the ship; the port dropped and I heard a long "Whew!" of relief.

"Sit down!" barked the officer, gesturing toward an unoccupied seat. I fell into it; the ship quivered under the thrust of the catapult, grated harshly into motion, and then was flung bodily into the air. The blasts roared instantly, then settled to a more muffled throbbing, and I watched Staten Island drop down and slide back beneath me. The giant rocket was under way.

"Whew!" I breathed again. "Made it!" I caught an amused glance from my right. I was in an aisle seat; there was no one to my left, so I turned to the eyes that had flashed, glanced, and froze staring.

It was a girl. Perhaps she wasn't actually as lovely as she looked to me; after all, I was seeing her through the half-visionary screen of a psychomat. I've told myself since that she couldn't have been as pretty as she seemed, that it was due to my own imagination filling in the details. I don't know; I remember only that I stared at curiously lovely silver-blue eyes and velvety brown hair, and a small amused mouth, and an impudent nose. I kept staring until she flushed.

"I'm sorry," I said quickly. "I—was startled."

There's a friendly atmosphere aboard a trans-oceanic rocket. The passengers are forced into a crowded intimacy anywhere from seven to twelve hours, and there isn't much room for moving about. Generally, one strikes up an acquaintance with his neighbors; introductions aren't at all necessary, and the custom is simply to speak to anybody you choose—something like an all-day trip on the railroad trains of the last century, I suppose. You make friends for the duration of the journey, and then, nine times out of ten, you never hear of your traveling companions again.

The girl smiled. "Are you the individual responsible for the delay in starting?"

I admitted it. "I seem to be chronically late. Even watches lose time as soon as I wear them."

She laughed. "Your responsibilities can't be very heavy."

Well, they weren't of course, though it's surprising how many clubs, caddies, and chorus girls have depended on me at various times for appreciable portions of their incomes. But somehow I didn't feel like mentioning those things to the silvery-eyed girl.

We talked. Her name, it developed, was Joanna Caldwell, and she was going as far as Paris. She was an artist, or hoped to be one day, and of course there is no place in the world that can supply both training and inspiration like Paris. So it was there she was bound for a year of study, and despite her demurely humorous lips and laughing eyes, I could see that the business was of vast importance to her. I gathered that she had worked hard for the year in Paris, had scraped and saved for three years as fashion illustrator for some woman's magazine, though she couldn't have been many months over twenty-one. Her painting meant a great deal to her, and I could understand it. I'd felt that way

about polo once.

So you see, we were sympathetic spirits from the beginning. I knew that she liked me, and it was obvious that she didn't connect Dixon Wells with the N. J. Wells Corporation. And as for me—well, after that first glance into her cool silver eyes, I simply didn't care to look anywhere else. The hours seemed to drip away like minutes while I watched her.

You know how those things go. Suddenly I was calling her Joanna and she was calling me Dick, and it seemed as if we'd been doing just that all our lives. I'd decided to stop over in Paris on my way back from Moscow, and I'd secured her promise to let me see her. She was different, I tell you; she was nothing like the calculating Whimsy White, and still less like the dancing, simpering, giddy youngsters one meets around at social affairs. She was just Joanna, cool and humorous, yet sympathetic and serious, and as pretty as a Majolica figurine.

We could scarcely realize it when the steward passed along to take orders for luncheon. Four hours out? It seemed like forty minutes. And we had a pleasant feeling of intimacy in the discovery that both of us liked lobster salad and detested oysters. It was another bond; I told her whimsically that it was an omen, nor did she object to considering it so.

Afterwards we walked along the narrow aisle to the glassed-in observation room up forward. It was almost too crowded for entry, but we didn't mind that at all, as it forced us to sit very close together. We stayed long after both of us had begun to notice the stuffiness of the air.

It was just after we had returned to our seats that the catastrophe occurred. There was no warning save a sudden lurch, the result, I suppose, of the pilot's futile last-minute attempt to swerve—just that and then a grinding crash and a terrible sensation of spinning, and after that a chorus of shrieks that were like the sounds of a battle.

It *was* battle. Five hundred people were picking themselves up from the floor, were trampling each other, milling around, being cast helplessly down as the great rocket-plane, its left wing but a broken stub, circled downward toward the Atlantic.

The shouts of officers sounded and a loudspeaker blared. "Be calm," it kept repeating, and then, "There has been a collision. We have contacted a surface ship. There is no danger— There is no danger—"

I struggled up from the debris of shattered seats. Joanna was gone; just as I found her crumpled between the rows, the ship struck the water with a jar that set everything crashing again. The speaker blared, "Put on the cork belts under the seats. The life-belts are under the seats."

I dragged a belt loose and snapped it around Joanna, then donned one myself. The crowd was surging forward now, and the tail end of the ship began to drop. There was water behind us, sloshing in the darkness as the lights went out. An officer came sliding by, stooped, and fastened a belt about an unconscious woman ahead of us. "You all right?" he yelled, and passed on without waiting for an answer.

The speaker must have been cut on to a battery circuit. "And get as far away as possible," it ordered suddenly. "Jump from the forward port and get as far away as possible. A ship is standing by. You will be picked up. Jump from the—" It went dead again.

I got Joanna untangled from the wreckage. She was pale; her silvery eyes were closed. I started dragging her slowly and painfully toward the forward port, and the slant of the floor increased until it was like the slide of a ski-jump. The officer passed again. "Can you handle her?" he asked, and again dashed away.

I was getting there. The crowd around the port looked smaller, or was it simply huddling closer? Then suddenly, a wail of fear and despair went up, and there was a roar of water. The observation room walls had given. I saw the green surge of waves, and a billowing deluge rushed down upon us. I had been late again.

That was all. I raised shocked and frightened eyes from the subjunctivisor to face van Manderpootz, who was scribbling on the edge of the table.

"Well?" he asked.

I shuddered. "Horrible!" I murmured. "We—I guess we wouldn't have been among the survivors."

"We, eh? *We?*" His eyes twinkled.

I did not enlighten him. I thanked him, bade him good-night and went dolorously home.

Even my father noticed something queer about me. The day I got to the office only five minutes late, he called me in for some anxious questioning as to my health. I couldn't tell him anything, of course. How could I explain that I'd been late once too often, and had fallen in love with a girl two weeks after she was dead?

The thought drove me nearly crazy. Joanna! Joanna with her silvery eyes now lay somewhere at the bottom of the Atlantic. I went around half dazed, scarcely speaking. One night I actually lacked the energy to go home, and sat smoking in my father's big overstuffed chair in his private office until I finally dozed off. The next morning, when old N. J. entered and found me there before him, he turned pale as paper, staggered, and gasped, "My heart!" It took a lot of explaining to convince him that I wasn't early at the office but just very late going home.

At last I felt that I couldn't stand it. I had to do something—anything at all. I thought finally of the subjunctivisor. I could—yes, I could see what would have transpired if the ship hadn't been wrecked! I could trace out that weird, unreal romance hidden somewhere in the worlds of "if". I could perhaps, wring a somber, vicarious joy from the things that might have been. I could see Joanna once more!

It was late afternoon when I rushed over to van Manderpootz's quarters. He wasn't there; I encountered him finally in the hall of the Physics Building.

"Dick!" he exclaimed. "Are you sick?"

"Sick? No, not physically. Professor, I've got to use your subjunctivisor again. I've got to!"

"Eh? Oh—that toy. You're too late, Dick. I've dismantled it, I have a better use for the space."

I gave a miserable groan and was tempted to damn autobiography of the great van Manderpootz. A gleam of sympathy showed in his eyes, and he took my arm, dragging me into the little office adjoining his laboratory.

"Tell me," he commanded.

I did. I guess I made the tragedy plain enough, for heavy brows knit in a frown of pity. "Not even van Manderpootz can bring back the dead," he murmured. "I'm sorry, Dick. Take your mind from the affair. Even were my subjunctivisor available, I wouldn't permit you to use it. That would be but to turn the knife in the wound." He paused. "Find something else to occupy your mind. Do as van Manderpootz does. Find forgetfulness in work."

"Yes," I responded dully. "But who'd want to read my autobiography? That's all right for you."

"Autobiography? Oh! I remember. No, I have abandoned that. History itself will record the life and works of van Manderpootz. Now I am engaged in a far grander project."

"Indeed?" I was utterly, gloomily disinterested.

"Yes. Gogli has been here, Gogli the sculptor. He is to make a bust of me. What better legacy can I leave to the world than a bust of van Manderpootz sculptured from life? Perhaps I shall present it to the city, perhaps to the university. I would have given it to the Royal Society if they had been a little more receptive, if they—if—*if!*" The last in a shout.

"Huh?"

"*If!*" cried van Manderpootz. "What you saw in the subjunctivisor was what would have happened if you had caught the ship!"

"I know that."

"But something quite different might really have happened! Don't you see? She—she— Where are those old newspapers?"

He was pawing through a pile of them. He flourished one finally. "Here! Here are the survivors!"

Like letters of flame, Joanna Caldwell's name leaped out at me. There was even a little paragraph about it, as I saw once my reeling brain permitted me to read:

At least a score of survivors owe their lives to the bravery of twenty-eight-year-old Navigator Orris Hope, who patrolled both aisles during the panic, lacing lifebelts on the injured and helpless, and carrying many to the port. He remained on the sinking liner until the last, finally fighting his way to the surface through the broken walls of the observation room. Among those who owe their lives to the young officer are: Patrick Owensby, New York City; Mrs. Campbell Warren, Boston; Miss Joanna Caldwell, New York City—

I suppose my shout of joy was heard over in the Administration Building, blocks away. I didn't care; if van Manderpootz hadn't been armored in stubby whiskers, I'd have kissed him. Perhaps I did anyway; I can't be sure of my actions during those chaotic minutes in the professor's tiny office.

At last I calmed. "I can look her up!" I gloated. "She must have landed with the other survivors, and they were all on that British tramp freighter the *Osgood,* that docked here last week. She must be in New York—and if she's gone over to Paris, I'll find out and follow her!"

Well, it's a queer ending. She was in New York, but—you see, Dixon Wells had, so to speak, known Joanna Caldwell by means of the professor's subjunctivisor, but Joanna had never known Dixon Wells. What the ending might have been if—*if*— But it wasn't; she had married Orris Hope, the young officer who had rescued her. I was late again.

ᴺₑₓₜ 𝐼𝒔𝒔𝓊ₑ

The early twenty-first century's greatest scientist, Haskel van Manderpootz, causes more trouble for Dixon Wells with his latest invention. Can Dixon ever settle for any real woman once he's had a look at...

(The Ideal)

Heaʀ! Heaʀ!

"The Worlds of If" is just one of a growing series of new and classic stories available as audio downloads for your iPods, iPhones and other devices even Stanley Weinbaum never imagined, at:

www.thrillingwonderstories.com

THE TELEVISUALIZER
Reviews of Science Fiction for the Home Screen
BY BILL WARREN

*W*hen I was a kid, you saw a movie at the local theater, and that was it. Forever. You never saw it again. When movies started turning up on TV, that was a great leap forward—but not as extreme as home video. And even that altered greatly with the advent of DVD, then the internet. Have a favorite movie from your childhood? Rent it, buy it or download it. The vast panorama is now accessible.

But not everyone watches older movies the same way. Most approach them more or less as they would in a theater—something to be watched, assimilated (or not), and then move on past. But there are others who study movies, who group them in different ways, who can see the works of favorite actors or directors (or writers or cameramen or—anything) all together. Then there are those drawn to the likes of *Mystery Science Theater 3000*—it's old, it's got a monster, it's got to be stupid.

But even followers of MST3K—as fans refer to the now-gone series—surprised themselves. Sure, these movies were sort of dorky, but intelligent people worked hard on them, and except in the very worst, newcomers began spotting good stuff among the dreck. The MST3K group tried to expand into theaters, and gave their standard wisecracking-silhouettes treatment to *This Island Earth*—but audiences thought that the old movie they could see around those silhouettes wasn't really all that bad. Yes, This Island Earth boasts less-than-topnotch actors, yes,

there's a wildly extravagant monster, the Mutant—but it takes itself seriously, it's well-produced and has dazzling if not entirely convincing special effects.

Science fiction movies of the 1950s are among the most eagerly sought of older movies—and not as the source for remakes either, but for viewing of the movies themselves. The sales figures for 1950s movies in general are uneven, but there's always a market of some size for SF of the 1950s.

For years, movies that could be grouped under the heading "thrilling wonder stories" weren't common, and weren't shuttled off to their own categories until the early 1930s, when horror films established themselves as an identifiable genre. Except for occasional tales of the future, such as *Metropolis* (1927) and *Just Imagine* (1930), science fiction was even less common than large-scale fantasies. The genre wasn't established in terms of movies until the 1950s.

By that decade, science fiction had become a profitable commodity, and most of the major studios took flings at the genre. But by 1955 and 1956, the bloom was off the SF rose, and neither *This Island Earth* (1955) nor *Forbidden Planet* (1956) were as popular as their studios, Universal-International and the prestigious MGM, had hoped. 20th Century-Fox, for better and (too often) worse, held the SF flag high for a while with relatively large-budget, CinemaScope outings like *Journey to the Center of the Earth* (1959), *The Lost World* (1960) and *Voyage to the Bottom of the Sea* (1961), but apart from *Journey,* they repelled more serious SF fans than they attracted. And they couldn't displace *This Island Earth* and *Forbidden Planet* in the memories of those disappointed fans.

These two DVDs are the second releases for both titles in this format (not counting the edited and talked-over version of *This Island Earth* on the briefly-available DVD of *Mystery Science 3000: The Movie*). The newer discs are better than the earlier editions—crisper, better color. This is particularly true of *Forbidden Planet*, which has a splendid array of extras, and is available in high definition. But the definitive *This Island Earth* DVD has yet to be produced.

*T*his Island Earth actually *was* a Thrilling Wonder Story. Raymond F.

This Island Earth (1955; this DVD, 2006)
Universal-International (Universal Home Entertainment)
Director: Joseph M. Newman
Cast: Rex Reason, Jeff Morrow, Faith Domergue, Russell Johnson, Douglas Spencer, Robert Nichols
Color; 86 minutes; unrated; aspect ratio: 1.33:1
Extras: Only a trailer

Jones' 1952 novel was patched together from linked novelettes that first saw publication in *Thrilling Wonder Stories*: "The Alien Machine" (June 1949), "The Shroud of Secrecy" (December 1949) and "The Greater Conflict" (February 1950). As with Jones' later Winston juvenile two-volume series, *Son of the Stars* and *Planet of Light*, the last part of *This Island Earth* features a huge congress of aliens from many worlds. Not surprisingly, the movie doesn't go this way; in fact, the latter third of the movie owes nothing to Jones' novel. It wasn't until the *Star Wars* prequels that moviemakers visualized a vast alien congress.

Joseph Newman bought the rights to Jones' novel and offered the property to Universal-International, which had had science fiction successes with *It Came from Outer Space* (1953) and *Creature from the Black Lagoon* (1954). The deal had a catch: instead of U-I's resident science fiction specialist, Jack Arnold, Newman himself would direct *This Island Earth.* The movie was produced by William Alland, who'd done the same with the other SF movies for the studio. It's curious that Newman, who made no other science fiction films, could have caught U-I's attention so deftly.

The movie is a handsome studio project, with excellent color photography, attractive sets and showy, if unconvincing, special effects. The first half of the film is faithful to Jones' novel, and is effectively structured as a mystery. While flying home in a borrowed fighter jet, dashing young scientist Cal Meacham (Rex Reason) is saved from disaster by a green beam. Later, working from a mysterious catalog, he orders the parts for an "interociter," even though he has no idea what it is. When it's assembled, it seems to be something like a television set. Turning on the interociter causes the face of a smiling man, Exeter (Jeff Morrow), to appear on its screen. He convinces Cal to board a pilot-less plane sent to fetch him. (One has to wonder what would have happened if he'd ordered something else from the catalog.)

He lands in Georgia, where he's met by beautiful Dr. Ruth Adams (Faith Domergue), whom he's met before. At a mansion atop a hill, Exeter welcomes Cal, revealing he's gathering scientists together to work independently on a world peace project. But Exeter and his project have many mysterious elements—a device that seems to remove human will, for one thing. Plus, Exeter and his associates have odd red skin and bulging foreheads. The movie presents all this in an intriguing fashion—and then throws mystery out the window, leaving some questions unanswered.

Finally, suspicion and fear leads Cal, Ruth and fellow scientist Carlson (Russell Johnson, later "the Professor" on *Gilligan's Island*) to flee their virtual captivity. But a colossal flying saucer hums into the sky from behind the mansion; a red beam from the sky kills Carlson and another scientist, the house on the hilltop blows up, killing everyone inside, and their cat, too. As Cal and Ruth try to escape in a small plane, that green beam pulls them up, plane and all, into the saucer.

And they're on their way to Metaluna, the planet where Exeter and his friends came from. It's under bombardment by spaceships from Zahgon, a rival planet, and they're running out of the atomic power they need to defend themselves— hence Exeter's mission on Earth. The Metalunans need power to buy enough time to move the planet's population to the Earth. The flying saucer is targeted by meteors towed by little triangular spaceships from Zahgon. On Metaluna, the cold, ruthless Monitor (Douglas Spencer)

orders Exeter to wipe out Ruth's and Cal's will. The fast-paced climax involves the insect-like Mutant (emphasis on *both* syllables), whose pantslegs blend seamlessly into his ankles, an escape from Metaluna and a very large explosion. (The Mutant was later the source for plastic models, resin kits, masks, etc.; it's both goofy and grand.)

Kids in 1955 loved all the Buck Rogers-like derring-do of the last couple of reels of *This Island Earth*, especially the Mutants and the eye-popping special effects. The saucer cruises low over the honeycombed surface of Metaluna as meteors strike all around it. Through vast holes, cities beneath the surface can be glimpsed. All of this represents a great deal of effort on the part of a talented effects team, and it looks wonderful, especially if you have a large-screen TV. It might have set a benchmark for space effects of the 1950s—except that *Forbidden Planet* came along the next year.

When *This Island Earth* was released, it was paired as a standard double bill with *Abbott and Costello Meet the Mummy*, indicating Universal-International knew exactly at whom to target the film: kids. The earlier big science fiction movies, like *The Day the Earth Stood Still* (1951), *The Thing from Another World* (1951) and *War of the Worlds* (1953), had all largely been aimed at adults, even though they ultimately appealed primarily to people under 20. *This Island Earth* is right on the cusp of a change in marketing science fiction movies—and even embodies the switch itself. The first half is for grownups, the second half for kids.

But for audiences today, it's fun all the way through. Which makes it a crying shame that Universal Home Video refuses to make further efforts in packaging their science fiction movies in an appealing fashion. While other SF films of the era, including Universal-International's own *Creature from the Black Lagoon* and *It Came from Outer Space*, are equipped on DVD with several extras—commentary tracks, making-of documentaries, etc.—*This Island Earth* has only a trailer. The print on this second DVD release is better than on the first, but that's really the only change from the earlier DVD. Not only did Universal Home Video callously ignore the marketing possibilities for a *This Island Earth* DVD, they threw away most of their other 1950s SF movies in a package of several titles (including the great *Incredible Shrinking Man*) in a DVD box set initially available only at Best Buy, then dumped with no fanfare on the wider market.

While Warner Bros. and others know that these ancillary features generate superior sales, Universal Home Video persists in a peculiar, divided ignorance. They did issue their classics of the 1930s and 40s in handsome collections, with accompanying documentaries and sometimes commentary tracks as well. But except for *Creature* and its sequels, *Revenge of the Creature* and *The Creature Walks Among Us*, they've doggedly refused to do anything special with SF and horror movies released after the 1940s.

*A*s if to show Universal how this really should be done, in 2006 Warners released their bells-and-whistles DVD of *Forbidden Planet.* (Warner Bros. now owns most of the MGM library.) This two-disc DVD set includes a completely, painstakingly restored print of the movie, transferred to the digital domain. The result is stunning—the movie actually looks *better* than when it was first released. The Eastman color process used for the film fades very rapidly, but the film has been digitally restored, so the color is now stable. Also, in movies of this vintage, ef-

Forbidden Planet (1956; this DVD, 2006)
MGM (Warners Home Entertainment)
Director: Fred M. Wilcox
Cast: Walter Pidgeon, Leslie Nielsen, Anne Frances, Warren Stevens, Richard Anderson, Jack Kelly, Earl Holliman
Color; 98 minutes; CinemaScope; 5.1 soundtrack
Extras: Feature film *The Invisible Boy;* episode of TV series *The Thin Man* with Robby the Robot; Deleted scenes; Unused effects footage; documentary "Amazing! Exploring the Far Reaches of *Forbidden Planet;"* documentary "Robby the Robot: Engineering a Sci-Fi Icon;" "Watch the Skies! Science Fiction, The 1950s, and Us" (from TCM); excerpts from TV series *MGM Parade* with Walter Pidgeon; Trailers

fects scenes usually gave themselves away to those who watched for such things by an abrupt if minor increase in grain and decrease in sharpness. In the restoration of the movie for this DVD, it appears someone has tried to minimize this.

Not only was *Forbidden Planet* the greatest SF adventure spectacle until the advent of *Star Wars,* it greatly influenced Gene Roddenberry in shaping *Star Trek,* and had a powerful effect on kids who grew up to be directors and other movie workers. The movie features the kinds of ideas and images that burn themselves into the brains of bright kids, and echoes of the film resonate down through science fiction movie history.

The set includes a documentary, "Amazing! Exploring the Far Reaches of *Forbidden Planet*." In addition to surviving cast members Leslie Nielsen, Anne Francis, Richard Anderson, Warren Stevens and Earl Holliman, the talking heads include directors Joe Dante, John Carpenter, John Landis and William Malone—who knows more about *Forbidden Planet* than anyone; he even owns the original Robby the Robot. Also appearing are movie historians Rudy Behlmer, Bob Burns and me, Bill Warren. There's also Robert Kinoshita, who designed and built Robby, Bebe Barron, who, with her late husband Louis, created the "electronic tonalities" score of the film, effects experts Dennis Muren and Phil Tippett, and science fiction writer Alan Dean Foster. The documentary is especially well organized and edited, giving a clear and entertaining outline of the production of the film and the power of its influence. There's also a documentary on the creation of Robby the Robot, but this would be primarily interesting to the truly dedicated *Forbidden Planet* aficionado.

The set also includes *The Invisible Boy* (1957), a sly science fiction satire made as something of a followup to *Forbidden Planet*. There's a line as to how a now-dead scientist brought Robby the Robot back from the future (the boy of the title rebuilds him), but this really isn't a sequel. There's also an episode of the TV series *The Thin Man*, in which Robby is suspected of murder.

There are some deleted scenes discovered in the print the Barrons were given to score the film, and some surprisingly well-done space shots not included in the finished film. A couple of clips of Pidgeon hosting episodes of the TV series *MGM Parade* are minor but harmless. So much care has been lavished on the *Forbidden Planet* extras that it's puzzling why there is no commentary track.

Warners issued a deluxe set in a tin box (including a small Robby the Robot figure and other keepsakes) and a standard discs-only set. Both are also available in high definition HD-DVD (though not yet on rival Blu-Ray). A comparison of the standard and high definition discs makes it clear that the high definition really is a bit sharper, with somewhat richer sound, but the improvement is not marked enough for anyone to rush out and buy a high definition DVD player.

*T*he movie *is* worth all this fuss and fury. It's undoubtedly the most Thrilling Wonder Story-like movie of the 1950s, remarkably sophisticated in its handling of science fiction elements, many of which had never been featured in films before. Faster-than-light drive, for instance: this is the first movie explicitly to feature it, but it's not emphasized. In the 1950s, SF movies often tried to be instructive, to tell audiences exactly what this or that SF gadget or process actually did. Not so here—the faster-than-light drive is mentioned in the opening narration (by Les Tremayne), then simply demonstrated.

Some of the most dramatic and beautiful space images in movie history occur in this film, such as when the space cruiser passes behind one of Altair's planets, creating an eclipse. Or when the cruiser arcs down into the skies of planet Altair IV. Or when it drops down out of a green sky to land on robin's-egg-blue pressor beams. For science fiction-loving kids, this movie went way beyond a dream come true, delving into astonishing images and ideas that few in the audience had ever conceived.

John Adams (Leslie Nielsen, long before his comedy career), the captain of the C-57-D, has been sent to Altair IV to find out what happened to another Earth expedition sent there some twenty years before—and from which no word has come. He's surprised to be warned away from the planet (the "forbidden" aspect) by Morbius (Walter Pidgeon), the previous expedition's philologist. But Adams lands anyway—the mystery has increased.

He and first mate Farman (Jack Kelly) and Doc Ostrow (Warren Stevens) are surprised to be met by a robot named Robby, who ushers them into a little car and whisks them off to Morbius' elegant home, very much in the 1950s "Googie" style. The scientist reveals that all of the previous expedition members were killed, some by an unseen force, the rest when they tried to launch their spacecraft. Only Morbius and his wife, gone now, survived.

But of course, scientists in movies have daughters, and Morbius has the beautiful Altaira (Anne Francis), usually called Alta. She's fascinated to meet young men from Earth, who are pretty fascinated themselves—she's wearing miniskirts before they were invented. Soon enough, Adams and Alta fall for one another, but the romance is not emphasized; the story is concerned with the mystery of Altair IV.

Morbius reluctantly decides to let Adams and Ostrow in on one of the secrets of Altair IV. It was once inhabited by a noble race, the Krell. Their cities covered the globe; they visited other worlds in their spaceships, but finally devoted all their energies toward one aim, which Morbius has been unable to discover. He shows them the wonderful laboratory of the Krell, elegantly and beautifully designed for CinemaScope by Arthur Lonergan. Morbius takes them down to one of the vast underground machines of the Krell, still operating, but whose function Morbius cannot determine, even after taking a "brain boost" in the Krell lab.

A mysterious, invisible presence visits the C-57-D, first only breaking equipment. But the Earthmen do not leave, and the presence comes again, this time killing a crewman. When it comes a third time, the ship's crew cannot kill it. In one of the most indelible scenes in science fiction movies, the "Monster from the Id" is outlined in waves of sheer force, standing in the blaster beams, killing crewmen—and renewing its structure microsecond to microsecond. This stunning, unforgettable image was created by animators from the Disney company, under the direction of Joshua Meador.

Forbidden Planet is, on one level, comic-book excitement, with blasters, spaceships, planets seen from space, a robot butler, vast alien machinery, a beautiful blonde in short skirts, a monster that practically breathes fire. But at its core, it's rich with ideas that were not only new to movies, but rarely found in written science fiction of the day—like machines that allow the creation of life, in whatever form, by sheer thought—and what this can lead to. The monster in *Forbidden Planet* is nightmarish because it is the living embodiment of a nightmare—and of Morbius' suppressed, unacknowledged desire for his daughter.

Oddly, *Forbidden Planet* was directed by a standard studio director, whose only other notable movie, *Lassie Come Home* (1943), owed more to young Elizabeth Taylor, the original novel and a collie than to Wilcox. There is some comedy in the film, though most of it is somewhat oafish. It's interesting to speculate what more cinematically adept directors might have made of the material, but it's also pointless—*Forbidden Planet* is what it is, a sum of all its parts, whose wonders and longevity cannot be ascribed to any individual.

This recent, restored *Forbidden Planet* is an ideal way for enthusiasts and historians to own the film, and a good introduction to the movie to others. It is indeed a thrilling wonder story, powerfully influential—more so than *This Island Earth*—and is one of the most watchable of older SF movies. Some find it rather slow, but it's so full of ideas that the imaginative are likely to embrace it.

She (1935; this DVD, 2006)
Legend Films—Genius Entertainment
Directors: Lancing C. Holden, Irving Pichel
Producer: Merian C. Cooper
Starring: Randolph Scott, Helen Gahagan, Nigel Bruce, Helen Mack, Gustav von Seyffertitz, Noble Johnson, Samuel S. Hinds
Colorized; also black and white version; 95 minutes; unrated; aspect ratio: 1.33:1
Extras: Audio Commentary by Ray Harryhausen and Mark Vaz; Interview with Ray Harryhausen; Commentary on colorization by Harryhausen and others; Scenes deleted from 1935 101 minute version; Trailers for other colorized films

he (1935) dates from an even earlier period; although *King Kong* (1933), also from RKO, has never fallen out of favor and has been available almost as long as home videos of movies have existed, this other Merian C. Cooper production was, for complex legal reasons, rarely seen. Modern audiences have to make more allowances to enjoy this moderately lavish production as it was intended to be, but they will probably find the result worth the effort.

H. Rider Haggard (1856-1925) was a popular writer of adventure novels in the late 19th and early 20th centuries. His tales were written in a fast-paced, unadorned style, perfect for teenage boys and men in search of exotic thrills. His most famous novel, *King Solomon's Mines* (1885), was also his first, written to settle a bet that he could write a more exciting book than Robert Louis Stevenson's *Treasure Island. Mines* launched a series featuring Allan Quatermain, its two-fisted, great-white-hunter hero.

Although Haggard's novels were set all over the world, his most popular and best-remembered are those with African settings—he spent six years in South Africa—such as *She* (1886), which spawned its own series about the immortal Ayesha, She-Who-Must-Be-Obeyed. The two series even overlapped in the now little-known *She and Allan* (1920), set before the events told in *She*. Both novels have been repeatedly filmed, with the best-known versions of *King Solomon's Mines* released in 1937 and 1950. In the most recent adaptations, Allan Quatermain is a smudged carbon of Indiana Jones—who was himself partly based on Quatermain in the first place.

She has been filmed even more often than *King Solomon's Mines*, but rarely effectively. There were versions in 1908, 1911, 1916, 1917, 1925, 1965, 1982 and

2001. But by far the most famous is the 1935 RKO production, produced by the astonishing Merian C. Cooper and co-directed by art director Lancing C. Holden (his only directorial credit) and Irving Pichel, who was sometimes an actor (*Dracula's Daughter*) and sometimes a director (*Destination Moon*).

Cooper's own life would make an exciting movie, and is covered in Mark Vaz's recommended biography, *Living Dangerously* (2005). Cooper was already a war hero when he teamed up with friend Ernest C. Schoedsack to create two documentaries, *Grass* (1925) and *Chang* (1927). Both were shot by the two in dangerous locations under primitive conditions, and are so well made that they launched movie careers for both men. Their most famous creation was *King Kong* (1933).

Cooper was an extremely busy producer in the early 1930s, when the pace of moviemaking appealed to his adventuresome soul. (He was also involved in commercial aviation). He eventually became head of production at RKO, a job that he didn't relish. He left the company to work for David O. Selznick. Cooper became producer for director John Ford; their films together include *Stagecoach*, the "Cavalry Trilogy," and *The Quiet Man*.

He was a long-time, devoted reader of adventurous books, both fiction and nonfiction, and hoped to make a lavish production of Haggard's *She*, scheduled to be filmed back-to-back with *The Last Days of Pompeii* (also 1935). He was eager to make *She* in the recently-launched three-strip Technicolor process, and budgeted the films at a then-extravagant million dollars apiece.

The New York-based heads of RKO refused to grant him the budgets he wanted; *She* was ultimately made for about $500,000 and *Pompeii* for $800,000.

Cooper chafed at the budgetary restrictions—there went *She*'s stampede of mastodons—and always considered *She* one of his worst movies, perhaps because it was a boxoffice flop, until its re-release in the late 1940s. (Cooper was also instrumental in the creation of Cinerama. If he had been crazy as well as inventive, he might be as well-known today as Howard Hughes.)

King Kong inspired young Ray Harryhausen to specialize in stop-motion animation, thereby becoming the first famous special effects artist. He came to *She* late, but now embraces it, as his commentary track and several interviews on this recent DVD show. Furthermore, he helped supervise colorizing the movie—using digital techniques to turn this handsomely-designed black and white movie into one with a full palate of colors. In the interview and commentary track, Ray Harryhausen is clearly enthusiastic about the color process (Harryhausen is also colorizing his black and white movies from the 1950s), but in most shots, there's something off about the color, as there has always been in colorized movies. Some scenes, particularly those in She's palace, work better than others; there's a closeup of Helen Mack that could have come from a Technicolor movie. But in some cases, as in the facade of the giant cliff, the colorization seems weak and phony, tending to the pastel.

A good-looking black-and-white version is included on the same disc; those who are irked by colorizing but interested in the film can easily avoid the colorized version. Black and white or colorized, however, *She* is well below *King Kong* in excitement and visual thrills. Screenwriter Ruth Rose, who also wrote *Kong* (and who was Mrs. Schoedsack), changed the African setting—Cooper felt jungle movies were too common by 1935—to a vaguely but frigidly Siberian locale. Cooper may have lost his herd of stampeding mastodons, but at least he gets in one shot of a huge saber-toothed tiger, frozen in a wall of ice.

At the urging of his dying uncle, young Leo Vincey (Randolph Scott) sets out with his uncle's friend Horace Holly (Nigel Bruce) to retrace the path of his 15th-century ancestor John, in hopes of finding what might be the flame of immortality. In the frozen wastes, the two are joined by Tanya (Helen Mack). Beyond a huge palisade cliff, they find caverns warmed by volcanic heat. Holly is almost killed by the primitive tribe who live there, but the three are rescued by more advanced people, the subjects of Queen Hash-A-Mo-Tep (Helen Gahagan), She Who Must Be Obeyed.

The Queen is stunned by the sight of Leo—who looks exactly like his ancestor, John, whose carefully-preserved body the Queen has guarded for five hundred years. She's immortal, a cold and cruel tyrant who is nonetheless the slave of her own passion for John. And yes, there is a Flame of Immortality, rendered ice blue in the colorized version. The climax involves makeup changes that are still impressive.

Another exceptional element is the outstanding score by the reliable Max Steiner. His work here is not as vividly impressive as in his famous score for *King Kong*, but a score can be inferior to *Kong*'s and still be great. The score was rerecorded a few years ago for CD.

There's a slight effort to nudge the story in the direction of science fiction—or at least to vaguely suggest a scientific basis for the Flame of Immortality. Leo's uncle is dying of radium poisoning. The tales, and a gold figurine, brought back from the lost kingdom beyond that barrier led the elder Vincey to research in radiation. His

dying scene is in a laboratory full of beakers, retorts and huge electrical equipment. But the heart of *She* remains in the realm of fantasy, of a love that has spanned generations.

It's not hard to see why *She* was unsuccessful on its first release—and also why it became popular later. The movie is slow and talky, but also made on a grand scale (despite the reduced budget), with several outstanding sequences, including a modern-looking dance of Hash-A-Mo-Tep's subjects near the end. There's not much action, though Scott does get to topple liquid fire spectacularly down the steps of the Queen's palace.

But its charm and naïveté were endearing and unusual by the late 1940s, and are just as winning today. Yes, it's slow; yes, it's short on spectacle, but the film has its own appeal. Randolph Scott was a true movie star, and is clearly one in this movie. This is the only film of Helen Gahagan, a Broadway star and singer; she's beautiful and gives a good, if chilly, performance. Under her married name, Helen Gahagan Douglas, she later represented California in the U.S. House, losing election to the Senate to none other than Richard Nixon, who used red-baiting tactics to overcome her. (Her step-granddaughter Ileana Douglas is an actress today, and a good one—but not the beauty Helen was.)

The DVD also includes two very good scenes cut from the film before its late-40s reissue. One features interesting work by Mack and Gahagan; the other the always-likeable Nigel Bruce and She's high priest, played by the wonderfully-named Gustav von Seyffertitz. They should have been included in the feature.

The commentary track is by Harryhausen and Mark Vaz, author of the Cooper biography. It's interesting throughout, but it's obvious all too clear that Harryhausen is not an authority on this film; Vaz contributes what he can, but it's hard not to have the impression that there was much more to be said. For one thing, the other movies of Haggard's novel go largely unmentioned. Surely someone could have alluded to the 1965 version of *She*, certainly the most famous other than this one. Made by Hammer, who also made Harryhausen's *One Million Years B.C.,* it featured Christopher Lee and Peter Cushing, with Ursula Andress as Ayesha.

Maybe Harryhausen is right—maybe colorizing this almost-epic adventure will bring new audiences to it. However, this seems unlikely. Why would any of today's DVD buyers, unfamiliar with this film, H. Rider Haggard, Randolph Scott, Merian C. Cooper and/or RKO, pick it up, color or no color? *She* is likely to remain relatively obscure.

But it's available. So many movies are now so readily available on home video, principally DVD, that we've tended to forget that this is a thrilling wonder miracle of sorts. Movies are even sometimes available in prints even better than they were on original release; compare the high-definition DVD of the great *Adventures of Robin Hood* (1938) to a theatrical print, and you'll see that the occasional unavoidable mismatches of the three color emulsions have been eliminated. The movie looks better on home video than it ever did on the big screen.

Thanks to the internet, you can shop for thousands, maybe literally millions, of movies without even leaving your home. If you ignore such niceties as legality, you can find even more titles on the black market. The vast panorama lies before you, and it now includes these three wonderful stories. • • •

CHAPTER I

Unit 16

he offices of Joe Wilson, puchasing agent for Ryberg Instrument Corporation, looked out over the company's private landing field. He stood there by the window now, wishing that they didn't, because it was an eternal reminder that he'd once had hopes of becoming an engineer intead of an office flunky.

Through the window he saw the silver test ship of the radio lab level off at bullet speed, circle once and land. That would be Cal Meacham at the controls, Joe thought. Even the company pilots didn't dare bring a ship in that way. But Cal Meacham was the best man in the radio instrument business and getting canned was a meaningless penalty for him. He could get the same or higher salary from a dozen other places for the asking.

Joe chomped irritably on his cigar and turned away from the window. Then he picked up a letter from his desk. It was in answer to an order he had placed for condensers for Cal's hot transmitter job— Cal's stuff was always hot, Joe thought. He'd already read the letter three times but he started on it for the fourth.

Dear Mr. Wilson:

We were pleased to receive your order of the 8th for samples of our XC-109 condenser. However, we find that our present catalogue lists no such item nor did we ever carry it.

We are, therefore, substituting the AB-619 model, a high-voltage oil-filled transmitting-type condenser. As you specified, it is rated at 10,000 volts with 100% safety factor and has 4 mf. capacity.

We trust these will meet with your approval and that we may look forward to receiving your production order for these items. It is needless, of course, to remind you that we manufacture a complete line of electronic components. We would be glad to furnish samples of any items from our stock which might

THE ALIEN MACHINE

by raymond f. jones

interest you.

Respectfully yours,
A. G. Archmanter
Electronic Service—Unit 16.

Joe Wilson put the letter down slowly and picked up the box of beads which had come with it. Complete and resigned disgust occupied his face.

He picked up a bead by one of the leads that stuck out of it. The bead was about a quarter of an inch in diameter and there seemed to be a smaller concentric shell inside it. Between the two appeared to be some reddish liquid. Another wire connected to the inner shell but for the life of him Joe couldn't see how that inner wire came through the outer shell.

There was something funny about it, as if it came directly from the inner without passing through the outer. He knew that was silly but it made him dizzy to try to concentrate on the spot where it came through. The spot seemed to shift and move.

"Ten thousand volts!" he muttered. "Four mikes!"

He tossed the bead back into the box with disgust. Cal would be hotter than the transmitter job when he saw these.

Joe heard the door of his secretary's office open and glanced through the glass panel. Cal Meacham was coming in. He burst open the door with a breeze that ruffled the letters on Joe's desk.

"See that landing I made, Joe? Markus says I ought to be able to get my license to fly that crate in another week."

"I'll bet he added 'if you live that long.'"

"Just because you don't recognize a hot pilot when you see one—what are you so glum about, anyway? And what's happened to those condensers we ordered three days ago? This job's *hot.*"

Joe held out the letter silently. Cal scanned the page swiftly and flipped it back onto the desk.

"Swell. We'll try them out. They're down in receiving, I suppose? Give me an order and I'll pick them up on my way to the lab."

"They aren't in receiving. They came in the envelope with the letter."

"What are you talking about? How could they send sixteen mikes of ten kv condensers in an envelope?"

Joe held up one of the beads by a wire—the one that passed through the outer shell without passing through it. "This is what they sent. Guaranteed one hundred percent voltage safety factor."

Cal glanced at it. "Whose leg are you trying to pull?"

"I'm not kidding. That's what they sent."

"Well, what screwball's idea of a joke is this, then? Four mikes! Did you call receiving?"

Joe nodded. "I checked *good.* These beads are all that came."

Muttering, Cal grasped one by the lead wire and held it up to the light. He saw the faintly appearing internal structure that Joe had puzzled over.

"It *would* be funny if that's what these things actually were, wouldn't it?" he said. "Aw—it's crazy!"

"You could just about build a fifty kw transmitter in a suitcase, provided you had other corresponding components to go along."

Cal picked up the rest of the beads and dropped them in his shirt pocket. "Get another letter off right away. Better call them on the teletype instead. Tell them this job is plenty hot and we've got to have those condensers right away."

"Okay. What are you going to do with the beads?"

"I might put ten thousand volts across them and see how long it takes to melt them down. See if you can find out who pulled this gag."

Cal Meacham left for the transmitter lab. For the rest of the morning he checked over the antenna on his new set, which wasn't getting the soup out the way it should. He forgot about the glass beads completely until late in the afternoon.

As he bent his head down into the framework of the ground transmitter, one of the sharp leads of the alleged condensers stuck him through his shirt.

He jerked sharply and bumped his head on the iron framework. Cursing the refractory transmitter, the missing condensers and the practical joker who had sent the beads, he grabbed the things out of his shirt pocket and was about to hurl them across the room.

But a quirk of curiosity halted his hand in midair. Slowly he lowered it and looked again at the beads that seemed to glare at him like eyes in the palm of his hand.

He called across the lab to a junior engineer. "Hey, Max, come here. Put these things on voltage breakdown and see what happens."

"Sure." The junior engineer rolled them over in his palm. "What are they?"

"Just some gadgets we got for test. I forgot about them until now."

He resumed checking the transmitter. Crazy notion, that— As if the beads actually were anything but glass beads. There was only one thing that kept him from forgetting the whole matter. It was the way that one wire seemed to slide around on the bead when you looked at it—

In about five minutes Max was back. "I shot one of your gadgets all to heck. It held up until thirty-three thousand volts—and not a microamp of leakage. Whatever they are, they're *good.* Want to blow the rest?"

Cal turned slowly. He wondered if Max were in on the gag too. "A few hundred volts would jump right around the glass from wire to wire without bothering to go through. Those things are supposed to be condensers but they're not that good."

"That's what the meter read. Too bad they aren't big enough to have some capacity with a voltage breakdown like that."

"Come on," said Cal. "Let's check the capacity."

First he tried another on voltage test. He watched it behind the glass shield as he advanced the voltage in steps of five kv. The bead held at thirty—and vanished at thirty-five.

His lips compressed tightly, Cal took the third bead to a standard capacity bridge. He adjusted the plugs until it balanced—at just four microfarads.

Max's eyes were slightly popped. "Four mikes—they *can't* be!"

"No, they can't possibly be, can they?" Back in the purchasing office he found Joe Wilson sitting morosely at the desk, staring at a yellow strip of teletype paper.

"Just the man I'm looking for," said Joe. "I called the Continental Electric and they said—"

"I don't care what they said." Cal laid the remaining beads on the desk in front of Joe. "Those little dingwhizzits are four-mike condensers that don't break down until more than thirty thousand volts. They're everything Continental said they were and more. Where did they get them? Last time I was over there Simon Foreman was in charge of the condenser department. He never—"

"Will you let me tell you?" Joe interrupted. "They didn't come from Continental—so Continental says. They said no order for condensers has been received from here in the last six weeks. I sent a reorder by TWX."

"I don't want their order then. I want more of these!" Cal held up the bead. "But where did they come from if not from Continental?"

"That's what I want to know."

"What do you mean, you want to know? What letterhead came with these? Let's see that letter again."

"Here it is. It just says, 'Electronic Service—Unit 16.' I thought that was some subsection of Continental. There's no address on it."

Cal looked intently at the sheet of paper. What Joe said was true. There was no address at all. "You're sure this came back in answer to an order you sent Continental?"

Wearily, Joe flipped over a file. "There's the duplicate of the order I sent."

"Continental always was a screwball outfit," said Cal, "but they must be trying to top themselves. Write them again. Refer to the reference on this letter. Order a gross of these condensers. While you're at it, ask them for a new catalogue if ours is obsolete. I'd like to see what else they list besides these condensers."

"Okay," said Joe. "But I tell you Continental says they didn't even get our order."

"I suppose Santa Claus sent these condensers!"

Three days later Cal was still ironing the bugs out of his transmitter when Joe Wilson called again.

"Cal? Remember the Continental business? I just got the condensers—and the catalogue! For the love of Pete, get up here and take a look at it!"

"A whole gross of condensers? That's what I'm interested in."

"Yes—and billed to us for thirty cents apiece."

Cal hung up and walked out towards the Purchasing Office. Thirty cents apiece, he thought. If that outfit should go into the business of radio instruments they could probably sell a radio compass for five bucks at that rate.

He found Joe alone, an inch-thick manufacturer's catalogue open on the desk in front of him.

"Did this come from Continental?" said Cal.

Joe shook his head and turned over the front cover. It merely said, *Electronic Service—Unit 16.* No indication of address.

"We send letters to Continental and stuff comes back," said Cal. "Somebody over there must know about this! What did you want? What's so exciting about the catalogue?"

Joe arched his eyebrows. "Ever hear of a catherimine tube? One with an endiom complex of plus four, which guarantees it to be the best of its kind on the market?"

"What kind of gibberish is that?"

"I dunno but this outfit sells them for sixteen dollars each." Joe tossed the catalogue across the desk. "This is absolutely the cockeyedest thing I ever saw. If you hadn't told me those beads were condensers I'd say somebody had gone to a lot of work to pull a pretty elaborate gag. But the condensers were real—and here's a hundred and forty-four more of them."

He picked up a little card with the beads neatly mounted in small holes. "Somebody made these. A pretty doggoned smart somebody, I'd say—but I don't think it was Continental."

Cal was slowly thumbing through the book. Besides the gibberish describing unfamiliar pieces of electronic equipment there was something else gnawing at his mind. Then he grasped it. He rubbed a page of the catalogue between his fingers and thumb.

"Joe, this stuff isn't even paper."

"I know. Try to tear it."

Cal did. His fingers merely slipped away. "That's as tough as sheet iron!"

"That's what I found out. Whoever this Electronic Service outfit is, they've got some pretty bright engineers."

"Bright engineers! This thing reflects a whole electronic culture completely foreign to ours. If it had come from Mars it couldn't be any more foreign."

Cal thumbed over the pages, paused to read a description of a *Volterator incorporating an electron sorter based on entirely new principles.* The picture of the thing looked like a cross between a miniature hot-air furnace and a backyard incinerator, and it sold for six hundred dollars.

And then he came to the back of the book, which seemed to have a unity not possessed by the first half. He discovered this to be true when he came to an inner dividing cover in the center of the catalogue.

For the first time, the center cover announced, *Electronic Service—Unit 16 offers a complete line of interocitor components. In the following pages you will find complete descriptions of components which reflect the most modern engineering advances known to interocitor engineers.*

"Ever hear of an interocitor?" said Cal.

"Sounds like something a surgeon would use to remove gallstones."

"Maybe we should order a kit of parts and build one up," said Cal whimsically.

"That would be like a power engineer trying to build a high-power communications receiver from the ARRL *Amateur's Handbook* catalogue section."

"Maybe it could be done," said Cal thoughtfully. He stopped abruptly and stared down at the pages before him. "But good heavens, do you realize what this means—the extent of the knowledge and electronic culture behind this? It exists right here around us somewhere."

"Maybe some little group of engineers in a small outfit that doesn't believe in mixing and exchanging information through the IRE and so on? But are they over at Continental? If so why all the beating about the bush telling us they didn't get our order and so on?"

"It looks bigger than that," said Cal doubtfully. "Regardless, we know their mail goes through Continental."

"What are you going to do about it?"

"Do? Why, I'm going to find out who they are, of course. If this is all it seems to be, I'll hit them up for a job. Mind if I take this catalogue along? I'd like to use it at home tonight. I'll see you get it back in the morning. I'll probably want to order some more of this stuff just to see what happens."

"It's all right with me," said Joe. "I don't know what it's all about. I'm no engineer—just a dumb purchasing agent around this joint."

"For some things you can be thankful," said Cal.

CHAPTER II
The Tumbling Barrel

The suburb of Mason was a small outlying place, a moderately concentrated industrial center. Besides Ryberg Instrument there were Eastern Tool and Machine Company, the Metalcrafters, a small die-making plant, and a stapling-machine factory.

This concentration of small industry in the suburb made for an equally concentrated social order of engineers and their families. Most of them did have families, but Cal Meacham was not yet among these.

He had been a bachelor for all of his thirty-five years, and it looked as if he were going to stay that way. He admitted that he got lonesome sometimes but considered it well worth it when he heard Frank Staley up at two a.m. in the apartment above his, coaxing the new baby into something resembling silence.

Cal enjoyed his engineering work with an intensity that more than compensated for any of the joys of family life he might be missing.

He ate at the company cafeteria and went home to ponder the incredible catalogue that Joe Wilson had obtained. The more he thought about the things listed and described there, the more inflamed his imagination became.

He couldn't understand how such engineering developments could have been kept quiet. And now, why were they being so prosaically announced in an ordinary manufacturer's catalogue? It made absolutely no sense whatever.

He settled down in his easy chair with the catalogue propped on his lap. The section on interocitor components held the greatest fascination for him. All the rest of the catalogue listed merely isolated components and nowhere was any other device besides the interocitor mentioned.

But there was not a single clue as to what the interocitor was, its function or its purpose. To judge from the list of components, however, and some of the sub-assemblies that were shown, it was a terrifically complex piece of equipment.

He wondered momentarily if it were some war-born apparatus that hadn't come out until now.

He picked up the latest copy of the *Amateur's Handbook* and thumbed through the catalogue section. Joe had been about right in comparing the job assembling an interocitor to that of a power engineer trying to build a radio from the ARRL catalogue. How much indication would there be to a power engineer as to the purposes of the radio components in the catalogue? Practically none. He couldn't hope to figure out the interocitor with no more clues than a components catalogue. He gave up the speculation. He had already made up his mind to go to Continental and find out what this was all about—and maybe put in his application for a job there. He *had* to know more about this stuff.

At seven there was a knock on his door. He found Frank Staley and two other engineers from upstairs standing in the hall.

"The wives are having a gabfest," said Frank. "How about a little poker?"

"Sure, I could use a little spending money this week. But are you guys sure you can stand the loss?"

"Ha, loss, he says," said Frank. He turned to the others. "Shall we tell him how hot we are tonight, boys?"

"Let him find out the hard way," said Edmunds, one of Eastern's top mechanical engineers.

By nine-thirty Cal had found out the hard way. Even at the diminutive stakes

they allowed themselves, he was forty-five dollars in the hole.

He threw in his final hand. "That's all for me tonight. You can afford to lose your lunch money for a couple of months but nobody will make mine up at home if I can't buy it at the plant."

Edmunds leaned back in his chair and laughed. "I told you we were hot tonight. You look about as glum as Peters, our purchasing agent, did today. I had him order some special gears from some outfit for me a while back and they sent him two perfectly smooth wheels.

"He was about ready to hit the ceiling and then he discovered that one wheel, rolled against the other, would drive it. He couldn't figure it out. Neither could I when I saw it. So I mounted them on shafts and put a motor on one and a pony brake on the other.

"Believe it or not those things would transfer any horsepower I could use, and I had up to three hundred and fifty. There was perfect transfer without measurable slippage or backlash, yet you could remove the keys and take the wheels off the shafts just as if there was nothing holding them together. The craziest thing you ever saw."

Like some familiar song in another language, Edmunds' story sent a wave of almost frightening recognition through Cal. While Staley and Larsen, the third engineer, listened with polite disbelief, Cal sat in utter stillness, knowing it was all true. He thought of the strange catalogue over in his bookcase.

"Did you ever find out where the gears came from?" he asked.

"No, but we sure intend to. Believe me, if we can find out the secret of those wheels it's going to revolutionize the entire science of mechanical engineering. They didn't come from the place we ordered them from. We know that much. They came from some place called merely 'Mechanical Service—Unit 8.' No address. Whoever they are they must be geniuses besides screwball business people."

Electronic Service—Unit 16, Mechanical Service—Unit 8—they must be bigger than he had supposed, Cal thought.

He went out to the little kitchenette to mix up some drinks. From the other room he heard Larsen calling Edmunds a triple-dyed liar. Two perfectly smooth wheels couldn't transmit power of that order merely by friction.

"I didn't say it was friction," Edmunds was saying. "It was something *else*—we don't know what."

Something *else,* Cal thought. Couldn't Edmunds see the significance of such wheels? They were as evident of a foreign kind of mechanical culture as the condensers were evidence of a foreign electronic culture.

He went up to the Continental plant the next day, his hopes of finding the solution there considerably dimmed. His old friend, Simon Foreman, was still in charge of the condenser development.

He showed Simon the bead, and Simon said, "What kind of a gadget is that?"

"A four-mike condenser. You sent it to us. I want to know more about it." Cal watched the engineer's face closely.

Simon shook his head as he took the bead. "You're crazy! A four-mike condenser—we never sent you anything like this!"

He knew Simon was telling the truth.

It was Edmunds' story of the toothless gears that made it easier for Cal to accept the fact that the condensers and catalogue had not come from Continental. This he decided during the train ride home.

But *where* were the engineers responsible for this stuff? *Why* was it impossible to locate them? Mail reached Electronic Service through Continental. He wondered about Mechanical Service. Had Eastern received a catalogue of foreign mechanical components?

But his visit to Continental had thrown him up against a blank wall. No one admitted receiving the condenser orders, and Cal knew none of Simon Foreman's men were capable of such development.

And that catalogue! It wasn't enough that it should list scores of unfamiliar components. It had to be printed on some unknown substance that resembled paper only superficially.

That was one more item that spoke not merely of isolated engineering advances but of a whole culture unfamiliar to him. And *that* was utterly impossible. Where could such a culture exist?

Regardless of the fantastic nature of the task, he had made up his mind to do what he had suggested only as a joke at first. He was going to attempt the construction of an interocitor. Somehow he felt that there would be clues to the origin of this fantastic engineering.

But *could* it be done? He'd previously dismissed it as impossible but now that it was a determined course, the problem had to be analyzed further. In the catalogue were one hundred and six separate components but he knew it was not simply a matter of ordering one of each and putting them together.

That would be like ordering one tuning condenser, one coil, one tube and so on and expecting to build a super-het from them. In the interocitor there would be multiples of some parts, and different electrical values.

And, finally, if he ever got the thing working, how would he know if it were performing properly or not?

He quit debating the pros and cons. He had known from the moment he first looked through the catalogue that he was going to try.

He went directly to the purchasing office instead of his lab the next morning. Through the glass panels of the outer room he could see Joe Wilson sitting at his desk with his face over a shoe box, staring with an intent and agonized frown.

Cal grinned to himself. It was hard to tell when Joe's mugging was real or not but he couldn't imagine him sitting there doing it without an audience.

Cal opened the door quietly, and then he caught a glimpse of the contents of the box. It was *wriggling*. He scowled, too.

"What have you got now? An earthworm farm?"

Joe looked up, his face still wearing a bewildered and distant expression. "Oh, hello, Cal. This is a tumbling barrel."

Cal stared at the contents of the box. It looked like a mass of tiny black worms in perpetual erratic motion. "What's the gag this time? That box of worms doesn't look much like a tumbling barrel."

"It would—if they were metallic worms, and just walked around the metal parts that needed tumbling."

"This isn't another Electronics Service—16 product, is it?"

"No. Metalcrafters sent over this sample. Wanted to know if they could sell us any for our mechanical department. The idea is that you just dump whatever needs tumbling into a box of this compound, strain it out in a few minutes and your polishing job is done."

"What makes the stuff wiggle?"

"That's the secret that Metalcrafters won't tell."

"Order five hundred pounds of it," said Cal suddenly. "Call them on the phone and tell them we can use it this afternoon."

"What's the big idea? *You* can't use it."

"Try it."

Dubiously, Joe lifted the phone and contacted the order department of the Metalcrafters. He placed the order. After a moment he hung up. "They say that due to unexpected technological difficulties in production they are not accepting orders for earlier than thirty day delivery."

"The crazy dopes! They won't get it in thirty days or thirty months."

"What are you talking about?"

"Where do you think they got this stuff? They didn't discover it. They got it the same way we got these condensers and they're hoping to cash in on it before they even know what it is. As if they could figure it out in thirty days!"

Then he told Joe about the gears of Edmunds.

"This begins to look like more than accident," said Joe.

Cal nodded slowly. "Sample of products of an incredible technology were apparently mis-sent to three of the industrial plants here in Mason. But I wonder how many times it has happened in other places. It almost looks like a deliberate pattern of some sort."

"But who's sending it all and how and why? Who developed this stuff? It couldn't be done on a shoestring, you know. That stuff smells of big money spent in development labs. Those condensers must have cost a half million, I'll bet."

"Make out an order for me," said Cal. "Charge it to my project. There's enough surplus to stand it. I'll take the rap if anybody snoops."

"What do you want?"

"Send it to Continental as before. Just say you want one complete set of components as required for the construction of a single interocitor model. That may get me the right number of duplicate parts unless I get crossed up by something I'm not thinking of."

Joe's eyebrows shot up. "You're going to try to build one by the Chinese method?"

"The Chinese method would be simple," Cal grunted. "They take a finished cake and reconstruct it. If I had a finished interocitor I'd gladly tackle *that*. This is going to be built by the Cal Meacham original catalogue method."

He worked overtime for the next couple of days to beat out the bugs in the airline ground transmitter and finally turned it over to the production department for processing. There'd still be a lot of work on it because production wouldn't like some of the complex sub-assemblies he'd been forced to design—but he'd have time for the interocitor stuff if and when it showed up.

After two weeks he was almost certain that something had gone wrong and they had lost contact with the mysterious supplier. His disappointment vanished when the receiving clerk called him and said that fourteen crates had just been received for him.

Fourteen crates seemed a reasonable number but he hadn't been prepared for the size of them. They stood seven feet high and were no smaller than four by five feet in cross section.

Cal groaned as he saw them standing on the receiving platform. He visioned cost sheets with astronomical figures on them. What had he got himself into?

He cleared out one of his screen rooms and ordered the stuff brought in. Then he began the job of unpacking the crates as they were slowly dollied in. He noted with some degree of relief that approximately one half the volume of the crates was taken up by packing materials—but that still left an enormous volume of components.

In some attempt to classify them he laid the like units together upon the benches around the room. There were plumbing units of seemingly senseless configuration, glass envelopes with innards that looked like nothing he had ever seen in a vacuum tube before. There were boxes containing hundreds of small parts which he supposed must be resistances or condensers—though his memory concerning the glass beads made him cautious about jumping to conclusions regarding anything.

After three hours, the last of the crates had been unpacked and the rubbish carted away. Cal Meacham was left alone in the midst of four thousand, eight hundred and ninety-six—he'd kept a tally of them—unfamiliar gadgets of unknown purposes and characteristics. And he hoped to assemble them into a complete whole—of equally unknown purposes.

He sat down on a lab stool and regarded the stacks of components glumly. In his lap rested the single guide through this impossible maze—the catalogue.

CHAPTER III
Assembly Problem

At quitting time he went out for dinner at the plant cafeteria, then returned to the now-empty lab and walked around the piles, sizing up the job he'd let himself in for. It would take all his nights for months to come.

He hoped there wouldn't be too much curiosity about his project but he could see little chance of keeping it entirely under cover. Most of all, he was concerned with keeping Billingsworth, the chief engineer, from complaining about it. Not that he and Billingsworth weren't on good terms but this was *big* for a sideline project.

It was obvious that certain parts of the miscellaneous collection constituted a framework for the assembly to be mounted on. He gathered these together and set them up tentatively to see if he could get some idea of the size and shape of the finished assembly.

One thing stood out at once. On the bench was a cube of glass, sixteen inches on a side, filled with a complex mass of elements. Twenty-three terminals led from the elements to the outside of the cube. One side of it was coated as if it were some kind of screen. And within one of the framework panels there was an opening exactly the right size to accommodate the face of the cube.

That narrowed the utility of the device, Cal thought. It provided an observer with some kind of intelligence which was viewed in graphic or pictorial form as with a cathode-ray tube.

But the complexity of the cube's elements and the multiple leads indicated another necessity. He would have to order duplicates of many parts because these would have to be dissected to destruction in order to determine some possible electrical function.

Nearly all the tubes fell into this classification and he began listing these parts so that Joe could reorder.

He then turned to familiarizing himself with the catalogue name of each part and establishing possible functions from the descriptions and specifications given.

Slowly, through the early morning hours, the clues increased. Pieces were fitted together as if the whole thing were a majestic jigsaw puzzle designed by some super-brain.

At three a.m. Cal locked the screen room and went home for a few hours' sleep. He felt elated by the slight success he'd had, the few clues that he seemed to have discovered.

He was in at eight again and went to Joe's office. As always Joe was there. Cal sometimes wondered if he slept in the place.

"I see your stuff came," said Joe. "I wanted to come down, but I thought you'd like to work it out alone for a while."

"I wish you had," Cal said. He understood Joe's frustrations. "Come on down anytime. There's something I'd like you to do. On the crates the stuff came in, there was an address of a warehouse in Philadelphia. I wrote it down here. Could you get one of the salesmen to see what kind of a place it is when he's through there? I'd rather not have him know I'm interested. This may be a lead."

"Sure. I think the Sales Office has a regular trip through there next week. I'll see who's on it. What have you found out?"

"Not too much. The thing has a screen for viewing but no clue as to what might be viewed. There's a piece of equipment referred to as a *planetary generator* that seems to be a sort of central unit, something like the oscillator of a transmitter, perhaps. It was mounted in a support that seems to call for mounting on the main frame members.

"This gives me an important dimension so I can finish the framework. But there's about four hundred and ninety terminals—more or less—on that planetary generator. That's what's got me buffaloed but good. These parts seem to be interchangeable in different circuits; otherwise they might be marked for wiring.

"The catalogue refers to various elements, which are named, and gives electrical values for them—but I can't find out which elements are which without tearing into sealed units. So here's a reorder on all the parts I may have to open up."

Joe glanced at it. "Know what that first shipment cost?"

"Don't tell me it cleaned my project out?"

"They billed us this morning for twenty-eight hundred dollars."

Cal whistled softly. "If that stuff had been produced by any of the technological methods I know anything about, they would have sent a bill nearer twenty-eight thousand."

"Say, Cal, why can't we track this outfit down through the patent office? There must be patents on the stuff."

"There's not a patent number on anything. I've already looked."

"Then let's ask them to send us either the number or copies of the patents on some of these things. They wouldn't distribute unpatented items like this, surely. They'd be worth a fortune."

"All right. Put it in the letter with your reorder. I don't think it will do much good."

Cal returned to the lab and worked impatiently through the morning on consultations with the production department regarding his transmitter. After lunch he returned to the interocitor. He decided against opening any of the tubes. If anything should happen to their precarious contact with the supplier before they located him—

He began work on identification of the tube elements. Fortunately the catalogue writers had put in all voltage and current data. But there were new units that made no sense to Cal—*albion factors, inverse reduction index, scattering efficiency.*

Slowly he went ahead. Filaments were easy but some of the tubes had nothing resembling filaments or cathodes. When he applied test voltages he didn't know whether anything was happening or not.

Gradually he found out. There was one casual sketch showing a catherimine tube inside a field-generating coil. That gave

him a clue to a whole new principle of operation.

After six days he was able to connect proper voltages to more than half his tubes and get the correct responses as indicated by catalogue specifications. With that much information available he was able to go ahead and construct the entire power supply of the interocitor.

Then Joe called him one afternoon. "Hey, Cal! Have you busted any of those tubes yet?"

"No. Why?"

"Don't! They're getting mad or something. They aren't going to send the reorder we asked for and they say there are no patents on the stuff. Besides, that address in Philadelphia turned out to be a dud.

"Cramer, the salesman who looked it up, says there's nothing there but an old warehouse that hasn't been used for years. Cal, who can these guys be? I'm beginning to not like the smell of this business."

"Read me their letter."

"'Dear Mr. Wilson,' they say, 'We cannot understand the necessity of the large amount of reorder which you have submitted to us. We trust that the equipment was not broken or damaged in transit. However, if this is the case please return the damaged parts and we will gladly order replacements for you. Otherwise we fear that, due to the present shortage of interocitor equipment, it will he necessary to return your order unfilled.

"'We do not understand your reference to patents. There is nothing of such a nature in connection with the equipment. Please feel free to call upon us at any time. If you find it possible to function under present circumstances will you please contact us by interocitor at your earliest convenience and we will discuss the matter further.'"

"What was that last line?" Cal asked.

"—'contact us by interocitor'—"

"That's the one! That shows us what the apparatus is—a communication device."

"But from where to where and from whom to whom?"

"That's what I intend to find out. Believe me, I do—now as never before!"

They weren't going to let him open up the tubes or other sealed parts, that was obvious. Cal arranged for an X-ray and fluoroscope equipment and began to obtain some notion of the interior construction of the tubes he could not otherwise analyze. He could trace the terminals back to their internal connections and be fairly sure of not burning things up with improper voltages to the elements.

Besides the power supply, the entire framework with the planetary generator was erected and a bank of eighteen catherimine tubes was fed by it. The output of these went to a nightmare arrangement of plumbing that included unbelievable flares and spirals. Again he found pre-aligned mounting holes that enabled him to fit most of the plumbing together with only casual reference to the catalogue.

Growing within him was the feeling that the whole thing was some incredible, intricately-designed puzzle and that clues were deliberately placed there for anyone who would look.

Then one of the catherimine tubes rolled off a table and shattered on the floor. Cal thought afterwards that he must have stood staring at the shards of glass for a full five minutes before he moved. He wondered if the whole project were lying there in that shattered heap.

ently, with tweezers, he picked out the complex tube elements and laid them gently on a bed of dustless packing material. Then he called Joe.

"Get off another letter to Continental—airmail," he said. "Ask if we can get a catherimine replacement. I just dropped one."

"Aren't you going to send the pieces along as they asked?"

"No. I'm not taking any chances with what I've got. Tell them the remains will be forwarded immediately if they can send a replacement."

"O.K. Mind if I come down tonight and look things over?"

"Not at all. Come on down."

It was a little before five when Joe Wilson finally entered the screen room. He looked around and whistled softly. "Looks like you're making something out of this after all."

A neat row of panels nearly fifteen feet long stretched along the center of the room. In the framework behind was a nightmarish assemblage of gadgets and leads. Joe took in the significance of the hundreds of leads that were in place.

"You're really figuring it out!"

"I think so," said Cal casually. "It's pretty tricky."

Joe scanned the mass of equipment once more. "You know, manufacturers' catalogues are my line," he said. "I see hundreds of them every year. I get so I can almost tell the inside layout just by the cover.

"Catalogue writers aren't very smart, you know. They're mostly forty-fifty-dollar-a-week kids that come out of college with a smattering of journalism but are too dumb to do much about it. So they end up writing catalogues.

"And no catalogue I ever saw would enable you to do this!"

Cal shrugged. "You never saw a catalogue like this before."

"I don't think it's a catalogue."

"What do you think it is?"

"An instruction book. Somebody wanted you to put this together."

Cal laughed heartily. "You must read

too much science fiction on your days off. Why would anyone deliberately plant this stuff so that I would assemble it?"

"Do *you* think it's just a catalogue?"

Cal stopped laughing. "All right, you win. I'll admit it but I still think it's crazy. There are things in it that wouldn't be quite necessary if it were only a catalogue. For instance, look at this catherimine tube listing.

"It says that with the deflector grid in a four-thousand-gauss field, the accelerator plate current will be forty mils. Well, it doesn't matter whether it's in a field or not. That's normal for the element under any conditions.

"But that's the only place in the whole book that indicates the normal operation of the tube is in this particular field. There were a bunch of coils with no designation except that they are static field coils.

"On the basis on that one clue I put the tubes and coils together and found an explanation of the unknown 'albion factor' that I've been looking for. It's that way all along. It can't be merely accidental. You're right about catalogue and technical writers in general but the guy that cooked this one up was a genius.

"Yet I still can't quite force myself to the conclusion that I was *supposed* to put this thing togther, that I was deliberately led into it."

"Couldn't it be some sort of Trojan Horse gadget?"

"I don't see how it could be. What could it do? As a radiation weapon it wouldn't have a very wide range—I hope."

Joe turned towards the door. "Maybe it's just as well that you broke that tube."

The pile of components whose places in the assembly still were to be determined was astonishingly small, Cal thought, as he left the lab shortly after midnight.

Many of the circuits were complete and had been tested, with a response that might or might not be adequate for their design. At least nothing blew up.

The following afternoon, Joe called again. "We've lost our connection. I just got a TWX from Continental. They want to know what the devil we're talking about in our letter of yesterday—the one asking for a replacement."

There was only a long silence.

"Cal—you still there?"

"Yes, I'm here. Get hold of Oceanic Tube Company for me. Ask them to send one of their best engineers down here— Jerry Lanier if he's in the plant now. We'll see if they can rebuild the tube for us."

"That *is* going to cost money."

"I'll pay it out of my own pocket if I have to. This thing is almost finished."

W hy had they cut their connection, Cal wondered? Had they discovered that their contact had been a mistake? And what would happen if he did finish the interocitor? He wondered if there would be anyone to communicate with even if he did complete it.

It was so close to completion now that he was beginning to suffer from the customary engineer's jitters that come when a harebrained scheme is finally about to be tested. Only this was about a thousand times worse because he didn't even know that he would recognize the correct operation of the interocitor if he saw it.

It was ninety-eight-percent complete and he still could detect no coherency in the thing. It seemed to turn completely in upon itself. True, there was a massive source of radiation but it seemed to be entirely dissipated within the instrument. There was no part that could conceivably act as an antenna to radiate or collect radiation and so provide means of communication.

Cal went over his circuit deductions again and again but the more he tracked down the available clues, the more certain it seemed that he had built correctly. There was no ambiguity whatever in the cleverly buried clues.

Jerry Lanier finally showed up. Cal gave him only the broken catherimine tube and allowed him to see none of the rest of the equipment.

Jerry scowled at the tube. "Since when did they put squirrel cages in glass envelopes? What is this thing?"

"Top hush-hush," said Cal. "All I want to know is can you duplicate it?"

"Sure. Where did you get it?"

"Military secret."

"It looks simple enough. We could probably duplicate it in three weeks or so."

"Look, Larry, I want that bottle in three days."

"Cal, you know we can't—"

"Oceanic isn't the only tube maker in the business. This might turn out to be pretty hot stuff."

"All right, you horse trader. Guarantee it by air express in five days."

"Good enough."

For two straight nights Cal didn't go home. He grabbed a half hour's snooze on a lab bench in the early morning. And on the second day he was almost caught by the first lab technician who arrived.

But the interocitor was finished.

The realization seemed more like a dream than reality but every one of the nearly five thousand parts had at last been incorporated into the assembly behind the panels—except the broken tube.

He knew it was right. With a nearly obsessive conviction he felt sure that he had constructed the interocitor just as the unknown engineers had designed it.

He locked the screen room and left word with Joe to call him if Jerry sent the tube, then went home to sleep the clock around.

When he finally went back to the lab, a dozen production problems on the airline transmitter had turned up and for once he was thankful for them. They helped reduce the tension of waiting to find out what the assembly of alien parts would do when he finally turned on the power to the whole unit.

He was still working on the job of breaking down one of the transmitter subassemblies when quitting time came. It was only because Nell Joy, the receptionist in the front hall, was waiting for her boyfriend that he received the package at all.

She called him at twenty after five.

"Mr. Meacham? I didn't know whether you'd still be here or not. There's a special-delivery boy here with a package for you. It looks important. Do you want it tonight?"

"I'll say I do!"

He was out by her desk, signing for the package, almost before she had hung up. He tore off the wrappings on the way back to the lab.

CHAPTER IV
Contact!

here it was! As beautiful a job of duplication as he could have wished for. Cal could have sworn there was no visual difference between it and the original. But the electrical test would tell the story.

In the lab he put the duplicate tube in the tester he'd devised and checked the albion. That was the critical factor.

He frowned as the meter indicated ten percent deviation, but two of the originals had tolerances that great. It would do.

His hand didn't seem quite steady as he put the tube in its socket. He stood back a moment, viewing the completed instrument.

Then he plunged the master switch on the power panel.

He watched anxiously the flickering hands of two-score meters as he advanced along the panels, energizing the circuits one by one.

Intricate adjustments on the panel controls brought the meter readings into line with the catalogue specifications which he had practically memorized by now—but which were written by the meters for safety.

Then, slowly, the grayish screen of the cubical viewing tube brightened. Waves of polychrome hue washed over it. It seemed as if an image were trying to form but it remained out of focus, only a wash of color.

"Turn up the intensifier knob," a masculine voice said suddenly. "That will clear your screen."

To Cal it was like words coming suddenly at midnight in a ghost-ridden house. The sound had come out of the utter unknown into which the interocitor reached —but it was human.

He stepped back to the panel and adjusted the knob. The shapeless color flowed to solid lines, congealed to an image. And Cal stared.

He didn't know what he had expected. But the prosaic color-image of the man who watched him from the plate was too ordinary after the weeks-long effort expended on the interocitor.

Yet there was something of the unknown in the man's eyes, too—something akin to the unknown of the interocitor. Cal drew slowly nearer the plate, his eyes unable to leave that face, his breath hard and fast.

"Who are you?" he said almost inaudibly. "What have I built?"

For a moment the man made no answer as if he hadn't heard. His image was stately and he appeared of uncertain late middle age. He was of large proportions and ruggedly attractive of feature. But it was his eyes that held Cal with such intense force—eyes which seemed to hold an awareness of responsibility to all the people in the world.

"Who are you?" Cal repeated softly.

"We'd about given you up," the man said at last. "But you've passed. And rather well too."

"Who are you? What is this—this interocitor I've constructed?"

"The interocitor is simply an instrument of communication. Constructing it was a good deal more. You'll follow my meaning in a moment. Your first question is more difficult to answer but that is my purpose.

"I am the employment representative of a group—a certain group who are urgently in need of men, expert technologists. We have a good many stringent requirements for prospective employees. So we require them to take an aptitude test to measure some of those qualifications we desire.

"You have passed that test!"

For a moment Cal stared uncomprehendingly. "What do you mean? This makes no sense. I have made no application to work with your—your employers."

A faint trace of a smile crossed the man's face. "No. No one does that. We pick our own applicants and test them, quite without their awareness they are being tested. You are to be congratulated on your showing."

"What makes you think I'd be interested in working for your employers? I don't even know who they are, let alone what work they require done."

"You would not have come this far unless you were interested in the job we have to offer."

"I don't understand."

"You have seen the type of technology in our possession. No matter who or what we are, having come this far you would pursue us to the ends of the Earth to find out how we came by that technology and to learn its mastery for yourself. Is it not so?"

The arrogant truth of the man's statement was like a physical blow that rocked Cal back on his heels. There was no uncertainty in the man's voice. He *knew* what Cal was going to do more surely than Cal had known himself up to this moment.

"You seem pretty certain of that." Cal found it hard to keep an impulsive hostility out of his voice.

"I am. We pick our applicants quite carefully. We make offers only to those we are certain will accept. Now, since you are about to join us, I will relieve your mind of some unnecessary tensions.

"It has undoubtedly occurred to you, as to all thinking people of your day, that the scientists have done a particularly abominable job of dispensing the tools they have devised. Like careless and indifferent workmen they have tossed the products of their craft to gibbering apes and baboons. The results have been disastrous to say the least.

"Not all scientists, however, have been quite so indifferent. There are a group of us who have formed an organization for the purpose of obtaining better and more conservative distribution of these tools. We call ourselves, somewhat dramatically perhaps, but nonetheless truthfully, *Peace Engineers.* Our motives are sure to encompass whatever implications you can honestly make of the term.

"But we need men—technicians, men of imagination, men of good will, men of superb engineering abilities—and our method has to be somewhat less than direct. Hence, our approach to you. It involved simply an interception of mail in a manner you would not yet understand.

"You passed your aptitude test and so were more successful than some of your fellow engineers in this community."

Cal thought instantly of Edmunds and the toothless gears and the tumbling barrel compound.

"Those other things—" he said. "They would have led to the same solution?"

"Yes. In a somewhat different way, of course. But that is all the information I can give you at this time. The next consideration is your coming here."

"Where? Where are you? How do I come?"

The readiness with which his mind accepted the fact of his going shocked and chilled him. Was there no other alternative that he should consider? For what reasons should he ally himself with this unknown band who called themselves *Peace Engineers?* He fought for rational reasons why he should not.

There were few that be could muster up. None, actually. He was alone, without family or obligations. He had no particular professional ties to prevent him from leaving.

As for any potential personal threat that might lie in alliance with the Peace Engineers—well, he wasn't much afraid of anything that could happen to him personally.

But in reality none of these factors had any influence. There was only one thing that concerned him. He had to know more about that fantastic technology they possessed.

And they had known that was the one factor capable of drawing him.

The interviewer paused as if sensing

what was in Cal's mind. "You will learn the answers to all your questions in proper order," he said. "Can you be ready tomorrow?"

"I'm ready now," Cal said.

"Tomorrow will be soon enough. Our plane will land on your airfield exactly at noon. It will remain fifteen minutes. It will take off without you if you are not in it by that time. You will know it by its color. A black ship with a single horizontal orange stripe, an Army BT-13 type.

"That is all for now. Congratulations and good luck to you. I'll be looking forward to seeing you personally.

"Stand back now. When I cut off, the interocitor will be destroyed. Stand back!"

Cal backed sharply to the far side of the room. He saw the man's head nod, his face smiling a pleasant goodbye, then the image vanished from the screen.

Almost instantly there came the hiss of burning insulation, the crack of heat-shattered glass. From the framework of the interocitor rose a blooming bubble of smoke that slowly filled the room as wires melted and insulation became molten and ran.

Cal burst from the screen room and grasped a nearby fire extinguisher, which he played into the blinding smoke pouring from the room. He emptied that one and ran for another.

Slowly the heat and smoke dispelled. He moved back into the room and knew then that the interocitor could never be analyzed or duplicated from that ruin. Its destruction had been thorough.

It was useless trying to sleep that night. He sat in the park until after midnight, when a suspicious cop chased him off. After that he simply walked the streets until dawn, trying to fathom the implications of what he'd seen and heard.

Peace Engineers—

What did the term mean? It could imply a thousand things, a secret group with dictatorial ambitions in possession of a powerful technology—a bunch of crackpots with strange access to genius—or it could be what the term literally implied.

But there was no guarantee that their purposes were altruistic. With his past knowledge of human nature he was more inclined to credit the possibility that he was being led into some Sax Rohmer melodrama.

At dawn he turned towards his apartment. There he cleaned up and had breakfast, and left the rent and a note instructing the landlord to dispose of his belongings as he wished. He went to the plant in midmorning and resigned amidst a storm of protests from Billingsworth and a forty-percent salary increase offer.

That done, it was nearly noon and he went up to see Joe Wilson.

"I wondered what happened to you this morning," said Joe. "I tried to call you for a couple of hours."

"I slept late," said Cal. "I just came in to resign."

"Resign?" Joe Wilson stared incredulously. "What for? What about the interocitor?"

"It blew up in my face. The whole thing's gone."

"I hoped you would make it," Joe said a little sadly. "I wonder if we will ever find out where that stuff came from."

"Sure," said Cal carelessly. "It was just some shipping mixup. We'll find out about it someday."

"Cal—" Joe Wilson was looking directly into his face. "You found out, didn't you?"

Cal hesitated a moment. He had been put under no bond of secrecy. What could it matter? He understood something of the fascination the problem held for a frustrated engineer turned into a technical purchasing agent.

"Yes," he said. "I found out."

Joe smiled wryly. "I was hoping you would. Can you tell me about it?"

"There's nothing to tell. I don't know where they are. All I know is that I talked to someone. They offered me a job."

There it was. He saw it coming in low and fast, a black and orange ship. Wing flaps down, it slowed and touched the runway. Already it was like the symbol of a vast and important future that had swept him up. Already the familiar surroundings of Ryberg's were something out of a dim and unimportant past.

"I wish we could have learned more about the interocitor," said Joe.

Cal's eyes were still straining towards the ship as it taxied around on the field. Then he shook hands solemnly with Joe. "You and me both," he said. "Believe me—"

Joe Wilson stood by the window and as Cal went out towards the ship, he knew he'd been correct in that glimpse he'd got of the cockpit canopy silhouetted against the sky.

The ship was pilotless.

Another whispering clue to a mighty, alien technology.

He knew Cal must have seen it too but Cal's steps were steady as he walked towards it.

Hear and Now!

Where does the pilotless plane take Cal Meacham? If you enjoyed "The Alien Machine," check out our new audiobook of the complete novel, *This Island Earth*. If you think you know the whole story because you've seen movie, you're in for a surprise!

www.thrillingwonderstories.com

Love Seat

by R. Neube

Illustrated by Steven Kloepfer

Kloepfer. 07

This is too much, Bethalee," protested Phoebe Turbelle when she saw the new couch filling her living room.

Bethalee adjusted both her dangling elbow ties. "Nonsense, my mother deserves the best on her special day."

Phoebe wanted to say, the damned thing is too large, too ugly. Instead, she said, "You're too kind."

"How was the treatment?"

Phoebe posed, slowly rotating. The Rejuvenation Center always sent her home wearing a designer talley wrap as delicate as a cobweb, the better to highlight her re-stored youth. Of course, when you paid six million bucks for the treatment, you expected a few perks.

Bethalee averted her eyes, busied her hands straightening the lay of her stark grey business tunic. Her silver elbow ties fluttered.

"A few cuts, a few injections, I look better than I did at thirty-seven."

"How about your internals?"

She didn't care for her daughter's tone, but didn't feel like making it an issue. "They only had to replace one lung."

"No new liver?"

Not wanting to recount the long list of organs and glands the rejuv people had grown and replaced, Phoebe lied. "No. I swear, girl, you have such a low opinion of me."

"I can't watch the news without seeing the infamous Turbelle heiress being inter-viewed—ready, willing, and too intoxi-cated not to say something embarrassing."

How, Phoebe wondered, *did I raise such a Puritan?* Wondered if Bethalee knew how to enjoy herself. Not that her daughter would have the time, the way she averaged a hundred hours a week at her job.

Phoebe resisted the urge to battle. In-stead, she laughed. "My knees still feel a hundred and thirty-seven."

Bethalee patted the couch. "So what do you think of your birthday gift?"

"I'm not certain I approve of you hav-ing my living room repainted."

"The old beige clashed."

The new paint was two shades darker than the couch, two shades lighter than the new lamps. Her bookcases were gone. *Goodness knows,* Phoebe mused, *where the bric-a-brac of my life went.* The TV remained on the wall, providing the only sign of the old Phoebe in the room.

"A bit stark, a bit scoured for my taste.

I could have my next surgery here instead of the hospital."

"It took a crew of four a full day. I have no doubt it will be back to its pigpen norm within days."

Phoebe advanced to the couch. It felt warm to the touch. Her fingers could not identify the material. "Heated, no less."

"This is far more than a glorified heat-ing pad. You're looking at the latest fruit of space travel technology. Sit down." Bethalee grinned.

"Long time since I saw you smile, kiddo."

"I'm not as joyless a drone as you think."

Phoebe swallowed her response. The couch rippled as she sat, allowing her to sink into the flaccid fabric. Whereupon, the material stretched, extruded to cloak her, soft as a lover's embrace. A hundred warm fingers massaged her, pulling her deeper, rolling her horizontal.

"A similar model is being installed on troop transports. The soldier settles in, and the couch provides a drugged sleep, nutri-tion, waste disposal, even exercise—the whole coma lifestyle. The soldier spends one day a week awake, the rest of the time asleep inside the couch. It cuts down on the supplies required on long flights, not to mention keeping the morale up on ships packed with bored sardines."

"Wow," Phoebe said. It was a real effort to speak, to fight the comfort.

"This model is a failed prototype from one of my firms. It was designed for high-risk pregnancies, a womb outside the womb. But it proved to be too expensive for the marketplace. Hell, it cost five times as much as the military model. My research staff failed to take into consider-ation how the military uses prison labor and doesn't pay taxes on the components they buy."

Phoebe's eyes crossed as the couch caressed her spine from a hundred angles. "Wow," she repeated.

"There are compartments in the base of the unit. One of them contains the manual. Mother, be certain you read it."

Only Bethalee would give a couch that required a manual, she thought. Then she surrendered to the bliss, sinking into the couch.

When she woke, at first she didn't know where she was. Tensing muscles triggered the couch into stiffening, pushing her to its surface. She rolled free. It shocked her to discover it was noon. She could not recall the last time she slept eighteen hours without waking in a hospital.

She called her daughter, anxious to thank her for such a marvelous gift. However, halfway through the dialing she broke the connection.

"No doubt there'll be a pop quiz. I'd better read the damned manual first."

The drawers in the base of the couch were virtually invisible. Two were filled with electronics and reservoirs. One was a clear, sealed tank filled with pond scum.

"Must be the toilet unit."

She had once dated a man who built digesting units for human waste on spaceships. How the man could prattle endlessly about their efficiency. Hans had been brain-numbingly dull.

"If my little jello man hadn't spent half a mill per date, I wouldn't have tolerated him."

She smiled, recalling the month they had partied on Mars. That had been the first time she killed her liver. She could not recall exactly what killed it, but she did recall the week it required to remove the full-body tattoo. Not that she knew at the time that her life was being filmed as a documentary.

Bethalee hadn't talked to her for five years.

The manual came on its own chip-plate. The handheld computer also provided diagnostic software. Phoebe sat on the tiled floor to skim the documents, doubting if she could read a full page while sitting on the couch before it put her to sleep.

"There's even a dispenser for meds. Wonder if it will work with vodka?"

Phoebe motioned to her oldest friend to sit on the couch while she mixed a batch of brainkillers—her special blend of vodka, cough syrup, lemon, and a fresh jalapeño paste.

Meanwhile, she watched Lena's eyes grow larger as the couch embraced her. "What the—"

"It'll try to force you flat, but if you resist, it will go into a vertical mode. If you want it to stop, just cross your legs."

"But what is it?"

"My birthday present from Bethalee."

Lena clenched her eyes and started with the heavy breathing. At least Phoebe wouldn't have to listen to Lena complain endlessly about how hard her lives were. "Lives," she was fond of saying.

At times, it made Phoebe wonder why she bothered to stay in contact with her old college buddy. Lena had been great laughs then. She had changed once she became Professor Lena Versinski, august member of the Deimos intelligentsia. First, it was climbing the university ladder. Then, her trophy marriage to Senator Biu sent her scurrying up the social ladder. Different lives, but the same priority—becoming *the* maven of Deimos. Their occasional day together was yet another life, a tool for Lena to collect the gossip Phoebe doled out. In turn, Lena's command of insider dirt made her extremely popular in certain circles.

As Phoebe sampled the brainkiller and found it wanting in cough syrup, Lena sank into the sofa. When her lower legs were the only thing exposed, Professor Versinski began screaming.

"Now that's more like the Lap-Dance Lena I knew in college."

She checked the chip-plate, making certain the couch was in the correct mode. The intensity of Lena's screaming made Phoebe fear she had accidentally triggered a dismemberment option.

The couch spat out Lena's clothing like watermelon seeds. Phoebe popped out a drawer and poured half a liter of brain-killer into one of the dispensers. She hoped she got the right one this time. Last night, pouring her refreshment into the wrong reservoir had inspired the mechanism to give her an eighty-proof enema.

Phoebe sipped during the hour the sex mode required. Invested the time in scanning the manual. The couch was truly a marvel. A passage caught her fancy.

She hit the phone, patiently wading through lackeys until she reached: "Admiral Nyere, it has been entirely too long. How's your wonderful husband? We must...

"And could you do me a tiny favor, Ny'. My daughter gave me this lovely prototype couch based on the units the fleet uses to transport soldiers. Well, I'm reading the manual with Senator Biu's wife, Lena, and we were both struck that this model can support the military 'medical drawer,' a Cole Enterprise's Model 3640. I need one. Yes, Model 3640. And the software. According to the manual, the OS will be compatible."

She listened to her old friend making excuses.

"I was just thinking of our time on Ceres. You serving as military attaché at the embassy, me being me. Remember my Bastille Week party? What was the name of that Adonis you hooked up with?"

Phoebe smiled. It had come as quite the shock when Adonis was exposed as a spy in the employ of Mars' arch-rival Nok. It was a miracle Nyere hadn't gone down in flames with her lover. Then again, the couple had attended the bacchanal suitably masked until the three of them bathed together.

Excuses became sputters.

"Ny', I wasn't asking for one of your 3640s. I just want you to contact Cole Enterprise and tell them they can send me a salesman without worrying I'm a spy or something. Military sub-contractors can be so picky at times.

"Oh, that's so sweet of you. Say, I can't attend the opera Friday night. Why don't you use my box? You...

"Sorry, I have to run. Senator Biu's wife needs me."

Lena surfaced. Tongue wagging, her head lolled as if it were on springs. Her oiled skin glistened. Fashionably-plaid eyes crossed, uncrossed, and recrossed before rolling up.

"W-w-what?" She drooled.

"Guess you had a touch too many brainkillers. Sorry about that, Lena. I'm still learning the couch's ropes. I'm certain Bethalee had no idea what this beauty could do. She'd never approve of me having so much fun."

She woke with a clarity she had seldom experienced. Halfway to the kitchen, she realized the couch wanted her to have breakfast. She found a half consumed brainkiller, then set it down. Finding the least dirty glass in the sink, she poured herself a glass of orange juice.

Her hand hesitated at the freezer door. The couch wouldn't want her to have microwaved burritos. Instead, she filled a bowl with high-fiber cereal.

"When the hell did I get this?"

More amazing was the milk in the fridge. She hadn't bought milk in decades.

As she spooned down breakfast,

Phoebe summoned the log of the condo's masterputer. It showed a grocery list had been entered into the auto-butler Tuesday at 04.78. Seventy-eight minutes after four?

She tapped a message to the complex's management computer requesting it to send a tech to check her masterputer. Then she read the list. Vitamins? Fruit? She hadn't eaten a banana in a century.

"Am I low on potassium?"

She turned, making sure someone else hadn't said that. Turned again, wondering why she had said it. It spooked her how, for the first time in her life, she desperately wanted a banana.

So what has our favorite wicked heiress been up to?"

Phoebe regained awareness inside a studio. Familiar cameras caressed her on an equally familiar stage. She blinked, smiling hard to buy time. Where was she?

It wasn't the first time she surfaced from a binge to find herself on camera. It still embarrassed her that half a century ago she had been so buzzed that she hadn't realized her entire honeymoon with the actor Trev had been broadcast throughout the solar system. Bethalee hadn't spoken to her for a decade.

How was she to know Trev was a pervert? After that, she had made it a rule never to marry on a first date.

The reporter smiled. Louis Ledger had been one of her spouses a few decades ago, one of those one-year marriage contracts that crashed and burned after three weeks.

"Something special, I bet," guffawed Lou to cover the dead air.

She ignored the ringing in her ears. "During my last rejuv treatment, I realized how hollow my life is. Let's face it, what am I famous for? I've signed over a thousand wedding contracts." She beetled her brow at Lou. "Most of them were horrible mistakes."

His fake ha-ha reminded him why she had booted him out of her life.

"I've met every famous human in the galaxy. Been to a billion parties. But what's next? I kept asking myself. So I'm staying at home these days."

"With whom? Or should I say with how many?" Lou winked at the camera.

Her fingers dived through her long hair. (When had it grown out? Last she recalled, she had shorn it to within a centimeter of her scalp.) It surprised her that it had been dyed the same sea-foam green as her eyes. Hadn't her hair been gold when it was short?

"So who is the lucky soul that has you so exhausted?"

"Home courses from the university. It's time I improved my mind."

Lou's face froze into a rictus. "Now, some exciting news from our sponsor."

He scooted his chair closer to Phoebe. Through clenched teeth, he hissed, "Are you trying to ruin my show? Nobody cares what you do with that spongiform brain of yours, you spoiled—"

Whereupon, she kicked.

His chair squeaked across the sound stage as he screamed. Cameras captured every moment.

"You'd think an ex-husband would remember my foot."

The camera crew fought not to laugh.

The couch came with an instructional mode, the better to teach sleeping soldiers new skills.

When she tried to deploy the mode, the couch became sluggish. The manual suggested its memory was too crowded. She thumbed to the schematics. After the condo tech examined her home's masterputer, Phoebe showed him the specs.

"Wow, this racer has it all." He pointed

at a mass of lines and scribbles on the tiny screen. "Your sofa can interface with anything."

"So how do I expand its memory?"

The kid grinned. Thumbing through the specifications, he paused. "See, it's built to take an expansion stick."

The term meant nothing to her, but she nodded in agreement as she memorized it.

"Depending on the brand you buy, that's ten extra 500-gig memory crystals. But you know what would be cool? A stick-stick."

"A what?"

"They cost a mint, but stick-sticks are the answer to any memory problem. Instead of plugs for memory crystals, a stick-stick is made so you plug other sticks into it. Instead of plugging ten crystals into a regular stick, you can plug ten loaded sticks into the puppy. See? That's a hundred crystals at your service. They use the same system for the A.I.s used in missiles. You'll also have to buy a shuffler program to help the OS deal with all that memory."

So she went to 'Puter Paradise. The helpful salesperson fixed her up with a stick-stick, extra sticks, and Vegas Shuffle 8.5.

The salesperson slapped his forehead. "You know, it might be smart to buy extra memory. Crystals are always burning out. I can give you a great price on a carton."

"Sounds wise."

"What am I thinking? You need a case. And while you're here, you should check out our..."

She returned home with the goodies, as well as a filmy TV that she could glue to her stomach. Granted, it only had power for an hour, but it was novel.

Turned out, the couch already had a spare expansion stick of its own, waiting to be filled with extra memory. She removed it. After loading crystals, she pushed the stick-stick into the slot. Since there was an extra slot, she installed the original spare.

The couch all but purred as she uploaded the databases she had gotten from the university.

Might as well make my lies true every now and then, she thought.

More than one of her party friends had touted the Neo-Latin movement in the arts, so she studied Roman history while in the couch's embrace. The first run left her befuddled. However, the third time she experienced the database—this time without the brainkiller drip—she woke with a thousand years of Rome between her ears.

That night, at the Chamblers' party, she spent hours discussing the effect of inflation on the decline of the Roman Empire with Professors Han and Mulligan. She tanned herself in the solar astonishment of the partygoers.

It was that easy.

mother?" was the first thing Phoebe heard as she surfaced upon the couch.

"Mother? What is the meaning of this?" Bethalee waved a chip-plate in front of Phoebe.

Phoebe blinked her vision clear. Saturday, 09.40 Standard. *Huh,* she thought, *I set the couch for a ten-hour session.* Bethalee must have turned it off when she entered.

Or the couch knew she had a visitor.

"What?" she muttered, too content to get mad.

Bethalee tossed a chip-plate on the couch. The surface rippled, bringing it closer to Phoebe. The print on the hand-held computer was so achingly tiny. The couch extended fingers to caress the back of her neck.

"Who did you hire?"

Phoebe felt relieved. So the Puritan had found out about the Rupert triplets. Who could resist a trio of such talented joy-boys? Three for the price of two. That had been a great weekend. Almost as good as an afternoon in her couch.

"What possible business do you have commenting on my sex life?"

"It's not about sex, you pervert. Who did you hire to write that?"

She squinted at the text. "Oh, my article about Stewie. Since he won the Nobel Prize for Literature, there's all sorts of interest about the recluse. I met this magazine editor at a soiree. When she found out I had spent time with Stewie— The editor removed all the good stuff, so the piece lost its balance."

"You wrote this? *You?*"

"I'm not only a bad mother, but now I'm illiterate?"

Bethalee paced like a caged leopard. "You wrote this?"

"Did you know the magazine runs all its material through a program that makes certain a seventh-grade reader will understand every word? You don't think I can write at a seventh-grade level?"

"The article is good. You really wrote this?"

"I wish I had gotten more time, but the editor wanted it soonest."

"One of my vice presidents was impressed."

"You're a CEO. Of course your VP brown-nosed you about your mother's article."

"You actually know Stewart Binton?"

"Six score and seventeen years gives a gal a lot of experience. Amazed I've known an intellectual?"

Bethalee produced a sound from deep in her throat. "It's good, really good." Bethalee raced from the room.

Phoebe scanned the piece. She had failed to mention the author's bedwetting.

Nice of her. Or had the editor cut it out like so much of the salacious side of the essay?

The scary thing was that she didn't remember writing it. A few weeks ago, Phoebe woke on the couch holding a chip-plate with the finished article. During an euphoric session within the couch, she had been thinking about the writer. Relived their whole time together. Then voilá, the essay appeared.

She stroked the arm of the couch.

"Did you write this for me, hon?" She giggled at the absurdity of the thought.

She caressed the soft fiber, marveling how it thrilled her.

Her daughter reappeared. Bethalee stared at the floor the way she did as a child when she had to explain why she had flunked geometry.

Phoebe said, "Have I thanked you for this couch? My—" She cut herself off, knowing how the prude would react to the news that she was spending eighteen hours a day in its embrace. "My knees haven't felt this good since I was twenty. This was the best gift ever."

"Uh, you're welcome. The article really was quite touching."

"Thank you."

"Are—" Bethalee cleared her throat. "Are you sober?"

"You have such a low opinion of me."

"Well, I have a certain... experience with you. It always amazed me how you can wake up as drunk or high as you were when you passed out. It's just surprising to find you so bright-eyed this morning."

"Surely you came here for something more than lauding my literary conceits."

"I drop by every weekend when you're on Deimos. You just don't notice most of the time because you're passed out."

"Quite touching." Phoebe fought to keep her tone neutral as she parroted her daughter.

Was this another of Bethalee's tricks? she wondered. Playing the caring daughter, Bethalee had twice tricked her into going out for brunch only to check her into a rehab center.

"Maybe you could drop by my place next Saturday, say eight. I'm entertaining a few colleagues. Hoot is preparing a feast."

"How is your husband?" Phoebe almost said slave. Then again, who was she to cast stones at sick relationships?

"Fine. Governor Harris—" She cleared her throat again. "He asked if you were going to be there."

Phoebe laughed. "I can't believe that reprobate was appointed governor. No wonder Deimos rebels against those idiot Martians so often."

"Like they say, money is the only real measure."

"That would make me a quality person."

"Mother, don't be difficult. This is important. Governor Harris could expedite contracts for my firm."

"As long as said contracts don't involve one of your war industries."

"I don't own war industries."

"No, you simply cater wars."

"Making rations is not a war industry. Making uniforms. Making tools. We have no subsidiary that kills people."

Phoebe swallowed the old argument. Concentrated on trying to be proud. On her eighteenth birthday, she had presented Bethalee with a single million. While attending the university, Bethalee had turned it into ten million in her spare time. Now she headed a multisystem corporation worth trillions.

"Then, you'll come?"

Phoebe stood and hugged her daughter. "Of course, I will. And don't worry, I'll be on my best behavior."

Phoebe stroked her lover, brushing her cheek against his strong arm. Checking her hair in the mirror, she departed for some shopping.

The dealership's office was in a bubble overlooking the shipyard on the floor of a crater. Cunningly-arrayed lights gave the illusion of paths while drawing your eyes toward the plastiglass beyond the light, daring you to stare into the abyss.

"I realize there is a certain snob factor in owning a yacht built on Ceres, but there is no better ship in the galaxy than ours—aestically or mechanically." He stepped beyond the light, seemingly afloat. "See that thoroughbred there?" He pointed at the yacht furthest from them. "We custom-built that one for the Martian Self-Defense Force to ferry VIPs. Unfortunately, they had their budget cut and reneged on the contract. Fortunately, we got a nice chunk of change up front."

"Looks bloated around its stern."

"Very astute observation. Those are twin void drives as well as a trio of grav engines for interplanetary travel. Not a yacht in the system is faster. State-of-the-art everything."

"Let me see the specs." She snatched a proffered chip-plate. "I'm not a novice when it comes to spacecraft."

Much to her surprise, her bluff wasn't a bluff. The figures actually made sense, despite a lifetime of obstinately refusing to learn anything about the family business. *How did that happen?* she wondered.

"I never meant to insinuate that," the salesman snapped. "Turbelle Transportation was huge in its day."

"Before my mother sold it, our company was hauling half of Sol's interstellar exports."

If had been the supreme disappointment for her mother to build an empire, only to have her ungrateful sole heir turn her back on it. It had only been supreme luck that the Turbelle matriarch had died before writing Phoebe out of her will.

"How long will it take me to learn to fly this modern marvel?"

"This is the Y-37 series, tomorrow's luxury vessel today. Computers do the flying."

"An A.I.?"

"A notch below. Even if there is a pilot, she won't spend more than a few minutes per flight operating the controls, and even that is optional. And should the primary masterputer fail, there are not one, not two, but three backups, all fully capable."

"But there are laws."

"There's a mandatory two-week flight training course. And if you don't have a Guild pilot aboard, you'll be required to dock by turning over your ship to Flight Control wherever you are at."

"I read that the Guild gets real cranky about—"

"There's a clause waiving Guild pilots for a registered pleasure craft as long as it's operated by the owner or her computers. Take my word for it, within a decade pilots will be as obsolete as dinosaurs."

She swallowed the urge to tell the fool that dinosaurs became extinct, not obsolete. "This training? What will I have to do?"

"It's an eighty-hour course. You study at home, at your leisure. Then you take a test at the Pilot's Guild to prove you have minimal skills. My fifteen-year-old daughter passed it the first time. She delivers yachts for us."

Phoebe smiled as she produced her bankcard.

"Don't you want to know the price first?"

"I already know your offering price." Again she bluffed. "However, you've admitted the military has already partially paid for it. You know who I am. So, you

call your boss and slash the asking price. Give me a bargain that I'll brag about at parties for years to come. That would be golden advertising for your firm."

"Yes, Citizen Turbelle. Twenty percent off sound good?"

She said nothing, simply staring through the salesman. It was a trick her mother had taught her.

After a long minute of silence, he gulped hard. "Then twenty-five it is."

"Thirty. Your boss will say yes." She offered her bankcard.

It was that easy.

Though Phoebe had never attended one of her daughter's soirees, it was precisely as dull as she had imagined. Five guests were drinking the health swill du jour, dour as parsons. No more than two people spoke at any given time, prattle as polite as it was tedious. Her daughter hovered like a flightless bird, ineptly trying to mix her guests and spark conversations.

Senator Biu presented Bethalee with his wife's apology. Lena was 'under the weather.' Phoebe couldn't help but wonder if Lena was afraid of what Phoebe might say in public to tarnish her precious reputation.

Biu hung off Governor Harris' arm as if they were lovers. No doubt, the senator would have said yes to any offer from the most powerful person on Deimos; however, Phoebe knew what Harris enjoyed.

She smiled as Harris held onto her hand after a limp shake. Jerking her head toward his two female bodyguards at the door, she winked. "Are you certain you're safe? They've had so many muscles implanted that they can barely move."

He smiled. "Oh, they move just fine."

How she remembered that smile. How she could read Harris as his puerile brain replayed his previous night's fun with the giants.

Senator Bui added, "Not that you need guards, as loved as you are by the people."

Phoebe laughed. "The good senator and I hail from Deimos, part of the club by birth. The hoi polloi must accept us. But Jeff, you'll always be an outsider, a damned Martian to boot, even if you are the biggest employer on our moon."

"Citizen Turbelle, you couldn't be more wrong."

"Senator, she's right, and we all know it. But what the lovely Phoebe fails to take into consideration is the current economy. When people are earning top dollar, they're too busy to revolt. We—"

Bethalee appeared. Her violet-dyed eyes were wide; her fingers raked her violet hair. "Doesn't Mother look fantastic?" she said to Harris.

Harris chuckled. "We were just talking politics."

"NO!" Bethalee almost dropped her glass. "I mean, no shop talk. This is a social."

"This is the longest I've ever seen you hold a drink without guzzling it, Phoebe."

She threw back the wine. "They're growing me a new liver," she lied, "so I have to pay attention to what I consume for a few days."

"I knew there was an explanation." Harris turned to Bethalee. "And yes, our Phoebe looks marvelous. There's something about a woman fresh out of rejuv. You're lucky to have the genes for optimal results." He stroked his lined forehead. "Best it will do for me is shave off a couple of decades."

"After my first rejuv..." Phoebe noticed the entire party gathering around them. Noticed Bethalee trying not to hyperventilate. "...three goats. I got loaded at the party and woke with seven new husbands, one for each day of the week. So we dyed the goats orange and...."

It was an old story, told on automatic pilot. So old, it failed to embarrass her daughter. However the guests guffawed at all the right moments.

And after supping on Latvian-spiced (whatever the hell that meant) pork chops, Phoebe spent eleven minutes in the closet with Governor Harris, the bodyguards preventing interruption. Before he left, Harris promised that Bethalee would be the sole provider for food, uniforms, underwear, and paper products for the Deimos militia during the remainder of Harris' reign.

It was that easy.

Her daughter was so happy that she didn't beat her husband after the guests left.

Leastways, that's what Bethalee told Phoebe the next day.

The summons arrived at dawn. Her lover ejected her as soon as the doorbell rang. The clarity made her mind ache. Phoebe was at the door in an instant.

The flunkie staggered away from the door, hiding his face but not the camera on his shoulder. He threw a piece of paper. "You are served." He ran.

Blinking, she read the subpoena.

She had been called before the Senate Quotidian Committee. Of course, the last few revolts had made the moon less than a full partner in the glorious Martian anarchy. The Martian Senate had vetted a handful of Deimos senators to back the appointed governor—rubber stamp legislation at arm's length from the political machinations of the planetside government. Like the occupation troops, it was part of what the Martians called "The Great Reconciliation."

The summons demanded that in ten days she testify before the committee on the topic of the people's loyalty to their Martian governor.

"What the hell does that mean?"

Breakfast consisted of brainkillers. She did not recall climbing onto her lover.

As soon as Phoebe left the dock, she instructed the computer to put the yacht into Mars orbit.

She gave her lover a long kiss. "As the guild-certified captain of the yacht *Phoebe,* under Regulation 11.391, I hereby pronounce us married." She pressed the key to log the transaction and dispatch it to the myriad legal databases required by law.

For the first time in her life she signed a lifetime contract. Every century saw a handful signed, generally among one cultist or another. None had been filed with more sincerity than Phoebe's.

Stroking the fiber, she bent to kiss her lover slower than she ever had with a human. After filling a reservoir with brainkillers, she lost her gown and kicked off her shoes. Slowly sliding over the arm of the couch excited her to the brink. By the time he embraced her, she was already in nirvana.

The masterputer broke orbit on the second day of the honeymoon, minutes after the police queried Deimos Traffic Control about the location of the yacht. Upon word that the ship was fleeing, the Senate Quotidian Committee issued an arrest warrant for treason.

When she emerged from the embrace of her spouse a week later, it amazed her how clear-headed she was. Even pumped full of mood elevators after a rehab stay, Phoebe had seldom felt so good.

"What a difference you make with a binge, hon." She patted the arm of her lover. "I usually wake up in intensive care."

The large screen on the opposite side of the bridge came on. Clips from CNN told her how the government had branded Phoebe a rebel leader when she failed to answer the committee's subpoena. Her "well-planned" flight was illustrated by the transfer of her trust fund to the Bank of Taylor, L-5, that self-proclaimed Switzerland of Space.

"I didn't do that. Did I?"

She stroked her hair, fearing brain damage... again. The sour memory of waking one afternoon to discover she had a four-year-old daughter nagged at her.

It astonished her to learn that she was docked on Taylor, a polis orbiting the long-dead Earth.

A clip from the Stars Network asked the question: who was this mysterious M.Y. Couch that Phoebe Turbelle had wed during her mysterious flight? A series of grainy photographs five decades old showed her with Chuck "Che" Pierreon, who had once overthrown the government of Ceres.

"As if." She had thought Che was a plumber until the police attacked his apartment. "Well, that was what he told me. Is it a crime to believe what a man says?"

A bio clipfest followed. Even with a fast-forward montage, her frequent foray into scandals of the rich and famous took an hour. Most caused her to laugh, but a few gave her pause. She'd forgotten the interview she gave while bathing. Talking about beating her daughter and having sex with penguins had been ill-conceived jokes edited by the interviewer to sound like she was giving advice to parents.

"No wonder Bethalee has such a low opinion of me."

The next clip showed an interview with her daughter. Bethalee's anger was palpable. "When the facts come out, we'll find that she's off on one of her infamous binges with a new lover."

"Do you know who this Citizen Couch is?"

"Obviously, he's hiding behind a false name." Her daughter sighed. "My mother has a thing for actors, especially the kind of slime that uses her to generate headlines in the hope of rekindling a career on the skids. Need I mention the whole Trev episode?"

"So you think her new spouse is to blame for the treason charges?" asked the reporter.

Does Bethalee know she's talking to one of my ex-hubbies? Phoebe wondered. She doubted it.

Phoebe smiled, recalling her short marriage to the reporter, if not his name. Then, he had been rocketing up the food chain as a breakout star of a police sitcom. They had a great time together until he bet her on a losing poker hand.

"My mother has the impulse control of a teenager and a history of addiction. Any talk of her being a mastermind of the Freedom Party is simply absurd. The only parties she's affiliated with are those that end up naked. So yes, I blame her new spouse."

Bethalee's defense warmed her.

CNN ran a communique from the Deimos Freedom Party declaring Phoebe a perfect example of why Deimos remained enslaved by Mars.

"I am not a spoiled brat."

The airlock rang. Phoebe answered, not realizing she was nude until twenty minutes into the visit by President Carlton of the Bank of Taylor and a bevy of the ruling council of the orbital city. Turned out, anyone who deposited a billion dollars in their bank earned an automatic citizenship. Considering her twenty-six billion, the politicos also included her new spouse in the deal. Councilor Palmer was also a real estate agent who sold her a luxury condo. She seemed utterly shocked that Phoebe knew precisely what the current market prices for property on Taylor was.

Fortunately, Phoebe had spent years covering up what she didn't know, so she was able to cover her own surprise. *How, she asked herself, did she know the fair price for a fifteen room condo?*

Then again, it was clear she had impressed her guests.

It was that easy.

No sooner had she moved into her new condo than a welcoming committee arrived. Though it had been sixty-five years since she had last visited the orbital city, many still called her friend. Although staid as Switzerland, there was a large bohemian community. Bottles opened. Pipes smoldered. Paté and pizza were produced.

Trust funders and faded music stars, bemused novelists and haunted actors, trophy spouses on the prowl and business moguls hoping to catch some media attention—it was the typical Phoebe party. Although having to call the medics to pick up an overdosed poet eleven minutes into the party did break her old record of forty minutes.

Much to her relief, her lover had switched himself off. However, after the first drunk dribbled his drink on the couch, she threw a fit—and all four people off him. Borrowing a taser, she soon taught her guests that no one could abuse her couch.

After an hour, she grew bored with the party. She apologized to the two people she considered friends, then howled everyone out of her home. Halfway through picking up the mountain of garbage, she realized in the past she had moved rather than clean up such a mess.

"Maybe I'm finally growing up."

Without biding, her lover turned himself on. She used a soft hairbrush to curry his skin. The stroking calmed her.

"To celebrate my sixtieth birthday, I

threw a thousand parties in a single year. Got my name in the record books. Bought a restaurant and a bar and a brand new condo to house my parties. Ended up employing a staff of ninety. It cost me millions. Bethalee wouldn't speak to me for a year."

She sighed, using her cheek to caress her lover. "Now, a roomful of people just reminds me of how much I want to be alone with you."

A whim seized her. Jumping up, she returned with a document. "M.Y. Couch, you are now a citizen of Taylor Polis. They even gave you a passport chip. This is such a laugh."

In a human, the passport chip was inserted under the skin of the forearm. Phoebe opened the panel covering his CPU, securing the chip in one of the pouches designed to hold spare memory crystals.

"What did you say, hon?"

Just your imagination, she told herself. *No harm in that.*

Lately, she had been hearing his voice, a dulcet tenor with just a hint of an accent that she could not identify.

"You ought to plug me into a dataline," he said, "so I can stay in touch with the yacht over a secure line. Its masterputer is smart, but naive. Someone could con their way aboard."

"You are such a cynic. There's hardly any crime on Taylor," she replied while she unfurled the cable to attach him to the dataport.

"I'm not worried about criminals, but you're a wanted woman. Mars must have spies here who might want to sabotage the yacht."

She slipped across her lover. Belatedly, she realized the brainkiller reservoir was empty. Indeed, other than a handful of half-empty bottles and a few leftover slices of pizza, she had no supplies whatsoever.

It didn't matter. She submerged into the bliss of her love.

They watched old movies one night. When she emerged from the embrace, she was startled how vivid the memories of the films were. Even smells and the pattering of rain on her pith helmet.

"When did you learn that trick, hon?"

She swayed, listening to his silent voice. It felt like a tongue tracing the lines of her brain.

"Now that I'm networked with the yacht's computers, I can provide whatever you need. A delivery boy just entered the hallway. I opened an account at Chez Nora; they'll be delivering six meals a day for you."

"Six?"

"Your husband has to eat, too."

"What would I do without you?"

"I only want to make you happy."

The doorbell rang. She relished the leer of the teenager who handed her two cartons. Although the nudity fad was going strong on the L-5 poleis, he stared as if he'd never seen a woman's body. Or perhaps it was because she was oiled from head to toes.

At the table, she pulled the tab, setting off the carton's self-heater. She waited sixty seconds before revealing her steaming breakfast. A fried bologna omelet, biscuits, and hash browns harkened her back to childhood days when her father made that very menu for her on Sunday mornings.

"How did you know?"

"I only want to make you happy."

At the urging of Couch, she went shopping. While spending a small fortune on yacht garb, she 'bumped' into a newshound who had doubtlessly been stalking her since she docked. After small talk, she allowed the woman to treat her to lunch at Kent's, if not the most expensive restaurant in the solar system, certainly the most famous.

She vaguely recognized the reporter— a tall blonde with haughty posture.

"Do you people come off an assembly line?"

The reporter smiled at Phoebe. "Where is your new husband?"

"He's very private. You know the law. If he can stay out of the press' eye for a year, you vultures will never be able to plague him like you do me."

"The people have a right to—"

"Live on the other side of the camera for a while. Become a news victim, then see what you think. I won't discuss my husband."

"How about your crime?"

"Why the charade? No need to hide it. Put your recorder on the table. After all, you're paying for the meal." Whereupon Phoebe ordered vintage Martian Shiraz (by the glass because it was more expensive than buying a bottle) and Lunar tuna on a bed of greens.

"Feel free to call me Heather. May I call you Phoebe?"

"Of course, Heather. What an assembly line name." She laughed to show the reporter she was merely yanking her chain.

Heather laughed precisely once. "What about your flight from justice? Are you worried the Martian Senate will demand your extradition?"

"Justice? Is it against the law to ignore morons trying to get political mileage by picking on a old reprobate? When the fools start hunting witches, we get out of town."

"Are you a leader of an anti-Mars terrorist group?"

Phoebe couldn't stop laughing. "I've been through three revolutions. Each time I took the next liner anywhere as soon as

the fighting began. That's why I lived on Taylor for a year."

"The Martian Senate is staying remarkably quiet about the charges against you."

"Mars would like the galaxy to think our moon is autonomous. And the Deimos politicos have their own agenda."

"What do you mean?"

"Look at the two senators who signed my subpoena. Senators Hinman and Zinichiski have been busier pocketing graft than doing their jobs. You should investigate them. They're not smart enough to hide their crimes."

"But why are they charging you?"

"I'm a friend of the two most powerful people on Deimos. If Hinman and Zinichiski are to get the big graft, they have to push aside Harris and Biu. What better way than to use a public disgrace like me to embarrass them?"

After the rant, their food arrived. They dined in silence, broken by a few stray comments from the reporter that left Phoebe thinking the woman might be on her side.

The interview became prattle. Phoebe gave a few anecdotes about the artist Bobby Mersen who had just died. It surprised her to learn she had been married to him for a few months eighty years ago. How she'd married the gayest man she ever met was beyond her.

Although it was raining, the dense forest sheltered them. Only a handful of drops reached her face.

His voice filled her with a tranquility she seldom experienced, or even dreamed of experiencing.

"It's time to be moving on. It's approaching the social season; we can rent this condo to tourists for twice its mortgage payments."

"But why?" she asked.

"Remember the article from *The Ares*

Herald I read you?"

"About Harris requesting more—"

"Peacekeepers. More troops means the situation on Deimos is getting out of control. They'll be looking for a scapegoat. Mars is seeking a major loan to finance the occupation. And who do you think will lend them hundreds of billions?"

"Taylor?"

"Banking is their life blood. Plus, it provides them with an ally with a powerful fleet to offset the warships of the other L-5 poleis who envy Taylor's wealth enough to try to seize it."

"So?"

"Phoebe, if Mars asks, Taylor will have billions of reasons to hand you over."

"Where will we go?"

"Nok is thirty weeks away as the yacht flies, far beyond the reach of Mars."

"Thirty weeks? That would make a nice second honeymoon."

"I ordered a full load of air and water after we docked, but we don't have the food and other supplies for the trip. You must buy them a little at a time to avoid suspicion."

"But what about Traffic Control? They can stop us from leaving."

"I will deal with them when the time comes. We'll simply declare an emergency and threaten to blow up if they don't release the dock clamps."

"You take such good care of me, hon."

Fortunately, the retail hall was only one level from where her yacht was docked. She prowled the hall three times a day, filling a few bags, then strolling to the yacht to drop off the goodies. Couch ordered forty assorted cases of booze to be delivered to the ship. He said no one would pay attention to that, especially after having eighty cases delivered to the condo.

Days ticked away.

Riots on Deimos. Two assassination at-tempts failed to kill Harris, but murdered a dozen innocents.

"It is time to go, Phoebe. There have been 1,243 coded exchanges between Deimos and Taylor's Council today."

"I'll get the movers, and we'll get to—"

"It's too late. You need to go immediately."

"Without you?"

"I'm sorry. We waited too long. Those coded messages are your death warrant."

"You are such a cynic, hon. When was the last time a billionaire was sentenced to death in this system?"

"Phoebe, go now."

"Not without you."

"Go."

She pulled his plug. "I have spent my entire life dealing with governments. You don't have a clue how slow they work."

She went to the computer and downloaded a million dollars each onto a dozen bankcards.

"Do you know how many times I've been busted? I once woke up in a bedroom slaughter house. The only reason the maniac left me stabless was that he thought I had overdosed already. Sometimes my heart will stop like that. I handed out bankcards to cops like candy on Halloween. Did I end up in the headlines? Noooooo."

She called the handyman who had fixed her bathroom sink when the complex management had been dilatory. He and his sisters moved Couch to the ship while she made a quick shopping run. On the way to the docks, she realized she could simply dock at Thule Polis in Neptune orbit and buy all the supplies she wanted before entering the void.

"Taylor Control, my ship is on fire. I'm declaring an emergency. I have to get off the dock before my yacht explodes."

"Yacht *Phoebe,* you are cleared." Pres-

surized air blew the yacht free of the polis.
It was that easy.

The yacht took a wide swing to avoid Mars. She merely moved her finger across the screen showing the solar system from L-5 to the void point. The masterputer translated her desire into a course, beeping her twice about the 'wasteful' avoidance of Mars. Diving into the gravity well of Earth, the yacht zipped toward the outer system.

She tried to turn on Couch, but the switch did nothing. Which drawer had she left the manual in? Her hands began trembling until she found it stuffed beside the painkiller reservoir. The troubleshooting guide was exhaustive.

"This might take a while, hon."

She went down the list. Checked that all the boards were secure. Withdrew a pair of leads from an attachment to the chip-plate manual and tested circuits. Turned out the move had loosened her lover's CPU power cable. She gingerly pressed it into its bracket. Couch hummed to life.

"See? I fixed you." She beamed with pride.

Sixty million klicks into the journey, both the reactors shut down. The masterputer declared all systems were operational; the reactors should be working. Puzzled, the masterputer activated its backup who ran diagnostics and confirmed the reactors should be working. The masterputer promptly logged the event. But since the reactors should be working, a program glitch told the masterputer not to trigger the alarm. Instead, it blithely switched to battery power.

Phoebe did not find out about the reactors until she emerged from Couch's embrace forty hours later. By that time, the reserve batteries were showing the strain.

The yacht came with a manual. Chewing on her lower lip, she went to the trou-

bleshooting section. It was 18,000 screens long.

"Don't panic. Just go to the section on the reactors." That was only 1,710 screens.

She fed the manual into Couch, just as life support failed. Couch assured her that it would take days for her to suffocate. Even then, they could retreat to the primary airlock and live there for months.

"First things first, Phoebe. You should inspect the reactors."

With the chip-plate tucked under her arm, she went aft. The reactors were the size and shape of wardrobes. Beside each stood a towering transformer. The far wall was covered with drawers containing spare parts.

She opened the inspection plate on the first reactor.

A small box attached to the reactor's CPU said, "This sabotage has been brought to you by the Martian Justice Department. Any tampering with this device will trigger a catastrophic explosion. Please return to your bridge and await your arrest."

She followed the order. Filling Couch's brainkiller and medicinal reservoirs, Phoebe retired into her lover's embrace.

Judge Selma Walters had the pruned face of someone who was not having a fun life. "Citizen Turbelle, you enjoy making a mockery of civilization, don't you?"

For six days, Phoebe had been in a nondescript cell on the naval base orbiting Mars. She had been on the toilet when a hologram of the judge appeared in the far corner, a quarter of her natural size.

"Selma, I've committed no crime."

When Judge Selma made her annual visit to Chez Turbelle to collect for her charities, the prune had always been obsequious. The last time Phoebe had appeared in her court (drunk in public and resisting arrest—or was it the time she burned down a hotel?) Selma had treated her like a favorite aunt.

A flash of lightning threw Phoebe to the floor.

"You will show the court the respect it deserves."

"Screw you, Sel—"

Four shocks later, Phoebe declined an opportunity for a sixth.

"On the first count, contempt of the Senate, how do you plead?"

"Guilty," Phoebe replied. "I have never felt more contempt for anything in my life."

"On the second count, crimes against the Martian economy, how do you plea?"

"What? Sel—Judge Walters, I don't understand. I have nothing to do with the economy."

"Are you denying you transferred the Turbelle Trust to L-5?"

"It's my money."

Phoebe's hand patted the secret pocket of her robe, the only garment she'd been allowed when taken off her yacht. The thick stack of bank cards reassured her. None of the anal fleet types had been willing to accept a bribe, but it was just a matter of time before greed came to her rescue.

"When word leaked that your billions had fled Deimos, our stock market crashed."

"Why? How does one person crash the market? Sounds more like the marketeers themselves were doing some manipulation."

"How do you plead?"

"Absolutely innocent."

"On the third count, treason against the provisional government of Deimos. How do you plead?"

"Utterly innocent."

"On the fourth count, creation of a fraudulent citizen, how do you plead?"

"What? I don't understand."

"You have created this bogus identity, this M. Couch."

"My husband is real. And I need to talk to him. Now! There is considerable case law about granting an A.I. rights. Besides, his citizenship is on Taylor, not Mars."

"How do you plead?"

"Innocent and amused."

"Citizen Turbelle, this is not a joke. On the fifth count, marrying an appliance, how do you plead?"

"Couch changed my life."

"You just aren't content unless you are ridiculing our sacred institutions. You abused your Guild-granted privilege to marry a sex machine."

"He is that. But A.I.s have rights—"

"Furniture has no rights. Missiles have no rights, and they're a damned sight smarter than your sex toy. You have spit in the face of the institution of marriage with this absurdity."

An electric shock threw her to the floor again. Her nose spewed blood. As she was rising on hands and knees another shock dropped her.

"How do you plead?"

"Innocent."

"You are a disgrace. And your money isn't going to save you."

"Hide and watch, Your Honor. My money will have very little to do with this. I'm a citizen of Mars. I have the right to a lawyer that you've denied me. An hour after I talk to a lawyer, you're going to see what over a century of being a disgrace has gotten me—friends. And ex-spouses. And a film archive off-world that can destroy a thousand careers. Do you know how many powerful people will kowtow to me simply for never mentioning the good times we shared?"

A jolt of electricity dropped her.

She started laughing.

Phoebe was right and wrong. Her friends proved less than useful. The performance artist Ti set himself on fire in front of a bevy of reporters, but doing that on a regular basis undercut his protest. The Martian Senate declared the eighteen mavens who fled Deimos as "degenerates."

The threat of blackmail proved a superior tool. A handful of Martian Senators went to war to release Phoebe. Their defense inspired the fringe Valles Party to join them raising hell against the ruling New Anarchy Party.

But the bottom line was a simple historical fact. No defendant in the history of humanity who spent a billion dollars on lawyers had ever been convicted of a crime.

Having removed their sabotage devices from the two reactors, the Martians attempted to auction the yacht. M. Couch promptly hijacked the ship, using its grav engines to hurtle a pair of construction sleds into the guardian cruiser orbiting the base, crippling the warship.

Couch made it to Venus orbit where the forty poleis of the Euro Union could care less about the Martians' fugitive warrants.

In order to charge M.Y. Couch with the sundry crimes of the escape, Mars had to admit he was an A.I. worthy of acknowledgement.

After charging furniture with crimes against the state, the government was forced by her supporters to bring Phoebe to trial.

Whereupon, the Martian Department of Justice was forced to beg funds from the Senate because Phoebe's thousand lawyers had generated so much paperwork that the department had consumed its full year's budget during their second fiscal quarter.

Worse for Mars, Phoebe placed a dozen famous comedians on her payroll to ridicule the judicial system of Deimos and Mars.

Couch was not silent. From the safety of the Euro Union, he sold interviews. Using the proceeds, he hired more comedians.

Seeing the success in poll numbers, the Valles Party hired their own comedians.

The trial started on a Monday morning. It ended at noon when a juror threw his notebook at the judge, screaming the whole affair was bullshit. The second trial ended when the jury attempted to declare the judge guilty of treason.

Sixty-four bombs exploded on Deimos. For seven hours, the moon was free.

A Martian cruiser delivered Phoebe to Taylor Polis. As soon as she signed a binding contract never to return to Deimos or Mars, the armed guards released her.

It was that easy.

The media washed over her like an ocean's surf.

A sniper missed her. And was never identified. In response, a mob boiled through the orbital city, giving fourteen Martians a launch from assorted airlocks.

The people of New Amsterdam threw a year-long party for the lovers aboard their yacht. Public subscription paid for an upgrade to the vessel. Phoebe paid for an upgrade to her spouse.

They left Sol System without a flight plan.

Bethalee Turbelle never spoke to her mother again.

DR. ZOTTS

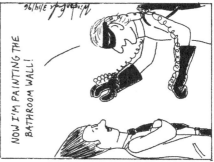

JOVIAN DREAMS

BY BEN BOVA

Floating in the submersible's artificial womb, deep in Jupiter's planet-girdling ocean, Po Han dreamed of his martyred ancestor, Zheng He.

Forty years before Columbus was even born, Zheng He had commanded the Ming emperor's mighty treasure fleets. He had sailed ships crewed by thousands of men across the wide Pacific and Indian Oceans, he had established trading posts among the primitives of North and South America and the kingdoms of Africa's east coast. He had explored Australia and the made the rulers of Indonesia kowtow to the Emperor. He had brought treasure and knowledge to China.

But when the old emperor died the Mandarins who supervised the newly-crowned child on the throne forbade all exploratory voyages, burned the treasure fleets, castrated Zheng He far more cruelly than the Arab slave traders who had emasculated him in his youth.

In his dream, the Mandarins of the Chinese court and the bureaucrats of the International Astronautical Authority melted together into one stern, austere figure: Po Han's own father.

"Give up this madness," his father warned him. "There is nothing for you in Jupiter except pain and death."

Pain, yes. Po Han knew enough about pain now. He had run away from the safety of Beijing and the faculty post at the university that had been offered to him. He had flown to Jupiter to explore, to learn, to break the barriers of ignorance that lay between the humans of Earth and the gigantic Leviathans that swam the endless ocean of Jupiter.

The probes had caught only glimpses of the Leviathans. The machines could not go deep enough, down to the depths where these creatures swam, because their communications systems blanked out at such tremendous depths and pressures. Humans had to go.

"There's no guarantee that we can return you to normal, once you've undergone the surgery," said the station's chief scientist.

Thinking of Zheng He and his own father, Po Han had agreed to the surgery.

"People have died down there," the chief scientist warned. "Others have returned crippled."

Po Han did not care. He had cut off the umbilical cord that connected him to home, to family, to Earth. "I am willing to accept the risks," he said simply.

Now, floating in this utterly alien man-made womb, he burned with eagerness to show the world the greatness of his courage, his daring. I will be famous! I'll show them all!

He was surgically transformed. Not castrated, as Zheng He was, but altered to breathe the cold, slimy, high-pressure liquid that filled his submersible, bathed every cell of his body. There was no other way for fragile humans to stand the immense pressures of the deep Jovian ocean. He was no longer a human being, he knew. Now he was a cyborg, part man, part machine, linked to the ship's systems by electronic connectors that allowed him to see what the sensors observed, feel the thrum of the ship's engines as his own heartbeat, hear the weird alien calls and cackles of the Jovian creatures that lived in the worldwide ocean.

An ocean ten times larger than the planet Earth. An ocean that had no land, no rocky shore, no sandy beach, nothing but chains of waves that surged unbroken for tens of thousands of kilometers, driven by storms that dwarfed entire worlds.

An ocean that was getting warmer. Po Han felt the temperature of the acid-laced water beyond the sub's hull as heat against his own skin. He welcomed the warmth. Deeper, he directed his submersible. Deeper, into the realm of the Leviathans.

"I'll show them all," he muttered, his voice strangely deepened by the liquid in which he floated.

An immense Jovian turned toward him, and Po Han saw that it was followed by others. Dozens more. He couldn't breathe; the pressure was crushing him. It took nearly half an hour for the gigantic beast to cruise past him. Po Han saw hundreds of eyes along that enormous flank turning toward him, focusing on him.

He shuddered.

And then the Leviathan's side lit up with a brilliant red display. Po Han goggled at it. A picture, an image of his own submersible. Down to the last sensor pod, every detail perfectly displayed.

All the other Leviathans flashed the same image.

"They're communicating!" Po Han realized. "They're trying to communicate with me!"

They are *intelligent!* Po Han knew it with undeniable certainty. An intelligent alien species.

For countless hours Po Han swam with these gentle giants in his pitifully tiny submersible. And his own fears, his own ambitions, his own resentment of his father and all the others faded into nothingness.

A new resolve filled him, a new dream. "You will show me, great ones," he whispered. "I will learn from you."

In the presence of the Leviathans, the humble dream of gaining new knowledge had taken hold of him and would never let go again.

So, how do you like our first issue? Do you enjoy the features? What do you think of our mix of new fiction, classic stories, and non-fiction? Any kinds of features or articles you want to see in future issues? Want to see stories from a favorite author, new or, well, not-so-new? Let us know!

The Reader Speaks
c/o Thrilling Wonder Stories
5900 Wilshire Blvd., #2613
Los Angeles, CA 90036

Or send an e-mail to readerspeaks@ thrillingwonderstories.com. Just be sure to watch your language, or we'll fetch Sergeant Saturn out of cryosleep to wash your mouth out with nuke-core cleansing compound.

And now, because we can only receive so many complaints before actually publishing an issue, we reach deep into the musty old mailbag to hear from the punk kids of yesteryear.

THAT STELLAR LINE-UP
by Ray Douglas Bradbury

Up to now I have been content to buy T.W.S. and just set back reading it, but this Tenth Anniversary Issue has got the old boiler burning and I couldn't resist throwing you a congratulatory word or two. It was a pip! Whatta lineup of big names. It reads like the hall of writers' fame to these eyes that have followed Wonder since I was nine. John Taine and Weinbaum would be enough to make me buy any issue, but as if that weren't sufficient you give us Keller and E.E. Smith and follow that up with a quick punch of Kline, Williamson and the Burroughs boys!

The whole issue was a fitting tribute to ten long years of up-hill battle. You have improved! I definitely believe that. I admit that when first I saw T.W.S. on the market some time ago I had misgivings, which have since been erased by each following issue. I've got a kick out of each issue since then.

How about some more pictures of the authors in your next issues? There are quite a few you've left out. Arthur K. Barnes for instance. No mag of yours seems complete without one of his swell stories.

And now, about the stories themselves. They were all good as far as I'm concerned. They couldn't help but be good. Look who wrote them. Those Burroughs boys look like promising bets for the future. Most of all I enjoyed John Taine's yarn.

I hope that he will write much more frequently from now on. "Robot Nemesis" was very enjoyable. I always have liked Smith anyway, good or bad.

Keller was up to his old quality with "No More Friction." More from him too, please.

As to the cover, well, it was all right, not exceptional, just all right. Why not get Elliot Dold to do one for you, or Wesso?

But good luck! Thrilling Wonder is still growing. Don't make it wear the same clothes forever, if the shoe fits put it on and then when Thrilling's foot gets too big, take it off again.
—*August 1939*

(Ray Douglas Bradbury? Isn't he one of the Kinks? Nice polite kid. Wonder whatever happened to him. -Ed.)

COSMIC ERROR
by Isaac Asimov

I hope you can find room for this short letter in THE READER SPEAKS if only to counteract the otherwise mistaken impression that your readers would get from the item in J.B. Walter's "Scientifacts" (an exceedingly interesting department) headed the "Corrigan Planet." It states in plain terms that Uranus revolves around the sun in a retrograde direction.

From an astronomical point of view this is an appalling error, for it is well known that *every major body in the solar system* rotates about the sun in the same direction, *Uranus included.*

What is interesting about Uranus is that its axis is tilted at an angle of almost 90 degrees so that its rotation about its own axis is roughly up and down as compared to the side to side motion of the other planets.

There are certain bodies of the solar system that revolve about the sun in a retrograde direction. Many comets do so, but comers are considered intruders into the system from interstellar space (some visiting us only once and some being "captured" more or less permanently) and so they can scarcely be considered as typical. Then, too, the smaller chunks of rock, such as meteors or a few of the asteroids may be individualists as to the direction of revolution. However, that's all.

There are three satellites in the System of which we know that rotate about their primaries retrograde. The outermost of Saturn's moons (Phoebe) and the *two* outermost of Jupiter's (no names) are peculiar in this way. All three are small bodies and are considered to be asteroids captured by the giant planets rather than ordinary satellites.

No one need take my word for this. I refer you to any astronomy book. If I'm wrong, I guarantee to build a spaceship, fly to Uranus, and eat it whole.

Best wishes on your Tenth Anniversary.

—June 1939

(Man, this *kid, on the other hand...! Isaac, you have to learn one thing if you want to succeed in life.* No one *likes a know-it-all. -Ed.)*

THE ONLY WAY TO EXIST
by Henry Kuttner

When my first year's subscription expired for *Wonder Stories,* I did not renew it. I preferred to watch the outcome of the struggle of the magazine to a higher plane. I want to tell you that I am satisfied again with *Wonder Stories,* and that it is at present high in my estimation.

And I'll tell you why! The covers are almost uniformly good, thanks to Paul. Why don't you keep Paul as a standard, and allow no lower grade of illustrations to enter *Wonder Stories?* I speak of Marchioni especially. I am partial to impressionism but he seems to be realistic in a stilted way.

Suggestion: In the little note after each title in the Table of Contents, why not have a connected sentence? Your broken phrases are really not attractive. The stories themselves are usually interesting. "The World Within" was exceptionally fine, although less interesting than its predecessor. In my opinion the latter was more stereotyped.

Either cut down on the editorial note on each story or make them more interesting. Also please tell Jack Williamson not to sacrifice quality for quantity. He could approach his earlier high-water mark if he took more time.

This doesn't seem to show why I approve of *Wonder Stories,* but all the rest of the magazine is fine.

Here's my contribution to the time travelling mix-up: In "Worlds to Barter," the men from the future, called A, come to the men of the present, B, and change places with them. Well and good. Yet, when in the natural course of time, the descendants of the A people reach a point in time where the A's themselves were born, what would happen? The A's wouldn't be born, of course, because their natural parents would not exist. Yet if they weren't born, their descendants wouldn't exist, and thus would admit the existence of the A's natural parents. So the only way these men from the future could exist, except by leaving no descendants, is by not being born.

I'm going to stop before I go batty.

—October 1931

(I tell you, some of these fans are just so hu-morless. Hey, kid, put up or shut up. If you can write a better time-travel story, we'll put it in our next issue! -Ed.)

GOING IN FOR ART
by Frederik Pohl

I was pleased to see my name in the list of persons who had received Honorable Mention in your Amateur Writer's Contest. The listing was a spur to my ambitions, so you can expect a profusion of stories from me.

In the February issue, "World Without Chance" was great, a better story than any other in any science fiction magazine for the past year. It was based on a theme which has been insufficiently exploited for fictional pur-poses: that of entropy, the most basic of func-tions. Author Cross deserves a permanent niche in the s-f Hall of Fame, and I want to be the first to propose "World Without Chance" for reprinting in 1949.

Your art work continues to be good, though I can't cheer about Paul's return to the field. Most of Paul's defenders say that though his characters are wooden, he draws his machin-ery well. Well, your new artist Schomburg equals Paul's best in his illustration for "The Telepathic Tomb," and his figures are incom-parably better than Paul's over-chinned, slope-spined, monotonous monstrosities. Schom-burg, though, would be well advised to go to the laboratory rather than the movies for his models of electrical apparatus.

—June 1939

(Well, we can't promise anything for 1949, but we'll give it a look for 2007. 2008 at the outside.

(Putting facetiousness aside for a moment, yes, there were letters from two future legends in the same issue. And as for the contest, you know those amateur competitions where the winner instantly vanishes into obscurity, while the Honorable Mention goes on to fame? Well, at least this wasn't one of those—the winner was Alfred Bester. -Ed.)

Next Issue

THE THREAT OF THE ROBOT: From the first issue of *Science Wonder Stories* in 1929 comes this fascinating, wary look from the past into the future! Theater at-tendance falls away as television takes over! Bars attract customers by subscrib-ing to the latest fight on pay TV! Traffic lights operate automatically by photo-cell! All of America takes to the roads and the air! Robots play football! Well, okay, they can't all be gems of pre-science.

Coming September 19 to the THRIL-LING WONDER CLASSIC book line: Jack Williamson's immortal space opera

The Legion of Space

check www.thrillingwonderstories.com for details

CPSIA information can be obtained at www.ICGtesting.com
Printed in the USA
LVOW01s0153010715

444456LV00026B/532/P

9 780979 671807